Three

Outback Wedding Wanted!

Three dramatic and enticing love stories from
one beloved Mills & Boon author!

Outback Wives Wanted!

MARGARET WAY

First published in Great Britain 2011
by Mills & Boon, an imprint of Harlequin (UK) Limited,
Eton House, 18-24 Paradise Road, Richmond, Surrey TW9 1SR

OUTBACK WIVES WANTED!
© by Harlequin Enterprises II B.V./S.à.r.l 2011

Wedding at Wangaree Valley, Bride at Briar's Ridge and *Cattle Rancher, Secret Son* were first published in Great Britain by Harlequin (UK) Limited in separate, single volumes.

Wedding at Wangaree Valley © Margaret Way Pty., Ltd. 2008
Bride at Briar's Ridge © Margaret Way Pty., Ltd. 2008
Cattle Rancher, Secret Son © Margaret Way Pty., Ltd. 2007

ISBN: 978 0 263 88435 7

05-0411

Printed and bound in Spain
by Blackprint CPI, Barcelona

Margaret Way a definite Leo, was born and raised in the subtropical River City of Brisbane, capital of the Sunshine State of Queensland. A conservatorium-trained pianist, teacher, accompanist and vocal coach, she found her music career came to an unexpected end when she took up writing, initially as a fun thing to do. She currently lives in a harbourside apartment at beautiful Raby Bay, a thirty-minute drive from the state capital, where she loves dining al fresco on her plant-filled balcony, overlooking a translucent green marina filled with all manner of pleasure craft from motor cruisers costing millions of dollars and big, graceful yachts with carved masts standing tall against the cloudless blue sky to little bay runabouts. No one and nothing is in a mad rush, so she finds the laid-back village atmosphere very conducive to her writing. With well over a hundred books to her credit, she still believes her best is yet to come.

WEDDING AT WANGAREE VALLEY

CHAPTER ONE

ALANA awoke before the birds. She had long since made it her habit. This was the time when the Valley was possessed of a special magic. Misty shades and depths cloaked the land, sliding down the ravines between the sentinel hills, only to vanish with the first slants of the rising sun. Occasionally a lone kookaburra beat her to it, but she managed her pre-dawn awakening pretty much every day of her life, even on Sunday, and Sunday was her well-deserved day of rest. She didn't need the hysterical wake-up call of the kookaburras or the ecstatic screech of flocks of cockatoos to rouse her. Her body clock was set. Besides, there was such beauty in the stillness, a wonderful *quietude* of the heart, that reached out and folded her in its soft arms.

Barefooted, she padded out onto the verandah, her spirits lifting as she was swept by cool little breezes. They whipped at her thin nightdress, moulding it against her body like petals sheathed a rose. She arched her back and stretched her arms, something sensual in her actions. The palest green mist hung over the densely treed hills, and the sky above was a transparent grey that was washed with pastel bands of yellow and amethyst along the horizon.

One twinkling star still blossomed, diamond-white with the faintest pink halo.

She had a wonderful unobstructed view over the Valley from the upper verandah. At all times of the day it presented a picture postcard of this part of rural Australia that was well beyond the precincts of the great Desert Heart. The garden beneath her was overflowing with colour: hibiscus, oleander, frangipani, giant bouginvillaea bushes in hot pink, purple and white. They spilled over arbours and walls and even climbed trees in their bid to reach the sun; close by, a rich diversity of nectar bearing native shrubs brought in parrots and brilliantly plumaged little lorikeets in their legions. It made a wild paradise of a garden that was now sadly neglected and in many places running rampant. The garden was huge by any standards. There simply wasn't the time.

Briar's Ridge was the centre of her life, but nowadays the homestead was hurting badly. Still, the Valley was the most desirable place on earth to live. This was where she was rooted. This was the place she had run wild as a child. She loved the fragrance of the eucalypts that dominated the high ridges, filling her lungs with their astonishing freshness. She felt she could even gargle on it, it had such antiseptic power. The eucalypts could be counted upon to flood the landscape with their marvellous aromatic scents and, when in flower, an amazing range of pods and blossom. Reluctantly she lifted her hands off the balustrade. It was *so* beautiful, a still dreaming world, but already the sky was lightening. Better get going.

Another day, another battle for survival. Over the past three years the farm had been going downhill, despite all their back-breaking hard work. Of course there was the drought. The man on the land was always fighting drought, but her father's decline into a grief-stricken, booze-fuelled lethargy was the crux of the matter. Inside she was torn by her suspicions over Guy Radcliffe—the man she privately dubbed Lord and Master of the Valley—who had been giving her father a helping hand. It was all done on the quiet, of course. That was Guy's way. Nevertheless, the thought oppressed her. Her feelings towards Guy—though she had known him all her life—were so strangely ambivalent they filled her with confusion; a confusion she was always at great pains to hide.

Guy Radcliffe, as Master of Wangaree, one of the nation's great historic sheep stations, was without a doubt the richest and most successful man in a highly prosperous region, and he was a well-known philanthropist. It was equally well known that he liked to keep his many dealings with his adoring subjects strictly under wraps. Dispensing largesse and a helping hand was a Radcliffe tradition, as befitting the Valley's leading family since the earliest days of settlement. Guy's ancestors had pioneered Wangaree Valley. For more than a century their wealth had ridden on the sheep's back. Then, with the downturn in the wool industry, the Radcliffes had been among the first of the sheep barons to diversify. These days Radcliffe Wine Estates had been added to the family portfolio. In a few short years it was already at the forefront of viticulture, with Guy as company chairman and brilliant CEO.

There wasn't much Guy couldn't do. He was *The Man*. No argument. Not only did he oversee the Radcliffe wine and olive production, he also still adhered to the old tradition of producing the world's best ultra-fine wool, prized by the textile industry and the world's great fashion houses. This most beautiful and expensive cloth was well suited to blending with silk and cashmere. Briar's Ridge, on the other hand, had until fairly recently produced excellent fine-medium wool, suitable for middle-weight suiting. If the coming wool sales went badly, the farm could slide into ruin.

Could they possibly hold on?

A few splashes of bracingly cold water brought her fully awake. She stared in the mirror unseeingly as she patted her face dry with a soft towel. She always laid her gear out the night before to save time: same old thing. Hers was a uniform of tight fitting jeans—she looked great in them, or so her good friend Simon told her—and today a blue and white checked cotton shirt. Seated on the side of the bed, she bent to retrieve her boots, pulling them on over grey socks. She didn't even bother to check her appearance. Who was to see her but the sheep and her dogs? The dogs were beautiful border collies, Monty and Brig—Brig being short for Brigadier. Border collies were special dogs, in her opinion. Though some sheep men in the Valley wouldn't have them. They thought them too temperamental, preferring sprightly kelpies or Australian Shepherds. Certainly Border Collies could seriously misbehave if they weren't getting enough exercise. They had quite a tendency to nip heels, which didn't make them popular with visitors, and they could be destructive, but their phenomenal intelligence, their wonderful herding ability and their infinite energy, willingness and capacity to work tirelessly all day long had won Alana's heart.

From long habit she quickly applied sunblock to her face, throat and the V above her shirt, and put protective gloss over her lips. A square of scarlet silk secured her thick honey blonde hair at the nape. She shoved her well worn cream Akubra down over her forehead as she made for the door. Barely ten minutes had elapsed, but the light had changed. The soft dove-grey of pre-dawn was taking on a solid blue cast as the sun leaned over the hills, flooding the Valley in golden dayshine.

Now the dawn chorus was up, building to a great crescendo. The noise was deafening to a city-dweller. *She* loved it. Nothing sweeter. Thousands and thousands of male birds in the Valley calling love songs to the thousands and thousands of females ready to listen. It usually took a good hour for the cacophony to die down, but some birds persisted for the best part of the day, pouring out their passion.

Today it was her job to ride up into the hills and round up the wethers—the castrated male sheep—before they started to scatter all over the hillside or moved deeper into the ridges with their tall trees. Usually she had her older brother Kieran's invaluable help, but Kieran was away in Sydney on business for their dad. Briar's Ridge was so deep in hock there was the real, sickening possibility they could lose it. These days their father rarely left home. He clung to the valley where his wife, their mother, was buried. Alana swallowed on the agonisingly hard lump in her throat. She couldn't afford to break down. She was no stranger to sorrow, but life went on—no matter what.

Downstairs the homestead was silent, except for the loud ticking of the English long-case clock in the entrance hall. It kept wonderful time and was actually very valuable. Her mother had brought it and all the other beautiful antiques in the house with her on her marriage. Some people in the Valley—her Denby relatives in particular—thought Annabel Callaghan-née-Denby had married beneath her. Like the Radcliffes, the Denbys were the old squattocracy.

One hand on the mahogany banister, Alana descended the central staircase, turning left to tiptoe along the wide, polished wood corridor, covered with its splendid Persian runner—her mother's. She moved past the big master bedroom—her father no longer slept there—and on to a much smaller room that in the old days had been the nursery. There their father—a big man, easily topping six feet—had set himself up, turning his back on all his old comforts and the crushing memory of having a much loved woman lying beside him, aching to hold her when she was no longer there.

The door was ajar, so she could hear him snoring. Even that was a relief. These days, almost three years after her mother's death, Alana dreaded the thought that one morning she would find her beloved father dead. Broken hearts killed. Guilt killed. Even his drunken snoring sounded desperate. She pushed the door a little more, saw him lying, his dark, tanned, handsome face squashed into a pillow, his raven, silver-flecked curls matted. He was covered by a very beautiful ultra-fine wool rug her mother had woven. One long brown arm was flung over the side of the bed, and an empty bottle of whisky lay on its side, a few inches from his fingertips.

Just how many empty bottles had she dumped, even hidden? He always bought more. On the small bedside table was a large studio portrait in an antique silver frame. A young woman's lovely smiling face looked out of it. The hairstyle was different, but the thick honey-blonde hair, the creamy complexion, the large hazel eyes that at different times had turned pure green, were the same. Then there was the smile. It could have been a photograph of *her*. Alana vividly re-membered how the close resemblance between them had de-lighted her mother.

"When you're older, my darling girl, you too will be named the most beautiful woman in the valley at the Naming."

The Naming was a special event at Wangaree's Wine Festival. The festival attracted large crowds from all over the State of New South Wales and beyond. Wine-lovers, food-lovers, music-lovers—they all came. And Guy always hired some famous artist to perform under the stars in the grounds of his lovely historic mansion, Wangaree. The Naming didn't happen every year, more like every three, but Guy had already announced, to great excitement, that it would be on the agenda this year. It wasn't just the honour—there was an all-inclusive holiday for two to California's beautiful Napa Valley with it, and spending money to boot!

She had no intention of entering. She thought of herself as a modest working girl. Besides, there was no money for a knock-out evening gown—though she could still get into the beautiful dress her mother had made her for her eighteenth birthday party. Let one of her Denby cousins carry off the prize. There were three of them: Violette, Lilli and Rose. All flower names, all born into a privileged world far removed from her own. Indeed, there had been little or no interaction between the families. Violette—never, *never* Vi—the eldest, at twenty-seven, and judged to be the most glamorous of the three girls, but not by much. All three sisters were extremely good-looking, although Rose was by far the nicest. Violette and Lilli were pure snobs, and Violette was one of Guy's *special friends*—but so far there had been no serious commitment, like an engagement.

Thank God! Something inside of Alana shied away violently from the thought of Violette's ever becoming Mrs Guy Radcliffe. But then she didn't want any other girl in the Valley to become his wife either. Now, that was a real puzzle. It wasn't as though she was in the running, or as if she wasted any time making herself unhappy about it. Her world was very different from Guy's. Violette was certain to win The Naming. Good luck to her.

As it happened, Alana's mother had been the inspiration for the original Naming, though the festival was the brainchild of the Radcliffes. She thought she would never be as beautiful as her mother, Annabel, and nor did she have her mother's wonderful craft skills. Her mother had excelled at quilting, rug-making, dressmaking, cooking, baking, making a house and garden beautiful, keeping her family well and happy. All those were art forms. Her mother had had them in abundance. Her own skills were with animals. Alana was an excellent rider. She had won many cross country and endurance races, beating Violette, who was a fine rider, on three separate occasions. That hadn't gone down too well with the Denbys. They had the born-to-win mentality of the Valley's social elite.

With the familiar tug of sadness she closed the door on her sleeping father, leaving him to his self induced oblivion. Every day of her life, while she was up in the hills within the cathedral of trees, she prayed he would break out of his prison of guilt and remorse. Everyone in the valley *except* Alan Callaghan knew it wasn't his fault his wife had died after a crash involving their station ute and a big four-wheel drive leisurely exploring the famous sheep and wine district. Holding to the centre of an unfamiliar valley road, the four-wheel drive had side-swiped the ute hard as it rounded a bend. Alan Callaghan and the driver of the four-wheel drive had literally walked away, with minor injuries—her father a broken wrist. Annabel Callaghan had not been so lucky. For some reason she hadn't been wearing her seat belt, though she had always been so particular with her children.

"Fasten up, Kieran. Fasten up, Lana. I don't care if we are on a back road. Do as I tell you now."

Her mother had not fastened up that day. That was the tragic part. A life lost through one careless mistake.

"I should have seen to it. Why didn't I?"

Alan Callaghan would never forgive himself.

In the big, bright yellow and white kitchen, Alana grabbed up a couple of muesli bars and an apple, then let herself out though the back door, heading for the stables. The stables were a distance from the homestead, on the far side of the home paddock. Her fastidious mother had not wanted a single horsefly to get into the house, so her father had had the stables relocated even before her mother had moved in as a new bride.

Buddy was already up and about, ready to greet her with his brilliantly white smile. Buddy, now around eighteen—no one including Buddy knew his exact age—was aboriginal, an orphan who had landed on their doorstep almost ten years ago to the day. Their mother had put the raggedy boy into a warm soapy tub, rustled up some of Alana's unisex clothes, dressed Buddy in them, then fed the starving child. Enquiries had been made, but no one had turned up to claim Buddy. The family had unofficially adopted him.

It was Buddy's job, among other tasks, to look after the horses and keep the stables clean and orderly. He did all his jobs well and conscientiously, immensely proud of the fact that the kindly Callaghans had not only taken him in and sent him off to school—which he had loathed from day one—but eventually given him a job and, above all, somewhere nice to live.

"Morning, Miss Lana."

"Morning, Buddy." Alana returned the greeting with affection. "Hard at it, as usual?"

"I like to keep things just so. You know that. How's Mr Alan this mornin'?" Buddy loved her father. He had *worshipped* her mother. Since she'd been gone Buddy had made time to religiously look after her rose garden.

"Not so good, Buddy." Alana shook her head, fighting off a wave of despondency.

"That's real sad. Devil-man's at 'im!"

"Sure is," Alana agreed. "I'll take Cristo this morning."

"Already got 'im saddled up." Buddy gave a complacent grin. He ducked back into the cool dim interior, then returned leading a rangy bright chestnut gelding—good bloodstock, like the other five in the stable.

"You're psychic, Buddy," Alana pronounced, believing it to be so.

"Never been sick in me life, Miss Lana," Buddy protested, his expression uncertain.

"Not sick—*psychic*," Alana answered, swinging herself up into the saddle. "Psychic means you've got spiritual powers."

"That's *me!*" Buddy visibly brightened. "Must have a teeny bit of Wangaree blood in me."

"Ah, the long-vanished Wangaree!" Alana gave a regretful sigh, looking up towards the surrounding hills.

The trees were standing tall, their silhouette greenish black against a radiant unclouded blue sky. The Valley had been the Wangaree's tribal ground. Wangaree Homestead had been named in honour of that lost tribe.

Alana toiled for hours, driving the wethers down from the ridge at a steady pace into the low country. The mustering of sheep and the directing of them to various locations around the property required plenty of patience and skill. Monty and Brig were in their element, with wonderfully eager expressions, floating around the mob and keeping them in a tidy, closely packed flowing stream. She provided the orders and her dogs carried them out, revelling in the chance to show her what they could do. A few sheep with a little more rebellion than the rest of the docile mob tried to make a break for the scrub, almost losing themselves in the golden grasses, but Monty—a low, near-invisible streak, his neck chain jingling—made quick work of herding them back into line, with a quick nip to a hapless hoof. The creek that wound through the property was glittering, as if a crowd of people were squatting beside it flashing mirrors. Alana always wore sunglasses. They were a must to protect her eyes from the searing glare.

These wethers were due to be drenched, but she would have to wait for Kieran to help her. Kieran was due home the day after next. She missed him when he went away. Life was pretty grim and enormously worrying, with their father the way he was. It broke her heart that the less compassionate people in the district had labelled her father "the Valley drunk." Grief affected people in different ways. Her father, once a light drinker, enjoying a few cold beers at most, had embraced the whisky bottle with a vengeance.

She lifted her head to the wide-open sky. It was an incredible lapis-blue, virtually cloudless. A hot air balloon was almost directly overhead, sailing through the air as free as a bird. The Valley was a centre for sky-diving and parachuting too. She put up her hand and waved. The tourists waved back. They loved seeing the Valley this way. Wangaree and the adjoining valleys were at the very heart of one of the world's great wine growing regions, and only a few hours' drive from the country's biggest and most vibrant city: Sydney.

Mid-morning, driven by hunger, she made her way back to the homestead. Two muesli bars and an apple didn't fill a hard-working girl's tummy. She stopped for a moment to admire her mother's rose garden and say a little prayer. It was a daily ritual. She didn't know if she believed in God any more, but she did it anyway. Her mother had been a believer. She missed her mother terribly.

Alana snapped out of it with an effort. How clever Buddy was! He had taken in everything her mother had taught him. High summer, and the roses were in extravagant bloom. The colours ranged from purest white through yellows and pinks to a deep crimson. Some of her mother's favourites, the old fashioned garden roses, were wonderfully scented. Drought or no, her mother's rose garden was putting on a superb display. For that matter the drought hadn't had a detrimental effect on the grapes. The yield was down, certainly, but the quality was up. They had experienced just enough winter rain, with no damaging summer storms that could wipe out a vineyard in less than ten minutes.

She could hear Guy's well-bred, sexy voice predicting, *"This will be a vintage year."* She could hear his voice so clearly he might have been standing right beside her. But then Guy was so vitally *alive* he seemed physically present even when he wasn't. At least that was what she believed. She even had to hold back a little moan, as though something sharp pricked at her heart. In his own way Guy Radcliffe was a god, complete with a valley full of worshippers. Certainly he was as splendid as any man might wish to be. Everyone adored him.

It fell to her to be the odd woman out.

Rounding the side of the house, she saw Simon's Range Rover making its way out of the tunnel of trees that lent beauty and shade to the long drive up to the homestead. Her heart lifted. He could stay and have something to eat with her. She and Simon were the best of friends. The bond had sprung up in pre-school. Simon had been a real dreamer then, and very, very shy. He still was, come to that, and rather a bit too much on the *intense* side. She had taken charge of him right from the beginning, almost like a little mother. Her role had been to keep Simon safe.

"You must have been put on earth just for me, Lainie!"

That had been when the two of them had been standing hand in hand before the manger at a midnight service one Christmas Eve. She had given him a big squishy hug. What a pair they must have been!

Simon had lost every playground fight when she wasn't around. The kids—and there had been some fair terrors around the Valley—had known not to mess with her. She'd been tough, and her big brother Kieran tougher. Simon was a Radcliffe—Guy's first cousin—and that should have made him bullet proof. But it hadn't—rather the reverse. Simon just seemed to be a natural-born victim. A big factor in his timidity could well have been the untimely loss of his playboy father before he was into his teens. Philip Radcliffe had died at the wheel of his high-powered car. His companion on that fateful day had not been his wife, but a Sydney socialite.

Simon's widowed mother had not gone mad with grief. She had become as bitter as ever a scorned woman could, clinging tight to Simon, her only child, and smothering him in an unhealthy possessive love. Simon, who was very bright, like all the Radcliffes, had eventually gone off to university, where he'd thought himself safe from his mother's excessive love—only to have to come home to Augusta Farm to a mother "terrified of being alone." Though anyone who saw Rebecca Radcliffe throw up her narrow dark head, flash her black eyes and flare her thin nostrils would have been forgiven for thinking she wasn't terrified of anyone or anything. It was the other way around.

Armed with an economics degree, Simon had been taken into the family firm as a matter of course. He worked on the business side of Radcliffe Wine Estates, which was now producing very high-quality chardonnay and shiraz wines. The estate's chardonnay was reaching near iconic standards. Everything Guy touched turned to gold. Another example of the rich getting richer, Alana thought. If only a bit of Guy's Midas touch could land on her father!

"It's wonderful just to see the grapes grow," Simon had once told her happily. "And Guy is the best boss in the world."

Of course he was! Guy was Simon's hero and his role model. Sometimes it put her teeth on edge, the way Simon drooled. She knew it wasn't fair of her. Guy had huge responsibilities. He took them in his stride. It was freely acknowledged that he was doing wonderful things for the Valley. Surely, then, he richly deserved everyone's devotion? There was no getting away from it. Guy Radcliffe was the driving force in Valley life. He drew people to him, men and women alike. Not that it made *her* love him the more. He didn't take any special notice of her either. Neither could she truthfully say she was invisible to him. There was something about the way he looked at her from time to time that caused moments of elation she tried hard not to show. Underneath, of course, she found Guy as impressive as everyone else. It was just that she felt compelled to keep it to herself.

"How's it going?" Simon called as he stepped out of his vehicle. As usual he had nosed it into his favourite parking spot in the shade of the lemon scented gums.

"Getting there," she answered, waiting for him to crunch across the gravel to join her.

A beautiful stone fountain was the central feature of the driveway: three tiers, topped by a life-size bronze of a little boy. It was the work of a famous Australian sculptor—another treasure her mother had brought with her, along with the urns and stone statues that were dotted around the fairly extensive garden. These days the fountain never played.

"I was about to get myself something to eat. Come and keep me company."

"Love to." Simon showed his sweet, vulnerable smile. He had been a delicate and sensitive little boy, and sometimes it still showed. "Well, for a little while. I have to be getting back soon."

"How did you get off in the first place?"

They mounted the short flight of front stairs.

Simon took off his hat and threw it onto the seat of a white wicker armchair. "I had to do a job for Guy. I was on my way back, but I thought I'd stop in here first. You look great."

"You're an awful fool!" she laughed. "I look terrible. I'm hot, sweating and starving."

"You *still* look great." Simon thought one of the best things about Alana was that she either didn't know or didn't care that her natural beauty was startling. Alana was his life. He had been running to her for peace and comfort ever since he could remember. "Your dad around?" His eyes slipped beyond her into the spacious entrance hall, as though Alan Callaghan was about to make another one of his slightly terrifying appearances.

"I guess he should be up by now," Alana said, leading the way into the house. "Go into the kitchen while I check. You could start the coffee if you like."

"Will do."

Simon was as familiar with the Callaghan homestead as his own. He made his way through to the big farmhouse kitchen at the rear. It looked out onto the summerhouse where he and Alana had enjoyed endless after-school snacks prepared by her lovely mother. How he had wished *he* had a mother like that! The white lattice sides were covered in a very beautiful climbing rose, a creamy yellow with glossy dark green foliage, and a heavenly perfume wafted into the kitchen. He would always associate it with Annabel Callaghan. He missed her too. She had been such a radiant woman—beautiful, warm, welcoming. She and his own mother, Rebecca, could not have made a greater contrast.

Alana found her father in his study. He was dressed in knee-length khaki shorts and a clean white singlet. His heavy brown-rimmed glasses were sliding down his nose as he made his way through a fresh pile of bills.

"How are you, Dad?" Alana walked around the king-sized desk to give him a kiss.

"Awful, if you must know," he grunted, putting an arm around her waist and resting his head briefly against her shoulder.

"Your own fault." It was a mistake to give too much comfort.

"I know, but it ain't easy," he commented dryly. "The wethers have to be drenched."

Alana slumped into a leather armchair. "Unless you can help me, it will have to wait until Kieran gets home."

"Of course I'll help you," he said, just a shade testily. In her whole life Alana had never heard a harsh word from her father. "If you're up to it we'll do it this afternoon."

"If *I'm* up to it? I like that!"

"Okay, okay—I know you're a good, brave girl. The very best." He broke off as emotion threatened to overcome him.

"My heart bleeds for you, Dad," she said, very gently. After all, she didn't know what it was to love someone like her father had loved and continued to love her mother. Passion between a man and woman was a different kind of love. She hadn't experienced it as yet, and maybe she never would. Not everyone found a soul mate at will.

Alan gave himself a little mental shake. "I'm not quite the weak blubbing fool I must appear, but your mother was my shining star. She was *there* for me. In the morning she was there. When I came back at night she was there. Always shining. I still don't know what she ever saw in me, the descendant of a wicked Irish convict."

"Who was transported for the term of his natural life to Australia because he'd poached a couple of rabbits to feed his starving family," Alana said darkly. "And who by the way went on to become a well-respected pastoralist."

Her father allowed himself a smile. "Be that as it may, my Belle could have had any man in the Valley and way beyond. She could have had David Radcliffe."

For a stunned moment Alana thought she hadn't heard right. She started up in her chair, her expression aghast. *"What?"* She couldn't control her rising tone. "Guy's father?"

"The very one—God rest his soul!" Alan Callaghan, hands locked behind his head, rested back in his chair, staring up at the pressed metal ceiling.

"B-b-but—" Alana found herself stuttering now. "I've never heard a word of this." In itself this was absolutely extraordinary. "Not one word, not from anyone in the Valley— and everyone knows everyone else's business."

"Obviously they don't know it all." Her father's tone rasped as he took in her stunned expression. "It wasn't common gossip. Neither your mother nor I ever spoke about it during our marriage. I'm sure the Radcliffes didn't either— especially after David married Sidonie Bayley a few months after we married. The rebound, of course. And she's a snob like the rest of them."

"Guy isn't. Simon isn't," Alana said fairly. "But this is unbelievable, Dad." She felt immensely disturbed. "Are you saying Guy's father could have been in love with *Mum?*"

"Is that a problem?" His eyes cut to her. "I don't know why I mentioned it. It just slipped out. *Everyone* was in love with your mother, sweetheart. She was a beautiful, beautiful woman—inside and out."

"And she'll always be remembered for it." Alana tried hard to pull herself together, but she was shocked. "Mum never made any mention of an old romance to me, and we talked about everything. That took in the Radcliffes as a matter of course. Why, she used to laugh whenever I made my little barbed comments about Guy."

"She knew you were kidding. Guy Radcliffe is a—"

"Don't tell me!" She passed a hand over her eyes. "A *prince!*"

"A real gentleman. There's your own Denby cousins, treating us like riff-raff—leave out little Rose—but I've always found Guy the most egalitarian of men. He could teach the Denbys a thing or two about courtesy and respect. His dad was the same way. No side to the man. The whole valley was devastated when Dave lost his life on the Ravenshoe site."

Alana nodded bleakly. It had been an appalling freak accident on a Radcliffe development site, when a ten-metre-high brick wall scheduled to be demolished later in the day had suddenly collapsed. David Radcliffe had been killed instantly, and his chief engineer, a short distance behind him, had narrowly escaped with significant injuries.

Alana began to wonder about certain things. "I remember coming upon Mum at the time," she confessed. "She was crying her eyes out, terribly upset. One didn't see Mum crying."

Her father took long moments to answer. "No," he rasped, and then inexplicably slammed his big hand down on a book. "David Radcliffe was a fine man, an honourable man. He left behind a fine son—a young man to be proud of. Let's leave it at that. I don't actually like talking about this, Lana. The drink loosens my tongue. I was very jealous over your mother when we were young. She was *mine*. I won her."

Was that belligerence in her father's dark blue eyes? Whatever it was, it made Alana swiftly drop the subject. "Simon is here, Dad," she said, rising to her feet. "He called in on the way back to work. Want to come and say hello? Have you had anything to eat?"

Alan shook his head. "Buddy wanted to get me breakfast earlier, but I said no. There's another good, loyal kid. I don't feel like eating, love."

"Well, you must. I insist. I'll make you a plate of sandwiches and a cup of tea."

"All right. But leave it until after Simon has left. I'll come and wave him off, but I don't want to spoil his precious time with you. He's hopelessly in love with you, poor fella. He has been for many a year."

Alana turned back at the door, her expression vaguely troubled. "Who says?"

"Me." Her father thrust a thumb at his chest.

"Well, you're wrong," she corrected him, emphatically. "Simon loves me like the sister he never had. Simon is not *in* love with me. There's a huge difference."

"Believe that, you'll believe anything," her father muttered dryly. "He's a nice boy. Always was. But he's not man enough for you, my darlin'."

The coffee was perking by the time she walked into the kitchen. Simon had set out cups and saucers.

"I didn't know what food you were going to have…" he said.

"Just a sandwich," she said. She considered then rejected questioning Simon about any old love affair in the Radcliffe family. Better let it lie. That was certainly what her father wanted. "Have you eaten?" she asked.

"Only about an hour ago. I will have a cup of coffee, then I must be off. All set for Saturday night?"

She flashed him a reassuring smile. Simon would have been devastated had she said no. "I'm looking forward to it. So is Kieran." Her brother got on a lot better with Guy than ever she had. They were of an age, with Kieran some six months or so older.

On Saturday Guy was giving a small function at Wangaree for visiting guests—an American couple, Chase and Amy Hartmann, members of a leading wine family in California's Napa Valley.

"Your mother's decided not to come?" she asked, striving

to keep her tone non-committal. Rebecca Radcliffe's presence would put a damper on anything.

The muscles of Simon's face abruptly clenched. "Yes, and I have to say I'm glad. Sorry if it sounds disloyal, but Mum can't be relied upon to say a pleasant thing in public. It's just endless barbed comments that seem to bring all conversation to a halt. Guy only asked her because she's family and he's Guy. Lately she's taken to criticising my friendship with you."

"But she's *always* done that." Alana looked up from pouring the coffee. "Heck, she used to blame me for all the bullying that went on with those awful O'Brien boys. Oddly enough, they've turned out quite well."

"Yes—can you believe it? But Mum's jealous of anyone I care about, and you're the closest person in the world to me."

"What exactly is she worried about?" Alana was attacked by concern.

Simon directed his grey glance out of the window. "She's terrified I might get married to someone she doesn't approve of."

Alana couldn't help laughing. "Well, that just about wipes out every girl in the valley. No question of marriage for me, thanks," she added briskly. "Put her mind at rest about *me,* at least. We're best mates. Darn near brother and sister. It would be incestuous."

Looking unbearably embarrassed, Simon grasped her hand and held it. "Can't we take a step up from that, Lainie?" he begged. "No, don't pull away. You mean everything in the world to me."

She didn't have it in her to be unkind. "Well, I'm happy about that, of course. But, Simon, dear, I'm *not* your girl-friend." Gently she removed her hand. "I'm your best pal. After The Man, Guy, of course. What's the matter with you, Simon?" she asked bracingly. The idea of making love with

Simon simply wasn't on. He was very dear to her, but no—decidedly *not*. "You and I, at twenty-two, are just babies in the marital stakes. You haven't actually met a lot of girls." Almost impossible with a psychotic mother. "I thought—I rather hoped—you liked Rose?"

Glumly Simon slumped back in his chair, stirring too much sugar into his coffee. "Come on, Lainie. Rose is really sweet—unlike the terrifying Violette—and I do like her, but she's not a patch on you."

"How do you know?" Alana challenged. She had previous knowledge that her cousin Rose thought Simon equally sweet. "You have to get to know her. Rose is not only sweet and seriously pretty, she has a lot of hidden depth." Or she *could* have, Alana thought. She had a soft spot for Rose.

Simon rejected that idea. "I wouldn't care to get mixed up with that family." He actually shuddered. A gesture, she suddenly realised, very reminiscent of his mother.

"Your beloved Guy squires Violette around," she reminded him, with a little touch of malice. Or could it have been envy? "Whenever it suits him, that is." Whatever did Guy see in Violette? Apart from the fact she was stunning, always marvellously turned out and she could ride. Violette knew all about sheep farming—and wine as well. Ah, heck. Violette's assets were starting to mount up.

"Violette, like many another, is praying that one day he'll pop the question," Simon answered. "But it's not going to happen." His tone couldn't have been more positive.

"Then isn't he being rather cruel to her?" Alana asked sternly. "I can hardly believe she confided in me, but she once told me he only uses her."

"Guy most certainly isn't a user. How dare she?" Simon burst out wrathfully. "He and Violette grew up together. That's all."

"Oh, *please!*" It came out with more vehemence than

Alana had intended. "Are you trying to tell me they've never been lovers?" She bit her lip, regretting her betraying outburst, though Simon—bless him—didn't appear to notice.

The very thought of Guy and Violette being lovers made her ill. There really was something weird about her feelings for Guy. On the one hand she pretended scorn; on the other hand just to catch sight of him induced the most extraordinary quickening in her body. Was it possible she was actually two people when it came to Guy Radcliffe? The Alana on the *outside* and the Alana on the *inside?*

"*Now* what deep thoughts are you thinking?" Simon startled her by asking. Mercifully he didn't wait for an answer. "Guy's no playboy, but he's no monk either. Women fall for him in droves. We all know that."

"He's too sexy for his own good."

There I go again!

"Lucky devil! I wish I had a bit of it." Simon spoke with a mix of admiration and lamentation. "But it's natural, Lainie—just like your sex appeal. You're either born with it or you aren't. Don't believe anything Violette has to tell you. She's only trying to put you off Guy, for some reason. Like I said—she's not the right woman for Guy." He put down his coffee cup, staring soulfully into Alana's eyes. "But *you* are the only girl in the world for me."

"Don't be stupid," Alana said.

Simon left soon after, leaving Alana feeling on edge and jittery. If Simon suddenly started coming over all romantic, she would have to join her father and take to the drink.

CHAPTER TWO

WANGAREE'S lovely mansion homestead stood on top of a knoll in the most beautiful part of the Valley. Everyone knew the magnificent rural property had been acquired by an Englishman, Nicholas Compton Radcliffe, in the early 1850's. Radcliffe, a man of vision and enviable private means, and set about building a homestead to rival any in the colony of New South Wales, and the style he'd chosen was Colonial Georgian. A double-storey central section dominated a serenely imposing façade flanked by one-storey wings with big handsome bays at both ends. To accommodate the hot Australian climate, canopied verandahs had been added at a later date. Rosy brick married wonderfully with the frosting of classical white pillars and beautiful white cast-iron lace. When the building had been completed it had been described in the colonial gazette of that time as "a splendid gentleman's residence."

These days only a rich family could maintain it, Alana thought, staring up the hill at the mansion. It was ablaze with lights, putting her in mind of the great liner *Queen Mary II* at night. She and Kieran had seen the ship make its majestic entry into Sydney Harbour a few months before.

They were late. She had fretted about it at first, and then she had begun to worry when Simon hadn't turned up on time.

Finally he had arrived at the farm, a good forty minutes overdue. He'd looked handsome in his dinner suit, but pale and upset. It had only taken Alana a few seconds to establish why. Simon and his mother—known rather cruelly behind her back as *The Widow*—had had "words". But then Rebecca would much rather have "words" than bid her son a fond, *Goodnight, darling. Drive carefully. Have fun.*

"About what?" Alana had asked.

"Oh, let's forget it," Simon had begged, putting his arm around her and giving her an exquisitely gentle kiss.

She hadn't been able to think of a thing to say that wouldn't have sounded dreadfully impolite. It was high time Simon stood up to his mother.

Now they were going to be the last to arrive. She could see all the parked cars, among them Kieran's. He had left on his own, almost an hour before, with the wry comment, "Simon won't want *me* along as a passenger."

Did even her own brother think she and Simon were an item? Alana found herself oppressed by the idea. As fond as she was of Simon, she shrank from being so labelled. The only one on her side appeared to be Simon's mother, who always greeted her so grimly she might have been hatching some plot to snatch Simon away. Even on the odd occasion when Rebecca offered afternoon tea, she never left them alone, but stood guard.

Together, they mounted the broad sandstone steps to the pedimented portico, waiting quietly in line behind other late arriving couples to gain admittance to Wangaree's delightful entrance hall. Alana had been inside the house often enough to be familiar with it—the black and white marble floor tiles, the coffered ceiling with rosettes, the dazzling chandelier and the romantic sweep of the staircase.

There was an antique console that stood against the wall

to the right of the front door, with its lovely fanlights and side lights, flanked by Chippendale chairs. She knew they were Chippendale. Guy had told her years ago when she had asked. A tall gilded mirror hung above the console, and tonight it reflected a marvellous arrangement of yellow and white liliums trailing green vines. Gilt framed watercolours of the valley had been placed precisely to either side of the antique mirror.

It suddenly struck her she really loved Wangaree home-stead. She just *loved* it. There was no question Violette that would look perfectly at home there. Perhaps not *perfectly,* she consoled herself.

"You look gorgeous!" Simon mouthed reverently.

She might have been a National Treasure. "Thank you, Simon."

It was maybe the fourth time she had thanked him, but she wasn't going to knock back a compliment. She thought she looked rather gorgeous too, considering it was her eighteenth birthday party dress, halter necked, golden green, with a tiny waist and a lovely full skirt. She hadn't put on an ounce of weight. Rather she had lost a few pounds since then.

For tonight she had gone to a lot of trouble. An *incredible* lot of trouble, for her. Who was she trying to impress? Not her best mate, Simon. The results, however, were pretty good, if she said so herself. And she could rely on her hair not to let her down. Great hair, inherited from her mother. Its honey-gold thickness and shimmer gave a girl a lot of confidence.

They were moving now. Alana counted herself lucky to be invited. Did Guy think she was Simon's girl? Perhaps she should seize a moment to set him straight? Why, exactly? Would the knowledge make him rush to rearrange his life? Hardly. Simon took her arm, drawing her so tightly to him she might have been trying to make a break for it. For a minute she considered socking him—but there was the mesmerising Guy.

She had never seen a man look so intensely, magnificently *male*. Guy Radcliffe could be the archetypal hero of some heart warming romance. She thought she could safely speak for all the women of the Valley.

With that, however, came a warning.

Fall in love with him at your peril!

Wasn't she blessed that she attended that warning? She had no intention of allowing herself to fall in love with Guy Radcliffe—not even in an abstracted kind of way, like a daydream. Nevertheless, her eyes absorbed him. He looked wonderfully elegant in his evening clothes. They fitted as though they had been cut for him by a master tailor—which they probably had.

She wanted to present herself in the best possible way, but instead of the cool composure she prayed for, she felt as though she had come madly alive, and shifted up several gears.

Warily, she continued her inspection. Charisma clung to him. What an asset! His beautiful sister, Alexandra, who lived and worked in Sydney, was standing beside him to receive their guests. She too possessed the same charisma. It worked like a beacon. How extraordinarily seductive was grace and breeding! And the Radcliffes had received more than their fair share.

Alexandra was the first to greet them, Guy being caught up with a few extra words to the couple in front of them. She flashed a lovely welcoming smile, putting out her hand. Huge soulful dark eyes lit up her magnolia-skinned face. "Lana, how lovely to see you again." It wasn't just the usual thing said on such occasions. Alana could see Alex really meant it, and felt warmed by it. "And how are you, Simon?"

Simon's tanned skin pinked with pleasure. He made a

funny little obeisance. "Great—just great, Alex." It was obvious Simon was in some awe of his cousins.

The two young women exchanged feather light kisses. "I'm only here for the weekend," Alexandra said, holding Alana's hands. "You must come over tomorrow and have lunch—mustn't she, Guy?"

Now the Lord of the Valley was free to give her his attention. He bent his face to her with languorous, almost regal grace.

It was the most stunning face imaginable. Alana put up a valiant struggle to meet that brilliant glance head on.

"It'd be a pleasure to have you, Alana!" he assured her, his veiled eyes moving over her.

She felt the impact of his gaze so keenly it might just as well have been his hands touching her. Part of her was ready to swoon. The weak, womanly part. Wasn't it the curse of womanhood to swoon over such men? She'd be darned if *she* would. She responded with a few graceful words of thanks.

"That's all settled, then." He smiled at her, rather ironically, she thought, but perfectly relaxed.

Oh, he had a beautiful mouth! It drew the eye irresistibly. Little brackets framed it on either side, drawing extra attention to its sexy shape. A touch ashamed, she fought down the little flares of excitement but found it a real effort. Everything about him sent a thrill through her. Her heart didn't just canter when Guy was around. It broke into a gallop. She just hoped to God he didn't know it. He had far too many female worshippers already. And a lot of them would be here tonight. She was bound to collide with her cousin, Violette. Violette had very sharp eyes.

"I want to know how life's been treating you," Alex was saying.

Alana turned to her. "I'm always kept busy, Alex." She smiled into that beautiful, poignant face.

Guy offered another comment designed to do damage. It never stopped. "May I say how beautiful you look, Alana?" He spoke in his usual smooth, self-assured way, yet she had never seen quite the type of look he was giving her. It was sort of full-on, and it provoked another chaotic flurry of sensations. She knew they were going to take a good while to settle down.

"Why, thank you, Guy!" she countered, almost as if they were sparring partners.

No use channelling your charm on me, Guy Radcliffe.

Yet his charm was drawing her into some powerful whirlpool. She had to make a serious attempt not to be caught up in it. She knew for a certainty it would be dangerous. She didn't need Violette to tell her that.

Simon chose that moment to clamp a firm arm around her shoulders, exclaiming with great gusto, "Doesn't she just? I love the dress she's wearing. Her mother made it for her eighteenth birthday party, remember?"

Alana could have kicked her dear friend in the shins—only she saw recognition of her annoyance in Guy's amused eyes. "I do," he replied. "Your mother was very gifted, Alana."

"Indeed she was," Alex added gracefully. "I treasure the beautiful shawl she made for me."

Alana blinked back a shimmer of tears. Guy had been invited to her eighteenth birthday party. Not Alexandra. Alex had already moved to Sydney by that time. Her abrupt departure for the bright lights had come as a big shock to the Valley. Everyone had thought Alex loved her home. But Alex had left them. Alana's party had been held at the Radcliffe Estate's award winning restaurant. It had been an unforgettable night. When Guy had presented her with her present—a porcelain Art Nouveau statuette of a nymph with long golden hair—he had bent to kiss her cheek.

It had been a token birthday gesture, but she still remembered how it had felt. What could she call it? The very *essence* of sensation? It had touched every part of her, as if she was naked, even reaching down into the most intimate part of her body. She had never realised until then that a kiss on the cheek could cause such an immense erotic rush. It had been quite scary. It still was, when she thought of it—which was usually at night. Guy Radcliffe was the one person who had ever had such a galvanic effect on her. It had to be what, exactly? Fascination? Infatuation? Neither answer satisfied. It certainly didn't venture into the realm of love. As she told herself frequently, there was a lot of distance between her life and Guy's.

"Come through and meet our guests," he invited now, his dark eyes still lingering on her in that special way.

What was she supposed to do about it? She wasn't in her element flirting.

"Yes, do." Alex took her arm companionably. "The Hartmanns are lovely people. I hope you're going to enter The Naming, this year, Alana. You could win the trip to beautiful Napa Valley."

Mercifully Alex didn't add, *You could take Simon.*

The huge reception rooms swam with bright faces and happy voices. It was a smallish function—only around forty people had been invited. Alana knew them all, except for Guy's special guests, who turned out to be a delightful couple in their early thirties, good looking, outgoing, and very friendly. The wife was wearing a particularly stunning yellow chiffon dress that moulded her willowy body beautifully. Alana caught Violette studying it in detail. For once she understood Violette's avid interest in fashion. She would have loved to own a dress like that herself—especially as yellow was her colour.

"Ah, there you are, Lana," Violette said, when she encountered her. "Surely you could have risen to a new dress, dear? What *is* that, exactly? Muddy gold? Or is it muddy green? I'm sure I've seen it before." Her blue eyes bored into the lovely shot-silk taffeta of Alana's dress. "You know, you've given a whole new meaning to the word *thrifty*!"

"And you to *bitchy,* Vi, dear," Alana returned, long used to her cousin's caustic style and almost bullet-proof against it. "But I do love what *you've* got on."

It would have been too churlish not to mention it. Violette was wearing a couture strapless number in aubergine. It suited her wonderfully well. All three Denby sisters were blonde and blue eyed, but they didn't boast Alana's magnificent honey gold mane. Rose came closest, but neither she nor Lilli were present that evening. They were staying with a socialite aunt in Sydney.

Simon took her into supper, which was simply scrumptious—as expected from the restaurant's top chef, who was handling the catering. Across a table laden with delicious food, she saw Kieran talking to Alex. The really odd thing about Alex and Kieran was that, although they had known one another all their lives, these days they acted like strangers. Even now, with their eyes glued on one another, neither was smiling. Alex was tall for a woman, taller yet in silver stiletto evening shoes that matched her short glittery dress, but Kieran, at six-three, easily topped her.

Both she and Kieran took after their mother, Alana thought with nostalgia. Kieran's blond hair was swept back carelessly from his broad forehead, thick and long, like a lion's, but it suited him. His eyes, though, were their father's, an unbelievable blue. He wasn't wearing a dinner suit—he didn't own one—but he looked great, in a summer-weight light beige suit. She had one handsome brother, she thought with pride.

And beside his goldenness, Alex's dark-haired, dark-eyed beauty looked very exotic.

Kieran had once called Alex, *"The most mysterious creature I've ever known."* Alana had thought at the time she understood. Alex had a way of looking at you, with her great lustrous, almost tragic eyes. Actually, there was something mysterious about the way her brother and Alex related to one another, Alana had often thought. Not that they met up frequently, living so far apart. They were both super-attractive people, but it was as if both of them had long since made the decision to walk separate paths.

Later, Alana was much in demand for dancing. Simon called her a miracle in a man's arms. Actually, it was just that she loved dancing when she got the chance. She found it astonishingly easy, but Simon found it extremely difficult.

"You've got to let yourself go," she advised. She really hadn't encountered anyone quite as uncoordinated as Simon on the dance floor.

"You're so brave!" he said. "If I let myself go I'd only be sorry. And so would you."

A familiar voice spoke over Alana's shoulder. "As host, it must be *my* turn."

It would be just her and Guy. So close! Instantly she felt that enormous rush. She could weep for her own susceptibility if she had the strength. Guy didn't have a loud voice, yet its special timbre, well-bred but a little edgy, sliced through the surrounding chatter.

Simon beamed at his cousin, ready to do anything he asked, and Alana spun around to face Guy, conscious of damp little tendrils of hair clinging to her cheeks and her nape. She could never look perfect when she wanted to. She knew she had a good clear skin, but it was inclined towards looking dewy instead of wonderfully matt, like Alex's or even Violette's.

Perhaps her foundation was all wrong? Oh, hell—what did it matter?

Guy took her hand.

It was like being zapped. She even fancied she could see little blue arcs of static electricity crackling between her hand and his. It made her feel strangely weak—as if all her strength was draining away and her legs were about to give way. She couldn't have moved even if she had wanted to, though her heart was pounding so hard even her ears hurt. This was madness, pure and simple. It would have been much wiser to have spent the evening safely at home, tucked up with a good book.

Simon gave her a much-needed moment to collect herself. "You won't find a better dancer than Lainie in the whole valley," he told Guy fondly, only too pleased to retreat from the dance floor and leave Alana to his celebrated cousin. "You can enjoy yourself at last, Lainie," he promised, giving them a wave that looked something like a Papal benediction.

Guy couldn't help it; he laughed. "He really puts you on a pedestal, doesn't he?"

"I don't know what you mean." The time was ripe to tell him she and Simon *weren't* an item.

"Oh, nonsense!" His tone was amused, those brackets beside his mouth deepening into sensual creases.

"Maybe Simon and I should split up for a bit," she said airily. "People seem to think we're a fixture."

He drew back his dark head, staring into her eyes. "Aren't you?"

Cool. Keep cool.

So much for that! She found herself answering with intensity. "What if I dared ask if you and Violette are an item?"

"Who says we ever *were*?" he challenged.

She drew a long breath. "Most of the Valley. Simon and I aren't and never will be an item, Guy. Simon and I are best…pals. Yes—*pals* is a good word for it. I've been looking after him ever since I can remember. Certainly pre-school."

"He loves you." There was a quiet seriousness in Guy's voice.

Uncertain, she searched his eyes. They were beautiful eyes, black as night, but with a diamond sheen. "You sound serious?"

"I'm always serious with you, Alana."

Heat swept her like a flame. She could feel the flush spread out all over her body. "Well, I never knew *that!* In fact, it's a bit too much to take in. Generally you speak to me as though I haven't made much progress since my eighteenth birthday."

"A bad habit I picked up," he rejoined suavely.

"So you admit it?"

"Absolutely. You didn't *really* want me to treat you like an alluring woman, did you?"

She nearly folded, deeply surprised. "Hey, I'm not the alluring one. *You* are." The heat off her body could be throwing off sparks.

"Alana, that's plain crazy!" He spun her then, in what felt like some elegant choreographed step. In fact the two of them were beginning to look like ballroom champions, she thought, aware people were looking their way, expressions openly admiring. "*Men* aren't alluring," he scoffed gently.

"Aren't they?" He gave off male allure in metre-high waves. "You should try reading some of Vi's romances."

"Violette reads romances? How delicious!"

As was his laugh. "Well, she might, for all I know. I was having a little joke. But, just so there's no misunderstanding, I want to make it perfectly plain. Simon and I have no plans that involve romance."

That little smile was tugging at his mouth. "Does one have to plan it?" he asked. "Surely it just happens? You wake up one morning wishing you could reach out for that special someone."

Her body quickened. She knew his hands would be just lovely. "Well, you must have done a fair bit of that—" There was the faintest trace of hostility in her voice. She broke off, horrified. He *was* her host.

He drew back to stare down at her. "It might be a good time to tell you, Ms Callaghan, that you've just about used up all my gentler feelings towards you."

"So I should start to worry?" she challenged.

For answer he pulled her in so close that the room around them started to blur.

"It might be an idea," he cautioned.

"Does that mean you can say and do what you like, but I can't?"

He didn't answer.

Silence had never seemed to say so much.

"Who would *you* reach for, Guy?" The words simply came.

"I won't terrify you and say *you*."

She, so wonderfully sure on her feet, stumbled. "You're terrifying me just thinking about it. You're joking—aren't you?"

He saw the bright confusion in her lustrous eyes. "Of course." His glance remained on her. It brushed her face and her throat, and her very feminine creamy shoulders. "But who could blame a man for wanting you near him, Alana?"

Every single nerve-ending in her body was wired. "You're taking me somewhere, Guy," she said, unable to control the tremble in her voice. "Where is it?"

"The big question is, do you *want* to come?" His handsome face was unusually intent.

"And leave my safe little world?" she asked shakily. She marvelled at the difference in him—in her. What had changed things so dramatically? Was this precarious kind of intimacy better or was she about to jeopardise her whole future? "It would be far too easy to fall under your spell, Guy," she said. "The result could be a lot of pain." Her sharp-talking, supremely self-confident cousin hid a lot of pain.

"And you're scared of that?"

"Absolutely." She released a pent-up breath.

"So what is it about me that scares you? You certainly haven't given that impression over the years."

"You've never invited me to come close."

"You were too young. Come closer now." He gathered her in. "You're a beautiful dancer, by the way."

"Have you just noticed?"

"I've always noticed."

"You could have asked me to dance with you hundreds of times over the last couple of years, but you never have."

"In the space of a few minutes the intervening years have disappeared. Maybe I thought you were being faithful to Simon?"

Her body abandoned all pretence, trembling in his arms. "Maybe I thought you were being faithful to Violette? Among others." She couldn't resist the little waspish sting in the tail.

His hand at her back exerted a little more pressure. "Remember what I said about being more careful?"

"Actually, I remember an astonishing number of things you've said to me," she found herself admitting. "At my eighteenth birthday party you told me I was sweet. And smart."

He gave her a disturbing smile. "Sweet, smart, and *tart*. Let's see—I remember now. I could have added passionate, argumentative, with a good sense of humour and sexy but innocent too. Sad, beautiful, a wonderful daughter and sister. The best woman rider in the valley, and that's saying something. I've always loved to see you competing. Poor Violette was always doomed to run second. Come to that, I love to see you working those Border Collies of yours. Not easy working dogs, but you instinctively know how to get the best out of them. You have a very attractive voice too. I've heard you singing to your own guitar accompaniment."

She was totally disarmed. "Now you're using your fabled charm on me, Guy."

"Is it working?" He flicked her a downward glance.

"I'm not sure it would be wise to tell you." She shook back her honey-blonde mane. "I feel sure you're pledged else-where. Or you soon will be."

Another couple whirled by, coming in too close. Instantly Guy's arms drew her out of harm's way.

Harm's way? Her heart rate had risen as though she had run halfway up Mount Everest. They had known each other such a very long time, but she couldn't imagine anyone who seemed so familiar yet so *new* to her. Her body fitted his so perfectly, it was beyond explanation. So perfectly she wondered if she should back off. All it needed was one tiny step over the dividing line. And there *was* a dividing line. She could never allow herself to forget that.

For the first time her graceful body offered resistance. "Cousin Vi's over there, looking like she wants to bury a tiny hatchet in my head." She tried to turn what must have been her perceptible withdrawal into a joke.

"I wouldn't let her."

Her breath shortened at his tone. "She could catch me on my own. Batter me in my sleep. Are you trying to make her jealous?" Did that explain his newfound manner?

"Don't be ridiculous." His reply was short. "I can't even see her. *You're* so dazzling."

She had a sensation she was floating. What was he trying to do to her? And why? There were so many unanswered questions spinning around in her head. "I'm dazzling all of a sudden?" she questioned, lifting sceptical eyes no longer hazel but pure green.

"Let's just say you've been dazzling me for quite a long time—though, very modestly, you've appeared unaware of it."

Modesty didn't prevent a highly explosive recklessness surging into her. Whatever it was that was happening between them, it was moving way too fast. Mistakes carried penalties, she reminded herself. "Who *are* you tonight, Guy?" She tipped her head back, to ask, "Do I really know you?"

"I don't think you do."

His voice held the faintest rasp to it, yet it was very seductive. His evident experience made her acutely conscious of her own lack of it. She was still a virgin, probably the last one left in the Valley, but that had never mattered to her. To date she hadn't met anyone she had wanted to enter into a serious love affair with. She hadn't even glimpsed anyone who didn't pale before Guy Radcliffe. Now she was discovering there was a lot of emotion locked up in her. Passion. Desperate hunger. She didn't want to feel this vulnerable. Up until now she had been rock solid, in control. A *whole* person, not part of someone else. Falling madly in love didn't guarantee happiness. Love could be abruptly withdrawn, leaving the rejected one to battle the pain.

"Wait." She placed a shaky hand against the snowy-white of his dress shirt

Immediately his expression turned to concern. "What is it?"

"Nothing really. I just feel a little odd." Her emotions, of course, were getting too hard to handle. But she couldn't tell him that.

"Let's go out onto the terrace. Get some air." His hand moved beneath her elbow guiding her outside.

* * *

The mingled scents from the garden were like incense on the warm air. Couples were standing laughing, talking, on the lush sweeping lawn; others were wandering the many stone paths, one with a little bridge that spanned a man-made pond where black swans sailed majestically and came at your call. The way was lit by hundreds and hundreds of twinkling white lights that had been placed in the density of the overhead trees.

The night was all around them, the vast dome of the sky thickly studded with glittering stars. There was Orion, the mighty hunter with his jewelled belt. The Southern Cross was so bright she understood perfectly why the aborigines worshipped it, and the Milky Way was a broad sparkling stream, the resting place of the great tribal heros.

Thoughtfully Guy produced a handkerchief to dust off the wide surrounds of a stone pillar—one of eight that supported the roof of the loggia. "Sit here. There's a lovely breeze."

"How good it feels!" she sighed, letting the breeze slide over her to cool her heated skin. Hadn't her inner voice always warned her it would be dangerous to get too close to Guy Radcliffe? And with good reason. Now that she had done so, however lightly, she realised she couldn't go back. His magic had already worked its way into her. She should do something to counteract it. But what?

He stood with his tall elegant body eased back against the pillar, looking down at her. "You're very like your mother," he told her quietly. "She was such a radiant woman. The Valley isn't as bright without her."

The gentleness and the compassion in his voice overwhelmed her. She was so incredibly touched she feared she might burst into tears. She remembered how her mother had always laughed merrily when Alana had made her tart little comments about Guy Radcliffe, Lord of the Valley. Of course her mother, skilled at recognising the truth of it, had seen through her. Now she thought there was a possibility Guy might tell her what she had so recently learned about her mother and his father. She desperately wanted to know.

Had they once had a relationship? Even a brief flutter that had burnt itself out? She had always felt a decided resistance to her from Guy's mother, Sidonie. Not that Mrs Radcliffe, who lived near Alex these days, wasn't always gracious. But she was ultra-*reserved,* withholding any real warmth.

"Guy?" She lifted her head to him, her voice betraying strong emotion.

He looked down on her. The exterior lights were making a glory of her beautiful hair, and burnishing the golden-green of her evening dress, its long skirt pooling around her. "If it's what I think you're going to ask, the answer is *no!*"

She felt the powerful rejection. "You can read my mind?"

"This time I can. You forget, I've known you since you were a little girl. I've a pretty good idea where you're heading. You were bound to hear something from your father at some point."

"And so I have—just a comment. I want *you* to tell me." She shifted position so she could look directly at him.

For a fraught moment he seemed to consider. "Alana, you shouldn't listen to gossip," he said finally.

"Gossip?" The tightness that had gathered in her throat was reflected in her voice. "There's always gossip in the Valley, but my father never gossips. I've never heard this before."

"And you're not going to hear it from me."

He said it so decisively it had the power and authority to stop her in her tracks. She rose to her feet, not knowing how to continue.

"Is that a warning?"

"No, of course not!" His brooding expression almost immediately lightened. "I'm simply stating my feelings. Leave it, Alana, please. There's nothing to be gained. Tell me how you feel now."

Rocked to my soul!

Her old self seemed to have disappeared for ever. "Much better," she lied.

The playful breeze sent a long golden strand of hair flying across her cheek. Guy reached out to smooth it back, his fingers making contact with her skin, electrifying it.

She inhaled sharply.

"Alana," he said, his hand slipping to the nape of her neck.

The depth of feeling in his voice dazed her. For a crazy minute she thought something cataclysmic was about to happen, something that would change her life. Was he going to draw her into his arms? Was he going to kiss her? Kiss her in front of all these people? Unbelievably, it felt like it. Her feelings were rubbed raw. She had a sudden overpowering urge to lift her mouth to him, but instead she moved back, the flutter in her voice betraying her state of agitation. "What am I getting myself into, Guy?" she whispered.

His answer was equally quiet and equally intense. "I guess it's about time to find out."

"You'll have to tell me what you mean." Her voice was charged with tension.

"Just let yourself go with it," he said, in a near-hypnotic voice.

Neither of them was moving. They were standing perfectly still, staring at one another; two people who were finally admitting they were powerfully drawn to each other. Alana felt her mind and body beginning to reel. She wanted to lie down. With *him*. She wanted his arms around her. Some part of her had always been tamped down. Now it was breaking out. Or trying to. She could feel it beating strongly against her ribcage. The safe option was to break the link—

only she wanted whatever it was between them to bind them closer together. The ambivalence that had been in her was no more than a defence. How long had she expected to hide behind those defences? She knew they wouldn't protect her anyway.

"Are you trying to hypnotise me?" The tension in her voice betrayed the emotional storm that was in her.

"I think you *could* be hypnotised," he said gently. "Are you brave enough to let me?"

"I don't think I'm ready…"

"Some part of you has always fought me."

"I can't deny it."

He smiled. "But it hasn't lasted. Are you going to enter The Naming?"

She dropped her head. "I like to keep a low profile. You know that. Besides, the competition is fierce. It's not fair that Alex has never been able to enter."

"Alex is family," he explained. 'Besides, she doesn't need a prize trip."

"But Alana Callaghan does?" She couldn't prevent the flare of resentment.

"All I meant is, you ought to do something different, Alana. Win a trip overseas. Enjoy yourself."

She didn't look at him.She turned her luminous head away, unaware that even in the semi-dark it glowed. " I couldn't enter even if I wanted to. I couldn't take up any prize even if I won—which is a long way from certain. I'm a working girl. I have to be around to give Dad and Kieran a hand. I have to keep my eye on Dad."

"How is he?"

Although his voice was full of real interest and concern, she was immediately on the defensive. Guy was a man of immense kindness, who did things for people without drawing attention to it, but she didn't want to talk about her father, burdened for so long with the worry, the hurt and humiliation of what he had become.

"You know darn well how he is, Guy," she said, soft vehemence covering her compulsion to cry. "Dad's a mess."

"Don't! I didn't mean to upset you. I'm sorry." His hand shot out to encircle her wrist.

She didn't have the strength to pull away. This man touched her in every way. "I'm not going to embarrass you!" Her pretty teeth were gritted. The light caught the sparkle of tears.

"Do I look like I'm embarrassed?" he challenged.

On the contrary, he radiated a richly sensual tenderness.

"I'm not *ever* going to cry in front of you," she vowed.

"You'll have to take the consequences if you do," he said enigmatically, not releasing her hand, but stroking her palm with his thumb.

She swallowed hard. *Consequences?*

"Your father has always resisted grief counselling." There was regret in his voice. "That's a pity. There are very good people who can help him. One in particular I'd like him to at least meet."

She bit her lip. "He won't do it, Guy."

"What if I talk to him one more time?"

She made a sad little face. "Dad thinks the world of you, Guy. And I have an awful suspicion you've been helping us out financially, but I know you won't tell me. Even so, I don't think your trying would do any good. Kieran and I have had to give up. Dad can be very stubborn. Sometimes I think he has a death wish."

Guy's hand tightened over hers, causing her to close her eyes at the mounting excitement.

"Don't say that," he told her quickly. "There's been enough tragedy."

How could she feel comforted and yet delirious with excitement at the same time? It was a fantasy. Did he know what it was doing to her, his thumb on her hand, skin on skin?

"My mother was tremendously upset when your father was killed." Once again she had strayed into dangerous territory. "When I think back, it was like something deeply personal."

"Your mother was a truly beautiful and compassionate woman. Leave it at that, Alana." His striking features were taut.

"I wasn't… Of course I wasn't… I wouldn't dream of…"

A disdainful drawl came out of the shadows, causing them to break apart.

"So there you are, Lana," Violette called. "Simon is looking everywhere for you."

"Why? Is there some emergency?" Guy turned his dark head as Violette, emanating a powerful jealousy, stalked up to them.

She gave Guy a playful smile. "Why, Guy, you know Simon can't let her out of his sight for a minute. He's mad about the girl. Goodness, they already *look* married. And I'm not the only one to think so."

"You *are* the busy little bee, spreading all these rumours," he pointed out dryly.

"Darling!" Violette protesting took his arm. "I think it's cute. Those two have been sweethearts almost from the cradle."

A scream felt like an appropriate response to Alana. Instead she found a smile. "Pardon me if I just run along."

Once she was inside the house, Simon dived back to her side. "How did the dance go?" he asked eagerly. "You and Guy were really, really good. Everyone was watching you."

"I loved it," she confirmed, in a massive understatement. "But actually I crave a cold drink."

"There's champagne," Simon suggested, smiling helpfully. 'It's really flowing."

"Cold water would do nicely."

"I'll get some. What about club soda?"

"Fine." She nodded her head.

"There's not a thing Guy can't do." Simon, his voice full of admiration, steered her towards the drinks table

"He's The Man, all right!" she agreed laconically.

"He sure is. Look, do you suppose we could get out of here soon? It's a lovely event, but I'm not much good with parties. I soon run out of chit-chat."

"You want to go?" Alana looked around for her brother. She spotted him, yet again with Alex.

They obviously preferred talking to dancing, and it was no trivial chit-chat either. They might have been about to face a firing squad together. Another mystery there. She hadn't seen them dancing together all night. But what perfect foils they were for each other! She supposed that might equally well apply to her and Guy. The striking difference in colouring, of course, the gold and the ebony. She had a presentiment that she should follow Kieran's direction and take a separate path from the Radcliffes. It wouldn't have escaped her so-proud brother's attention that Alex was an heiress. It pretty well put a sign around her neck that read, *strictly off-limits*. Besides, when Alex was at home she was never without Roger Westcott in tow. A lot of people thought *they* would marry. The Westcotts were old squattocracy. It was the same old story. Money married money. People with a position in society married their own kind. It helped keep the family fortunes intact.

"Look, I'll stay if you want to," Simon was saying selflessly, though he didn't really enjoy himself when Alana wasn't around. And all the fellows he knew were looking their way, no doubt awaiting an opportunity to dance with her. "You're so good with people. I envy you. I always get the feeling people don't know what I'm saying. The only person in the world I can really relax with is you."

Sadly, it was true. Rebecca's brand of mothering had had a disastrous effect on him. Simon had made reticence an art form.

"And I worship Guy," he tacked on, quite unnecessarily.

"Simon, dear, I don't have the slightest doubt of that!" She wondered for the first time in her life if she didn't worship Guy herself?

"Yet I always feel I should recharge the batteries when I'm around him. He's so vital, so focused. And Alex is a lovely person, but I don't really know her—she's so deep. Kieran always gives me the impression he'd like to see me do a stint in the army. Little Rose, now, is sweet. I can see a little bit of *you* in her."

Here was an opportunity. Alana seized it. "Well, isn't that what I keep telling you? You have to get to know Rose better."

"Let's go. Let's get out of here," Simon said by way of an answer.

When they arrived at Briar's Ridge, Simon, very properly, got out of the Range Rover to escort her to the door. "I won't see you tomorrow if you're going to Wangaree for lunch. You could come over for tea?" he suggested, giving her a beseeching look.

"Doesn't your mother require a month's notice?" Alana put up a hand and pinched his cheek, something she'd been doing since the First Grade.

"What about fish and chips down by the river?"

"My very favourite place! Down by the river it is."

She reached up to kiss his cheek, before sending him on his way, only Simon decided it was his moment to act. The light of battle was in his sky-blue eyes.

"Simon!" she gave a warning wail, not wanting to hurt him, her dearest friend, yet at the same time possessed of a fierce urge to push him away.

But Simon wasn't about to be put off. He was all buoyed up. "Lainie, I love you," he declared. "I'll kill myself if you don't let me kiss you. You're the most beautiful girl in the entire world!" He was almost choking with emotion. "Please... please...a proper goodnight kiss." He placed his hands on her shoulders—she could feel his arms trembling as he gripped her—and dipped his dark head.

What followed was actually quite sweet. In fact Alana nearly thanked him. She'd had a lot of kisses worse than Simon's. He could easily find a girl to love him, she thought, but no way were *they* on the cusp of a grand passion.

"I think I hear Dad," she whispered, thinking that was a sure-fire way to get Simon mobile. Simon was marginally terrified of her father.

"I'd better go, then," Simon whispered back. "Promise me I'll see you tomorrow."

"I'll ring you." Inside the darkened house there was a noise, as if something fairly light had toppled over. Alana latched on to it. "Could be Dad!" she warned, knowing full well it was most likely their cat.

"Night, then!" Simon took off down the short flight of front steps, then broke into a run.

CHAPTER THREE

BRIAR'S Ridge was into its first week of shearing. For most of the preceding week the brunt of getting the barracks ready for the shearing team had fallen on Alana. The men brought their own cook, and there was a kitchen, bathrooms, and a large communal shower room, but it all had to be cleaned, swept and dusted, mattresses aired, then beds made up with fresh sheets. Alana had had to dig deep to get through it all, but the last sheep was expected to be shorn by the end of the following week.

Wangaree, by far the biggest property in the valley, was already underway, with its shearing expected to go on for weeks.

Alana had loved shearing time from when she was a little girl, and the itinerant shearers—all regulars to Briar's Ridge—had made a little mascot of her. An extra bonus for this week was the gratifying way her father had managed to remain sober and on the job.

When Alana wasn't droving sheep to the shed, or taking shorn sheep back to the paddocks, part of her time was spent with the shearers—much to the delight of the men, in particular a newcomer to their ranks, with an excellent reference from a big Western Queensland station.

Even dressed in unisex jeans and a cotton shirt, there was no mistaking Alana for anything else but a beautiful, vibrant young woman with a powerful sex appeal that was entirely natural. Admiring glances came her way aplenty, but no man was fool enough to look at her directly with lust in his eyes. Alan Callaghan was still a daunting presence in the sheds and around the yards. There was her brother Kieran too, a great bloke, but fiercely protective of his sister. And then there were Alana's dogs, a formidable pair. The upshot was that Alana went where she pleased without a moment's hassle.

Apart from her golden beauty, the men admired her for her proven abilities and capacity for hard work. Alana could shear a sheep with the best of them. Maybe she didn't have their strength and endurance, and she couldn't keep up the count or the pace—she was a woman after all, very fit and in splendid shape but at the end of the day no match for a man—but she came into her own instructing her dogs to draft the sheep through the yards. It was fascinating to watch the dogs in action. Up, under, around, running along the sheeps' backs. In the shed Alana worked hard, picking up the shorn white fleece the instant it was ready, then throwing it in a smooth arc onto a long slatted table.

That particular day when the men were more than ready for their mid-morning break—although there were no smokers any more, like in the old days, no pollution of human lungs let alone the wool—Thommo, their best and fastest shearer, even if he was the oldest, let her have a go finishing off the last sheep. Thommo had given her and Kieran lots of tips about shearing over the years, which they had taken on board.

"Come on, love. Your go," Thommo said encouragingly.

"Thanks, Thommo." There was still plenty to learn.

Beneath her blue shirt Alana was wearing a sports bra and

a yellow singlet. All the exterior doors and windows were open, but it had grown very hot in the shed. Without a thought, unselfconsciously she ripped off her cotton shirt.

"Sheep-o!" Thommo yelled as he pulled a fairly hefty ewe from the pen. "You're on the clock, love."

And this, then, was how Kieran and Guy found her, when they walked down to the shed to check on how the wool was coming.

"Well under four minutes!" Thommo congratulated her, well pleased.

He took a closer look. She had freed the wool cleanly in one piece, nice and close to the loose kinky skin. He threw her a clean towel and she moved forward to catch it. Sweat was running down the side of her face from her temples, trickling into her cleavage. She was positively *glowing.*

Guy gave no indication of it, but he was deeply rattled. This wasn't the Alana he had seen a few weeks back, at the party for the Hartmanns. She had been so beautiful then, in her golden-green dress, hair and make-up immaculate. This was the tomboy Alana Callaghan Guy remembered from only a handful of years before, but the luminosity she had inherited from her mother was a thousand times more potent. She didn't seem at all uncomfortable, yet the tight yellow singlet drew attention to her small, beautifully shaped breasts, her taut midriff, tiny waist, and the slender strength of her arms. Her lovely, glossier-than-satin skin was dewed with sweat, the ponytail at her nape a damp honey-gold tangle.

She looked incredibly erotic.

Guy felt a hard knot tightening in his chest. He felt a powerful impulse to strip off his own shirt and cover her up. His eyes whipped around the shed. Most of the men he knew.

They were regulars on the circuit. One fellow he didn't: young, heavy build, heavy wrists and shoulders, good-looking in a rough sort of way, dark overnight growth on his face. *His* response to Alana was showing only too starkly.

Guy found himself jamming his hands so they came together like fists. He loathed violence. He'd never had to employ it—he knew he commanded a lot of respect that precluded it—but he had a driving urge to run the shearer not only out of the shed but off a property that wasn't even his. He had to force himself to calm. If he had *his* way, Alana would be barred from the shed.

His sister Alex had been treated like a princess from birth. *Alex* had never been allowed to wander at will around the shearing sheds when the men were there working. *She* certainly didn't know how to shear a sheep and class the wool, much less work energetic sheep dogs. Alex's place had been at the homestead with their mother. She had gone on to university, after which, armed with an arts degree majoring in Fine Art, she had been offered a job at arguably the best art gallery in the country, owned and run by a family friend. A smooth ride—as Alex would be the first one to admit.

Alana too had had her chance at university, but when her mother had been killed there had been nothing else for it but for her to come home. For the past three years she had been a full-time, hard-working farm girl, coping valiantly with a guilt-ridden father with a potentially fatal drinking problem. No easy life for a twenty-two-year-old girl. It came to Guy, not for the first time, that *he* was powerfully protective of her.

The shearers' cook, a wiry little Chinese man, entered a side door, calling out, "Smoko!" to the men. Morning tea was ready, which meant a mountain of sandwiches, fresh dampers with butter, golden honey or strawberry jam, and a gallon of billy tea.

As she towelled herself off, Alana caught sight of the two

men in the main doorway. Their tall, lean figures, wide in the shoulders, narrow in the hips, were silhouetted against the brilliant sunlight.

Guy! He had only to appear and she came unstuck. Settle down, her inner voice advised. She shouldn't let him do this to her, but so much of life just *happened.*

Totally unselfconscious only a few minutes before, now she threw the towel down and made a hasty grab for her shirt, pulling it on but letting it hang loose.

"Hey, Lana—want to organise some morning tea for us?" Kieran called to her in a cajoling voice. "I'll have a few words with Thommo, then I'll join you both back at the house. Don't worry about Dad. He and Buddy are flat out at the Second Paddock."

"Fine. I'll wash up first." She walked towards Guy, while Kieran followed the shearers outside into the sunlit courtyard.

"Morning, Guy," she managed brightly, although her throat had gone bone-dry. "This is a surprise." She led him off on the shortest route to the house.

Brilliantly enamelled parrots squawked overhead; and a fresh gust of wind sent spent petals flying from the seductive smelling flowers.

"I wanted to have a word with your father."

"Oh?" She looked up at him quickly, trying to decipher what lay behind those fathomless dark eyes. He sounded very distant for Guy. Indeed, he looked daunting. His eyes were clouded— but with what? Some strong feeling, that was for sure. It unnerved her. Was it anger that overwhelmed him? If so, about what? She kept her head tilted towards him, feeling enormously heated—and it wasn't just from her recent physical activity. Emotions were running dangerously high. She had never seen Guy this way. She tried to cover her inner agitation with whatever veneer she could muster. "What about?"

"We want to keep it to ourselves." His expression lightened, but it still troubled her.

"Now you've got me really interested."

"While keeping you out of the loop?" He gave her a faint sideways smile. "No, it's just private stuff, Alana. Nothing to worry or concern you." His glance swept her, increasing her jitters.

She was wearing some light gloss that made her heart-shaped mouth look moist and luscious, Guy thought. He knew there were many young men in the Valley in love with her, his own cousin included, but she wasn't looking to get rescued from the farm. She loved Briar's Ridge. She was a true country girl, but just too damned desirable to work with the men.

"Shearing is gruelling work," he said, hearing it come out a lot more tersely than he'd intended.

"You mean you don't approve of my taking part?" She stared up at him with a little questioning frown. His attitude had taken her by surprise.

He was silent a moment. "Actually, I don't. There's a new fellow on the team. What's his name?"

She gave a little laugh. "Gosh, you worked that out pretty fast. He's a New Zealander, and he's good. Great co-ordination. I can't remember his name. I think it's Dean."

"Then *Dean* had better keep his eyes off you."

It was preposterous. He was *jealous*. "I never thought you so arrogant, Guy Radcliffe!"

His mouth compressed. "It's not that I'm arrogant. To put it simply, I'm older and wiser than you."

"Oh, yes! You're my superior in every way."

"At various times I might be. You should consider keeping your shirt on around the men."

She made a sound of intense irritation. "What a sensible suggestion! You're really jealous, huh?"

He shrugged a shoulder. "No, just concerned. Your father and Kieran can't keep their eye on you all the time."

Alana could feel her temper go from simmer to boil. "Gee, Guy, it's so nice you called in. Don't you think I can look after myself?"

"Sorry, Alana. You can—better than most. But I wouldn't like to see anyone bothering you."

"What would you do?" she challenged, thinking that the elegant Guy Radcliffe, who never raised his voice, wouldn't be the man to cross. At that very moment the Lord of the Valley looked mighty tough.

He held a bougainvillaea bough freighted with hot pink blossom away from her head. "You've seen me cracking a whip haven't you?" he asked. Whips were used by stockmen to assist in the mustering process. Alana knew better than most that it wasn't anywhere as easy as it looked. Guy was wonderful to watch.

"I've got a big brother, Guy," she pointed out sweetly.

"I don't feel in the least brotherly."

It took a full minute for her to respond. "How about cousinly?" she suggested.

"Not even close. Kieran is enormously protective of you, and he worries when he has to go away."

It was the truth. "You Valley men are all so old fashioned. Don't deny it. You are."

He surprised her by coming to a halt, then turning her towards him. "Men have always been attracted to beautiful women, Alana. Most are civilised and keep their admiration within prescribed bounds. *Some* don't."

Her hazel eyes sparkled as she lifted her chin. "You sound like you want to sack my new man on the spot?"

"I'm going on instinct." His dark gaze was very serious.

"What was he doing?" She broke away angrily.

"It's called arousal," he responded bluntly.

Alan couldn't control her flush. "Listen, Guy," she said tightly, "I'm confident I can handle the men, thank you very much. Our regulars wouldn't let any new man get out of line. Besides, Dad is sober these days. He's out and about, and Kieran is always around. I have three favourite men in my life. And, no, one of them isn't *you*."

"Lord of the Valley?" he queried, very dryly.

The fact he knew mortified her. "Okay I admit I call you that sometimes."

"You've been calling me that for years," he jeered softly.

"Be that as it may, my three favourite men are Dad, Kieran and Simon—in that order."

He didn't look in the least slighted. In fact he laughed, showing his beautiful even white teeth. "Then, Ms Callaghan, you're in the best of all possible hands."

Inside the house, Alana excused herself quickly. "I won't be more than a few minutes. I'll just wash up. Go into the living room. Make yourself at home."

"Is that one of Kieran's?" Guy made a beeline to the wall hung with a huge, unframed canvas. It was an abstract, yet unmistakably the light-filled Australian bush. It sang of it. It even seemed to smell of it. "Of course it is," Guy muttered to himself. "Couldn't be anyone else's. It's astonishing! It radiates!" He suddenly wanted to buy it, knowing if he suggested such a thing Kieran would have the painting off the wall in no time, gift-wrapped and delivered to him.

"Tell *him* that," Alana called, dashing away.

God knew, Alex had tried often enough to tell him, Guy thought, studying the work of art even more intently. How did Kieran get so much *light* into it? Annabel Callaghan had not painted, to the best of his knowledge, but she had been a very "arty" woman, enormously gifted at craftwork. One of Annabel's Denby cousins was a well-known painter, Marcus Denby, who had lived in England for the past thirty years. So it was in the genes, in their nature, Guy thought. Though it was only since his mother's death that Kieran had found release in these riveting landscapes, "knocked up"—in his own words—in one of the farm sheds. Kieran painted. Alana read books. Alan drank himself to death.

Guy had known Kieran all his life. Kieran was clever, insightful, extremely hard-working but he wasn't meant to be a sheep farmer. It was at Alex's instigation that Guy had discovered Kieran Callaghan's great gift. He simply hadn't known. But Alex *had*. He knew Alex and Kieran, remarkably close in their teens, had long since gone their separate ways. Something hadn't worked out, and he often felt that was a great pity. He had tried at one time to find out what the big rift had been, but both, independently of one another, had let him know he was breaching boundaries. After that he had backed off. Alex had more than her share of admirers anyway. He just hoped she wouldn't settle for poor old Roger. Roger Westcott was a good man—they had gone to school and university together—but he wanted someone with a lot more going for him for his beautiful, artistic sister.

Guy was still standing in front of the painting when Alana flew down the staircase.

"There—what did I tell you? A few minutes!" she announced breathlessly.

He let his eyes rest on her, aware of a powerful desire to reach for her, fold her in his arms, let what might happen, happen. Instead he said lightly, "You look like you've had a shower." She was wearing different clothes—a red tank top and beige shorts that showed off her long beautiful legs. Her honey-blonde hair was damp, little tendrils curling around her hairline like golden petals.

Her face lit up with a smile so beautiful it took his breath. "Just a quick one. In and out. Come through to the kitchen," she invited, almost dancing ahead. "You like that painting of Kieran's, don't you?" she asked over her shoulder. The delicious scent of boronia wafted to him in her wake. Probably the soap she had used. No wonder that new shearer was drooling over her. Was there ever such a bloom on a woman?

"Kieran might be on the wrong track, sticking to wool production," he risked saying. "He has it in him to be a very fine artist. To make it his career."

Alana considered that quietly. "Of course he has," she agreed, very proud of her brother's outstanding ability. "Do you think I haven't told him that? And I'm sure Alex is tired of telling him. I think they had a big bust-up about it."

"When was this?" He frowned.

She met his eyes. "I have an idea Kieran might have taken to looking in on Alex whenever he's in Sydney. They could have made up, but if they have he's not saying. He goes there a lot at the weekends. He was there recently."

"And he doesn't tell you if he sees her?" Guy's frown deepened.

"Kieran plays his cards very close to his chest when it comes to your beautiful sister," Alana said. "There was a time they were close, but then she moved away, and now Roger Westcott is always in the picture. Alex will never be short of men in love with her. But the specific occasion I'm referring to was last Easter, when we were all in Sydney for the Royal National. They were feinting around one another like a couple of boxers."

"Don't they always?" Guy asked laconically. "Over the years both of them seem to have built up an impenetrable wall. Now, can I help you with anything?"

Alana laughed. "Please sit down. I'm not short, but you *tower* over me."

"Kieran and I are of a height," he pointed out reasonably, pulling out a chair. "Your dad is a big man."

"That's all very well, but you're different somehow. Kieran started painting just after Mum died, when the pain was almost too much to bear. He's very artistic, like Mum. She always used to encourage him with his drawing, from when we were kids. Kieran can draw anything. He's marvellous with trees. A few strokes and he's created a whole hillside of eucalypts."

"Alex is right. He's brilliant."

"Hey, *I'm* right too," she reminded him, pausing in what she was doing. "I know good art when I see it, thank you, Guy."

"Of course you do." His tone soothed. "It's one of the reasons I admire you. You're getting to be a woman for all seasons. All of us are right about Kieran, but Alex is the one in an ideal position to help him."

Alana's expression was sad. "Kieran doesn't *want* to be helped, Guy."

"What does your dad think?"

Alana set out cups, saucers and plates from her mother's best Royal Doulton dinner set. This was Guy Radcliffe, after all. "Dad does his best to understand, but he can't critique Kieran's work. He can't relate to abstract depictions. He doesn't want to see the soul of a tree, or the spirit of the bush. He wants photographic realism. Dad is a bit out of his depth with art. He'd be the first to admit it. What do you want to talk to him about?" She changed the subject to what was really on her mind. "He hasn't borrowed money off you, has he?" She was very fearful he had.

Guy looked back at her directly. "I thought we'd agreed it was a private matter?"

"You know *everything*—we're in a lot of trouble," she said bitterly.

"If your father needs help, I'll give it to him," Guy responded. "Are you going to put the coffee on?"

"You're here to give orders, are you?"

"No, only trying to be helpful."

"Dad has put his whole life into Briar's Ridge," she said, doing just as he suggested. "We were doing just fine until Mum died. Since then, of course, Dad has made a few really bad mistakes."

Guy knew about all of them. "Forgive him for them, Alana. Grief is a terrible thing. The mind doesn't function as well as it should."

"I do forgive him," she said, flashing her beautiful glittery eyes at Guy. "He's my father. I love him. But Kieran and I know we may be forced to sell if we don't do well at the coming sales. The two of us have poured so much hard work into the place—" She broke off to look at him. "I had an idea we could do something like Morgan Creek, in the next valley. What do you think?" She had intended talking to Guy about this at some stage—why not now?

"You mean offer day trips to a working station? Show tourists and visitors the ropes, let them learn about our oldest and biggest industry, give them a great barbecue lunch, let them enjoy whip cracking and boomerang-throwing and then send them on their way?"

"I'm ready to try my hand at it."

"Alana, you're ready to try your hand at *anything*," he said, rather quellingly.

"Like Superwoman?" Her response was sharper than she intended.

"You already work far too hard. Have you given any thought as to how you're going to fund it?" he challenged.

She gave him a look that was hurt and disgusted. "Guy, we have to *fight* to save this place."

He saw behind her aggression to the pain. "Maybe your father has lost the will to fight?" he said gently. "Maybe Kieran would like a crack at another life? And you? What about you, Alana? Are you going to fight to save Briar's Ridge, and then settle down some place else? You'll marry. I'd be surprised if you weren't married by this time next year."

That made Alana grit her teeth. "Are you *nuts?*"

He laughed. "I can't believe someone else hasn't ever suggested it."

She waved that fact away. "If you mention Simon, I tell you, you're on very dangerous ground."

"In that case I'd better back off. I'm fond of my cousin, Alana, but no way is he a match for you. You like bossing everyone around."

It took her half a minute to see he was teasing. "I have to confess to bossing Simon," she said wryly. "But in my own defence I had to do it. If you're so fond of him, why don't you get him away from his mother?"

Guy looked back with his usual calm concentration. "Alana, I *could* get him away from Rebecca—but it would take a miracle to get him away from *you*. Simon has invested everything in you. I don't mean this unkindly, but he's rather like your favourite Border Collie, Monty. He's one-woman loyal. You're Simon's dearest friend, his greatest interest in life—his only love."

She slumped into the chair opposite him, unaware that the oval neck of her tank top had dipped into her lovely young cleavage. "Once upon a time I would never have believed you. Now I think it's scary. Simon *can't* channel all his love into me. Suppose I fall in love with someone? Suppose Dad has to sell the farm and we have to move away? Suppose I die? People get killed all the time. We know that better than most people. He *can't* love me. Besides, his mother wouldn't stand for it. She's drilled it into him that she doesn't even approve of me as a friend. I know she's a relative of sorts, but she's a horrible woman. She's all but broken Simon's spirit."

"Then he ought to hit on some motto—like *Be A Man*. Simon has to develop a little backbone, Alana," he offered crisply, wondering if Simon had ever worked up enough courage to kiss her.

"That's all very well for you to say. Simon is scared of his mother." She hesitated a moment, then soldiered on, "You know Rose quite likes Simon…"

The brackets around his mouth deepened in amusement. "I can see the wheels turning in your golden head. But *you* can't play matchmaker."

"Why don't *you* try your hand at it, then?" she shot back. "You're so highly successful at everything you do."

"Okay!" He leaned back, considering, linking his strong tanned arms behind his crow-black head. "Why don't *I* show a little interest in *you?*" he suggested.

The expression on Alana's face abruptly changed. "What? Pretend a romantic in…ter…est?" She stumbled over the word.

"Why make it sound like there's more chance of getting struck by lightning?" His tone mocked. "Surely it wouldn't be all that difficult? You're a smart girl."

"Men don't like smart girls," she said bluntly.

'Ah, yes, but you're as beautiful as a dream. That helps."

Her eyes looked frightened. "Would you like to walk that by me again? I'm *beautiful?*"

"Would you settle for sexy?"

His gaze tantalised her. "Thanks, but no, thanks, Guy." She whirled up from her chair. "I'll do anything in the world for Simon except fall in love with *you.*"

Kieran was greeted by the incomparable aroma of rich, dark roasted coffee. Alana had made a stack of sandwiches that looked really good, as well as producing a plate of triple chocolate brownies she had made only the night before. Alana was a good cook. Their mother had seen to that. The brownies were a favourite with their father, who nowadays mostly preferred to drink than eat.

Kieran poured himself a cup of coffee, then sat down beside his sister. The pair of them were so golden they delighted the eye. "It's good to see you, Guy." Kieran spoke with warm sincerity. "You don't get over often enough."

"Things will start to slacken off as winter approaches," Guy said. "I was admiring your new landscape in the hallway. It's quite something."

"It's yours!" Kieran declared, strong white teeth biting into a ham sandwich with relish.

It was just as Guy had expected. "I'd be very happy to own it, Kieran, but I'm speaking to you as a buyer. I'd like to pay for it."

Kieran shook his leonine mane. "That's not going to happen. You've been too good to us, Guy."

"Could you elaborate on that?" Alana looked quickly from one to the other.

"Haven't you noticed all the nice things I do?" Guy told her smoothly. "I've lent you various equipment from time to time. I've sent wine, table grapes, our very best extra virgin olive oil. I've given Kieran here plenty of advice when he's asked."

Kieran spread his arms wide. "You're brilliant, Guy. No wonder Lana's little puppy dog Simon calls you The Man. If you like the painting, Guy, it's yours. I can knock up another one."

But Guy was minded to be serious. "You know you have a considerable gift?"

Kieran's smiling face sobered. "My talent for painting won't keep Briar's Ridge going, Guy. You know that."

"But your talent for painting might carry you far."

"You sound just like Alex." Kieran gulped rather than sipped at his steaming hot coffee. "If Alex had her way I'd be mounting an exhibition before the end of the year. She's guaranteed me a sell-out."

"Alex knows what she's talking about," Guy pointed out, in his quiet, authoritative voice. "She can help you."

Kieran kept silent.

How mysterious were the connections of the heart, Guy thought.

Alana looked across the table, feeling bewildered. "Do you two know something I don't?"

Guy managed a lazy smile. "Lots of things I expect."

Kieran too grinned. The smiles didn't fool her. Alana turned to her brother. "Are we in deeper than you've told me?" she asked, sounding worried.

"We'll know more after the sales, Lana." Kieran picked up another sandwich.

She drew a quick breath. "I've spoken to Guy about my idea of turning Briar's Ridge into a show farm, like Morgan Creek."

Kieran glanced across the wide pine table at Guy, then back at his sister. "Lana, we've been over this. It might work with a big influx of money, but even if by some miracle we could borrow it, Dad wouldn't sit still for it. You know that. He wouldn't want people wandering around the property. He'd hate it."

"So we go under? Is that it?" She blinked furiously, amazed she was so emotional these days.

Kieran laid an arm around his sister's shoulders. "We haven't gone under yet, kiddo!" Brother and sister stayed that way for a moment, then Kieran rose, pocketing a couple of brownies. "That was great. Just what I needed." He looked at Guy with his extraordinarily blue eyes. "Dad's in the

Second Paddock, if you want to find him. We're supposed to have a meeting with Bob Turner at three." Bob Turner was the local wool representative. "Want me to drop you out there?"

Guy shook his head. "I won't keep you. I know you've got plenty on your hands. Any of the other locals been around yet?" he asked. The local wool growers usually turned up to check out the quality of their neighbours' clip.

Brother and sister nodded golden heads in unison. "Harry Ainsworth and Jack Humphrey," Kieran said. "The stack's growing, but it's nothing like our best quality. Dad is disappointed, though he really should have been expecting it. I'm keen to see what's happening on Wangaree."

Wangaree's clip always attracted enormous interest. At the important wool sales in Sydney buyers representing the leading woollen mills and the famous fashion houses of the world usually found their clip close to perfection, which meant Guy had a good idea of what Wangaree's clip would bring even before it was auctioned off. No matter the slump in prices, wool of the quality produced by Wangaree could be eagerly snapped up.

"Why don't we make it one day next week?" Guy suggested. "The clip will have grown even taller by then. It's superfine, and unbelievably white. Bring Alana. Stay to lunch. Your father is very welcome too, but I'll speak to him myself when I drive out to see him."

Kieran moved off with the grace of a trained athlete. "That'll be great! By the way, I meant what I said about the painting. It's yours. I refuse to take money for it."

"Then I'll just have to find another way to pay you back," Guy called after him. "I'll have it framed."

"Sure." Kieran waved a hand. "I couldn't run to a frame. Good ones cost the earth."

"After which I'll hang it in a prominent place at the house," Guy promised. "In the years to come I'll be able to say, *Yes, that's a Callaghan. He's a good friend of mine. I was one of the lucky ones. I got in on the ground floor.*"

CHAPTER FOUR

THINGS didn't go well for Briar's Ridge at the sales. Brother and sister sat together at the Wool Exchange in a tense silence as wool worth millions and millions of dollars was sold off. The market was down. No big surprise. Everyone had anticipated that. But mercifully it kicked up quite a bit when the first of the Wangaree Valley clip came up for sale.

"This is awful—the waiting." Alana was so anxious she felt sick to her stomach.

"Listen, it's not that bad." Kieran, nervous himself, but hiding it extremely well, tried to comfort her, even though he had the gut-wrenching feeling it was going to be. This sale represented twelve months' growth of wool and a hell of a lot of hard work from him and Alana. They had virtually carried their father, once such a dynamo.

Wangaree's clip, one of the star attractions of the sale, was recognised as superb. Everyone in the Valley had seen it, marvelling at the quality. Another top producer from the ad-joining State of Victoria had called it perfection. Guy's comment had been, "It's better than that. It's *damned good!*" One didn't hear him say that all that often. Guy wasn't one to commit himself, but the Exchange was abuzz with excitement. People in the know were predicting a record price for Wangaree's clip, and as a spin-off maybe others in the Valley.

If she turned her head she would be able to see him, Alana thought. He was sitting with the top people of the industry. In his group would be her uncle Charles—her mother's brother, Charles Denby. Uncle Charles was as good as a stranger to her and Kieran, though their resemblance to their Denby mother was most apparent. In fact, Uncle Charles was so remote he mightn't have been their relative at all. It was no secret he had been deeply shocked when his beautiful sister, Annabel, the apple of everyone's eye, had married a struggling sheep farmer, an Irishman, "rough diamond" Alan Callaghan. And Denby brother and sister had been near enough estranged since the day of the wedding, which unhappily no Denby had attended. A lasting wound.

The three Denby sisters, Violette, Lilli and Rose, dressed to kill and turning heads, fresh from a splendid lunch at one of Sydney's top restaurants, had been present at the inspection earlier, but two had since disappeared—most likely to hit the fashion boutiques. Only Violette remained with her father and—need it be said?—Guy. Violette wouldn't want to miss out on the Denby sales, let alone miss the frenzy of bidding when Wangaree's clip came up.

"I'm glad Dad's not here," Alana sighed, her spirits wilting. Their father had been too nervous to come. Once upon a time he had been right in the thick of it, so proud of having his beautiful wife and family beside him, receiving handshakes and congratulations when his sale prices were good.

An hour later Wangaree's lot came up. It was sold, as predicted, in the blink of an eye, once again to a leading European fashion house. Italian designers had a wonderful way of mixing wool with silk. Alana loved the top designers, their work cut and tailored by people whose ancestors had been handling the finest fabrics for hundreds of years. She remembered how her untrained mother had cut and woven fabric so it fell into the most beautiful soft folds.

By four o'clock the sale was over, with hundreds of lots having gone under the hammer. Alana and Kieran, though heartsore over Briar's Ridge's downspiralling fortunes, remained behind to shake Guy's hand. All eyes were on him as he stood in the centre of the floor, surrounded by prominent people within the industry, head and shoulders above most of them, clearly The Man. Simon had been spot on when he had found this name for his illustrious cousin.

"Don't look now, but Uncle Charles and Vindictive Vi are coming our way," Kieran muttered. "Of course there's the strong possibility they'll spot us and shoot off in the opposite direction."

"And who would care?" Alana asked wearily, fully expecting to be ignored. Charles Denby knew nothing about the milk of human kindness. He was a civilised monster.

"When do you suppose dear old Charles is going to make the transition to a *real* person?" Kieran asked, with a flash of black humour. "I mean, I've never understood a damned thing about the big estrangement. What was so shocking about Mum breaking with family tradition and marrying Dad? The Denbys aren't Royalty, for goodness' sake. Even hell bent on wrecking himself, Dad's still a handsome man. So he was a nobody on the social register? He must have been really something when he was young. Big, handsome, strong. He was hard-working, perfectly respectable. People liked him. He'd even managed to buy himself Briar's Ridge, though it was mortgaged up to the hilt. He didn't take Mum to a hovel. And she loved him. Wasn't that all that mattered?" Kieran broke off angrily, visibly upset.

"One would have thought so!" Alana sighed.

"Oh, no—they haven't spotted us," Keiran groaned in dismay.

Charles and Violette were so busy talking, heads together, probably planning a night out on the town with Guy's party, they all but walked into Alana and Kieran.

"Oh, it's you two!" Violette reacted with her usual hateful disdain. She looked Alana up and down, her gaze deliberately pitying, as though Alana were dressed by charity shops instead of a smart-casual designer.

Alana, well used to her cousin's intended put-downs, took no notice. What consumed her was the look in her brother's eyes. Slow to anger, Kieran had been known to go off like a rocket if sufficiently provoked. It was their father's temper— nearly always under control, but always there. She gave her brother a beseeching look. It would do no good at all for Kieran to lose his temper right here and now.

Ignoring Violette, she addressed her distinguished-looking, ultra-remote uncle. "How are you, Uncle Charles?" she asked politely. "You look well. Congratulations on the Denby prices."

A tall man, Charles Denby stared down at his niece with the strange intensity he always bestowed on her. "Everything we wanted," he announced with ice-cold suavity. "You, on the other hand, mustn't have liked what you heard for the Briar's Ridge lot? I saw it myself. Not up to scratch, my dear. Or rather it'll make up darn scratchy."

Kieran broke in, the heat of anger coming off his powerful, lean body. "Why, sir, do you go out of your way to be so damned cutting?"

Violette's breath exploded in shocked indignation. "I beg your pardon, Kieran?" she huffed. "You apologise to my father this *instant*."

Kieran gave her a sidelong look that blazed with contempt.

"Tell me, *Vi,* you silly, pretentious creature, what is there to apologise for? All our civility, all our polite overtures, get met with freezing dislike. My mother and your father were brother and sister. I could never treat my sister the way your father treated his—no matter what! And my mother did absolutely nothing but marry the man she loved."

Charles Denby's only reaction was a narrowing of his glacial blue eyes. "Your mother brought disgrace on herself and the family," he said finally. "Alan Callaghan was a nothing and a nobody who put my sister in her coffin. Now the whole Valley knows him as a hopeless drunk. Get out of my way, young man. I have better things to do than talk to an upstart like you."

Upstart? The irony was that Kieran looked more like their uncle than he did their own father. Alana sucked in her breath, fully expecting the rocket to launch.

Only Kieran surprised her. He spoke quietly, but his body language was immensely threatening. "There's plenty of room for you to walk around me, sir. Another word and I can't guarantee your safety."

Alarmed, Alana took hold of Kieran's hard-muscled arm— but not before Guy, aware of a mounting crisis, moved swiftly to join them.

"It might be an idea to cool it, Kieran." He came alongside the younger man, keeping his voice low and level. "This *is* the Wool Exchange, and every eye is on us. You're my friend, and I don't want to see you get into trouble."

Kieran shook his leonine head, as if to clear it. "This man here—" he gritted.

"It might be time, Charles, to walk away." Guy glanced meaningfully at Charles Denby.

"That's the trouble with people like you Callaghans," Violette sneered, hot red colour staining her cheekbones.

"You simply don't know how to behave. Come on, Daddy, they're not fit to speak to." She spoke as though Alana and Kieran's natural habitat was the gutter.

"Yes, run away!" Kieran told her in a furious undertone, looking as if he was about to give her a good shove. "It's my sister who's the lady around here. Never *you!*"

"Kieran, *please*—if not for our sakes, for Mum's," Alana implored. She was excruciatingly aware a number of people were turning to stare. "Wouldn't she have been horrified to see us make a spectacle of ourselves?"

"Sadistic man!" Kieran rasped, as Charles Denby and his daughter stalked off. He turned his burning blue gaze on Guy. "What have we ever done to them to warrant such treatment?"

Guy's answer was immediate. And it sounded as if it came from the heart. "Your uncle has never been able to face down his demons, Kieran. Charles Denby is a very bitter and unhappy man. It has to be said there was a time he adored his sister, and he continued to do so though he became warped and bitter. What you have to do is let your anger settle. There's nothing you can do to change your uncle. His rigid attitude has deprived him of so much happiness in life. You can't hope to engage his liking or sympathy." He spread his hands. "Charles hasn't anything left to give. He's to be pitied, really."

"I don't pity him," Kieran fumed. "We're sick to death of being ignored and humiliated, Guy, of having our father spoken about with such contempt. How callous can a man get? If he weren't an old fogey I'd have socked him." He stared at his friend, so angry there was a red mist in front of his eyes. "Listen, would Lana be all right with you?" It came out in a plea. "There's someone I must see."

"But of course," Guy answered, as though surprised Kieran would even have to ask.

Alana looked at her brother in consternation. "Who is it?

Where are you going?" They hadn't planned anything but a quiet evening, most likely pondering their losses.

"I feel bad, Lana." He looked to her for understanding. "But I need to see someone."

"A woman?" Alana stared at her brother, thinking it quite possible Kieran had a secret life.

"Yes. Of course a woman." He bent to kiss her cheek. "You'll go back to the hotel? I really don't know what time I'll be in. It could be an hour or hours. But we'll leave as scheduled—first thing after breakfast."

Alana kept her head tilted to him. "What's happening here, Kieran? Who is this mystery woman? She sounds pretty important to you."

"Well, I'm not much use to her," Kieran said with great bitterness. "Look, I have to get out of here."

"Then go," Guy urged him gently. "I'll look after Alana."

"I don't need *anyone* to look after me." Alana turned on Guy, her own temper going up a dozen notches. "Anyway, Guy, you must have plans of your own."

"Which just so happen to include you." He rested his hand briefly on her shoulder. "Off you go, Kieran. Everything's okay here. You, however, look like a man who's in dire need of comfort."

Kieran's blue eyes flashed. 'Thanks, Guy." He transferred his gaze to his sister. "I'll make it up to you, Lana." With that he turned on his heel and stomped away, his tall, powerful body all tightly coiled fury.

They were out on the street, and strong sunlight, even at late afternoon, bounced off the pavement. The sidewalk was busy with people hurrying to and fro; traffic streamed bumper to bumper.

"There's no need for you to bother about me, Guy," Alana

said, trying to keep her enormous upset down. Who exactly did her uncle think he was? The next Pope? *"Your mother brought disgrace on herself and the family!"* What did *that* mean? Some words, once uttered, could never be called back. The man was paranoid about family, and insufferably sanctimonious. "I'm perfectly all right on my own."

"I don't think so." He was finely tuned to her mood, and deeply sympathetic.

"You'll want to be with your friends," she persisted doggedly.

"I regard you and Kieran as my friends."

"Gosh, I don't know if we're *fit* to be your friends," she muttered bitterly. "What the hell was my uncle on about? You know everything that goes on in the Valley. I adored my mother. She was a beautiful, dignified, gracious woman. How could she have brought disgrace on herself? Forget her awful family. They're the *real* disgrace. They act like the enemy—except for Rose. How did Rose miss out on their worst characteristics? My mother marrying my father can't possibly explain Uncle Charles's attitude."

"I told you. Charles is a tortured soul. And his wife and daughters have been affected to a greater or lesser degree. Rose, the youngest, is the most fortunate. Most of it has rubbed off on Violette, for which I pity her. Now, why don't we go and grab a cup off coffee?"

"I don't want one," she said mutinously, unaware that the sparkle in her eyes and the colour in her cheeks made her look extraordinarily beautiful.

"Okay—a stiff drink. Don't argue. I want one, even if you don't. You can't do anything about your mother's family, Alana. Don't even try."

"Why do you just pick up and then drop Violette?" she accused him. "You sound on side with her, yet she's so horrible. Could it be you're only interested in her body?"

He glanced down at her rebellious face. "I'll forget you said that, because you're so upset. Here—this will do." He drew her off the pavement into the foyer of one of the city's leading hotels.

"Why don't we check in while we're at it?" she suggested, putting her hand out to catch his arm. "Kieran has a mystery woman. I'm going to get myself a mystery man."

"Well, that lets me out," Guy said evenly." I've known you all your life."

In the handsomely appointed lounge, Alana sank into a comfortable chair. Only a few tables were occupied. Smiles and quiet conversation. It would be another hour before the regulars and the after-work crowd arrived.

"What will it be?" Guy remained standing, his face showing its own brooding tension.

If anything, it only made him look even sexier, she thought, feeling angry, nervy and very, very *physical*. No one brought it out in her like this man.

"Perhaps it's time I took to the whisky?" she said.

"Let's settle for a gin and tonic—or a glass of white wine?"

"It really ought to be champagne. For you, anyway. Congratulations, Guy." She lifted her hazel eyes to him, angry, unshed tears making them diamond-bright. "Kieran and I were waiting behind to tell you that when my awful, *awful,* malevolent relatives walked into us. I have to say it was by mistake. I think they were discussing what was happening tonight."

"It definitely wasn't happening with me," Guy said. "Just try to relax. You've got enough burdens without taking your relatives on board. I'll be back in a minute." He walked away to the bar, with every female eye in the vicinity tracking him. A woman would have to be blind to miss him.

An animal lover, Alana always saw her brother as a golden lion and Guy as a sleek black panther. And where was Kieran going, so completely and utterly furious? It had been blindingly obvious. Of course he had a woman in Sydney. He was a virile young man. Sydney was little over a two hour drive from the Valley. The big hurt was that he hadn't confided in her. She tried to accept that, but the hurt gnawed deep at her. Why hadn't he told her about something so important? He told her just about everything else. Was it possible the mystery woman was married? Oh, that was *so* risky. She would be beautiful, of course. The artist in Kieran would be drawn like a magnet to a beautiful woman. But she couldn't be more beautiful than Alexandra Radcliffe. Alex was really and truly a classic beauty. Although Alex and Kieran operated on different planes.

Guy returned empty handed. "What about my G&T?" she asked in surprise. "Not even a bowl of nuts or a packet of potato chips?" She tried to fight her edginess with banter.

He sat down in the chair nearest her. "There you go again! I've ordered a bottle of champagne."

"Good heavens! Isn't that a dumb thing to do? I'm just so angry and despondent I might get drunk."

"I won't let that happen." He very gently patted her hand, his dark eyes glinting. "You had a good lunch, didn't you?"

"Not as good as yours, I bet." It was usual for the pastoral houses to take the big wool producers to lunch on sales day. "Oh, God, what a day!" she lamented. "We're going to lose Briar's Ridge, Guy. We needed good sales. We're drowning in debt—as if you didn't know."

"Something can be worked out," Guy said.

She looked at him with a sharp sense of humiliation. "You've been propping us up, haven't you? I feel it in my bones."

"You didn't *want* me to try and save you?" He studied her face intently.

She glanced away. Wherever his eyes touched her she felt little jolts of electricity. Even when he took his dark eyes from her, she still felt the after-shocks. "I'd much prefer it if we saved ourselves," she said, in an agony of helplessness, hopelessness—and, it had to be admitted, burning resentment.

"Well, let it go for the moment," Guy advised. "You're right on the edge. So, for that matter, am I."

"*Never!* Not Guy Radcliffe?"

"You don't even know me."

"Yes, well, I know as much as is safe to know. Ah—here comes the champagne."

"Two glasses and I'll take you back to your hotel. I'd like you to have dinner with me tonight."

Her heart almost leapt into her mouth. "You can't be serious? I expect Uncle Charles and Vi will have muscled in?"

"I had the pleasure of Charles and your cousins at lunch."

"If I didn't know better I'd say you found 'the pleasure' quite an ordeal. Has Uncle Charles ever turned the conversation to wedding bells?"

"Nothing so alarming." A waiter, who bore more than a passing resemblance to a well known English comic, arrived with the bottle of champagne, presenting it for Guy's inspection like a character in a skit. After a quick glance, Guy nodded.

"Surely you've sown your wild oats by now?" Alana asked, after the waiter had waltzed his way back through the tables. Was it possible the comedian really was in town and there was a hidden camera?

"Dinner for two," Guy said, watching the waiter's comic progress himself. "Just you and me. I'd much rather listen to you—even if you do like to cross swords." He lifted his glass. Their flutes clinked. "Loosen up, Alana. There are always some compensations available."

She took a quick sip. It was delicious. "Believe me, I want to. But I can't. I'd love to have dinner with you, Guy—not that I've got anything halfway decent to wear—but I suddenly feel I'm wanted at home." She spoke with such urgency she might actually have received a phone call. "Kieran did ring Dad to let him know how things went. Dad's been good for weeks, but I fear he won't be able to handle this. He'll start drinking again." She sought understanding in his eyes. "You couldn't possibly drive me back tonight, could you?" She was so nervous her tongue seemed to be cleaving to the roof of her mouth. "I understand perfectly if you can't. You probably have commitments. Not to mention breakfast with Violette," she added, even though she recognised it was foolish.

"Is this the right way to go about asking me?" He looked steadily back.

"I guess not. But I'm nervous. It's difficult not to be nervous around you."

His mouth compressed. She had a mad urge to lean forward and kiss it, though neither of them were acting in the least flirtatiously.

"I have to say you hide it remarkably well. There's nothing that can't be taken care of at a later date. You really want to go home? You're absolutely sure?"

She took a deep, fluttery breath, then nodded her head. "If you'd be good enough to take me, Guy," she said meekly.

Now he smiled—half-amused, half-mocking. "I rather enjoy seeing you this way, sweet and pleading. But just how do you think you can help your father?"

She stayed quiet, took another sip. "At least I'll *be* there. You know how he is. I can't help worrying. I'll ring Kieran.

Let him know. He has his mobile with him. I'm guessing he won't be able to drag himself away from his mystery woman. That's if he finds her. You wouldn't happen to know who she is?"

Guy's eyes were brilliant, but unreadable. "The whole thing is pretty damned weird. But, whoever she is, she clearly has a lot of power over Kieran."

CHAPTER FIVE

SHE wasn't in the apartment when he arrived. Kieran hadn't expected her to be. It would probably be another hour before she got home. He considered ringing her, decided not to. He had his key. He let himself in, instantly inhaling the lovely scent of her. He could almost see her floating towards him. Sometimes he got so frustrated he could punch a hole in the wall.

He turned on a few lights. It was a beautiful apartment. No minimalist approach here. Everywhere one looked there was something beautiful to admire. The colours were white and a delicate shade of green, with accents of sunshine-yellow; there were lots of silk cushions with expensive fringes, tall *famille vert* porcelain vases, valuable antiques someone had turned into lampstands for her. *Lampstands,* mind you. The rich really were different. A glorious cyclamen orchid with five bracts sat in another deep *famille vert* bowl on a glass-topped table.

A beautiful setting for a beautiful woman. He crossed to the sliding glass doors, opened them. Beyond the plant-filled balcony set with a circular table and chairs was Sydney's magnificent harbour, the breeze fresh off it. She had a splendid view, fanning three hundred and sixty degrees. And why not? The apartment had cost millions. Well, they had it. He shrugged. Old money. Nothing ostentatious.

He ripped off his jacket and threw it down over the back of a sofa. He loosened a couple of buttons at the neck of his shirt, jerked his tie down. Next he moved to the cabinet where he knew the drinks were housed. God, how he needed one! He almost began to see how their father had made the tragic slide into alcoholism. Yet hadn't love been the cause of it? The intensity of that love? Surely there was something a little noble about that? He hadn't just lost his money or his farm. He'd lost a woman—his beloved wife. Their father was grieving so profoundly over the loss of their mother he couldn't seem to face life without her. How would it feel to love someone like that and know you could never have them, let alone have them *back?* Kieran thought he knew.

Whisky came to hand. Great! He poured himself a good shot of it, then walked through to the bright and open kitchen for a little crushed ice from the refrigerator door. This was one neat woman. Not a thing out of place, and lovely little feminine touches everywhere. She loved flowers. He had never seen the apartment without flowers in every room, and that included the en suite and the guest bathroom. Today there were yellow tulips on the glossy black granite flecked with gold. There were lots of crisp white cupboards, some glass-paned to show off fancy bone china, but the *pièce de resistance* of this beautiful apartment, with all its art works and *objets d'art* was always *her.*

Gradually, under such a benign influence, he was calming. What a terrible day! No way could they afford to hold on to Briar's Ridge now. The bank would foreclose on them. And what then? He had come to realise the farm wasn't everything in life to him, as it was to their father and Alana. Alana was a true country girl. She revelled in life on the land. He had always enjoyed it too, but in his heart of hearts he knew he wouldn't mourn the loss of it deeply. He could always visit it when he wanted. He could always paint it when the urge took him.

The truth was, he recognised inside himself that he had a gift. His mother had always told him he did.

"Why, I do believe, my darling Kieran, one day you'll have it in you to become a fine painter. I'd be interested to see what Marcus thinks of all these drawings. Next time he's in the country I'll ask him."

He might never rise to Marcus Denby's lofty heights, but then he had a *different* vision. He wouldn't mind struggling for a while. Just about everyone had to struggle for a while. His abrupt laugh sounded strangely harsh in the silence of the lovely room. He wouldn't have to struggle with Alex by his side. Alex was a Radcliffe, an heiress, a glittering, impossible prize. He threw back the whisky with one gulp. A vision of Alex flashed before his eyes. Skin like a pearl. Eyes and hair like ebony. The pure face of a Madonna, yet she had sinned deeply. He walked to one of the upholstered custom-built sofas and eased his long body into it, staring sightlessly at the exquisite spray of cyclamen orchids. He felt his heart contract with his own kind of grief. That whisky had gone down too quickly. He'd have another…

Immediately he heard the key inserted into the deadlock he jumped to his feet. His heart was thudding, picking up knots. It was dark now. He had turned the lights on. How many times had he entered her apartment before she'd arrived home? He couldn't begin to count.

She must have realised he was there, because she called softly, "Kieran?"

He covered the distance that separated them in a couple of

long strides, watching her drop her leather handbag to the silk rug. He reached for her, pulling her into his arms, kissing her feverishly, hotly, hungrily, forcing open her softly cushioned lips.

"I'm crazy about you!" he muttered "Crazy. Is it ever going to stop?" He didn't seem to care that he was overwhelming her with his intensity.

He had her moaning in his arms. To hear her moan meant everything to him. Somehow he had lifted her clear of the ground, crushing her in his powerful grip. She was tall, but so slender, she was a featherweight to him. Her beautiful pale pink suit had little covered buttons down the front. She wore a white silk camisole beneath the jacket. His hand swept rapaciously across her breasts as though it had a life of its own. "Alex, Alex," he whispered. "What am I going to do about you?"

She breathed into his neck. "Just keep on putting me through hell?"

His response was to swing her off her feet, carrying her down the passageway into the master bedroom. He was desperate to be inside her. He couldn't see straight until he was. He threw her down on her marvellous big bed, pausing for a moment to stare down at her as she lay back against the opulent cream and gold quilt. Oh, the *ache* in him! Every time he laid eyes on her he had the sensation that his heart was breaking. Her wonderful dark eyes were huge with emotion. He never felt guilty at seeing her drowning in it. *She* was the one who should feel guilty but refused to. Her arms were thrown back above her head, outstretched, imploring, pleading. She was imperceptibly trembling. Her long silky hair that had been arranged in some elegant knot was coming loose. A skein fell like a black satin ribbon across her pearly cheek.

"How beautiful you are," he rasped. "*Too* beautiful!" But she could never wipe the slate clean.

He reached down to her, his long fingers beginning to burrow at all those little buttons. She made no effort to stop him. She lay quietly while he undressed her, wondering if there was ever going to be an end to this unquenchable desire.

"Why didn't you let me know you were coming?" she whispered.

He made no reply. Instead he pulled her up so he could release the catch on her rose lace bra and expose her exquisite white breasts. How incredibly seductive a woman's breasts were. Every time he undressed her it was like the first time. Such beauty! Always for *him*.

"Kieran—Kieran, do you love me?" Tears filled her large oval eyes.

He kissed them. "How can I love you after what you did to us?" he answered jaggedly. "I *want* you. I *need* you. Be content with that."

They had everything and nothing. All the world lost. "How easily you've condemned me all these years. You had no difficulty at all, even when I told you the truth."

He choked off a bitter laugh. "*Don't*, Alex," he said. "I'm supremely indifferent to your lies. They've all been done to death anyway."

A glistening tear slid down her cheek. She arched her back to make it easier for him to take off her panties—rose lace to match her delicate bra. She always wore the most beautiful underwear. He thrilled to strip the delicate garments off her.

Finally she was naked, her white body as remarkably virginal as when he had first seen it when they were innocent teenagers. There had been no adolescent yearning, no clumsy gropings. It had been full on, wildly passionate sex—she surrendering herself completely, he taking her, penetrating her, as if he wanted his whole self to disappear inside her. Neither of them had been able to get enough of the other. Drunk on sex. Drunk on love. Alex had been his sun, moon and stars.

But almost seven years had passed. Years spent apart. Time they could no longer spend together. He wanted her more now than he had then—barely believable but utterly true. Not only that, he knew how to get more of her. Oh, yes, he did. Alex was *his*. His incurable addiction.

He fell to his knees beside the bed, still fully clothed, taking a coral pink nipple sweet as a fruit into his mouth, lightly between his teeth… "Alex, Alex, Alex…" he whispered, his voice fierce even to his own ears.

She shaped his golden head with her hands, sinking her fingers into his thick mane of hair. Her eyes were filled not only with an overwhelming desire, but with a deep, dark tenderness. She would have died for Kieran. He knew that. But he didn't care.

He put one strong hand beneath her back, raising her to him.

"Why do I let you do this to me?" she gasped.

He pressed his open mouth all over her. "You know why," he muttered, without a shred of sympathy. "Because neither of us can *stop*."

The big car ate up the miles. Alana thought she might close her eyes briefly, but was stunned when she heard Guy's voice murmur near her ear. "Wake up, Sleeping Beauty."

She blinked and sat straight, looking around dazedly. "I can't believe that! I fell asleep."

"I'd say you needed it." He didn't mention she had been making little distressed whimpers that smote his heart.

"We're home!"

"Right at your door, my lady!" Guy looked very soberly

towards the darkened homestead. There appeared to be only one light on, towards the rear of the house. "I'll come in with you." He released his seat belt.

Voices said such a lot about a person, Alana thought. Who you were. What you were. Where you lived, even how you lived. Were you confident, self-assured, charming? Warm or cold, diffident, abrasive, a person to steer clear of. Her father was right. Guy Radcliffe was a *prince.*

They were walking towards the front steps when Buddy, stick-thin no matter how much he ate, emerged from the interior of the house and moved out onto the verandah. He lifted a hand to turn on the verandah light, splashing himself in a dull golden light.

"Miss Lana, I didn't know you'd be comin' home," he called, then tiptoed over to the timber balustrade. "Good evening, Mr Radcliffe," he added respectfully.

"Evening, Buddy." Guy's tone was warm and approving. He knew that approval gave the loyal youngster pleasure and confidence. "Everything okay here?"

They all knew it was nothing of the sort. Alana ran on ahead, up the steps, disappearing into the house.

Buddy's liquid black eyes cut to Guy. "Mr Alan—he start drinkin' a few hours back," he confided in an unhappy voice. "I came to check on 'im. He likes me around."

"I know he does, Buddy." Guy nodded, feeling the keenest sympathy for Alana. "You're a good man to have around."

"I do me best." Buddy glowed at Guy's praise. "I'm afraid Miss Lana is going to find her dad collapsed in his armchair. I wanted to shift him into bed, but he's a big man." He spread his arms an unbelievable distance, to demonstrate just how big. "Didn't have a chance of lifting 'im. It's all so sad."

It's that! Guy thought to himself. What had happened to Alan Callaghan came under the category of "survivor's guilt."

Callaghan blamed himself terribly for surviving when the wife he adored hadn't.

"Mrs Annabel, she's up there." Buddy pointed towards the glittering river of diamonds that was the Milky Way. "She's fine. She's not alone. Mr Alan should find somethin' good."

Guy couldn't help but agree. It would allow the man some release. "You can go along now, Buddy," he said. "And thank you. I should be able to get Mr Callaghan into bed."

"Need a hand?" Buddy, thin as a whippet, even in riding boots only five-five, was desperate to help in any way he could.

"Thanks, Buddy, but I'll manage." Guy made a movement to go inside, paused. "Have you eaten yet?"

"No, sir. Been here." Buddy's coal-black curls bobbed as he shook his head. "I had to attend to Mr Alan first."

"Do this for me?" Guy said, as though asking a favour. "Drive out to the estate restaurant and get yourself a really nice meal? Whatever you want—three courses. You can take it away if you feel shy being on your own. I'll ring ahead so they'll know you're coming."

Buddy gave a funny little whoop. "Me?"

"Yes, Buddy," Guy confirmed. "You must be starving by now."

"I am a bit hungry," Buddy admitted. Actually, he had a growling stomach. But the Radcliffe Estate restaurant! He'd only poked his head in a couple of times. Never been in there, of course. It was way too grand for the likes of him. Could he really order up a three course meal? Maybe oysters and a fillet steak? Some crazy wicked chocolate dessert? Mr Radcliffe said he could, and Mr Radcliffe owned the place. Cool!

Alana knelt beside her father's armchair. Alan Callaghan sat in it, looking hellish, one large brown hand resting on the top of her shining head.

"Guy!' Recognition leapt into the bleary red-rimmed eyes as Guy approached. "God, I'm sorry." Her father's normally attractive voice was nothing more than a slurred croak.

"Why don't we get you to bed, Alan?" Guy said, calm as a stone Buddha on the outside, deeply perturbed on the inside. He stripped off his checked jacket.

"Sall right!" Alan Callaghan made a pathetic attempt to heave himself out of the armchair and fell back, looking worse than ever.

"Come on—we'll help you, Dad." Alana fiercely wiped a tear from her cheek with the back of her hand.

"It's okay, Alana. Just get out of the way," Guy told her, in a kindly but authoritative tone.

She didn't argue. Guy said he could do it. Simple. She did what she was told, running ahead to make sure her father's bed was ready and the room was fit to be seen. She was agonisingly embarrassed, but at least she always did her best to make sure her father's bolt hole—for that was what it was—was clean.

They came slowly down the hallway, Guy supporting her father by the shoulders as though Alan Callaghan were a drunken dancing partner. Both dark heads were bent towards their feet. Her father was muttering incoherently to himself. Guy wasn't even breathing hard. It only took a few minutes for Guy to lower the older man onto the narrow bed.

"What is he doing in *here?*" Guy looked about him. "It's a monk's cell."

"With Dad the penitent?" Strain and mortification were showing on Alana's face. "I'm only surprised he doesn't scourge himself."

"I'll undress him," Guy said. "Or at least make him more comfortable. No problem. Go along now."

Alana turned, but hesitated near the door. Her father blew

out a harsh, spluttering moan, then seemed to come alive. He lifted one still powerful arm and began to wave it with a vigour that surprised her.

"She was in love with him, you know," he said, in voice that was almost normal. "I'm telling the truth here. I made her pregnant. I made my beautiful Belle pregnant. Can't say anything in my own defence. I did it. I *did it*." Alan Callaghan made a futile grab for the front of Guy's shirt. "You're a gentleman, aren't yah? And your dad was a gentleman. I'm just a bog Irishman. Anything to say?"

Guy's expression transfixed Alana. It had turned from compassionate to granite. Would this man who had always been so kind to her father now turn and condemn him for being a pitiful drunk? "You're shocking your daughter, Alan," Guy said quietly.

Alan Callaghan stared blearily past Guy, the full weight of what he had just said seeming to fall on him. "Are yah still here, darlin'?" he asked in dismay.

Alana didn't answer. She stood frozen on the spot, more vulnerable than she had ever been in her life.

"Leave this to me, Alana," Guy repeated, putting his tall rangy body between her and her father.

"What?" She stared at him dazedly. "You *know* what Dad's saying. You *know*—don't you, Guy. And my uncle knows. That's why he hates us."

"Doesn't he just?" Alan Callaghan suddenly bellowed. "He's never tried to conceal it. Idolised her, he did, his beautiful sister. Loved his dear friend David. But I didn't care how I got her. I was mad for her. Just couldn't back off. I always had a touch of the prize fighter in me."

"You're not putting up any fight now, Alan." Guy's dark eyes were blazing with light. "I see no sign of the fighter. Look at you. A big man—what? Fifty-five, fifty-six years of age?—collapsed in your bed like you've been defeated."

Alana was seized by agitation. "Dad's no coward, Guy!" she cried. "He has courage." Or once he had had it, she thought mournfully. But now her father had lost all direction.

Guy bent his gaze on her. "Someone once said courage in a man is enduring in silence whatever heaven sends him."

"What about what heaven takes away?" she retorted fierily. "Takes away so you can never get it back?"

Guy sighed deeply. "We all bear the weight of our losses, Alana. I miss my father every day. He was a fine upstanding man. The *finest*."

At that, Alan Callaghan's broken laugh exploded. "That he was!" he roared, and then, as though all played out he rolled away without another sound. Face to the wall.

It was the worst of all possible scenarios. Alana sat rigid, arms clasped around her, in the living room, waiting for Guy to come out of her father's room—the cell of the condemned man.

What had her father done all those years ago? What tricks had he used to get the woman he had always looked at so adoringly? How had her mother agreed to marry him, have his baby, when she'd been meant for somebody else? Had *loved* somebody else? Or was there little truth in that either? What else could she hope to find out when her father was drunk?

Guy had known what had been hidden from her and Kieran all along. He had never breathed a word. Surely other people in the Valley knew of the old love triangle? Why had everyone, including her uncle, kept the old story so deeply hidden? And the stark way Guy had spoken! Should he have rubbed in her father's defeat? Could she forgive or forget that? The real nightmare was that Guy himself might hate them underneath. How would she know? What really lay in the depths of his unfathomable dark eyes? And what of Guy's mother, always civil, but maintaining her distance? Guy loved his mother. Sidonie would have known about an old love affair of her husband's, surely? It hadn't gone as far as an engagement, but it now appeared to have been serious. Maybe her mother and David Radcliffe had never patched up a violent quarrel? It happened. Maybe they had argued about the Irishman Alan Callaghan? Was the truth more shocking yet? Whatever it was, it haunted her father—maybe to the grave. It was his choice to walk a self-destructive path.

"He's dead to the world," Guy announced when he returned.

It couldn't have sounded more grim. "Who? The coward?" she retorted, feeling the stinging heat of humiliation.

"I didn't use that word, Alana," he said almost wearily.

"You did. But isn't he, in a fashion?" Guy's tone was extraordinarily bitter for him.

He sank onto the leather sofa opposite her, the teak chest that served as a coffee table between them.

"And I thought you were a compassionate man." She stared at him with deeply wounded eyes.

"Compassion isn't working, Alana," he responded bluntly, finally convinced of the fact. "Your father has taken a tremendous blow in life, losing his beloved spouse. But so have others in the Valley—including my own mother. The world is full of people who have had massive blows to overcome. Your father calls himself a fighter? Well, as a fighter, he has hit the mat. Anyone can forgive him that. But he's never tried to get up, Alana. That's the thing. He has you and Kieran. He has Briar's Ridge. He's as good as lost it."

Her voice shook with emotion. "You think I don't *know* that?"

He leaned forward, focusing on her distressed face with its large expressive eyes. "You've put your heart and soul into the farm, Alana. Don't you deserve some consideration? And

Kieran has worked like a slave. Though Kieran will fall on his feet. Kieran has inherited the Denby gift."

"No sign of any gift in *me?*" She flashed him a look that was more poignant than bitter. Did he despise her?

"Alana, you're beautiful, and gifted in so many ways," he said with a curious sadness. "What I hate is that so much weight has been put on your shoulders. You should be enjoying a better life, not spending your time fighting off ruin."

The humiliation of it all rendered her abruptly furious. "I *love* my life, Guy!" she said, leaping to her feet. "The last thing I need from you is *pity!* I *hate* it! And never, *never* from you!" Easier that the entire world should pity her.

His response came fast. In a single explosive movement he was on her side of the table, towering over her, his own disturbed emotions in full view. "That's how you see it? *Pity?*"

She stared up at him with a thudding heart, knowing that a challenging answer would change everything in one indelible second. Still she threw out the challenge. "What *else* is it?" She lifted her chin, trying to hold her nerve, yet knowing she was in some kind of jeopardy.

Black eyes that smouldered caught fire. "Well, here's where we find out!"

She couldn't look away The intensity of his expression chopped off her breath. She had set herself against him for years now, but he was about to prove who was in control.

He hauled her to him so her head snapped back, then seemed to fall in slow motion into the crook of his arm. Her hair spilled everywhere in a wild golden mass.

She had the disorienting sensation she was falling… falling…toppling from a very high place with no way to stop. Or would he save her? But this was a wholly different Guy.

One she had barely glimpsed. She was confronted by the dominant male pushed that little bit too far. The hunter in him was about to take what he wanted. She couldn't get her breath for the overwhelming excitement.

"Guy—please don't!" It would be the end of their relationship as she had known it.

"Stop me if you can!"

Pulses of electricity were running up and down her thighs, pooling in the delta of her body, alive with raw nerve-endings.

"Guy!" Her voice shook with panic. She felt the *force* of him, the inner energy, the demands he was going to make on her. Everything about him gave her to understand beyond any possible doubt that he desired her above anything else.

Her heart beat as if wings were unfurling in her chest. It was as though she had never been up close to a man in her life, had never known the violent eroticism of a man's hard body, so powerful, so aggressive, so very different from her own.

He was deaf to her involuntary cry—if he even heard her. This was all about getting what *he* wanted. His mouth, poised over hers, abruptly came down, opening her lips beneath his, pressing without crushing, gaining control and then mastery. She had no defence against him. Not even the desire to protect herself. What was happening was *ravishing,* far from gentle, and deeper than hunger. What could it be? The only possible answer was *passion.* She had no recourse but to yield to it— because in the end wasn't this what she craved? All she could do was cling to him, trapped by a sexual pleasure that was nigh on unbearable.

The scent of him was in her nostrils. She felt the indescribable warmth of his mouth and his mating tongue, the taste, the texture, the faint rasp from his tanned polished skin on her tender flesh. She thought dazedly that their mouths were refusing to part. Refusing to surrender the fabulous thrill. Her back arched at the same time as she let out a whimper. What she feared that was she would lose all coherent thought.

His voice, strangely laboured, came from above her head. "Not much pity there, Alana," he said, with unfamiliar harshness.

She thought if he took his encompassing arms away she would simply fold. "No…" She couldn't deny it. There were tears in her eyes. "What *was* your intention?" she whispered. "To teach me a lesson?"

His spread fingers pressed along her spine. "I don't want to discuss it."

"You're so very good at it. Would you like to feel my heart?"

She hadn't believed for one moment that he would respond to what was no more than a taunt. Instead he confounded her. He pushed his hand inside the printed silk of her shirt, the palm of his hand taking the weight of her breast, thinly covered by her bra.

She gasped, instantly suffused in heat. His fingers, man-like, sought her naked flesh. She gripped his wrist tight. She had to stop him, even though she desperately wanted him to keep going. It filled her up with a reckless passion she had never experienced before. Where was her life going? She thought wildly. She had never thought of him as a lover.

Liar, said that inexorable voice inside her.

"Your heart's racing," he murmured, continuing to caress her. His expression was drawn taut, intent, as if he had started on a long-awaited voyage of discovery of her body.

Speech was impossible. Indeed, how could they ever speak to each other after *this?* The tips of his fingers had found her sensitised nipple, full of colour, were rolling it between them so it became a swollen bud of pure want. With one arm he brought her closer into him, staring down into her flushed face.

"You're a beautiful, beautiful woman, Alana!"

"One you shouldn't be putting at risk."

"Close your eyes. I won't hurt you," he promised. "I only want to make love to you a little."

Couldn't he see her agitation? Her flesh was threatening to catch fire. "And if I say you can't?"

"I know I can." His kisses moved to her throat. "Your father will sleep well into the morning. I want to take you home with me." His voice was so low and seductive it could have melted stone.

She knew if she went with him it would be momentous turning point in her life. "Don't think I'm so foolish." Caution welled. She *was* a virgin. She had no protection.

"I won't do anything you don't want. Instinct tells me you're a virgin?" He came at it directly.

A groan escaped her. "What am I, anyway? An open book?" She tried to pull away, but he held her tighter.

"A book I desperately want to read," he said, the note in his voice making her senses swim. "I'll call the house. You've had nothing to eat. I'll get Gwen to make us something."

"And for the rest of the night?" She threw back her golden head, the spirit of challenge showing in her eyes.

'I'll make love to you a little," he said softly. "Though the time's fast approaching to make it real."

"It's real enough for me now," she said, feeling her every last defence had been shaken loose. "Besides, I'm not in such a hurry. I should stay here—where I belong." Her feelings were so intense, so out of control, she felt she had little option but to push the panic button.

"You're too frightened to come with me?" He looked deeply into her eyes.

Insane as it was, it was true. "I have to think ahead, Guy," she answered, grappling with her heart's desire. "If I go to Wangaree with you, the whole Valley will know by the morning."

"Don't be ridiculous," he said. "My people will see you for exactly what you are. A lifelong friend."

"Of course—you *would* command absolute loyalty. Is that how I've never heard even a whisper about my mother and your father? Were they lovers?" She stepped closer, staring into his eyes.

"What would be the point of discussing it?" he said sombrely.

"Point being some people are feeling the shock waves to this day. How did your mother manage to live her life with such a secret in the background?"

He didn't answer for a moment, his striking face taking on a daunting expression. "Why don't we leave my mother out of this, Alana?"

"I'm sorry," she apologised. "But can't you see I have a need, indeed a *right* to know? I'm not a child. I can't be kept in the dark. You wouldn't accept being shut out for a half a minute. Why should I? Your mother must have known. For that matter, when did *you* first find out? Does Alex know? Or was she kept in the dark like me?"

"Keep probing and you'll finish up in a dark forest," he warned, reaching for his jacket. "For the last time—are you coming?"

She braced herself against the intolerable weight of longing. She knew she couldn't resist him. And, to make her position even more vulnerable, she knew of the powerful forces that had gathered in him.

"No, Guy," she said, as though she had sworn an oath. She turned away with a little broken laugh. "I can't think *any* woman has said no to you before."

"Is that why you're doing it?" he asked, his black eyes glittering.

She struggled to frame the right words. "You know why I'm doing it, Guy. You say you don't want to hurt me, but I fear somewhere deep down inside of you, you *do!*"

CHAPTER SIX

KIERAN returned from Sydney, strained and on edge. Although he apologised to Alana for having disappeared on the day of the sales, the name of his mystery woman remained a secret.

So many secrets, Alana thought, herself so troubled in her mind that she left her brother well alone. Kieran would confide in her when he was ready, she reasoned. Until then she would keep out of his private affairs. They only appeared to hold anger and pain. Besides, hadn't her own life turned into a mess?

Like Kieran, she couldn't bring herself to discuss it. She couldn't imagine what Kieran would think if she suddenly confided she was totally in love with Guy Radcliffe. She thought after the initial shock he would advise her to leave well alone. That was the way it must have been with him and Alex. *Leave well alone.* Clearly Kieran believed the Radcliffes were out of reach. The Radcliffes were rich folk. The Callaghans were battlers.

Their father had fought his way out of his binge, but he had lost so much weight for a man previously so strongly built that Alana began to worry his alcohol addiction over the past three years had done significant damage to his body—in particular, his liver. She began to read up all she could about the chronic liver disease cirrhosis, and found her way to an important medicinal herb, St Mary's Thistle, which had been used to good effect for liver ailments, indeed all sorts of ailments, since the time of the ancient Greeks and Romans. Her father refused point-blank to see a doctor and undergo any tests, but he did consent to swallowing the liquid extract the long-established village pharmacist recommended.

"Your dad really needs to see one of the doctors at the clinic, Alana." Kindly eyes were fixed on her. "Don Cameron is a good man. This Milk Thistle here could be no help at all."

Alana thought it was worth a try.

Out of the blue her cousin Rose rang to invite her to lunch at the hugely popular Radcliffe Estate Restaurant.

"I have some news for you!" Rose trilled excitedly down the phone. "I'm up in the air about it, actually. See you Tuesday—say about one p.m.? My shout. I'll make the reservation. It's usually packed out."

Tuesday morning, Alana dressed with care in a brilliantly white linen shirt with a small stand-up collar, over narrowly cut black pants. She had just the legs for the cut, and the right kind of derrière. Around her waist she slung a wide patent leather black belt with a big silver buckle, and she slipped on a pair of high heeled black sandals—her best. Her mother's black bag was dateless, never out of fashion. She thought she looked pretty good. She had inherited her mother's chic, and that actually meant a lot. Money wasn't synonymous with style.

She was looking forward to seeing Rose. All dressed, she presented herself to her father, who was sitting aimlessly in a planter's chair out on the verandah, staring up at the blue hills.

"How do I look?" She struck a model's pose, trying to get

a smile out of him. Off the wagon, Alan Callaghan was more morose than on it.

"Beautiful!" he said, putting his arm out to her and gathering her in around her slender hips. "Remember me to little Rosie. Some people just suit their names."

Alana remained in her father's embrace. "Like some people look exactly what they are." Of course she was thinking of Guy—The Man. "What are you going to do with yourself, Dad?"

He grimaced. "Well, let's see. Where shall I start? I thought I might go into town."

"Really?" Alana was pleasantly surprised. Her father rarely wanted to go anywhere. "Why didn't you say? I could have run you in and picked you up later."

"Only just thought of it," he said. "Might call in on Father Brennan. Make me confession."

"Dad?" Alana bent to stare into her father's face, feeling a shock of alarm.

"Only jokin', darlin'." He raised the ghost of a grin. "I haven't been to confession for many years. Hardly time to be starting up again now. But I like Terry Brennan. He's a good bloke."

"Mum thought so." Her mother had been raised a Catholic.

"God bless her!" Alan Callaghan sighed. "She was a saint to put up with me."

"You weren't so bad!" Alana shook him lightly. In fact in the old days their father had been full of fun and good cheer—the most affectionate of fathers. "Mum loved you."

"Did she?"

That struck a badly discordant note. "What are you saying, Dad? Of course she did."

"There's love and there's *love*," Callaghan pronounced flatly.

"So what are you trying to tell me?" Alana asked in distress. Oh, God!

"I let a *dream* rule my life, me darlin'. The dream that your mother loved me. I know she settled for me. I know she was absolutely loyal to me. But I wasn't what she wanted."

Pain slashed all the way through her. "Who *was?* I'm really confused about all this, Dad. We were a happy family. It wasn't a dream. It was a reality. And Mum *did* love you. She *had* to. She laughed at all your jokes. Don't shatter what we had with maudlin thoughts. Maybe she was in love with David Radcliffe at some stage, when they were very young. But she didn't marry him, did she? She married you."

Alan Callaghan let out a strangled sigh. "Things happen, Alana."

"*Tell* me." She waited, breathless. "It's obviously eating away at you, whatever it is."

"Sorry, darlin'!" Her father sat up straight. "I'm a bit hazy on it myself. You go off now and enjoy yourself. God knows, you deserve a bit of pleasure."

Alana glanced at her watch. She *had* to go, or she would be running late. She had intended taking the car—the air-conditioning in the ute was on the blink—but now she changed her mind. "I'll take the ute. You take the car," she suggested, in her usual generous fashion. Her father didn't know the air-conditioning in the ute was shot. There was so much he didn't know or care about.

"Doesn't matter to me, darlin'," Alan Callaghan said. 'You're all dressed up. *You* take it."

"The car will suit you better," she replied. Alan Callaghan was six-three, like his son, and his skin had a peculiar flush. "I'm fine in the ute." She bent to kiss his cheek, resting one hand on his shoulder. "You have clean shirts in your wardrobe, all ironed. Blue always looks so nice on you. Take care now, Dad. Love you."

"Love you too, my darlin'," Alan Callaghan said, rising to his feet, then going to the verandah balustrade to wave her off.

Alana saw pleasure leap into Rose's eyes as she walked towards her. Rose was already seated at the table, having arrived some minutes earlier. She jumped up to hug and kiss her cousin.

"Oh, isn't this great? I'm so happy to see you, Lana," she said in her affectionate way. "You look *gorgeous*—as usual. *Très chic!* You're easily the most stunning girl in the Valley. It puts Vi's nose out of joint I can tell you." She giggled.

"Is it any wonder I love you so much?" Alana asked indulgently. Rose herself looked a picture, in a designer dress that must have cost the earth. Her Italian handbag alone would have set her trust fund back a few thousand dollars. With maybe another thousand or more tied up in the shoes. The Denby girls weren't cheap dressers. They were fashion icons. In fact Alana rarely saw them in the same thing twice.

Predictably, they had been allotted one of the restaurant's best tables, beside the huge floor-to-ceiling plate glass windows. The building was shaded by extensive covered verandahs that commanded a splendid view over the sun drenched vale of vines that marched in precise lines right up to the base of the green foothills. What a visual delight! Alana felt herself calming. It was marvellous paintable country! The ripened chardonnay grapes were to be harvested at any moment, which accounted for the palpable air of expectancy that permeated the air, and it was a sparkling scene laid out for their delectation beneath a shimmering blue sky.

"You're going to have a glass of wine, aren't you?" Rose asked, fixing her cousin with her huge, heavily lashed blue eyes.

Rose was so very, very pretty, Alana thought. Rather like the pin-up girls of old, with her thick blonde hair cut in a bob and her rosebud mouth painted fire-engine-red. And she was sweet. She'd be perfect for Simon. Even the Draconian Rebecca couldn't object that much to Rose Denby.

"Just the one, Rose," Alana said with a smile. "I'm driving."

"Simon is going to run me home," Rose confided, looking just the faintest bit anxious, as if Alana might have some objection. "We'll soon be working together." She held up a hand. "You can't tell him yet, it's not set in stone, but Guy has offered me a job."

"That's your news?" Alana wondered at the reason behind Guy's sudden action.

"Yes!" Rose came across as thrilled. "I think it's right down my alley, but I wanted to get your take on it. You're the one with the good head on your shoulders. I'm a twit."

"That's not right, Rose," Alana protested right away. Pretty as she was, Rose didn't have a lot of self-esteem. "When did you stop believing in yourself? You were an excellent student."

"Sure!" Rose sighed, looking away, across the luxuriant vineyard. "It's hard to believe in yourself with sisters like mine. They gang up on me, those two. I know I was good at school but I've never amounted to anything, have I? You've been working your butt off since Aunt Belle died. People speak of you with such admiration. They dismiss *me* with a little knowing nod—*airhead, featherbrain, fluttery little playgirl.*"

"Hey, that's not true!" Alana caught her cousin's hand and shook it. "You're so hard on yourself, Rose. You're not reaching out, that's all. You can *do* things. You don't have to party all the time. I think it's great Guy has offered you a job. I'm so happy for you."

"You always did have a lot more faith in me than anyone else." Rose leaned across the table, speaking in such a confidential voice that all the people in the huge room might have been dead set on eavesdropping. "I'll be the PR person. I wouldn't be waiting tables or anything like that. Mummy and Daddy would have a fit. It's the social scene I'm good at, but I suddenly realise I *want* a job. I think it's a dumb mistake, the way I've been living the life of a playgirl. Just like you said, I want to *do* something. Not something terribly serious, or really hard work, like you, but something I can enjoy. Something I can shine at. I'm good with people. Unlike my snooty sisters, people seem to like me."

"Well, there's a very good reason for that, Rose," Alana said. "You have charm. You're lovely to look at. You're warm, friendly, intelligent. If you knew anything about mustering sheep I'd hire you myself. But you know everything about the Valley. And you've been just about everywhere in the world, so you can relate to all the overseas tourists. I think you'd be great! Congratulations. I'm proud of you."

Guy's hand is behind everything, Alana thought.

Rose blushed. "Gosh, it makes me happy to hear you say that, Lana. Guy has faith in me too. That means such a lot. I won't let you down. I'll be organising tours of the estate, making sure everything is working smoothly. I expect my duties will grow—Guy said it's up to me. And I can help Simon in the office when I have the time. I've always had a soft spot for Simon, but he can't see *anyone* outside you," she lamented.

Alana shook her head. "Rose, it's high time I told you I have *no* romantic interest in Simon. None whatsoever. We're pals."

Rose blinked, clearly having difficulty accepting what Alana had just said. "But Vi has been telling everyone you two are just biding your time before you get married. Simon's mother is a bit of a pain in the neck, no?" Rose looked at

Alana sympathetically. Rebecca Radcliffe, The Widow, had terrified her as a child. Rebecca looked just like the wicked stepmother in her illustrated book of *Snow White*.

"You're not listening, Rosie." Alana placed her hand over her cousin's, giving it several little emphasising taps. "I-am-not-and-never-will-be-in-love-with-Simon."

"Oh, thank you—thank you!" Rose put a hand to her breast, as if she was about to have a heart attack. "Just when I thought you were two steps away from the altar."

"I'm two steps away from punching Vi in the nose," Alana said as though ready to do it.

"But he worships you…" Rose could barely take in this new development.

"He would worship *you* if you played your cards right." Alana looked her cousin directly in the eye.

"But this is crazy! Lana, don't torture me. I'm already hyperventilating. You *really* don't want him?"

Alana picked up the leatherbound menu, which was quite extensive. She studied it for a moment before answering. "As a husband, no; as my lifelong pal, yes. I'd be excited to be a god-mother, though. Maybe chief bridesmaid before that. Don't take any notice whatsoever of anything Vi says. She's a born trouble-maker, I'm afraid."

"You're telling me!" Rose huffed. "And Lil's just the same. It will blow up in their faces one day."

Simon was thrilled to have the opportunity of seeing Alana in the middle of his working day. He kissed her on both cheeks with Gallic aplomb, and smiled benignly on little Rose, who was looking remarkably pretty and flushed.

"Good lunch?" he asked, walking them to the parking lot.

"Great lunch!" both young women said together, then laughed.

"Well, the restaurant boasts a much-lauded chef," Simon pointed out with satisfaction. "What did you have?"

"Rose will tell you in the car." Alana lightly touched his arm. "She says you're driving her home?" Actually, Alana could easily have done that, but Rose obviously didn't want to miss out on a little private time with Simon.

"I wouldn't want her to drive after a few drinks," Simon said. "Our Rose can be quite naughty!"

"I like to enjoy myself, Simon, darling," said Rose, suddenly feeling free to take his arm. "We had a brilliant time." She puckered up to kiss Alana goodbye. "Just double-checking—you're entering The Naming, of course?" she asked. "Will I *ever* get a chance to shine? Everyone thinks I'm pretty cute, but *you're* something else again."

"I'm not entering, Rosie," Alana said firmly. "And I'm thinking it would be absolutely wonderful if *you* won."

"Truly? You want me to win?" Rose's big blue eyes widened.

Alana nodded. "I'll take loads of photos of you wearing the crown."

Simon, however, was searching Alana's face with a frown. "You're joking, aren't you, Lana?"

"No, Simon, I'm not,' she said sweetly, resisting the urge to pinch his cheek.

"But I've already entered you," Simon burst out, near broken-heartedly.

"You shouldn't have done that, Simon. It's my decision not to enter."

"Well, that's good news of a kind." Rose was looking on the bright side. "It gives the rest of us a chance."

Alana was walking, head down, to the ute, when a tall figure loomed up in front of her, his height blocking out the sunlight. "Hi," Guy said in a perfectly calm voice. "Lost in thought?"

She was glad her eyes were hidden behind the dark lenses of her sunglasses. "Why, hello, Guy. Is this the way it's going to be from now on?"

"And how's that?" He took her arm with unbearable gentleness and moved her into the shade of a trellis that was covered in a prolifically flowering white vine.

"We're not friends any more?"

"Were we ever friends?" he asked ironically, his dark eyes moving slowly over her.

She averted her head. "Maybe not. I've just had lunch with Rose."

"So I heard," he answered smoothly. "She thinks the world of you, Alana."

"And I'm very fond of Rose. It's Violette I like to keep a million miles from. Violette is still telling anyone who will listen Simon and I are two minutes from the altar. At least that's what Rose just told me."

He was looking at her white shirt, at the first three buttons undone, allowing a mere glimpse of the shadowed cleft between her breasts.

She felt she was burning alive, unable to lock out the memories of his hands on her.

"Well, I do hope you put her right!" he said.

Alana gave in to a wry laugh. "You should have seen her rush off with Simon. She told me about the job. She's thrilled. It's wonderful you're giving her a chance, Guy. It's what she needs. Rose is capable of so much more."

"I did it for *you*, Alana, as you well know," he returned bluntly.

"Excuse me?" She threw back her head, aglitter in the sunlight.

"Don't play dumb. It doesn't suit you in the least. I did what you suggested. I set it up so Rose and Simon are thrown together. I understood that's what you wanted?"

She heard the birds calling to one another, the bees droning, inhaled the nearly overpowering sweet scent of the cascades of white flowers. "Do you want me to go down on bended knee and thank you?"

He smiled. "Actually, that could be nice. Why don't I drive you home instead? It's damned hot, and I know for a fact the air conditioning in your ute has broken down."

"Is there anything you *don't* know? Anyway, there are such things as windows," she pointed out. She who had been forced to spend several minutes fixing her windblown hair when she'd arrived.

"If you could manage a smile, I'll get someone to fix it and deliver it back to the farm. Probably by tomorrow afternoon."

She would be a fool to turn such an offer down. "I can't let you do it, Guy."

"But you *can* let me play matchmaker to get Simon off your back?"

She smarted—just as he'd intended. "I love Simon."

"As a friend. Simon needs to be strong about recognising that fact. I'm sure Rose will do her very best to offer sympathy. I like Rose. As you say, there's so much more to her than she's been allowed to show. I think she can do this job, and do it well."

"So do I!" Her note was overly emphatic, as though he might change his mind. "She's ecstatic about it."

His mouth twitched. "I think she's more ecstatic about coming into daily contact with Simon. They're both gentle people. I need hardly say you're not!"

"Neither are *you!*" she shot back, affronted.

"You *are* going to let me drive you home, though?"

She stared up at him. "You're an intimidating man when you want to be, Guy Radcliffe."

He took her arm, leading her off to the reserved parking

area, under shelter, where his car had pride of place. Once there, he opened the passenger door for her—but before she could make a move to slide into the leather seat he suddenly caught her chin, turned her face up to him and kissed her mouth.

She didn't know if it was fierce or tender or a combination of both, but her legs turned as wobbly as a toddler's.

"Lucky for you I'm not intimidating all the time," he said, placing a hand on the top of her head and guiding her down into the passenger seat as though she were his prisoner.

The countryside revealed itself in gentle swells of hill and dale, in every possible shade of green. Alana was very sensitive to all the different shades of nature. Graceful, broad-domed shade trees lined the valley road, and in the huge paddocks some species of wattle had already begun to burst into the glowing masses of golden blossom that outstripped the display turned on by the red and pink flowering gums.

Alana stared through the window of the gently purring car as the Valley landscape flashed by. The interior was beautifully cool. The top-of-the-range car was a far, far cry from the farm utility or indeed anything she was used to.

It was the bluest of blue days. A day to rejoice in—though if the truth be known numerous anxieties were tugging at her heart. A few shape-shifting white clouds were gathering over the hills. One looked like the dove of peace, with its wings outstretched. She didn't feel in the least peaceful. She was trying hard to resist the urge to touch her still pulsating mouth. Every kiss he gave her was more devastating than the last. If only she could read their *true* meaning. Tease away her doubts.

"Dad said such a strange thing to me before I left," she confided.

Guy glanced at her with a quick frown. "Oh? What?"

"He said he was going to see Father Brennan to make his confession."

Guy, being Guy, cut right to the heart of the matter. "What are you afraid of?"

"I believe Dad has a death wish." Her tone betrayed her sorrow.

"It's possible," Guy agreed quietly.

"Kieran and I are always on guard, but we can't be with him all the time."

"Where is Kieran today?"

She rested her head back. "He's gone over to the Mangans to give them a hand. Mr Mangan isn't properly on his feet after his operation."

"Yes, I know," Guy murmured, his mind clearly on other things. "You know your farm will have to go?"

She nodded in abject resignation. "Maybe you can give me a job, like Rose?" She heard the bitterness in her voice, then felt appalled by it. "I'm sorry. I know how that sounded."

"I could buy Briar's Ridge," Guy said.

She turned her head to look at him in amazement. He had sounded serious. "You don't need it."

"No."

"So why would you do it?"

A muscle clenched along his clean jawline. "I'd do it if it would get your father back on his feet." So she did mean something to him. But what?

"I don't believe it would," she answered, on reflection. "Dad is sunk in—not apathy, it's despair. He tried to make that 'confession' a joke but he can't fool me. He told me, 'There's love and there's *love*.' He said he'd let a dream rule his life. That he wasn't the one my mother wanted."

"Isn't *that* a confession?" Guy said with a strange note in his voice.

"You know it all, Guy. That's why I'm telling you. In a way, your family and mine are bound together The richest family in the Valley, descendants of the old squattocracy, and an Irish immigrant who arrived in this country as a penniless boy with only a kindly great-aunt to take him in. Why did my mother choose the man she did? Why did my mother choose my father when even my father believes he wasn't her heart's choice?"

Guy took his time before he answered. "Your mother was pregnant at the time of her marriage, Alana. She married the father of her child. It's as simple as that. She did what she believed was right."

Tears choked her throat. "Do we even know *that* for sure? Why do Kieran and Alex act so strangely whenever they see one another? If I didn't know better, I'd say Alex was Kieran's woman of mystery. She certainly looks the part. Maybe they think they're related? Maybe that's what they're afraid of?" She broke off, emotionally exhausted.

Guy's dark eyes cut to her distraught profile. "Alan Callaghan was the father of Annabel's child." His voice had the ring of certainty. "Don't make yourself sick toying with a fantasy. Although there *is* something odd in Kieran's relationship with my sister. Whatever it is, it's definitely not what you've just thrown in. You can get that out of your head right now. However your father won your mother—whatever method he used—it has haunted him. Believe me, Alana, Kieran is his son. Do you really think my father would have let his own child get away from him? Your mother alone made the decision to marry your father. She could not be dissuaded. Anyway, as a family you always gave the appearance of being happy. You *were* happy. Leave it at that, Alana. There's nothing to be gained by asking too many painful questions to which you might never get an answer."

Even so, immense frustration was building in her chest.

"When I was a girl I used to hero-worship you," she said in a tight voice.

He kept his eyes on the road. "You said that with such a mix of emotions. Am I going to have to do battle for you, Alana? You know I want you. I'm having trouble thinking of anything else *but* wanting you." He lifted a hand off the wheel to touch her cheek.

Her body was swept by the sharpest aches and longings. *Don't you dare cry,* she admonished herself. But her feelings were reflected in the melancholy tone of her voice. "So we start an affair? Is that it? Because *you* want me? For how long? What happens when it's all over?" She turned her head to stare at him. "What could be the terrible result? For that matter, how do you know I won't trap you into marriage? Even for you, someone renowned for never making a mistake, it wouldn't be difficult. I could swear to be on the pill when I wasn't. It's been done before today. We both know of cases in the Valley."

"You could never trap me," he said. "The man who gets you, Alana, will be walking off with a prize. And let me correct you. I've made plenty of mistakes. Not, however, with women. Anyway, that's not the way you are. You don't have a dishonourable bone in your body."

"I hope not." Everything about him went deep with her. It was so much worse since they had crossed that dividing line. This man had the power to break her heart. She might be like her father. Some broken hearts never mended. "Do any of us truly know what we are until crisis time?" she asked. "Was Kieran's conception just an accident?"

Guy's face darkened. "Please, Alana, forget it."

"Easier said than done. Maybe much of life is a series of accidents? What do you really want of me, Guy? I must tell you I'm no plaything to be enjoyed and then thrown away."

"You think I see you as a plaything?" he asked with a flare

of anger. "I don't fall into the emotionally screwed up category, Alana. And in case you've started thinking revenge; forget it. Revenge is not in my heart. We both know we've always had a connection, though I suppose both of us have done our best to cover it up. I was older when you were just growing up. It made a difference. *Then.*"

Hadn't his position, his charisma, his experience and sophistication kept her in awe for a long time? She stared out of the window for a few moments. "Were you ever sleeping with Violette?" she asked finally. She couldn't stop herself. That was the other thing. His relationship with her cousin.

Guy's mouth twisted. "Okay—yes! I was for a while. I won't lie to you. My mother was very much in favor of Violette. I guess you don't understand why. I don't know that I do myself," he said wryly. "But Violette can be very charming when she puts her mind to it. She knows how to insinuate herself with the right people. I'm sure you know what I mean. But our relationship couldn't go beyond a certain stage. We're very different people. Violette will find someone to suit her. I've had plenty of girlfriends. You know that. Most of them are still my friends. I've never deliberately hurt a woman. The very *last* person I want to hurt is you."

"But despite your best intentions it could all turn out very differently," she said quietly. "If we became close, our differences might stand out.'

"Does that worry you?" he asked. "I've known you all your life, Alana. I haven't seen any essential differences. We're not opposite poles. We both love the land. Not everyone sees it as we do. We need this life. We love Nature. We feel its healing power."

"It hurts me to know you slept with Violette," she admitted. "Your affair—whatever it was—lasted quite a while. She must be good in bed."

A groan came from the back of Guy's throat. "Alana, even for you I can't kiss and tell. Did you want me to lie to you? Sex happens. I made no promises to Violette. I didn't lead her astray. We really weren't half as close as you seem to think. There's a thousand times more excitement in touching your cheek."

"So we're going to have a sexual relationship?" If so, she might lose herself for ever!

"That's what *I* want! I think we've gone past the stage where we can remain good friends."

"Would you like it if I said I've slept with Simon?"

He turned his head briefly. "No, I wouldn't," he said, unmistakably emphatic. "But you haven't. I'm thinking Simon *has* to be the Sir Galahad of the Valley. He adores you. It must have been very hard for him, treating you all this while as his best pal."

"He *is* my best pal, that's why!"

"What would I be, then?" He shot her a challenging glance. "Come on—tell me, so I'll know."

She began to count out on her fingers. "You're a man with a lot of influence. You have a lot of power. And, yes, you have loads and loads of money."

"Would you marry me for my money?"

"Of course I wouldn't. Anyway, I'm not thinking of marriage at this stage."

"What about six months from now?"

"You're fooling," she said shortly. She could see the sparkle in his eyes. "Go on, have your fun."

"You never know! Anyway, you and Simon are wrong for each other."

A little wave of sadness swept through her. "Simon is going to be dreadfully hurt."

"I know that, and I'm sorry. Simon is my cousin—he's

family. But we both know Simon and Rose are much better suited. Besides, Rebecca will take a completely different view of Rose."

Alana gave a brittle laugh. "Rose is a Denby."

"So are you. Rebecca is an odd person," he commented unexpectedly.

"My mother used to say Rebecca 'wasn't quite right.'"

"And she was being kind. Keep away from Rebecca as much as possible."

She turned her head in surprise. "Why do you say that? Anyone would think I was considering moving in."

"Well—" Abruptly, Guy broke off what he'd been about to say. He further startled Alana by putting a warning hand on her arm. "Looks like there's been an accident up ahead. I can spot skid marks, and there's a gouge in that big tree that looks fresh. A vehicle might have skidded on the gravel, hit the tree, then flipped. We'll need to take a look."

Instantly Alana was riven by dread. Some part of her recognised that she had always been prepared for something like this. Her mother had lost her life not very far from here. Her father had told her he intended driving into town. That meant he would have had to travel this very road. Full-blown panic entered her bloodstream. The beauty of the day gave way to nightmare.

Guy stopped his car at the top of the rise, a few feet from the towering gum. An area of bark had been gouged out of the trunk, long strips of it lying around the base. Swiftly Guy got out of the car and came round to her. "Stay where you are. I can smell petrol."

She responded by trying to get out. "I'm coming too. You can't stop me."

"I can and I will," Guy said, looking grim and well capable of using force if he had to. "This is a dangerous situation,

Alana. Stay put. You're needed to ring the police and an ambulance."

"Just tell me it's not our car," she implored, her hopes dimming.

Guy lifted his hand, then dropped it as if in futility. Despite himself he too was giving in to a peculiar dread. He moved off while Alana sat there, door open, making heartbreaking little keening sounds.

He was back to her in moments. "It *is* your car," he said, a world of regret in his voice. "I can see your father slumped over the wheel. The petrol fumes are strong. I have to get him out of there."

"But, Guy, the danger!" She stared up at him, wild-eyed. Could she lose Guy and her father too?

"I'll be fine," he insisted. "Just do what I tell you. Make those calls. There's no real help you can give. You'll only be in the way."

Urgently he moved down the woody slope. The smell of petrol was worrying him dreadfully. Alan Callaghan could be incinerated—a fate not to be borne. He was either unconscious or dead.

Guy reached the vehicle, tugging with all his might at the door handle. Finally he got it open. He reached in over Alan Callaghan's dark head to turn off the ignition, his heart flipping at the moan that issued from the injured man's throat. *Thank God!*

Guy withdrew his head for a split second, shouting back to Alana, who was standing at the lip of the slope, staring down at the crash scene. "He's alive!" *But in what condition?*

Blood was running from a wound high up on Alan Callaghan's temple. Working swiftly, fearing the situation, Guy released the seat belt, then got his arm around the man. There was no way he could leave Alan Callaghan where he was.

The car could catch fire at any minute. It would explode. Too gruesome a death! One to be avoided at all costs. There was nothing else for it but to carry the semi-conscious man up the slope. To Guy's immense relief, Alan Callaghan roused himself, then made a definite effort to stand on his own two feet.

"I've got you, Alan!" Guy cried. "We have to get up the slope as quickly as we can."

Just as he had done once before, Guy slung his arm around the big man, half pulling, half dragging him up the slope, which mercifully wasn't steep.

Oh, Dad—Dad, what's to become of you? Alana shook her head, her nerves raw. Was this an attempted suicide? Or had her father simply lost control of the vehicle when he'd skidded on the gravel? Going on the strength of the petrol fumes, she was terrified he and Guy wouldn't make it up the slope until it was too late. And she was in danger herself, standing so close to the lip. But she couldn't bring herself to move away.

I can't face life without these two.

If anything bad happened now it would break her. There had been so many losses, her spirit would simply call it quits.

"There's a rug in the boot," Guy called to her. "Be quick, Alana. Get it and drape it over the back seat. I'll put your father there. We can get him to hospital much faster than waiting for the ambulance."

Alana ran.

Less than a few minutes after that, with Guy's car speeding back towards the town, the Callaghan's car exploded. It went up in a solid wall of orange flame, with sections of buckled steel flying like missiles through the sulphurous air.

CHAPTER SEVEN

THEY were sitting in the waiting room, hoping for news of Alan Callaghan's condition.

Alana knew she would have been locked into a dark world if Guy hadn't been with her. His strong, calm presence lent her tremendous support. He was, in fact, holding her hand. She didn't know when he had taken it, but she wasn't going to let go. Some time in the future, when her father had made it, she was going to thank Guy for saving her father's life. It had been a very brave thing to do. Not everyone would have taken such a risk. Most people would have been thinking, quite naturally, of their own survival. Now her mind was dulled with shock, replaying the incident over and over, trying to fathom what had been in her father's mind. She was leaning against Guy, her head resting on his shoulder, but she was no longer fully conscious of what she was doing.

"Lana?"

They both looked up as Kieran, with a visibly upset Buddy in tow, came into the waiting room. News of the crash had travelled with the speed of lightning. It had reached the Mangan farm in no time at all.

Alana stood up, throwing herself into her brother's arms. They closed around her powerfully, conveying the state

Kieran was in, but there was a faintly bitter edge to his voice. "What's all this about, Lana?" he asked, his handsome face pinched. "Was it an accident, or Dad deciding to call it a day?"

She could only murmur helplessly, "I don't know. I don't know."

"Well, the police will soon sort it out," Kieran said grimly. "God, I'll have to stop Buddy blubbing. It's really getting to me."

Alana looked towards the sobbing youngster. "He loves Dad."

"Well, I love Dad too, but I'm fed up with all this. What was in Dad's mind? Doesn't he care about *us* at all? Doesn't he care how we would feel *afterwards?*"

Clearly Kieran thought it was a failed suicide attempt.

Guy, on the other hand, was by no means sure of that. He decided to intervene. Alana looked pale enough to faint. "It could well have been an accident, Kieran," he said, joining them.

"Or Dad determined on taking his last ride," Kieran said in a choked voice. "We can't thank you enough, Guy. You're a hero."

"Forget that!" Guy brushed all mention of heroism aside. "I did what you would have done in the same circumstances."

"You're a hero in my book," Kieran repeated firmly, suddenly turning on the weeping Buddy. "For goodness' sake, Buddy, quit it!" It was obvious he was in no mood to listen to Buddy's choking sobs, which had started the very minute they got the news.

Guy twisted about to get an arm around Buddy's slight shoulders. "You've got to be strong now, Buddy. Think you can do it?"

"I'm a bit of a mess right now, Mr Radcliffe," Buddy said pitifully.

"We *all* are, Buddy. But we mustn't slip into despair."

Buddy rolled his eyes. "You were willin' to go down to a rolled car that was threatenin' to blow up! I call that mighty brave."

Incredibly brave, Alana thought.

"It wasn't about bravery, Buddy," Guy said, finding being labelled brave a burden. "It was doing what had to be done. Now, let's forget it."

I'll never forget it! Alana thought.

Minutes later Simon and Rose hurried in, both showing their concern. "When we first heard there had been an accident Simon nearly went off his head," Rose confided to Alana quietly. "We had absolutely no idea at that point it was your father. Simon thought it was you. Maybe there's a lesson to be learned in that. He loves *you*, Lana. Only you."

Alana looked into Rose's blue eyes. "He's there for me, Rosie as I'll always be there for him. Oh, look—" her gaze went past her cousin "—it's Dr Pitman."

They all rose to their feet. They all knew Bill Pitman, who was in his early fifties and had a shock of pure white hair. He was the hospital's cardiologist and head of the emergency team.

"Okay," Pitman announced briskly, but with sympathy and understanding. "Alan has had a heart attack. It was that which caused him to lose consciousness at the wheel. Our immediate goal has been to ease his pain and discomfort. Now we have to clear the blocked coronary artery and restore bloodflow to the heart." He turned to Guy. "Only you acting so quickly, getting him to the hospital in time, Guy, after pulling him out of the car, has ensured his survival. I won't beat about the bush. Alan is a sick man. We all know he hasn't been looking after himself. I'm going to keep him here for a day or so. I want to run more tests. He'll need bypass surgery, so be prepared for that."

"Can we see him?" Alana asked, experiencing a degree of relief that it had been an accident and not attempted suicide.

"For a moment only." Bill Pitman smiled gently. "You and Kieran. Your father is groggy. He needs to be kept quiet."

"Of course." Guy, who had saved Alan Callaghan's life, nodded his head on behalf of the rest of them.

The fact it had been an accident made quite a difference, Guy thought. He could see the relief neither Alana nor Kieran was able to keep out of their faces. Bypass surgery had a high success rate. With the proper care Alan Callaghan had many more years of life left. What he had to do was make huge change to his lifestyle. That was if he really wanted to live.

Alan Callaghan's quadruple bypass was scheduled for ten days' time. He was sent home on medication. There was no question of his touching alcohol. Alana was certain he'd make no attempt to, even when no one was around. Not that he was left on his own for any length of time. Kieran was managing the farm almost single-handedly. She devoted her time to her father watching him like a hawk, and when she took a short break Buddy, who had moved into the house from the cottage, was at hand.

"A man's never alone for five minutes!" Alan Callaghan pretended to growl. "Can't even go to the lavatory on my own." It was true Buddy followed him there, on sentry duty outside the door.

The Wine Festival Dinner-Dance was to take place on the Saturday night, but Alana had no thought of going. She had to be home with her father. She was going to be extremely nervous until he had his operation, and stood over him while he took his medication. Simon came over frequently—mostly to see Alana, but genuinely concerned for her father's health.

"Surely Buddy can watch your dad for a few hours?" he

suggested. "He looks all right to me. In fact much better." That at least was true.

"There will be other dinner-dances, Simon," she said. "Take Rose. You and she have been spending a bit of time together, I hear."

"Bless her. She's been a big help when I'm really busy," Simon said quite fondly. "It's just as you said. There's a lot more to Rose than meets the eye."

"Gosh, I would have thought what meets the eye was good enough for most guys," Alana said. "Maybe Rose is having a calming influence on you? As for me—one part of me is really sorry I'm missing out, the other knows where love and duty lie."

But her father when he found out, wouldn't hear of her missing out on the big night. "Alana, I won't sleep until you tell me you're going. I'm as right as rain, my girl. Haven't you been noticing how much better I am? Would you deprive your father of the pleasure of seeing you all dressed up and winning The Naming? Think about it. I'd be far happier seeing you go off to the ball than seeing you sitting home with me. I can watch some television. Buddy will keep me company. Buddy's perfectly capable of keeping an eye on me. As if I need it! I can't have you worrying yourself sick about me. I *want* you to go."

Alana had a problem. She didn't have a dress.

Kieran worked close to the homestead while Alana took a quick trip into town. There were two excellent boutiques. Maybe she could find something to fit her budget?

She was coming out of the first boutique, having tried on several lovely but too expensive garments, intending to move on to another shop to check out what they had in stock, when a well-bred but severe-sounding voice hailed her.

"You're going to the dinner-dance, then, Alana?"

Alana spun to look into Rebecca Radcliffe's obsidian eyes. Of all the rotten luck! "Oh, hello, Mrs Radcliffe." Hastily she put a smile on her face. "Dad doesn't want me to miss out."

"How is he?" Rebecca asked, with little show of concern.

"Much better, thank you." Alana moved into the arcade for privacy. Rebecca followed suit. "He's due to have a bypass on the fourteenth."

Rebecca smiled thinly. "I know. My son tells me everything. I'm not quite sure what it is you want from my son, Alana. Perhaps, since we're on our own, you can enlighten me?"

Alana knew a challenge when she heard it. She began a slow count to ten. "Mrs Radcliffe, Simon and I have been friends since we first started carrying school bags. Friends are what we are. I thought that was understood."

"Oh, please." Rebecca gave a nasty little jeer. "You know, I can't figure you out, Alana. You don't want my son, yet you can't bear to let him go. You give him no chance to be with other girls, you demand his constant attention, and all the time you have your eye on Guy. No, don't attempt to deny it. I'm no fool. Guy's one of your little secrets, isn't he? You've been infatuated with him for years now. I remember as if it were yesterday you looking up at him at your eighteenth birthday. I remember his kissing your cheek. I remember how you touched it afterwards. A dead give-away to anyone watching, as I was. Guy, of course, has an understanding with your cousin, Violette. You know that. But I suppose a girl can dream. You won't get him, my dear. Though I suppose he can't help being fascinated. You *are* beautiful. A heartbreaker, like your mother. But you won't get Guy, mark my words. There's bad blood there."

Alana wasn't as profoundly shocked as she once would have been. Nevertheless, she felt as though an arrow had pierced her heart. She stared back at Rebecca's face, with its fine, cold features, for the longest time. "How dare you attempt to defile my mother's memory?" she said, her voice low and vibrating with emotion. "I'd have a care, if I were you. Someone might start dragging out *your* secrets, and I bet you've got a few. What are you talking about anyway? Bad blood?" The anger that was in her showed in her sparkling eyes.

Rebecca Radcliffe gave another one of her thin, hateful smiles. "You're such a passionate creature, aren't you?" She made it sound like a serious character defect. "I know when to keep my mouth shut. There's plenty that has been kept hidden. Plenty that has been kept within the family. *I'm* family. You forget, I was married to David Radcliffe's brother."

Alana's Irish temper unfortunately got the better of her. "Who seemed pretty desperate to get away from you," she shot back, then immediately apologised. "I'm sorry, I shouldn't have said that. But I can't stand here being insulted by you, Mrs Radcliffe. I've been through a pretty emotionally worrying time with my father. I won't let you upset me further, though upsetting people *is* your specialty. If you've got concerns about Simon and me, speak to Simon. Personally, I think Simon's big problem in life is *you!*"

That was all wrong, she fumed, as she rushed away. But didn't Rebecca deserve it? Alana didn't want to look at dresses any more. She didn't want to go to the dinner-dance. Thoroughly upset, she kept on walking, past where she had intended to go and on to where she had parked the ute. What a dreadful woman Rebecca was. No wonder Simon lacked backbone, with a mother like that to drive him crazy. Alana was doing Rose a huge disservice, pushing her in Simon's direction. Razor-tongued Violette was much better suited to dealing with a potential mother-in-law like Rebecca.

She had almost made it back to the ute when Guy, who was driving through town spotted her bright head. It really was a beacon, that mane, he thought—not for the first time. There was a parking spot just behind the utility. He pulled into it, getting out of the car and greeting her across the bonnet. "So—what are you doing in town?"

Her heart did its usual flip. This love of mine, she thought. This *secret* love of mine. "I haven't been here for long," she said, the tremble in her voice betraying her agitation. "I ran into Simon's mother."

"Aaah!" Guy expelled a long understanding breath, joining her on the pavement. "That must have been like running into an iceberg. So, what did she say?"

Alana put a hand to her temple. "Let's see. Where shall I start?"

"Come and have a cup of coffee with me," he said. "You can tell me then."

"I should get home to Dad."

"Coffee will give you a kick. We won't be long." He took her arm. "Actually, I wanted to suggest getting a trained nurse in to watch him this weekend. You are coming to the function?"

"I wasn't." She allowed herself to be steered towards the town's newest and by far best bistro, run by an Italian family, newcomers to the district. They had turned an ordinary little café that had been losing money into a thriving business. The coffee was everything coffee should be, the light meals were delicious, and the specialty breads, the luscious little tarts, slices, mouth-watering cheesecakes, were all made on the premises by different members of the family.

"So, what changed your mind? Guy asked.

"Dad persuaded me. That's what I was doing in town. I was after a dress."

"Why don't you let Alex pick a couple out for you in Sydney?" he suggested, as if that was the perfect solution. "She'd know exactly what would suit you."

"I'm certain she would. Alex has superb taste. But perhaps I should tell you I'm on a budget." Of course the Radcliffes didn't know what budgets *were*. They had millions.

"I'm sure Alex could find you something ridiculously cheap and gorgeous at the same time," Guy said smoothly. "She'd love to help out. You won't find what you're looking for here."

"Most women aren't prepared to pay *astronomical* prices for dresses," she pointed out. "Anyway, I'm not going."

"Yes, you are," he coolly contradicted. "Personally, I'd be shocked if you didn't win the title of most beautiful girl in the Valley wearing something run up from a hessian bag."

Guy opened the glass-paned door of the bistro, allowing Alana to step into the relaxed charm of a large open room, decorated very much in the Italian style. The lunchtime wave was over—the bistro had been packed—so there were tables available. The grandfather of the family, Aldo—a big man, slightly overweight, still handsome in his early seventies, with warm, expressive brown eyes and a head of tightly furled white curls—hurried over to greet them, shepherding them happily towards the best table available.

They settled on the same thing. A slice of *timballo,* a marvellous home made chicken and mushroom pie in a pasta case. "And Mamma has made her famous hazelnut and chocolate cake," Aldo confided, as though no one could possibly resist.

Alana looked up to smile. "Then I can't say no."

Guy gave a relaxed nod. "I won't say no either, Aldo." He'd had nothing since seven o'clock that morning. He didn't normally stop for lunch, preferring to wait for dinner. "A glass each of one of your good dry whites with the *timballo,* one long black with the chocolate cake, and—what?—a cappuccino for you, Alana?"

"Perfect," she sighed, realising not only how hungry she was but what wonderful restorative powers even the mention of food had. She recalled how her mother had adored reading cookbooks.

"Have you heard from your granddaughter?" Guy asked pleasantly, watching Aldo's face light up with love and pride. Daniela Adami, at twenty-six, had worked with famous chefs in Paris and Rome. Guy had learned at present she was sous chef to the executive chef at a famous London hotel. The entire family were excellent cooks, but Daniela had taken things to an even higher level. She was a young *cordon bleu,* fast making a name for herself.

"She rang only last night," Aldo told them. "She's well and happy, but she's missing the family. She's been away from us for nearly five years now. Always climbing the ladder. One of these days she'll come home and open her own restaurant. She is a *real* chef, our Daniela. Even the male chefs don't mind taking orders from her in the kitchen. She's as good with people as she is with food. We sent her back to Europe to learn, but there's so much happening here in Australia. Great Australian chefs. Great Australian restaurants. Marvellous ingredients—ah, the sea food! Nothing short of superb!" He kissed the tips of his fingers. "We must pay homage to the great chef you have at your estate restaurant, Mr Radcliffe."

"Why don't you and your wife visit on Saturday night?" Guy suggested, knowing other members of the family would keep Aldo's restaurant going. "I'll arrange for a table. You'll come as my guests. Who knows? Daniela might one day bring her culinary art to Wangaree Valley."

Aldo burst into a flood of lyrical Italian, raising his hand over them like a priest giving a blessing.

"You've made his day," Alana commented, as Aldo moved off to attend to their order.

"I like this family." Guy looked around him. "They're good for the town. I want them to fit in."

"I think they already have."

Thirty leisurely minutes later, they were walking back to their cars. "Feeling better?" asked Guy.

"Much," Alana said, visibly perked up. "Simon's mother is such an upsetting woman. She goes out of her way to be unpleasant. How did she come to have a sensitive, gentle son like Simon?"

Guy shrugged. "One of life's great mysteries."

"I pity the woman he ends up marrying," Alana said, looking up at Guy with a frown. "I think we've done entirely the wrong thing, trying to set him up with Rose."

"It must have slipped your attention that a girl like Rose wouldn't offer Rebecca any challenge. You, on the other hand, do. Rose will know how to handle Rebecca. She's by no means as empty headed as she acts."

"Empty-headed?" Alana looked at him aghast. "I don't believe you said that."

"Just an observation. Let me rephrase it. Rose, however pretty, comes across as a little vapid when compared with you."

"Damn it, Guy, *you* gave her a job!"

"Of course I did. It's as I said. She's pretty. She's friendly. People like her. And she's been given the opportunity to prove she's a lot smarter than people give her credit for. I like Rose—I *do*. We get along well. Besides, it's only my opinion."

Alana broke into a wry laugh. "Lord only knows what your real opinion of me is, then."

He glanced down on her head. "I can't lie. You'd be flattered." He used the remote to open his car. "Hop in for a moment," he said, his hand on the passenger side door. "I have something I want to discuss with you. Won't take a minute."

"Why so mysterious?' she asked, feeling more and more exposed the closer she got to him.

"Hop in," he repeated.

"Whether I like it or not," Alana muttered, doing as she was told.

A moment later Guy slipped into the driver's seat beside her, all radiant male energy, completely in charge of himself. *And her.*

"I wanted to get your reaction first." He turned to her, his dark eyes signalling serious business. "I know someone who would very much like to buy into the Valley. His family has been long established in the New England area. They own and run a well-known sheep station, Gilgarra."

"Of course I've heard of it," Alana said.

"Yes, well, I went to school and university with Linc, but he has an older brother. He wants a place of his own. He never did get on with his father anyway. I don't think Alan would have any difficulty selling Linc Briar's Ridge for a good price."

Alana sat clutching her handbag in her lap. Her face showed a whole range of emotions. "You've gone ahead and discussed it with this Linc?" she asked.

"I'm discussing it with *you*, Alana. Linc is a good friend of mine. I know his ambitions."

"Linc who?" Her beautiful hazel eyes were throwing off sparks. "What's their name again?"

"Linc Mastermann," he said calmly. "His first name is actually Carl. His mother was Barbara Lincoln, of the

Victorian pastoral family. Somewhere along the line Carl got to be Linc."

Alana looked straight ahead of her. She wanted to stop this conversation, but knew that she should listen. The farm had to go. They all knew that. Even if it weren't so deeply in the red, and her father's bypass operation was a great success, she wouldn't want her father returning to a life of hard physical work.

"I'm sorry, Alana," Guy said, giving her a tender look she missed. "I know how much you love your home."

"And what about the horses? And my dogs?" she burst out emotionally, turning her head accusingly, as though it were all his fault.

"You won't have a problem finding the dogs a good home. I'll even take them myself. And Linc would want to keep the horses. It's not the time to talk to your father yet, though. He simply isn't well enough to handle it. I've spoken to Kieran, of course."

"Of course!" Her tone held bitterness. "Let the *men* settle it!"

"It's not that at all." His own tone turned terse. "Kieran has been living a life that doesn't altogether suit him. He's an artist. He's only just come to the realisation he could be very, very good. Kieran won't have a big problem making the transition to a different lifestyle."

She knew that was probably true, yet she was filled with a boundless sense of loss. She put her hands to her head. It seemed to be spinning. "And what about me?" She was determined to hold back the tears. "I love this life. I don't want to go off to the city. Work in an office. Hemmed in. I don't want that."

He leaned towards her, his voice deep and soothing. "Don't get angry. I'm not suggesting that at all. Why don't we take one thing at a time, Alana? Your father's operation first, and then we must give him time to recuperate. All I'm saying is I have a buyer for when the time comes. At least I can take that worry off your mind. The sale could be handled smoothly and privately. I'll do everything I can to make that happen."

The tenderness in his voice, the sheer seductiveness of it, quite undid her. "And what do you get out of this, Guy?" she demanded, throwing out an emotional challenge. "What do *you* get out of it?"

His eyes were brilliant with intensity. "I get *you.*"

"Me?" Her voice broke.

"You," he repeated, taking hold of her nerveless hand, straightening out her curled-over fingers, exercising the power he had over her. "We started out talking business. Let's stick to that. It's time I married. I want a wife who can be many things, and I believe you can easily fill that role. You can give me what I want and need. That definitely includes children at some future time. As for me, I can give you security and the right environment to blossom. I don't like seeing you work so hard, Alana. You're young now, so you're not feeling it as much as you should. You won't always want to work a six-day week. I want to look after you. I want you to look after me. Both of us can look after Wangaree. I don't just want a beautiful wife, I want a full partner. I want a woman I can talk to about everything. I don't even mind if she wants to fight me from time to time."

"And you think *I* can handle all that?" she erupted.

"I *know* you can."

"So what about love? L-O-V-E?" She spelled it out. "Oh, Guy!" She moaned as though her heart was breaking. "Do you want love at *all?*"

His long fingers suddenly laced into her thick golden hair, turning her face to him. "I want everything you can offer me," he said.

CHAPTER EIGHT

KEIRAN saw her sleek car picking up speed as it moved away from the homestead and down the gravelled drive. So she didn't intend to stick around to say hello to him? The more fiercely he wanted her, the less it worked. He was desperately close to deciding to put half a world between them. Would he *never* get rid of the feelings of remorse, the sadness of it all, the loss? Even that hadn't separated them. The two of them were locked in the most passionate of hells.

He knew she had brought Alana a dress to wear for the big function tonight. The whole Valley was *en fête*. He wasn't going. He couldn't bear to see her there, an impossibly beautiful orchid on the shoulder of that oaf Roger Westcott. Westcott wasn't going away. Westcott would grow old before he let Alex go. He wanted her, and he was prepared to hang in there for as long as it took. Forget Westcott. Think Sidonie Radcliffe. Sidonie and her party of socialites were staying at Wangaree for the gala weekend. He couldn't bear to come into contact with the great Sidonie Radcliffe. He'd sooner be thrown into a cellar full of snakes.

His expression softened as he thought of Alana. She would be certain to win the crown of most beautiful girl in the Valley. But her own family wouldn't be around her.

Their adored mother was gone. Their father has a mere shadow of what he had once been. Keiran was terribly worried about their father. Everyone kept telling him the operation had a high success rate, but did their father have any positive feelings left to pull him through? Of course the ever faithful Simon—who was a nice guy, but kind of gutless—would be there to partner Alana. Alana had had numerous admirers over the years she'd never seemed to take any notice of. It hurt to be deprived of the pleasure of seeing his beautiful sister in the Naming. His own Dark Lady was too perfect to be allowed to enter. It wasn't nice, her driving away; it was oddly out of character. She knew how badly he would want to see her. He kicked the gelding into a gallop.

She saw him coming, riding hell for leather down the steep slope. He and Alana were splendid riders. Not many could touch them. Guy. Violette Denby, a few others. There was beauty in Violette, but malcontent marred it. He was coming so fast that for a heart-stopping moment she thought he was going to gather his mount and fly over the sloping hood of her car as if he was clearing a jump. Swiftly she pulled off the unsealed road, nosing into the shade of a feathery acacia. Nerves jingling, she turned off the engine and lowered the passenger window—ready to confront him, but with some protection. Not that he had ever, or would ever, physically hurt her, but on occasion he had a very tough persona.

He reined in a few feet away, dismounted, then looped the reins around a low branch of the tree, trying to calm himself to no avail.

"Get out of the car," he said. There was urgency and anger in his taut handsome face. "Get out of the car, Alex," he repeated, blue eyes blazing.

It was useless to defy him. She stood out of the car, head bent, her slender shoulders faintly slumped.

He hauled her right into his arms, his chin coming down hard on her gleaming head. "You weren't going to wait and say hello to me?" he accused her, with burning intensity.

She threw up her head, inching it back so she could stare into his face. "Sometimes I can't take what you do to me, Kieran." There was such a sad and haunted look in her beautiful dark eyes it would have melted a heart of stone.

"You think it's easier for *me?*" He locked his steely arms around her, staring down into her face with an expression that bordered on anguish. "I've tried and tried to blot out our past, but something—God, what is it? Conscience?—won't let me. All I know is despite what you did to us, I have a boundless hunger for you. I can't think it will ever be assuaged."

He gave way to his longing and brought his mouth down over hers, a driven man, covering it in a furious kiss that plunged him into white-hot arousal. Her hold over him was so powerful, was it any wonder it struck fear into him?

"When am I going to see you? How?" He rubbed his thumb up and down her white throat. "I *have* to be with you."

She too was engulfed, trying hard to speak. "Maybe you should do something drastic and start afresh. Things don't have to be the way they are, Kieran. We've wasted so much of our lives. We've sought what we want in others, but neither of us could ever find it. We're no good together. No good apart. There has to be an end to it. We have to break out of the prison." She lifted her head. "Alana told me you've decided not to come tonight?"

He let his hand cup her breast, openly claiming it. "And watch you from a distance?" He gave a rasping laugh. "Watch that fool Westcott drool all over you? He never takes his eyes off you. How often have you claimed you were going to marry him? Why haven't you? You're just trying to torture me, that's all. Anyway, do you think I would go with your mother there?"

She moaned. "Oh, Kieran, you're so hard on us all. Please don't start on my mother again."

"She started on *me*. I was the boy from the wrong side of the tracks with a sword in his heart." Tears stung the back of his eyes. Darkness surrounded all his thoughts of Sidonie Radcliffe. Such was the drama of the past he had become so traumatised he couldn't speak of certain things. It was as though that woman had sewn his lips shut.

"*Don't,* Kieran!" Alex shook her head so violently the soft knot at her nape came loose, sending her hair swirling down her back. "You've stuck to your belief she forced me into having an abortion. I've told you in vain it didn't happen. My mother didn't even know until afterwards. No one knew I was pregnant but you, me and Dr Moreton."

"Who, conveniently, is long dead," Kieran said, the chaos of it all still in his head.

Alex was well beyond frustration. This had gone on too long. It had all but wrecked their lives. "I've told you and told you—Dr Moreton would never have consented to performing an abortion, or steering me to some other doctor who would. I *wanted* our precious child, even if we were hardly more than kids ourselves. We could have handled the situation with a little help. As it is, neither of us can move on. We can't be happy together. We can't be happy apart. I should hate you for it, because it's *you,* Kieran, who is driven to punish us both."

Tragically, there was truth in that. "Do you think I *want* to be the way I am?" He pulled her to him, staying very quiet for a moment. "I'll always have the death of our baby on my conscience, Alex. I can't help it. It's my nature. For years I had nightmares about it. I even made drawings of our child inside your womb, as though the pictures could help me communicate with it. I've had lost children hidden in my paintings. *You've* seen them, if no on else can. I'm not an uncaring man. The trouble is I care too much. You say we could have managed? We could have managed with *my* parents. *Your* parents would never have allowed it, no matter what you say. They couldn't have coped with the disgrace. Their beautiful only daughter pregnant by a nobody? That was how your mother saw me. I could never be a fitting partner for you."

"That's ridiculous, Kieran," she said fiercely, at the same time knowing he was right about her mother. "You're a very *special* person. Only you're unbelievably stubborn. You believe what you choose to believe." She lifted a hand, hit it helplessly against his chest. "We've battled this for years and years. Why?" She struck him again. "You've condemned me for having an abortion without your knowledge or approval. The truth is as I told you from the beginning. I had a miscarriage."

He pinioned her arms. "Please stop, Alex. It does no good."

Pain twisted like a knife inside her. "You can't think *Guy* knew?"

"I accept Guy didn't know," he answered quietly. "Guy was away at university most of the time. In any event, he would have stood by you."

Every word rained on her like a fresh blow. "Where have our dreams gone, Kieran?" she asked tragically. "You can't live without me, even though you've branded me a liar. And I love you, God help me. I've always loved you—only you. But I can go on like this any more. I want children. *Your* children. But you deny me."

There was such a glitter in his brilliant blue eyes. "It wouldn't be the same, though, would it? We ended one life."

Before she could stop herself her hand flashed up, cracking across his cheek. "Stop it, Kieran!" she cried. Blood was rushing in and out of her heart. "*Stop it!* I want the pain lifted. I want an end to the nightmare. I want someone to love me unconditionally. I want to be a *mother*." She twisted away from him violently, making a dive into her car.

Kieran gave way to remorse. "Alex, don't go." He held the door fast.

"I must. Please stand away from the car, Kieran," she said with hard determination. "You have to let me go."

"It's too late for that. You're the pattern of my life." He continued to stare down at her. "I've thought of going far away. Travelling halfway across the world to forget you, let both of us get on with our lives, but I know in my heart the world isn't big enough."

Slowly he shut the car door. Alex switched on the ignition, put the car into reverse, and once on the road drove away swiftly, sending dust and debris flying out from the spinning wheels.

She was weeping.

Kieran could hear his own agitated breathing. His tears had to remain silent, unshed. They fell, as they had fallen for so many years now, down the walls of his heart. Alex never lied, but in this one desperate instance she *had*. She had never changed her story—perhaps understandably blinding herself to her shame and her guilt. He knew she *had* had an abortion, though he had never told her his unimpeachable source. A few times he had come desperately close. But he had sworn an oath to Alex's mother he wouldn't. She had insisted it be a binding oath. He was not to tell Alex. *Ever.* Alex had to be left alone to grapple with her own grief. She had made the decision. She had thought it the only one open to her. Maybe she had believed life as she wished to live it would have been drastically altered had she borne his child?

Only his child had had a right to life. That fact took
precedence over every other consideration. They could
have weathered the storm together. In all likelihood the
storm would have passed over quickly. But Alex had failed
them both. She had made an irreversible decision. Her
choice. Her own mother had admitted it, sobbing broken-
heartedly as she did so. Mothers didn't lie. The loss of a
grandchild, she had told him, was a tragic event, the cruellest thing. She too suffered. She had wanted him, her
daughter's seducer, to be very aware of that. But Alex alone
had made the decision. He had to live with it. Moreover,
they had to break up. He had done enough damage to her
beautiful daughter.

From that day on he knew he had made a powerful enemy
in Sidonie Radcliffe. The great irony of it was some of the
time he didn't even blame her. He was the one, after all, who
had got Alex pregnant.

Parental love blazed out of Alan Callaghan's face as he looked
at his daughter, twirling before him. She was wearing a long
gauzy gold dress that made her look extraordinarily radiant.
He was quite certain she would win the title of the most beautiful girl in the Valley, as her mother had before her. He
decided there and then that from now on he was going to do
his very best to get back on his feet. He had given not only
himself but his children hell. Time now to throw off despair.
Father Brennan had talked sense to him, as he always had.
And he would have his operation. He had been told he should
come through it well. And he would stop drinking. He had
never really liked the taste of whisky anyway. It was only to
keep his heart and mind still. He would have to sell Briar's
Ridge, but maybe the farm held too many unquenchable
memories.

Guy had told him he would do everything he could to help

him. What a man was he? Guy had to know Alan had once stolen the much-loved Annabel Derby from his own father.

He and David Radcliffe had had one thing in common. Both of them had been madly, irrevocably, in love with Annabel. That was how the split between David and Annabel had come about. Alan had been waiting—with some cunning, he had to admit—in the wings, ready to step into whatever little void opened up. Annabel's anger with David—they had fought about *him;* David had been right to be jealous—had not burnt itself out. Pride had kept David away overlong. The proud and high-spirited Annabel had been looking for comfort. Alan Callaghan had provided it, overcoming her in the end, but never forcibly. That one night—magical for him—had been consensual. Hadn't it? He'd been a fine-looking guy in those days. He knew if there hadn't been a David Radcliffe Annabel would have let herself fall in love with *him.* For one night the world of the senses had swallowed them up. They'd been young. Hot-blooded. Kieran had been conceived.

So be it!

Now Alana, arms extended, danced before him, looking the image of her mother. He whispered her name. *"Annabel!"*

"It's me, Dad." Alana broke off her twirling, sending him a poignant glance. She moved to where her father was sitting, in his favourite armchair, his face illuminated with pride. She bent down to kiss him lovingly on his cheek. "So, what do you think. A front runner?" She tried to joke, but her heart wasn't in it. Kieran was staying at home with their father, so she wouldn't have to worry about him, but she had been carrying countless nagging anxieties all day.

"A clear winner!" Her father gave her the thumbs up.

"Belle of the ball!" Kieran said, truly affected by his sister's beauty. "You look ravishing. That's one helluva dress, I can tell you. It suits you perfectly."

"I have to thank Alex for that." Alana smiled at him, conscious her brother was in as much inner turmoil as she was. "She has exquisite taste."

"Sure!" Kieran shrugged laconically. "I won't ask how much it cost."

Alana pulled a little face. "I think Alex fibbed about that."

Kieran glanced away. Twice he had picked up the phone to call her. Twice he had put the phone down. The only place he could have her to himself was in Sydney. He had put Alex under enormous pressure for too many years now. Unless he could set the spirit of their lost child free he would destroy her. And with her, himself. Like his father, he had to change.

Alana was conscious as she and Simon entered the glittering restaurant and threaded their way through to their allotted table that everyone was smiling at her.

"See—you're the favourite!" Simon snorted with pride. "Told you so!"

An old friend of her mother's caught her fingers. "Don't you let us down now, Lana," she whispered cosily, thinking but not saying, because that would be too emotional, how she wished Alana's mother could have been there.

So I'm expected to be Named? Alana thought, sliding gracefully into the cushioned chair Simon pulled out for her. Most of the tables, apart from the main table where the judging committee was seated, were set for ten, with floor-length tablecloths and napkins, seat cushions as well, in alternating colours of soft pink and yellow that lifted the room, with all its dark polished timber, and made it glow. Glass bowls of glorious pink and yellow roses adorned the centre of each table, with tapering white candles set to either side. The huge room had taken on a decidedly glamorous air—a fitting setting for this gala function. Whoever was responsible for it had done a splendid job.

Rose arrived, looking marvellously pretty in hyacinth-blue, which that drew attention to her eyes. She greeted everyone happily, looking down at her dinner card. "Oh, look—I'm next to you, Simon," she said, as though it were a big surprise instead of scrupulously planned. "Lana! You look like a film star—seriously *sexy!*" she announced, eyes wide. She had never seen so much of her cousin's yummy figure. Alana had such a beautiful bust. She should show it more often. "Where did you get that dress?" she demanded to know. "Violette will be *livid!*"

Alana smiled sweetly. "Sorry, I can't tell you. It's a secret."

"It's to die for!" Rose let her expert eyes move over her cousin's shimmering silk organza strapless gown. "Believe me, you're going to win!"

Alana tried not to laugh. "It's not a matter of life and death, Rosie."

"It is to Violette!" Rose hissed from behind her hand.

Heads turned, as Alex rose from the main table to come over and say hello. She looked exquisitely beautiful, in a décolleté white gown with big South Sea pearls hanging from her ears, and another large pearl on a long shaft appended to a glittering white-gold chain around her throat.

She greeted everyone around the table, exchanged a few pleasantries, then spoke quietly to Alana as everyone turned back to their own conversation. "You look wonderful!" she said softly.

"So do you. Thank you for all your help," Alana said sincerely. Alex had lent a her gold evening bag, and the topaz and diamond earrings that swung like miniature chandeliers from her ears.

Alex inclined her head, her heavy raven hair drawn back into a classic chignon. "Kieran is home with your father?"

"He knew I'd be anxious," Alana explained.

"Of course." Alex touched her shoulder gently. "I just wanted to say hello, and tell you how lovely you look. I'd better get back to our guests now."

"Your mother is here." Alana looked towards the main table, arranged to seat twenty, where Sidonie Radcliffe in midnight-blue, looking light years younger than her age and sparkling with sapphires and diamonds, sat with her adored son, her Sydney friends, some VIP guests and the other three members of the committee besides Guy.

"She likes to come on these occasions," Alex murmured with a poignant smile. "Good luck now, Alana. You're the clear favourite—as you should be," she whispered, bending her head close to Alana's ear. "I'll see you later."

Alana wasn't the only one who kept their eyes on Alexandra Radcliffe as she walked back to the main table.

"Will you *quit* it, Rose?" Simon was saying, almost angrily, his face flushed.

"No, I mean it!" Rose replied earnestly.

"Mean what?" Alana intervened.

Rose fingered her pretty three-tiered earrings. "I was just telling Simon how handsome he looks. Anyone would think I was trying to proposition him."

"It's true, Simon," Alana chided him lightly. "You *do* look great." She turned her attention to their friends, Sally and Greg, asking if they had set their wedding date yet. Sally had already promised she and Rose they would be bridesmaids.

"Come on, now—you've been engaged six months," Rose said. 'Time to get married. Start a family. I can't wait to pick out my dress."

"To *help* pick out your dress," Sally said.

They were treated to a superb three-course dinner. Alana didn't feel hungry, although she had hardly eaten anything all day. A feeling painfully akin to dread seemed to be weighing her down.

"Laine, you're not eating anything," Simon murmured, looking at her with concern. "Try a mouthful of dessert. It's absolutely delicious!"

It certainly looked it. Luscious-looking strawberries had been arranged on a disc of crisp hazelnut shortbread, with a generous amount of champagne sabayon spooned over. A richly coloured strawberry coulis was spooned artfully around the plate, and there was a tiny sprig of fresh mint.

She picked up her spoon, intercepting a glaring look from Violette, who—surprise, surprise—hadn't managed to make it to the main table. She was seated a short distance away among her own crowd, and was wearing an electric-blue gown with a high straight neck, wasp-waisted. The severity of the top made much of the flounce of the full skirt that fell from her narrow hips. When she turned, most people gave a gasp. Almost the entire back was scooped out, revealing a good deal of smooth skin. A large sunburst brooch of diamonds, which Alana happened to know belonged to the girl's mother, was pinned to one side of the bodice. Alana thought she looked beautiful and very sophisticated. If only she could get that scowl off her face! Poor Violette. She hadn't yet discovered how to relax. If it were up to me, Alana thought, I would hand the prize to Violette. She wasn't trying to win anything. Violette *was*.

After the dessert had been served, serious table-hopping started as the dancing began. Rose and Sally had gone off together to the powder room, but Alana discreetly repaired her lipstick at the table, with Simon looking on with such reverence she might have been a religious icon.

"Okay?" she asked him, pouting a little. She couldn't figure out how to get through to Simon that although she loved him it wasn't and could never be a romantic love. It was much more sisterly. Her heart ached. The last thing she wanted to do was make Simon miserable, but she was going through a really difficult time now herself. Rose would have to do the nurturing for a while. Rose was so pretty she'd catch any man's attention.

Why, oh, why did people make the wrong choices?

"Perfect." Simon laughed, his eyes on her beautiful mouth. He positioned one of his hands over hers. "You look so wonderful I don't dare ask you to dance. I don't want to tread on your toes. I love your shoes. What do you call them?"

"Shoes. Or, if you want to get specific, slingbacks. If you don't want to dance, we can sit it out," Alana said, fully prepared to reject an over-enthusiastic admirer heading her way.

Simon glanced past her to smile. "Well, you can count your lucky stars. Guy is coming over. From the look of him, he seems set on changing your mind. I don't blame him. You two are really something to watch."

"Fred and Ginger!" Alana said, a little discordantly.

She glanced over her shoulder, watching Guy make his way towards them, looking as good as any man could or should. He was a real heartbreaker. She started to wonder if she had dreamed he had proposed marriage just a few days ago. If it wasn't a dream, what was she supposed to *say? I love you very, very much, Guy, but no.* She had always suffered from the sin of pride. He hadn't said a single word about loving *her.* Instead, he had come up with a serious proposal. An arrangement; a business deal. He was, after all, a high-profile businessman, a master of strategy. She had just about accepted he wanted her. Those kisses didn't lie. Did he count on falling in love with her eventually? Or had he seen too much of love destroying lives?

She had known Guy Radcliffe all her life. A decade ago she had hero-worshipped him. By the time she was sixteen it had morphed into an enormous adolescent crush. At around nineteen, to counteract the crush, she had taken to trying to take the mickey out of him. Now he had asked her to marry him. Not only that, he was waiting for a response from her. And she had to make it snappy.

She *had* dreamt it. It was possible to dream with one's eyes wide open.

The closer he got, the more her pulses throbbed. She might well faint by the time he arrived at their table. She could hear the adoring voices raised to greet him as he passed the tables. He would have a special smile for everyone. Guy was so charming he could sell ice-blocks to Eskimos.

"Marvellous evening, Guy!" Simon exclaimed in his familiar worshipful tones. "Everyone is having a great time."

"Seem to be," Guy responded warmly, one hand coming to rest on the curved rim of Alana's chair. "Alana, am I going to have to talk to your back?" he enquired with soft mockery.

"Of course not, Guy!" She turned slowly towards him.

Their eyes met. "You take my breath away," he said.

Simon's smile wavered uncertainly. Guy and Alana were looking at one another with a strange intensity. If he didn't know better, he'd say they appeared to be fascinated with one another. What could it mean? It wasn't simply friendly. It looked as if they had a secret understanding. That *couldn't* be the case…

Alana didn't answer, but she did let Guy take her hand as she rose.

Simon watched them move away as if he didn't exist. Was there something here he needed to worry about?

Softly, so softly it was almost inaudible, Rose tiptoed up behind Simon and whispered in his ear, "I can't help thinking Guy's got his eye on our Lana."

"*Guy* has?" Simon croaked.

"Well, yeah." Rose slipped into Alana's abandoned chair.

"No way!" Simon shook his head vigorously. "*I've* got feelings for Lainie." That settled it. Mother-dominated Simon might be but he had always managed to get pretty well everything he wanted.

"Well, of course you have," Rose soothed. "You've been friends since you were kids. But Lana's all grown-up now, Simon. She's following her heart."

"Her *heart?*" Simon repeated numbly. "You've got it wrong."

"You have to trust me." Rose sweetly patted his cheek. "Just look at them. Are they dancing or making love? Anyway, you can't sit here moping." She grabbed his hand. "Come with me. I'll teach you to tango!"

Simon wasn't the only one watching Guy and Alana as they moved with such spellbinding grace around the dance floor, Guy's dark head bent over Alana's, her long golden mane, centre-parted, curling sinuously around her face and down her back. The effect was quite magical.

Sidonie Radcliffe didn't see it that way. "What's going on *there?*" she demanded of her daughter, steering Alex to the cover of a handsome clump of golden canes in glazed pots.

"You disapprove?" A blind woman could see her mother wanted to break it up.

"Of course I disapprove." Sidonie made no effort to hide her dismay.

"I don't think Guy could make a better choice," Alex said, not terribly surprised at the turn of events.

"Well, you would, wouldn't you?" her mother replied sharply. "You've let her brother ruin your life. Beautiful as you are, I can see you still unmarried at forty." A ripple of malice passed across her striking face.

Alex had thought the same thing herself. Nevertheless, she managed wryly, "One isn't old and ugly at forty, Mother. You really hate them, don't you?" Did anything ever change?

"Why wouldn't I?" Sidonie sounded frighteningly bitter. "They're Annabel's children. Your father might have married me, but I was his second choice. Annabel was his great love."

"I'm sorry, Mama," Alex felt her mother's pain and lifelong resentment. "But he did love you, and he was faithful to you. Dad wasn't the sort of man who dishonoured his marriage vows. He wasn't the sort of man who would touch another man's wife."

Tears sparkled momentarily in Sidonie's eyes. "I don't need you to tell me that, thank you, Alexandra," she said tightly. "But we all know what kind of man Alan Callaghan is."

"A very sick man," Alex said. "I have an awful feeling he won't pull through this operation."

"Perhaps that's just as well," Sidonie muttered cruelly, her face pale beneath her impeccable make-up. "Roger won't wait for ever, Alex. He's devoted to you, but he wants you to make up your mind. So do I. You can't waste any more of your life on that seducer. I know he's got a powerful hold on you, but it's all sexual."

"It generally *is*," Alex commented wryly, her eyes following Alana's and Guy's slow, sensual progress.

"At least you've never let yourself fall pregnant to him again," Sidonie said, barely controlling the bitter resentment she still carried. Her best-laid plans—and she had had *such* plans for her beautiful teenage daughter—had been ruined. Alex, her perfect girl, had allowed herself to be seduced by an utterly unacceptable young man. Sidonie hated him. She had no more moved on than her daughter. But at least Keiran had stuck to the promise she had wrung from him. In Sidonie's view it was the only decent thing he had ever done.

Alex's face had that poignant look again. "You always blame Kieran, but it took the two of us, Mother. We mightn't have shown much wisdom in the timing, but we were mad for each other."

Sidonie's eyes flashed contempt. "I never thought you were *weak,* Alex," she said. "Why don't you try asking him if he'll marry you?" she challenged, with a chilling smile.

To Alex, it was like an actual slap in the face. She felt herself turn to a pillar of ice. What she saw in her mother's eyes caused her to gasp. "My God!"

Her mother stood motionless.

"What a fool I've been! What a *trusting* fool." The bubble had finally burst. The sound was like a crack of thunder.

Even the supremely self-confident Sidonie felt the vibrations. She suddenly became agitated, even though she knew agitation diminished control. "What? What is it?" she demanded, tugging on her spectacular necklace.

"I look at you, Mother, and I see a stranger," Alex said painfully. "I told Kieran the truth of what happened. I think you may have told him something different."

Sidonie's released breath was like the hiss of a snake. "Like what?" She spoke aggressively, but those glacial eyes of hers looked trapped.

Alex felt as though she was awakening from a nightmare. "Of *course!* Who would Kieran believe if not my mother?" she asked. "Oh, I bet you made it good. You can be very convincing when you want. It was *you* who invented the story of an abortion, knowing full well all the anguish that would bring. *You,* the mother I trusted with my life. And he believed you. Why not? You were Mrs David Radcliffe, a woman who would never stoop to sordid lies. I bet you swore him to secrecy as well? Told him to keep questioning me would only put me on the rack? God, Mother! What have you *done?*"

Alex held up a hand as Sidonie went to speak. "No—please don't deny it. It's right there in your face."

Indeed it was, and with terrible clarity. Sidonie tried very hard to gather herself. "This is not the time or the place to have such a conversation, Alex," she said harshly. "Everything I've ever done has been in your best interests. All I'll say is this. The Callaghans, brother and sister, are a dangerous pair. Guy would be making a very serious mistake if he got involved with that girl. It would never work out—any more than your sick relationship with her brother has." She went to stalk off, her face tight, only Alex caught hold of her arm.

"Sick relationship?" she queried, keeping her voice very low. "I've heard you say that so many times. I've hated it, but I've tried to see where you as my mother are coming from. I trusted you absolutely. I was under the ridiculous impression you loved me."

"I do love you, Alex," Sidonie flashed back. "Even though you've made it hard. I repeat: everything I've done has been for you. Now, stop this right now—before people start to notice."

Gently Alex released her mother's arm. "Tonight has been a real eye-opener for me, Mother. A shaft of light has suddenly come into my life. You've kept your hateful secret a long time, but tonight, seeing Guy and Alana together, you were provoked into giving that secret away. Your plan to destroy my relationship with Kieran almost succeeded. We've wasted years—trying other relationships that could never go deep. Well, you'll have to forget Roger as a son-in-law. I've already told him his hopes are in vain. I love Kieran. I always will. The wicked part is you used any means at your disposal to drive us apart."

"There's nothing a mother wouldn't do to protect her child," Sidonie said, and gave a strange laugh that held no humour at all.

"Only, *Mother,* you have a heart of lead." There was infinite sadness in Alex's response.

No one would have dared to break in. Quite a few people were transfixed, watching Alana in Guy Radcliffe's arms. It wasn't just their expertise that was riveting the eye, their body language was even more revealing.

Violette's mother, Constance, moved in close to her daughter, giving her an ironic sideways look. "I can't imagine what he sees in her, can you? I mean, it can't be her looks!"

Violette rose from the table and dashed away.

On the area of the restaurant converted to a dance floor, even Alana felt defined as Guy's "woman". They hardly spoke. Neither of them was smiling. But Alana could feel herself falling deeper and deeper in love. What was happening to her was tremendous. She had often pictured herself dancing in Guy's arms, but she had found the reality physically breathtaking. She vaguely remembered all the other partners she had had over the years. She had gone along to all the dances. She had always been very much in demand. The difference between Guy and all those others was mindblowing. It wasn't just his physical grace and sense of rhythm that was exceptional. She felt as if she was actually being made love to. If she lifted her head and he lowered his they could touch mouths. They were not kissing, but they might have been.

"I wish there was some place we could go." Guy looked down at her, his dark gaze intense. "I want to make love to you." So badly he was consumed by a primitive urgency. "I don't want to wait."

His words thrilled her so much Alana's eyelids fluttered closed. If his arms hadn't been encompassing her she thought she might even have fallen. She didn't want to wait either. She was ready. Waiting. Open. Desperate to be taken to his bed. She had made it her business to seek protection, so that she would be ready when he wanted her. There was such an inevitability about it.

They were standing still now. The music had stopped. Guy's warm hand brushed across the bare skin of her back. Her nipples were so hard she felt their peaks must be showing through the silk organza of her dress. What she felt for him was so overwhelming she was dizzied.

"Time to return to the world," Guy murmured wryly, as though he too was being wrenched from some deeply intimate secret place. "Oh, well—there's always tomorrow. And tomorrow. And tomorrow." He smiled at her ruefully, then escorted her back to her table.

Some twenty minutes later, the lights in the huge room were dimmed room and all voices stilled as Guy walked to the podium and held up his hand. A spotlight rained down on his dark head. He glanced at the card in his hand, then looked up to give the audience his marvellous smile, the flash of white teeth offset by the polished bronze of his skin. Guy Radcliffe was no ordinary man. He was Lord of the Valley.

"And now, ladies and gentlemen," he began, the special timbre of his voice working its magic, "it's my great pleasure to announce, on behalf of the committee, the winner of the title Most Beautiful Girl in Wangaree Valley."

He paused, a moment of drama, and the spotlight skipped from him to the table where Alana was sitting with her friends. Three of the other young women there had entered the contest— Rose, Sally and Louise—all charming, and very attractive. Guy put out an arm. A fanfare went up, then a slow drumroll.

"And the winner is…" He spread it out, in time-honoured

fashion. "Miss Alana Callaghan." His voice, had he known it, held tremendous satisfaction.

A few young women expelled disappointed sighs. One, the glamorous Violette Denby, actually turned up her nose—a gesture that didn't go down well with the guests seated around her.

"Alana would you come up to the dais, please?" Guy invited.

Simon helped Alana to her feet, the first one to kiss her cheek. "Congratulations, Lainie!" he said, bursting with pride. Genuinely thrilled for her, Rose, Sally and then Louise followed suit.

"When you go to the Napa Valley you're supposed to bring a friend," Rose prompted. "Keep me in mind!"

From around the large room there was so much clapping and cheering and loud whistles the noise almost raised the rafters.

"Go on, sweetie—you're on!" Rose gave Alana, who was standing rather shell-shocked, a little push. "Breathe in, breathe out!" she instructed.

People stood up as Alana made her way through the tables on her way to the dais. "*Bravo, Alana. Well done!*" Her mother's friend, Helen, embraced her warmly.

There was a bursting sensation in Alana's chest. She was that rare thing: a beautiful young woman who didn't dwell much on her looks.

When she moved past Violette's table she almost expected her cousin to poke out her tongue, but Violette confounded her by growling, "Congratulations!"

Alana kept her eyes trained on Guy's tall commanding figure as though he were her guiding star. Finally she reached him. He took her hand, staring down at her, then he carried it to his lips.

"Congratulations, Alana." He bent his head, his hair under the lights as shiny as a crow's wing, to kiss her cheek.

The audience loved it. Pretty well everyone rose to their feet, and as the volume of clapping increased the rest didn't dare remained seated. This was a great occasion for the Valley. The harvest was over. It would be a vintage year.

A gold diadem of exquisitely wrought gold vine leaves with a gold medallion at its centre, studded with a cluster of glittering garnets to represent the fruit of the vine, was held high by Guy. The crowd went quiet as he placed it gently on Alana's head, finding exactly the position that suited her best.

There were little cries and gasps of admiration and delight. Another boom of applause. Alana appeared so bright and beautiful—so much like her mother. A few wounds around the room opened up, then miraculously closed.

She walked a little way, so everyone could see her.

The clapping got harder. There couldn't have been a more popular choice. Then the cheering and laughter broke into, "Speech, *speech!*"

Alana moved back to Guy, "I don't have a speech prepared," she whispered in a worried voice.

He leaned towards her. "Just say what you're thinking right at this moment."

Her speech was short, but it turned out to be brilliant. It was funny. It was touching. It started out and finished with thoughts of her mother.

When she was finished, many people in the room who had known Annabel Callaghan, born Denby, discreetly blew their noses. Charles Denby, extraordinarily enough, was one of them. Things had to change from this point on, he thought.

Her father was asleep when she finally arrived home. She looked in on him, then closed the door gently, going back to the living room, where Kieran was waiting for her. They talked about the function, and Kieran was full of brotherly pride in her win.

"Uncle Charles actually came over to offer me his congratulations."

"Good grief. I wonder what it cost the old man to do an about-face?" Kieran laughed. "How did Alex look?" He turned away, seemingly casual, to switch off lights.

"So, so beautiful." Alana sighed. "A beautiful, tragic woman, like the heroine in an opera. You know—the one bewailing the loss of her lover? It's there in those great dark eyes. She wore a superb white gown with pearls. Anyway you'll be able to see all the photographs. What time did Dad turn in?"

"Not long after your call. That was the big excitement of his night. We watched the football earlier. I asked Buddy over. He's a good kid. He broke into a dance when I told him you'd won. Dad wept tears of joy. He's much more at peace with himself these days."

"Isn't he? Thank goodness!" Alana murmured fervently.

Around eight o'clock the next morning—she'd had a rare sleep-in—Alana took a tray into her father's room. On it was freshly squeezed orange juice, a slice of papaya, two soft-boiled eggs, wholegrain toast, and a little pot of Vegemite to go with it.

She was about to call *wakey, wakey,* when she realised with a shock her father wasn't in his bed. She knew he wasn't in the bathroom. The door was open. There was no sound. So where had he spent the night? Her heart began an ominous thud. Still carrying the tray she retraced her steps, pausing outside the master bedroom. The door was very slightly ajar. She used the edge of the silver tray to push it open.

Her father lay on his back, his hands folded across his chest, his eyes shut, his face serene. He hadn't turned back the quilt. He lay on top of it. It was one of her mother's beautiful patchwork quilts—a work of art.

Her heart felt as if it was being entombed in ice. Her limbs went numb. She was frozen in position, yet she called with quiet anguish, "Dad?"

No response. But then she hadn't expected one, had she? A great winged being had come for her father; one that had caused him no fear.

She thought she might have cried out her brother's name. Kieran should be here with her now. The silver tray started to wobble dangerously. Soon it and its contents would crash to the floor. But that was nothing. She didn't care.

"Lana?"

Through a fog, she heard Kieran's voice. He had returned home.

Kieran was to tell her later he had felt such a chill, even in the bright sunshine, he had returned to the homestead without completing his chores. Now he moved swiftly along the passageway, his every movement urgent. He took the tray out of his sister's shaking hands and set it down on a hall table.

"Dad won't wake up," she told him, sounding to his ears as she'd used to as a little girl.

He could see she was already going into shock. Alana had had to endure so much. He threw his arms around her and she clung to him desperately.

"Dad will never be unhappy again, Lana," he tried to console her. "His life was over when Mum died."

Her heart broke.

CHAPTER NINE

THE day of the funeral was one of stifling heat, although everyone in the Valley had thought the worst of the high temperatures was over. Father Brennan, the village priest, presided at the Mass, and later at the graveside. It seemed as if everyone in the Valley had turned out, filling the church and spilling out into the grounds where the golden wattles were at the height of their beauty.

As though it was perfectly reasonable, and there had been no estrangement whatever, the Denbys were in attendance. Charles Denby, in fact had shepherded his family to the pew directly behind Alana and Kieran, murmuring condolences to them as he passed. They even sounded sincere.

"God!" breathed Kieran to his sister, not one to forgive and forget.

When the time came Guy spoke movingly—emotionally in control, but with such a sensitive, comforting intonation.

I could have fallen in love with your voice alone, Alana thought, biting down hard on her lip. Many tears had fallen in private. For the service she had decided to be strong.

Others came forward. Alana knew her mother's friend, Helen, was to speak. Helen had offered. Simon, who sat beside her, held her hand.

If Alana isn't going to fall *in* love with me, at least she will always *love* me, Simon thought, feeling some small degree of consolation. We're *pals*. Alan Callaghan's death had brought about a few radical changes, though the night of The Naming had turned Simon's thoughts around. He would take another look at Rose…

At one point in the graveside service Kieran Callaghan distracted everyone's attention by suddenly throwing out an arm and clasping Alex Radcliffe to him as though they couldn't be apart. Alex Radcliffe further distracted the mourners by adhering tenderly to his side. There was no real explanation for why she had been standing right next to him, other than the fact her brother Guy and their cousin Simon were flanking Alana. No one had a clue Kieran Callaghan and Alex Radcliffe were still such good friends. Or more accurately, so close.

"Well, we needn't wonder who Kieran's woman of mystery is any more," Guy murmured to Alana as he led her away to his car. "It's Alex."

Even in the midst of her grief Alana hadn't been slow to pick up on that. Of *course* it was. How could she have been so stupid? In one staggering moment of revelation Keiran and Alex had shown themselves to be powerfully involved. They had even walked off together, Kieran's arm around Alex's slender shoulders as though he couldn't bear to let her go.

Somehow Alana got through the wake. Yet again Guy had come to the rescue, organizing the food and drink which seemed to be expected on even the most mournful occasions. Alana couldn't for the life of her work out why. Couldn't people function without cramming down food? Still, the people who packed into Briar Ridge's homestead were for the most part good, caring people she and Kieran had known all their lives.

Simon's mother, Rebecca, had even stunned the throng by showing she had a smile. Pale-faced, she had taken Alana's hand, telling her if she ever needed someone to talk to she was "just up the road". In the space of a few days Rebecca had turned from an enemy to a friend. A phenomenon that was unique—although Guy's strengthening presence in Alana's life *would* have appeared to her as taking the heat off her son.

A further shock was in store when Charles Denby offered to lend his niece and nephew money to "keep the farm going."

"I haven't done enough for you, Alana," he told her heavily, as though he felt the guilt. "I adored your mother, my only sister. You're *so* like her."

"Adored her, did he?" said Kieran wrathfully, his blue eyes burning. He was about to continue in that vein, only Alana looked so utterly spent he kept the rest of what he was going to say to himself.

Finally the last of the mourners, who happened to be Uncle Charles and his family—now apparently *their* family—left.

"Hypocrites, the lot of them!" Kieran said, the expression on his handsome face an indicator that he had endured more than enough.

Only Guy and Alex remained, sitting quietly in the living room, behind the scenes.

"I'm taking Alana back to the house with me, Kieran," Guy said. "You're very welcome to come too." Although he meant it, Guy had a very good idea Kieran would stick with Alex, who had to make the return trip to Sydney for a big art showing the following night.

Alex confirmed it. "Kieran's coming back to Sydney with me," she explained quietly. "I know it's a sad time, but a big international art dealer is in town for only a very short while. I'd like Kieran to meet him and perhaps show him some of his work."

"What? Bring the dealer back here?" Alana asked in surprise.

Alex's magnolia skin flushed. "*I* have some excellent examples of Kieran's work at my apartment, Alana."

"Oh!" How had she never seen what had been happening? It hadn't been right under her nose, but still…

"Well, well, well!" said Guy, as Alex and Keiran drove away.

"There was always a flock of girls after Kieran," Alana said. "I used to wonder why he never settled on any of them for long."

"The same with Alex and the boys. The truly extraordinary thing is given the way they feel, why haven't they *done* something about it?" Guy asked. "You saw what they're like when they don't bother to put up the usual front. They're long-term *lovers!*"

Alana looked at him with shadowed hazel eyes, wondering how she would have got through these days of trauma without his presence and splendid support. "Alex has always seemed to me as though she has some tragic secret. Could I be wrong about that?"

"Like what?" Guy asked, his black brows knitting. He sat down beside her and took her hand in his.

"How should I know? You're her brother." She was close to tears.

He drew her head onto his shoulder, feeling a torrent of emotion himself. "All I can tell you is I'm pretty sure Kieran was Alex's first love. When they were teenagers they were inseparable—don't you remember?"

"When they split up, and Alex went off to Sydney, I thought Kieran had decided she was way out of his league."

"Whatever that league may be?" Guy murmured in a wry voice. "Do you think I'm way out of *your* league?" He looked down on her, utterly vulnerable, utterly his object of desire.

"I thought you wanted to make do with me," she responded.

Guy stood up, gently drawing her with him. "You're exhausted. I'm taking you home."

They fled the Valley chased by grief. Kieran drove Alex's powerful car faster than he should, as if it gave him the best chance of losing whatever was in pursuit. She didn't have to glance at his sculpted face, illuminated by the glow from the dashboard, to recognise the pain and sorrow that consumed him. They were approaching the outskirts of the city before he slowed down. She breathed a sigh of relief. The last thing she wanted was to catch sight of a police car on their tail. Kieran was an excellent driver, but rules were rules. Still, he manoeuvred through the traffic, changing lanes until they drove into the underground car park of her apartment block in record time.

Inside the apartment Kieran threw off his jacket, trying to get hold of himself. He felt like crashing on to the bed with Alex—his beautiful Alex—locked in his arms. Whatever had happened to them in the past, it suddenly didn't matter now. If he lost Alex he would be the loneliest man on earth. He loved her. He always would. She was his only chance at happiness. Hadn't his poor father been a one-woman man?

"God, I'm a mess," he said aloud. "One big emotional mess. But I swear I'm going to get myself together." He thrust a hand through his thick blond hair, dragging it back from his broad forehead. He was deeply conscious of his change of attitude. Something almost supernatural was giving him a second chance.

"Why wouldn't you be?" Alex comforted him quietly, removing her black jacket to expose a delicately ruffled white chiffon blouse. "It was a simply terrible day."

"I'm sure I couldn't have got through it without you," Kieran said, moving to the drinks cabinet. "The same goes for Lana and Guy. I always knew Guy mattered to her, however much she tried to hide it, but she *loves* him!"

"Aren't you happy about that?" Alex searched his burning blue eyes, herself very pale.

"Oh, yes!" Kieran exclaimed in surprise. "You don't think I'd leave my sister with just anyone? Guy is the best bloke in the world. *I'm* the bad guy who is so self-righteous! What would you like to drink?" He turned. God, she was beautiful! Her beauty broke his heart. He had been working on a portrait of her. He had to have it finished by her birthday. A big surprise! He hadn't thought he would be any good at portraiture, but he was happy with what he had done so far. Even to his highly critical eye it was good.

"Don't worry about me." Alex shook her hair free so it cascaded around her face and down her back. "I think I'll have a shower to unravel."

"Neither of us have had anything to eat," Kieran commented, his glance tender. "It was impossible to think of eating at the house. Would you like me to order something in?"

Tears were standing in the corners of Alex's dark eyes. She turned away, raising a furtive finger to wipe them away. There was something different about Kieran. It was as though they were drawing closer now, rather than moving apart. Was it possible he was close to forgiving her? Forgiving her for something she had never done?

"I've got plenty of eggs and smoked salmon, if that would do?" she called, beginning to move down the corridor. She was exhausted—not only from the funeral, that had filled her with sadness, but from her own concerns. Plus, there would be a lot of running around to do for the following night's art showing.

Kieran sigh was deep in his throat. "Fine," he called back, swallowing a mouthful of bourbon neat. "Don't be long. I can't bear you out of my sight."

Warm water cascaded all over Alex's face and body. It went a way towards restoring her calm. She tried to think of the right way to tell Kieran the truth. Her mother had *lied*.

As with all lies, there had been a reason. She knew her mother well. Her mother loved her. She had been shocked out of her mind when she'd gone to her to confess she had carried Kieran's child for almost three months. And in the space of a few minutes she had lost it. She knew her mother had had so many dreams centred on her. She had destroyed them by getting pregnant so young, without even finishing her studies. Her mother had decided there and then to wipe Kieran out of her life. And she had chosen what she had considered the most effective way to do that. She had made Kieran believe the girl he loved and trusted totally had given him no say whatsoever in what happened to their unborn child. She had given him no chance to try to talk her out of an abortion that had never happened. She had made her decision without him. It was her life, her body. She was too young for such responsibility. There were profound consequences to reckless behaviour. It happened in life.

True to his promise, Kieran had laboured for years to say *nothing*. He had stuck grimly to his promise not to betray her mother's confidence. Only her mother's lie had left a huge standing obstacle in their lives. Kieran, so volatile on the surface, was underneath a deeply sensitive man.

She had her head tilted back, letting the water run over her face and down over her breasts, when he entered the bathroom.

"Come out of there," he said thickly, already rock hard at the sight of her. Her slender arms were raised to her temples in a motion that lifted her chest. Her long raven hair was knotted and pulled back tightly from her face. She looked as though she had been out naked in the rain. Beads and rivulets of water glistened all over the curves and planes of her body, her satin smooth buttocks, that little silky triangle of intimate hair. He picked up a bathtowel as she turned off the tap. "Come on out to me." He walked to the shower door, opening it for her.

His tone of voice told her he wanted her. Right then. Kieran was a very sexual man.

"I'll dry you."

She stepped onto the bathmat with a leap of the heart. He used the soft towel on her as well as his mouth, slowly covering every inch of her body, the little swells and dells, the insides of her thighs and legs, her intimate flesh, sliding to his knees to do so.

"Kieran!" she whispered, enveloped in an indescribable heat. She moved her hands down in a near frenzy, to lift his golden head. Saw his eyes. He let the towel fall to the tiles, then he rose to his commanding height, opening the petals of her soft, moist lips as he held her crushed against his demanding body.

"I could never be separated from you for long." A sound like a low growl issued from his throat.

He stood kissing and caressing her, but the time came when he could no longer contain himself. He lifted her into his arms, exulting in her exquisite womanliness. It fell all around them like a silken enveloping cloak.

At Wangaree's splendid homestead, Alana was sitting in the dream of a kitchen, watching Guy, CEO of Radcliffe Enterprises, move about it as though preparing a meal was child's play. Wangaree might be his castle, but he had taken it upon himself to make them both a Thai stir-fry chicken dish that was to be served with jasmine rice.

"Where's Gwen?" she asked, too worn out to take her elbows off the table. Gwen was the housekeeper. She had worked for the Radcliffes for over forty years.

"I said it was okay if she spent a few days with her daughter."

"It's pretty funny, your doing the cooking," she remarked wryly.

"Sometimes I surprise myself." He gave her a half smile. "When you try it, you'll find it's good."

"It smells good. Chilli, coriander, ginger… I'm sorry I can't help you."

"I don't want you to help me. I want you to just sit there and do nothing. Why not drink that glass of wine? It might help relax you."

"I don't feel like a normal person," she said sadly, taking not a sip but a gulp.

"You'll feel a little bit better after you've had something to eat," Guy commented. He was trying hard to comfort her, while understanding there was precious little comfort to be offered on such a day. There would be a great deal of mourning over this bereavement. The situation was just too painful.

A few minutes later Guy put a beautiful blue and white bowl in front of her. It contained a steaming mound of jasmine rice with the fragrant stir-fry ladled over it.

"Thank you." She looked up at him gravely. "You're being awfully kind to me."

"You're awfully easy to be kind to." He was afraid of saying any more. Now wasn't the time to burden her with his overload of emotion. Instead he resorted to an encouraging briskness. "Okay, then—off you go!"

She rewarded him with a laugh. "You should ring a bell."

She took hold of her fork. Because he had gone to so much trouble, she made a real effort to eat.

"It *is* good," she said, after a minute, finding him watching her as if she was a difficult-to-please child.

"Thank you. Thank you very much, Ms Callaghan. I don't know that I like the note of surprise, though." He sat down opposite her.

"Oh, come on—you know I'm joking." Her smile wobbled. She gave a shuddering sigh.

"Don't cry," he said. *"Please."* He remembered how she had once said she would never cry in front of him. But then she had not been expecting this further tragedy. He knew if those tears started rolling he'd lose it and pull her into his arms. "No need to talk. Just finish your dinner."

"You're a wonderful man," she said. "You sound like you might feed me like a baby."

"Take it seriously," he warned. "I just might do that, before you droop into sleep. By the way, I got hold of some sleeping tablets for you—just in case you feel like taking one."

"So I can fall into oblivion, you mean?" Her beautiful eyes met his. "I'm not a weak woman, am I, Guy?"

It took every last bit of his self-control not to move around the table and gather her up. He wanted to carry her upstairs. Show her in every way he knew, how much she meant to him. But it seemed like sacrilege to have these primeval urges when she was so supremely vulnerable.

"Of course you aren't," he said, his tone a little harsh, from the strength of his feelings. "You're really brave. Uncommonly brave. Now take another mouthful."

"Yes, Sir Guy!" She gave a plangent laugh. "I won't have one of the sleeping pills, thank you. I don't like taking things unless I absolutely have to."

"Well, we'll see," he said, and left it at that.

* * *

Alana moved out of her bedroom into the spacious hallway of the upper level. It was more like an art gallery, with its fine paintings, valuable antiques on carved stands, and its chairs set at intervals. She stood looking around her for a minute or two, trying to get her bearings. It was such a big house—a true mansion. She had thought as a child she could easily get lost in it. She could get lost in it now.

It seemed hard to believe, but she had fallen asleep the moment her head hit the pillow. Had Guy given her a sleeping draught after all? He had made her a glass of warm milk accompanied by a shortbread biscuit at around ten o'clock, after which he had walked her upstairs to the luxurious bedroom that had been made up for her. It was Alex's bedroom. Her mother had had it redecorated to encourage Alex to come home more often. It had a very "French" feel to it, Sidonie Radcliffe being a self-confessed Francophile. Now *she* was occupying the room specially prepared for Alex.

Sidonie Radcliffe didn't like her. It was easy to understand why. Sidonie most probably had strong feelings about the role her own mother, Annabel, had played in the Radcliffe marriage. Yet surely her own parents had been happy? Hadn't they? They had hardly ever argued. When they walked about Briar's Ridge they had walked hand in hand. Her mother had laughed at all her father's jokes, especially the Irish ones. Alana *had* to believe they'd loved one another. Her mother had been the very centre of her father's life.

Guy had left the hall sconces on. That would be for her benefit, of course. It was obvious he hadn't wanted her to feel lost in a strange house. Even the corridor seemed very, very long.

What was she doing out here in her nightgown? Suddenly she felt seriously befuddled. She turned about, taking a few halting steps back into her room. She wasn't like this normally. She wasn't prone to confusion. But from the moment she had come awake in the semi-dark she'd realised she hated to be on her own. Kieran had his Alex. She had a powerful urge to be with Guy. She wanted the wonderful comfort of his arms around her. He had offered her marriage, hadn't he? He shouldn't be surprised, then, if she went to him.

The main problem was she didn't know where he was. She turned around and then walked on uncertainly. The bedrooms to either side were empty. She knew there were twelve bedrooms in the mansion. She wasn't sure if Guy had told her which one was his. If he had, she couldn't recall which.

God, she felt dreadful—weaker than she had ever felt in her life. She came to a halt, then called out tentatively, "Guy?"

There was absolute silence. She felt a complete fool. He would be fast asleep—though she wasn't at all sure what time it was. What was she supposed to do? Walk up and down for the rest of the night, crying out his name?

Please, Guy, where are you? I need you.

She knew she was acting oddly. However, she had some excuse. She was in an intensely emotional state.

"Alana?" It was a voice she would know if she heard it anywhere.

Thank goodness!

"What are you doing there, wandering about? Are you okay?" He had come by way of the staircase, which meant he had been downstairs. Now he was moving swiftly towards her, the embodiment of the protective male.

"No, I'm not!" She shook her head. "Were you sleeping downstairs?" The curious thing was he looked virtually the same as when he had shown her to her room hours earlier. He hadn't gone to bed at all.

"I had a bit of a problem sleeping," he admitted. "Actually I was reading."

"Gosh, it must be a good book. You'll have to lend it to me." She stared up at him with over-wrought eyes. "What time is it?" She wasn't aware she was whispering.

"Not all that late," he said. "Two o'clock. Do you want a little company?" He said it in his usual fashion, though he knew he could be putting himself in a situation that would require all his will-power.

"Oh, yes, *please*," she said gratefully, turning to retreat to her room.

"I'll stay until you fall asleep again," he told her gently. "I did suggest a sleeping pill."

"You should have taken one yourself."

"Then I wouldn't have heard your voice."

"I need you, Guy," she said.

It sounded more aggrieved than desirous. "Good. I like to be needed." They were inside the room now, sumptuous by any standards.

"Take off your robe and hop into bed," he said. "I'll spread out on the chaise."

His voice, the voice that fascinated her, was absolutely gentle, yet his face looked tense. She was beginning to think she had made a big mistake. Did he *really* want to be here with her? Was that what was bothering him? Maybe he wanted to finish that great book?

She slid the silk robe off her shoulders, then stood beside the bed in her nightdress. It was a virginal white, pure cotton, with pintucks and little pearl buttons, and bouquets of pink roses in blue baskets embroidered here and there.

It wasn't a seductive or glamorous garment, Guy thought. Nothing like his sister's exquisite lingerie. But she was pretty and *so* innocent, with her long flowing hair a glittering gold in the light from the bedside lamp. Guy felt a great rush of protectiveness at war with the white heat in his loins.

He took a step towards the bed. "Come on, now. I'll tuck you in." It was amazing how normal his voice sounded when he was having to deal with an aching hunger.

"Please don't talk to me like I'm a child," she said.

"Poor little one!"

She was in the bed and he was looking down at her. Her beautiful hazel eyes were swimming with tears. She put out a hand to touch his. "I don't want you over there on the chaise, Guy. I want you *here*."

It took everything he had in him to clamp down on his desire. He spoke carefully. "Alana, I can't lie beside you and not want to make love to you. You surely must know that?"

She looked up into his taut face. "I'm not in the least sure. You've been treating me like a favourite cousin all evening, when I thought you were thinking about marrying me?"

His brilliant eyes flared. "Not *thinking* I want to marry you, Alana. I *am* going to marry you—in as short a time as is decent."

"You think I'll grow on you?" she asked ironically.

"Don't be silly." If he kissed her now he'd be lost. He began to move away.

"Unless you lie beside me I *won't* marry you," she called, as though issuing an ultimatum. "Are you going to do it?"

She felt so strange! Sad, disoriented, yet madly excited too. She wanted to feel the full length of his body beside her. She wanted to move right up against him. He didn't even have to touch her for her whole body to tremble.

"Okay," he said crisply, as though coming to a sudden decision. "Move over."

She did so immediately, her expression indicating she had won a victory. "Aren't you going to feel uncomfortable in your clothes?"

He couldn't help it. He groaned. "Alana, I have no intention of removing them until you're in a stronger frame of mind. I have, however, removed my shoes."

He lowered his long lean frame onto the bed beside her, taking care to lie on top of the bedclothes while she was under them. With a grunt he settled a couple of pillows behind his head, then dared to look down at her. She was turned on her side towards him. He could see the upward swell of her breasts, delicate as roses. One arm reached across him.

"Now go to sleep," he admonished.

She sighed. "If you add *like a good girl*, I'll scream."

"I might join you," he told her tersely.

A moment's silence, then, "*Hold* me."

I can't do this, he thought, his heart and senses and mind desperate to give in to the driving, shocking urge to take her. She was there to be taken. His living desire. Only how could he when she was in this state of enormous distress? That alone made him draw back. He wanted her to know exactly what she was doing when they came together. But she was making it impossibly hard. He wasn't a saint. His thoughts weren't saintly in the least. He was a man who urgently wanted the beautiful young woman lying so trustingly beside him. He wanted the exquisite pleasure of a mating with her beautiful virgin body. Who would have dreamt she had kept herself for him?

When she spoke, her voice was soft and sad. "I'm sorry. I didn't mean to embarrass you. I know it isn't the time." Not for intimacy.

Her eyelids shut to close him out, and slowly, carefully, he drew her body towards him, so her honey-gold head was lying against his shoulder.

"Dad has gone and left us," she murmured, snuggling in closer in an acute need for comfort. "I'm going to miss him terribly."

Guy's expression was infinitely tender. "Of course you are. I'll miss him too." He began to stroke her hair very gently, wanting so much to make her a part of himself but, beyond that, wanting what was best for *her*.

Finally, as he continued to soothe her, she slid into sleep.

Just as at home, a lone kookaburra signalled the dawn. Alana whirled up from sleep, her mouth opening in a gasp as she realised where she was. She vividly remembered Guy's stroking her hair with exquisite gentleness the night before. Nothing after that. He wasn't in the room, but a featherlight rug bordered in satin lay in a heap on the chaise. Obviously he had spent some part of the night there. Her memories were all tangled up. Hadn't she invited him into her bed? On the very night her father had been laid to rest? She pressed a hand against her heart, feeling it break. Both Guy and her father must be deeply ashamed of her—as she now was of herself. What had got into her? She flinched away from her advances, and from Guy's rejection. She wasn't the object of his desire. She was the young woman he had chosen for his own reasons to marry.

She felt gutted.

Four minutes later she had put on the clothing she had brought with her—jeans and a white tank top—and pulled a pair of flatties on her feet. She would pick up the rest of her things later. She was going home. She had made a fool of herself, even if the aftermath of the funeral was a hazy blur. The pain was awful. She could have been forgiven for clinging to him like a drowning woman in a stormy sea, but not for trying to seduce him. That now seemed to her profane. She was pathetic and ridiculous.

She made it out of the house via the verandah, then down the rear stairs. No one was about.

Horses were in the home paddock. She whistled one up, throwing herself up on its bare back.

"Come on, boy!" She clutched the gelding's mane, thumped its sides with her heels. A born horsewoman, she didn't hesitate for a minute to ride bareback. Briar's Ridge was barely a mile away.

She had only been home a few minutes when the phone rang. She made no move to answer it. It wouldn't be Kieran. Not at this hour. He had rung from Sydney the previous night. Besides, she was supposed to be with Guy. She let the phone ring out. She had to get a grip on herself. But how? she wondered. Nothing about her seemed to be functioning properly—her heart, her mind, even her legs. She walked into the kitchen to make herself a cup of tea and maybe a slice of toast. It was a terrible thing to lose all good sense. But that was what falling in love had done to her. For the first time in her life she felt inadequate in her own eyes.

The kettle had scarcely boiled before she heard a car pull into the drive. She stood rooted to the spot, recognising the sound of the engine. She couldn't hide. She had to go to the door. She had no other option. She had actually stolen one of his horses.

Guy came up the short flight of steps, a faint pallor beneath his tanned skin. "Well, at least you're okay," he said tensely. "What the hell did you think you were doing? One of the boys saw you riding hell for leather bareback across the Valley."

"No harm to the horse," she said, tossing her head. "Is that what you've come to check on? Your horse?"

Guy frowned darkly. "Why are you like this?"

"Why are you like *you?*" she hurled back at him, almost running back inside the house. Anything to get away from him.

He literally zoomed after her, spinning her around against him. "Alana, what is it? Tell me and we can sort it out."

"I'm telling you nothing," she gritted, loving him so much she hated him too. It was a grim feeling. "But I do have to thank you, Guy—for everything you've done for us. So thank you." She might as well have added, *and good riddance.* "You've been wonderful—as befitting Guy Radcliffe, Lord of the Valley—but—"

"Shut up!" His hands tightened on her. He was outraged. All the ardour he felt for her, held repressed for so long, was suddenly, fatally, violently ignited. Every man had his limits. He had reached his. To add to his outrage, he had stayed awake the entire night, battling the punishing desire to go to her, take her for himself. What a reward! She had insulted his integrity. He had *not* succumbed to his elemental passion, yet she was looking at him as if he had brutally ravished her, stripped her of that virginal little nightdress and taken his fill of her, mindless of her cries.

It was not to be tolerated.

"Guy!"

A rising panic was in her voice. She had never seen this dark side of him.

"I'm not going to hurt you, you little fool!" His black eyes flashed. "Look at me."

Her heart was knocking fiercely against her ribs. "You're holding me so tight I can't run away and hide."

"Nor are you going to. I love you. I would never hurt you," he said furiously. "Why are you shivering and shaking?"

"It's the way you're holding me," she moaned, past all pretence.

Immediately he gentled his grip. "I'm sorry."

"Don't be. I *want* you to hold me. But with love. I'm desperate for you to love me. I thought…last night…I thought…"

"Tell me?" His hand slid to her satiny throat, half enclosing it with his long fingers.

"It must have seemed to you I was trying to seduce you into my bed. I'm sorry. I'm so ashamed. My only excuse is I was so dreadfully lonely. The house is so big, and it felt like you were a couple of blocks away. I couldn't seem to stop myself."

For a few moments he looked at her with a tense, questioning stare. "Then you'll understand if I can't stop myself either." His strong hands slid down her body to grasp her hips. He pulled her in to him, leaving her in no doubt of his arousal.

But there was something she desperately needed to say. "I love you," she exclaimed ardently, as if he mightn't quite believe her. "I think I've *always* loved you. You're someone I can love and honour. Someone I want to—"

His mouth covered hers so completely she couldn't get to finish. *Someone I want to share my life with.* He seemed to know all the same. All she had to do was hold on to him and never let go.

At some stage kissing wasn't enough. He picked her up, carrying her up the stairs with little effort. She stretched out on her bed.

"Do we need protection?" he asked, his voice urgent.

She shook her head. "It's perfectly okay."

For a moment he stayed where he was, sitting on the side of the bed, saying nothing. He stared down at her as she lay, her eyes huge, her breasts rising and falling, her beautiful hair fanning out over the bed cushions.

"There's nothing I wouldn't do for you, Alana," he said. "I wanted you desperately last night, but I felt I would be taking advantage of a very sad situation. Never think for a second I was rejecting you. I was electric for you—as I am now. Tell me. You want this, don't you?"

How could he doubt it? Her expression was one of immense longing. "I want nothing more in the world," she said.

He swooped then to kiss her deeply, ardently, his hand moving to her shoulders, pushing the straps of her tank top and bra down her arms.

It was the beginning of an ecstasy that was to mount and mount, turning her into a creature of pure sensation. He removed her clothes, very slowly, very gently, all the while studying her, his dark eyes deeply desirous, and when he was finished he stood up and began to strip off his own clothing.

Excitement poured into her, flooding every artery. Her heart beat and flapped wing-like in her ears. Finally he was with her, the splendid male, spreading her arms wide as his mouth went down on her breast...

"I'll go slowly," he murmured tenderly. "Just say what you want, what you don't want, what you're comfortable with, what you're not. I want this to be the most marvellous experience for you. One we'll remember all our lives." The voice she loved vibrated with something akin to wonder. "I can't begin to explain it, my beautiful Alana, but I feel like this is the very first time for me too."

That evening Sidonie Radcliffe made a late entrance to the art showing, along with a select party of friends. As expected the gallery was crowded. As expected, red stickers were all over the paintings—thirty in all, displayed to perfection in two interlocking rooms. Morris Templeton was a long-established artist with a cult following. Sidonie had a few of his paintings in her own apartment, all increasing handsomely in value. Across the room she saw Alex, looking absolutely wonderful. She was so proud of her beautiful, clever daughter, talking to the artist himself. Like all men, Templeton, a known womaniser, looked fascinated.

A few moments later she caught sight of Keiran Callaghan as he moved with Colin Scholes, an art critic, into the main room. He stood head and shoulders over poor Colin, making him look like a rotund puppet. She had to hand it to her daughter's lover—he was a very glamorous looking young man. That leonine shock of blond hair—too long, of course—suited him. No one looking at him in his designer suit, black with a black shirt and no tie, would believe he was a humble sheep farmer. He looked like a film star.

Well, she had come here with a job to do. She had to do it. Like it or not. She didn't lack guts. She had done everything in her power to split the two of them up, but in the end it hadn't worked out. She had put the well-documented "aversion therapy" to the test, but although it had worked on him to a degree, it hadn't proved powerful enough to keep them from re-finding each other. Her beautiful daughter and Annabel Callaghan's son were bound together. She had to accept it or lose her daughter altogether. It was terrible what a parent was expected to do. But hadn't the whole business over the years begun to weigh increasingly heavily on her conscience? Everything had spun out of her control. When it came down to it, life itself was out of anyone's control. That was the terror if it.

The very last thing she had ever anticipated as all four were growing up—Guy and Alana, Kieran and Alex—was that they would fall in love with each other. She had seen her adored son with Alana, the mirror image of her mother. He *loved* her. Oh the irony! Moreover, Guy would marry her. She fully expected it would happen, after a period of mourning for the father. Like Charles Denby, Sidonie had decided she had to make a complete about-face. If she didn't she would not be able to retain the love and respect of her son and daughter. The prospect was unthinkable. Besides, she would make a marvellous grandmother.

Sidonie saw that Kieran was for the moment free. She had to move fast. A man who looked like that generally got mobbed. Swiftly she forged a path towards him. A beautiful, powerful, mature woman, the source of ongoing strife and pain, was ready to eat the humblest of humble pies. The really strange thing was, it brought with it an unexpected sense of freedom.

Confession really was good for the soul!

EPILOGUE

Four months later

THE wedding of Guy Radcliffe and Alana Callaghan took place at the bridegroom's splendid, sprawling country estate, historic Wangaree Station. The actual ceremony was held in its charming old private chapel, built in the Gothic revival style in the late 1880s for the Radcliffe family and their servants. It hadn't been in use as a place of worship since the late 1940s, when the two Radcliffe sons and the men of the Valley who had survived had returned home from World War II, but it had been splendidly maintained.

Guy's mother and father had been married in a Sydney cathedral, to much pomp and glory, but Guy and Alana had wanted their wedding to be a country affair. This was their way of showing their love for each other and for the Valley. The Valley in turn was thrilled by their decision.

Family and close friends had the privilege of attending the wedding ritual. They packed the chapel, lavishly decorated for the occasion with a veritable Eden of cream and white flowers, and with huge satin bows tied to the end of the polished cedar pews. The chapel, though small, was really very handsome, standing in its own grounds, with beautiful surrounding rose gardens that had been brought to the peak of perfection for the big day. Other guests, close to three hundred, had been invited to the reception, which was held in the magnificent grounds, which now looked more like the Botanic Gardens, under vast cream and gold marquees which appeared magical, floating on top of the lush green lawns.

The beautiful bride—none could eclipse her—wore a ravishing gown in the grand romantic fashion. Everyone said it was glorious, and it suited her to perfection. The bodice was strapless, encrusted with sparking crystals and seed pearls and with a tiny handspan waist, and the skirt was wonderfully billowing. The bride had elected to have an extravagantly full veil to shimmer around her and follow her in a train as she walked down the aisle on the arm of her stunningly handsome brother, Kieran. The Valley had recently learned that Keiran was making a mark in, of all places, the *art* world. Everyone suspected Alexandra Radcliffe had a lot to do with that…

The bridal veil was held in place by an amazing headdress, featuring at its centre a large, very valuable antique diamond brooch the bridegroom's mother had lent the bride to wear on her great day. Two little flower girls had been chosen, adorable in cream silk and cascades of tulle with long ribbons in their hair, and there were four bridesmaids in all, to match the bridegroom's tall, handsome attendants: the three cousins of the bride, Violette, Lilli and Rose, and, the fourth and chief bridesmaid, the beautiful sister of the bridegroom— Alexandra Radcliffe.

The bridesmaids, all blessed with perfect figures, wore elegant satin gowns cut like slips, which clung to the hip then fell to the floor in softly draped folds. The bride had proposed dawn shades—silver-grey, palest golden pearl, a beautiful blueish pink, and the softest amethyst. The bridesmaids, at first caught a little by surprise, had been thrilled with the finished gowns. It was the chief bridesmaid, Alexandra, who had hunted up a beautiful array of long vintage necklaces that lent additional glamour to the deep V of their gowns. All wore drop earrings of lustrous Tahitian pearls—a gift from the bridegroom—the iridescent colours of the pearls harmonised wonderfully with the particularly beautiful shades of their gowns.

When the moment came for the radiant bride to put back her veil and face her bridegroom, resplendent in his wedding finery of a grey morning suit, tears sprang to the eyes of every woman in the chapel and, it had to be said, quite a few of the men. The bride's uncle, Charles Denby, was even seen to discreetly blow his nose on a snowy white handkerchief.

It was that kind of wedding. Visually exquisite, tender and immensely moving. The love bride and groom felt for each other was so palpable it rayed over the assembly like a glorious heaven-sent light. Everyone in the chapel later swore they had felt the power of the ceremony, the utter seriousness of the vows. This was a couple who were in an enviable state of grace. Their union would bring even greater things to the Valley.

"Do you, Alana Maree Callaghan, take this man, Guy Balfour Radcliffe…"

Alana had thought in all the emotion of the moment her voice might fail her when the time came for her to say *I do*. But it emerged with the sweet clarity of her pure loving heart.

Finally the ceremony was over, and Guy—her wonderful Guy, her *prince*—took her in his arms.

"I adore you," Guy whispered emotionally against his wife's softly yielding mouth. "My wife—my beautiful Alana." Overwhelming happiness shone from his brilliant dark eyes.

"I adore *you*, Guy—my husband," she whispered back, thinking she was utterly blessed.

Together they turned as man and wife to face the beaming

congregation. Immediately the organ, tuned to perfect pitch, sprang into rich, triumphant life. It filled the flower-decked chapel with the exuberant strains of the "Wedding March." Not to be outdone, sunlight chose that moment to pour like a benediction through the tall stained glass windows of the west wall of the chapel, creating a magical kaleidoscope of colour that caught the bride's veil and bathed it in jewelled lights.

An audible wave of delight swept through the chapel. Surely that was a good omen for the future?

Joyously, the beautiful bridesmaids followed after them. Alexandra was thinking it wouldn't be long before her own wedding day. Out of deference to Guy, his position, and all that he had achieved for the Valley, she and Kieran had decided they would wait until after he and Alana had celebrated their great day. Kieran had always scoffed at weddings in the past, but today she had caught his eye too many times to ever let him get away with that again. He had been as moved as she was, both of them touched by the power of love.

As the bridegroom's mother was heard to murmur to an elderly relative, swathed in lavender with pearls, "I simply can't imagine a more perfect wedding!"

"And Sidonie, dearest," the smile-wreathed relative responded, "their happiness has just begun."

* * * * *

BRIDE AT
BRIAR'S RIDGE

CHAPTER ONE

LINC checked out of his Sydney hotel after a late breakfast. An easy two-hour drive later he was cruising through the beautiful Hunter Valley, wedged snugly between the blue-hazed Brokenback Ranges, dominated by the native eucalypts. He had an idea the word eucalypt came from the Greek for 'covered'. Maybe it had something to do with the way the buds covered themselves, as though seeking shade. There were over six hundred species of eucalypt at the last count—Australia's gift to the world. It was the fine drops of eucalyptus oil in the atmosphere that gave off that marvellous purplish-blue haze. That was how the beautiful Blue Mountains some forty miles west of Sydney got their name.

To his mind, trees made the landscape. He loved them. He was first and last a man of the land. Sometimes he thought he and the land were one—pretty much the same primal feeling of the first Australians, the aboriginals who had managed the land for 40,000 maybe 60,000 years. The white man, with his need for progress now almost out of control, was doing great harm to nature. The planet was screaming out for urgent change.

It was a brilliantly fine day, all blue and green and gold,

and the unfolding landscape was like one of Hans Heysen's famous rural paintings that found their way on to calendars and postcards and the like. Miles of sun-drenched vine-yards met his eyes, expanding to the horizon. Here and there he caught glimpses of glorious big rose bushes, bearing a profusion of flowers. He knew roses were grown in close proximity to the vines because their presence pro-tected the vines from certain blights. Fruit and flower gave off a heady rich perfume and a riot of colour.

The Hunter was Australia's oldest wine-growing region, probably the most visited, and it produced wonderful wines. In fact the Hunter was a Mecca for those who relished gourmet food washed down with plum-coloured Shiraz, golden Chardonnay, citrusy Semillon or classic Cabernet with its blackberry flavour; a superb wine to complement every type of cuisine. He wasn't behind the door with the vino, having sunk a bottle or two in his time, but he still had a taste for a good cold beer.

Some parts of the landscape were reminding him of Italy: the imported eucalypts, the golden sun soaking into the fertile soil, the intoxicating aromas of fruit and flowers, the open grassy meadows filled with wild poppies, scarlet and yellow, their papery petals bobbing in the breeze. He was halfway to feeling good when for many years of his life he had been swept by restlessness. He had a dark side to him. Linc had come to accept that. Now he took his time, savouring the laid-back atmosphere of the valley. It held more than a hint of the wild bush he loved. Every country had its own landscape. The Outback was Australia's, but the *real* Outback was farther on—the Back O'Beyond.

He slotted in another CD and drove along with it as he continued on to his destination. Wangaree Valley. Wangaree was the legendary stronghold of the mighty sheep barons and their descendants, in particular his old friend, Guy Radcliffe. He and Guy had been through school and university together, and Guy had been a role model for him in those days—a calm, steadying hand when he'd really needed one. He remembered Dr Mallory, the headmaster of their school, describing Guy as 'the perfect gentleman'. There was no getting away from it. Guy *was* impressive. Linc, on the other hand, was kind of wild—especially since he and Chuck, his elder brother, had lost their mother to breast cancer a few years into their boarding school stint.

It had torn his heart out. He still wasn't over the shattering blow. Never would be. He had been very close to his mother, even more so than Chuck. Their father had favoured Chuck. The moment he thought of his mother Linc's breath caught on a moan. In those last heartbreaking days she had become so wasted—parchment skin stretched tight over delicate bones, hardly a vestige of her beauty left to her. But even at the end she had been so incredibly loving, so selfless and *brave*, thinking only of them, her two boys, and his heart broke all over again. Suffering seemed to happen to the best people. His mother had been the one who'd held the family together. He was going to miss her until the end of his days.

Right now he had to make an effort to clamp down on his upsetting memories. No one seemed to realise it—he knew he projected the misleading super-confident image of a man right on top of things—but he was a pretty complicated guy, maybe even messed up. Only his mother had truly understood him. His father had been antagonistic even when Linc was a kid. He knew he had always asked too many questions—not trying to be the smart-ass his father had long since labelled him, he had actually wanted to *know*. He'd always had an enquiring mind. But his father hadn't seen it that way. To him, being questioned about anything was rank insubordination. Ah, well! He wasn't the first and he wouldn't be the last not to get on with his dad. But that was all over.

He was in the valley for the best of reasons. Guy had asked him to be one of the groomsmen at his wedding. Something he had kept from the family. He had wanted to tell Chuck, but Chuck could unwittingly be conned into admissions he would never have made on his own. The wedding was to be celebrated the coming Saturday. Guy was marrying a very special girl by the name of Alana Callaghan—'the most beautiful girl in the valley'—or so the legend went. Linc had been delighted to accept his friend's invitation. Besides it would give him the opportunity to view Briar's Ridge.

Alana and her brother, Kieran, had inherited the sheep farm from their late father. Guy had told him it was a good buy, and Guy was the man in the know. Guy also knew Linc was anxious to strike out on his own. Briar's Ridge just might work.

It would be a huge challenge, even so. He did have money of his own, plus a nice little nest egg he had inherited from his maternal grandad—God rest his gracious, loving soul. His father, Ben, as tight-fisted as they came, would have refused point-blank to lend him a stake. *Giving* was out of the question. The only thing his father would have given was a few tips to Scrooge. Except where Cheryl was concerned. Linc felt a burning in his chest at the thought of Cheryl, who could have answered to the name Jezebel. Cheryl was another pressing reason he had to get away from Gilgarra. Cheryl, the third Mrs Ben Mastermann, had taken no time at all to fix her predatory china-blue eyes on *him*, of all people. He had taken it as a tremendous insult—both to his father and him.

Now nowhere was safe. A woman hell-bent on pursuing a man who in no way wanted her wasn't a pretty sight. He might have earned himself a bit of a reputation with the ladies, but he considered himself an honourable man. Hell, he *was* an honourable man. His only option had been to approach his father and let him know of his ambition to strike out on his own. He wasn't about to tell him that day was at hand. Ben Mastermann had been known to wreck more than one property sale.

'Your place is right *here*!' his father, angry as a bull, had bellowed, veins like cords standing up in his neck. Ben Mastermann had been furious that his younger son was willing to abandon their family heritage, even though everyone in the district knew father and son were nearly always at loggerheads.

What his father *didn't* know, and Linc could never tell him, was the problem he was having freezing out Cheryl. Their mother had only been dead two years before their father had taken Valerie Horden, a socialite divorcee and a long-time acquaintances to wife. That hadn't lasted, although Val hadn't been a bad sort—kind to him and Chuck in an off-hand sort of way. Not that they'd seen much of her, what with school and university. The marriage was over after six years, with a ritual exchange of insults, laying blame, and a hefty settlement for Valerie. Nothing like marriage to bring out the best and worst in people. Val, a dedicated sportswoman, had plunged in, but had soon found herself way out of her depth with the demanding and autocratic Ben Mastermann.

Then had come a long hiatus, but just when Linc and Chuck had thought they had good reason to believe their father had abandoned any search for another wife, without warning along came Cheryl—who had *seriously* been searching for a rich husband along with the meaning of life. That had been a little over two oppressive years ago, and even now Cheryl was only a few years older than Chuck, which put her in her early thirties. The two brothers had spotted her as a gold-digger on sight. Chuck had put on a tortured smile for his father's benefit—Chuck was such a good-natured guy, and he loathed confrontations—but Linc, who had adored his mother, had stood well back, realising there was going to be trouble. Big-time.

Their father still believed Cheryl had fallen as madly in love with him as he had with her. He even joshed her about her 'chasing him'. That was something Linc and Chuck definitely believed. Not that their dad wasn't a fine-looking man, but he was in his late fifties to Cheryl's thirty-two or three, and of course there was the tiny fact their dad was *loaded*. Some ladies appreciated that sort of thing. A rich older guy was infinitely better than a young guy who wasn't. There had even been talk of their having a baby. He'd wait for *that* to happen. The luscious Cheryl was obsessed with her figure, and he'd bet the farm Cheryl had no intention of getting pregnant. She would even convince his dad it was *his* fault without saying a word. Wasn't that the way with older guys who had so much to prove?

It was all kind of sad. Worse yet, *dangerous*. Linc wasn't a guy who frightened easily, but Cheryl had freaked him out when she had burst into his bedroom.

'You can't go, Linc!' She had thrown herself headlong at him, clutching him around the buttocks, kneading his behind through his tight jeans with her talons, her pretty face contorted with what he'd been supposed to interpret as passion. *'You can't go and leave me. Just play it cool, okay, baby?'*

Play it cool, baby? He'd marvelled at her language, let alone her damned effrontery. And he hadn't been able to fault her nerve.

'You're married to my father, Cheryl. Or was that just for the money?'

She had looked at him with an injured little smile, indicating that was *so* unfair. *'I think you'll find I'm making him happy,'* she'd claimed, china-blue eyes smouldering not for his dad but him.

He couldn't disagree with what she had said about making his dad happy. His father was still at the honeymoon stage, and thought all his Christmases had come at once.

What else could a man do? He had pushed her aside, leaving her staring at him like some vamp in a 1940s Hollywood movie. Probably a calculated piece of play-acting. Either way, he hadn't been able to get out of his bedroom fast enough!

Not that woman trouble hadn't been a part of his life. He didn't go looking for trouble; it came to him. Married women had offered—cold-hearted, toffee-nosed ones too—but they had never been accepted. Married women were off-limits in his book. Not that he had even met one who had inspired an uncontrollable urge. It was Cheryl who was at the uncontrollable urge stage. She had shelved all caution. It all went to show she didn't really know his father. Any man fool enough to lay hands on Cheryl would finish up a corpse, with his dad going to jail.

How good it was, then, to make his escape! He'd have made it long, before only the entire district knew he was the one who actually ran Gilgarra. He was the ideas man, the power behind the throne. Chuck was a fine sidekick, a good hard worker, but he wasn't an ideas man—as he freely acknowledged. Their father had all but retired to give his sole attention to Cheryl. He had left them with it. And not before time.

Wangaree Valley was distant enough from his family turf, in a region called New England in the north of the state, bordering Queensland. It encompassed the largest area of high land in the country. His mother's family, the Lincolns, had quite a history in the area. They had raised merino sheep and bred cattle for generations. The Mastermanns had come later, and they had prospered on the sheep's back. Now Linc was looking to raise a dynasty of his own.

He wanted kids. He really liked kids. Two boys and two girls. He didn't care what order they came in. Just let them be healthy. But he just hadn't run into the right woman yet—even if he'd never been lacking in girlfriends. There were those who claimed he had broken too many hearts, but that had never been his intention. Some girls just wanted to settle down the moment he met them. As for him, he realised at this stage of his life he *wanted* marriage, even as he feared some wild cat still prowled within him.

He glanced at the time on the dash. He had told Guy he would be arriving mid-afternoon, so he had plenty of time. Hunger pangs were starting up again. He would stop to eat somewhere—the Hunter abounded with fine restaurants. He knew Guy owned an award-winning restaurant on the Radcliffe Wine Estates, but what he was looking for was more like a good café; a fresh ham and salad roll would do, with a nice cup of coffee. A man needed a good café or restaurant run by Italians for that.

Australia had become almost a second Italy, which was okay by him. He had spent an entire year in Europe after he had left university, and been back many times since. Paris was Paris—unique—but he absolutely *loved* Italy.

Italy appealed to the exuberant side of his nature. He was not a quiet man. Neither was he the hell-raiser he had once been. The hell-raising had really got a kick start with the death of his mother and the escalation of the abrasive relationship he had with his father. He had been overlong in kicking free, but then Gilgarra had needed him.

By one-thirty he was driving through Wangaree's town centre. It was a very pretty town, a showpiece for rural Australia. There were some well-preserved classic heritage buildings on wide, tree-lined streets, and from what he could see a few lovely little parks. He was almost at the end of the main thoroughfare, Radcliffe Drive, when he spotted a place called Aldo's. With a name like that it was sure to offer good Italian fare and a decent cup of coffee. He was very fussy about his coffee. His long stay in Rome had assured that. There was even a parking space just outside.

He drove up beside a shiny black SUV, then put the sports car into reverse, slotting it in as neat as a pin between the SUV and an old battered ute with the obligatory bull bar.

He was a long way from home and he couldn't feel happier.

A few moments later, he opened the handsome glass-panelled door to the bistro, inhaling the fragrant fug of good coffee, strong and fresh. There was a small curved foyer, and beyond that two steps leading down to a seating area. The area was barred by a young woman wielding a broom.

Casual, seeking nothing but a meal, he was now jolted into full alertness. In its way it was like being slammed up against a wall. He had grown cynical about a woman's beauty. But *this*! He had to drag in a breath as a force more powerful than he reached for him and held him in place.

The very air trembled!

The impact this young woman was having on him

seemed to be dictating his every move, or lack thereof. He found it thrilling and disquieting at one and the same time. He knew he was staring—but then weren't beautiful women used to stares? This woman was his idea of physical perfection. Even his lungs were scrambling for a breath. Damned if it wasn't like a mystical experience. The thought amused and awed him.

Just as he was deciding how best to proceed, the Dream turned, enabling him to study her full-on.

Sensation rushed through him with the speed of light.

She didn't speak. Neither did he. He couldn't think of anything to say anyway. Neither of them made a move. Instead they looked across the span of brightness, staring at each other for what seemed an awfully long time. It was one of those moments that go on for ever, locking a man in. For all his reputation as a ladies' man, he had always held a pretty effective shield against woman magic. In no way was he guaranteed protection now. He didn't relish the thought. There was nothing wrong with being fascinated. Unless it reached the point where it upset his emotional balance. At the moment that was pretty precarious. He had sworn off women while he got his life on track. Yet here he was, caught like a moth in this creature's golden glow.

How had she arrived in this country town anyway? She looked more as if she had stepped out of a medieval painting. Her beautiful classical features were absolutely symmetrical. Wasn't that rare?

He canted a black brow, unaware his silvery green eyes held a mocking challenge. 'I hope you're not going to take that to me?'

If he was expecting an answering smile—a lightening of the fraught atmosphere—he got none. There was more than a touch of dismissiveness in her great dark eyes. It sent the silent message that she had met his like before.

'Don't worry, you're safe.' She spoke for the first time.

Daniela had, in fact, taken swift note of the stranger in town even before he entered the bistro. What she decided now was to disregard the dimpled smile, however sexy, and the languid, yet highly athletic set of the stranger's tall, rangy body. Six-footer-plus. Copper-skinned. Jet curls. Startling contrasting eyes.

Linc, for his part, had no difficulty registering that he had been summed up and found wanting. It didn't, however, temper the shock of sexual excitement. It was like a hot wire in the blood. He felt the sizzle, the palpable thrill that stroked the hairs on his nape, causing him to shiver. The thrill moved to his scalp. Hell, what a reaction—and with such speed and power! He liked pretty women, sure, but not one of them had ever affected him like this. He was even having difficulty not reaching out just to touch her.

She had only the faintest suggestion of an accent, but he had spotted it right off.

'Buon guiorno!' he said. His Italian was fairly fluent and he had kept it up. Italian-speaking communities were all over Australia. He held her gaze—indeed he couldn't look away—plotting how he could get her to smile. He was used to smiles. He began to picture her smile in his mind. 'Like me out of the way?' He gestured beyond, to the main room.

'If you would.' Daniela inclined her head. 'A customer accidentally knocked an ornament off the counter here.'

'I'm relieved to hear it. You look the type that throws things.'

'Me?' She eyed him, letting him know she was question-ing his impertinence. He was probably well-used to women fawning on him. She wasn't about to join the ranks. Daniela was far less trusting of men than she had once been.

'Just a joke, ma'am. I see you don't like jokes,' he said, with a touch of self-derision.

'I have to *get* the joke first.' She put a little more distance between them. 'Unusual—a cowboy who drives a sports car?'

She spoke as though the vehicle might be a serious rite of passage for a guy like him. Cowboys obviously weren't high on her *wow* scale. 'I'm a sheep man, actually.'

'Really?'

He watched her press her beautifully cut lips together— fine, sensitive upper lip; full, sensuous lower lip—as though she feared she would burst out laughing. He was only surprised she didn't say, *How absurd!*

'Don't you like sheep men?' he challenged, hardly giving a thought to lunch now. Conversation was way better.

'I have to confess you struck me more as a cowboy.' She didn't mention her first impression had been that of a rock star. He had that same air of glamour, wearing his vibrant masculinity like a second skin. He would fit neatly into the Outback as well. Not as your average stockman. Dear me, no! Boss Man was more like it. Young as he was—and he couldn't yet be thirty—he had the *command* presence, the easy male authority. It was written all over him. Then there was the educated accent, the self-assurance he wore like a cloak, the pulsating energy. A bit of a dynamo, she thought; the kind that loved women but didn't really need them.

Linc thought he was holding up well under the judgmental waves that were coming full at him, but he was a little baffled by her attitude. He wasn't *that* bad, surely? He glanced down at himself wryly. He was wearing black designer jeans, an upmarket bush shirt, elastic-sided boots.

Maybe his hair was too long. He never paid a lot of attention to his jet-black curly hair. It sort of looked after itself. And he hadn't missed the little flashes of antagonism either. This was a woman who could erupt! And, hell, she was the rarest of creatures: a woman who had taken an instant dislike to him. He liked that. It put him on his mettle.

If the trace of accent hadn't alerted him, her looks did: Northern Italian colouring, wonderful thick, swirling blond hair, side parted, curving in to just below her chin. The colour could have come out of a bottle but he didn't think so. There wasn't a dark root in sight. Her complexion was perfect—honeyed Mediterranean. The lovely features were classical, her aura passionate but restrained—as if she deliberately held herself in check. Her eyes were really beautiful beneath arched black brows—so dark the iris rivalled the pupil. She wasn't tall—maybe five-five in her high wedged heels—but her body was beautiful. Slender, but with shape.

The glory of women, he thought, slowly releasing his breath. 'You're beautiful!' he said, unconsciously investing it with real meaning. He hadn't meant to say it. It just came out as a simple statement of fact.

'Thank you,' Daniela answered him gravely.

She had been called beautiful many times in her life. Unfortunately beauty often came with a high price tag. It didn't always draw the right people. She had left London and a great job because she was being hounded by a man obsessively attracted to her and her looks. Sometimes, back in London, she had thought she would go mad thinking and worrying about it.

Linc had intuitively tuned in to her wavelength. How men's eyes must cling to her, he thought. Maybe that was a reason for her being so wary. And she *was*. No mistaking it. He could actually hear the defences going up. So what was a Renaissance beauty doing in a small country town wielding a broomstick? She obviously worked here. A cute little white apron was tied around a waist he thought he could span with his hands. Her dress, sleeveless with a short skirt—showing off great legs—was navy. A sort of uniform, he thought. She made it look chic. But the aura she gave off was downright patrician, even a touch forbidding, as befitting someone who had stepped out of a medieval masterpiece.

Maybe she owned the place? Maybe she owned a whole chain of bistros? Though she barely looked old enough to be a big success. Twenty-four? Twenty-five? As well as being beautiful, she looked highly intelligent. That had conveyed itself to him. A confident, competent young woman who knew how to keep mere mortals like him in his place.

His gaze came back irresistibly to centre on her face. 'Do you believe in love at first sight?' he asked, as though it was the easiest question in the world to answer.

'Doesn't everyone?' Daniela answered, calmly enough, transferring her midnight-dark gaze over his shoulder. 'Ah, here is my grandfather to take care of you.' She sounded relieved.

'You work for your grandfather?' It really wasn't like him to hit on a girl in this blatant fashion.

'In this case I am helping out.' Clearly she was making an effort to be polite. Far more the *principessa* than the waitress.

'So who am I talking to?' he persisted, watching a big, handsome grandfatherly figure with a crown of tight snow-white curls hurrying towards them.

'Daniela Adami,' she informed him, turning to pick up a dustpan filled with pieces of broken china.

'Carl Mastermann. My friends call me Linc. I've come to look over a valley property.'

'Ah, yes? Which one would that be, Mr Mastermann?' She spoke as if there were hundreds on the market.

Couldn't she risk a smile? It was important to him to see her smile. 'Briar's Ridge. It's owned by the Callaghans—brother and sister. Do you know them?'

'I have that pleasure.' She dipped her head formally, then made a move to walk by him, a determined action that managed to be enormously seductive at the same time.

He eased back, resisting the strong impulse to swing an arm around her and no doubt receive a painful electric shock for his trouble.

'Nice to have met you, Mr Mastermann.'

It sounded as if she didn't want to lay eyes on him again. *But that*, Principessa, *isn't about to happen.*

CHAPTER TWO

WEDDINGS had a knack of working their magic on everyone. Linc had lost count of the number of weddings he had attended over the years, but the wedding of his old friend Guy, and his beautiful Alana, a luminous creature, with happiness shining out of her eyes, was turning out tops.

Wangaree was one of the nation's finest historic sheep stations, a splendid estate and one that fitted the courtly Guy right down to a tee. The wedding ceremony had been held in the station's private chapel—a marvellous place to hold it, Linc thought. Flower-decked for the great occasion, the old stone building was wonderfully appealing within its surrounding rose gardens, all coaxed into full bloom. The chapel had been built way back in the early days and was the perfect place for bride and groom to take their vows. In fact, his own throat had tightened during the moments when the bridal vows had been exchanged. The utter seriousness with which those vows had been exchanged he had found intensely moving.

The good thing was he felt he had absorbed a lot of the happiness that shone out of bride and groom. It had happened without his working at it. The best man was the bride's brother, Kieran, a terrific-looking guy; the chief bridesmaid was Guy's beautiful, elegantly refined sister, Alexandra. Guy had told him early on Alex and Kieran would soon be tying the knot themselves. He just hoped Kieran, whom he had only just met, would agree with his sister to sell Briar's Ridge to him.

He was sure Guy was going to put in a good word. Nevertheless he was feeling a bit nervous the deal might fall through. The property had been allowed to run down—he understood their late father had been ailing for some time before he died—but he knew it could be rescued and brought back to its former high standing. He couldn't say yet if he would stop at Briar's Ridge as he had big plans, but it would be an excellent start.

It was as they were coming out of the chapel to the joyous strains of the organ and the peal of the chapel bells that he saw *her*—with extraordinarily sharp focus.

She was looking exquisite. She stood out from the beautifully dressed crowd around her, as one would expect such a woman to do. Even the glorious multi-coloured lights that were now spilling through a stack of tall stained glass windows sought her out, suffusing her face, her glowing hair and her bare shoulders in radiance.

If his eyes had found her, her eyes had found him.

There was an expression that seemed to fit how he felt: being struck by a lightning bolt from heaven. He couldn't say if that was a good thing or not, but it sure as hell raised big questions. He didn't for a moment doubt it.

She looked away, as though she had seen his thoughts on his face, her thick blond page boy falling against her slanted cheekbones. If he were smitten, she was making sure he knew she wasn't. He had to change that. He didn't know if it was a wise decision or not. He didn't care. Despite all his plans he had been shot down in flames.

Remarkable it should happen when he least wanted or expected it. He even had an idea he couldn't return to the man he was. Maybe the right woman might be able to save him, make all the pain go away?

A big *might*, was the cynical whisper in his head. She had said she knew the Callaghans. What she hadn't said was she had been invited to Alana Callaghan's wedding to his friend Guy Radcliffe. Now, why keep that a secret? Why act as though she was never likely to see him again? Perhaps she was as troubled in her way as he was in his?

He found he wanted those maybes resolved. It might shock and amaze him, but he wanted to know all there was to know about this woman. *All* of it. Even if he wasn't ready.

Outside in the brilliant sunshine—the sun was blazing out of a cloudless opal-blue sky—the rest of the guests, those not able to fit inside the chapel, were milling all over the manicured green lawn. It was as big a wedding as he had ever attended. There were quite a few children, all dressed up for the occasion—especially the little girls, in their pretty party frocks—laughing and bobbing in and out of the crowds, playing games as children had always done and always would. Massive cream-and-gold marquees had been erected in the extensive home grounds. In the shimmering heat they seemed to float above the emerald grass.

She had to be deliberately holding back, because he didn't see her again until they were all seated in the bridal marquee.

It didn't take him long to locate her. She was at a table for eight flanked by two men, one around forty-five, the other his age. Both were dancing attendance on her. The food was superb, as were the wines—lashings of both. He was seated between two cousins of the bride, Violette and Lilli. Both of them were extremely good-looking. Perhaps Violette had the edge, but even she couldn't hold a candle to her cousin Alana, Guy's beautiful bride. Linc yielded to their harmless flirtations, effortlessly doing his bit. This kind of thing he was long used to. Both sisters appeared to find him worthy of their attentions, but in reality his antennae was constantly twitching, almost completely given over to tracking *her*. By some magic means he was now a woman-watcher. And that was just plain dumb. He was a guy who liked to hold the whip hand.

The speeches were over—all of them excellent, hitting just the right note. Guy had very movingly opened his heart to his bride and all the guests were applauding, everyone was so touched. Looking down the bridal table, decked with what looked like thousands of exquisite white orchids flown in from Thailand, Linc could see a little tear run down Alana's cheek. He knew it for what it was—a tear of overwhelming happiness. Weddings were times of high emotion. What he hadn't expected was to get all emotional himself. He tried to stand back from that kind of thing. Much better to keep all the emotions locked up inside. Grief, abandonment... As a boy he had been so crazy he had even *blamed* his mother for dying, for going away and leaving him. And his highly confrontational relationship with his father he had to paste over. He couldn't bear to think about that poor silly creature Cheryl.

At last the formalities were over, and everyone was free to roam from table to table, meeting up with old friends, making new ones, joining in the dancing. A great five-piece group was playing. The guy on the sax was so good—the sound, the form, the phrasing—he would have been happy just to sit there, listening, champagne glass topped up regularly. Only Lilli caught hold of his shoulder, urging him to his feet. Someone with a professional-looking video camera started to film them. He guessed the

Radcliffe-Callaghan wedding would make it into the glossy magazines. He might even make it himself. He didn't look too bad in his classy suit, with a pink rose with a bluish tint in his buttonhole to match Lilli's sexy satin gown. All four bridesmaids were wearing drop earrings of large Tahitian pearls with a fair-sized diamond above—a very generous gift from Guy.

'This is wonderful, isn't it?' Lilli gushed. 'Alana is my favourite cousin!'

He wondered about that.

After a while he felt as if he had danced with every girl inside the marquee except *her*. Every time he made a move towards her some other guy beat him to it, or one of the sisters clamoured for another dance. The elder one, Violette, was being rather forceful about it. Lilli had confided in him that Violette had been a long-time girlfriend of Guy's.

'He nearly married her, you know.'

He took that with another cup of salt. He had a feeling Guy was a one-woman man, and that woman was now his wife.

She must have moved outdoors.

Pleasant as it was, he was continually trapped by pretty girls, eyes shining, cheeks flushed. He couldn't be rude and turn them down. He needed to keep up his role as groomsman.

'Don't disappear on me,' Lilli begged, her bright blue eyes locking on his. 'I promised Mike here another dance.'

It was his moment to make a move. His decline into sheer neediness was so dramatic, it was mind-blowing. He actually *needed* to see the woman. He actually wanted to see her smile.

A lovely gentle breeze was blowing, carrying the mingled scents of Wangaree's spectacular gardens. A lot of other guests had drifted outside, most still hugging their champagne glasses.

Where was she? She couldn't have gone home. Guy and Alana hadn't left yet. Alana, as tradition demanded, hadn't yet thrown her bouquet. The honeymoon was to be spent in Europe, but the happy couple were staying overnight in a suite at one of Sydney's luxury hotels, before flying out to Paris via Dubai the next day.

Obviously she had decided to lose herself. It didn't make him mad, but intrigued. He continued on his way, skirting the main paths bordered by banks of azaleas and rhododendrons, a positive sea of them, pink, white, ruby-red. He traversed a small ornamental bridge that spanned a glittering dark green lily pond before heading towards what looked like a secret garden. He was enormously impressed with the way Guy kept the place. The maintenance of the gardens alone was a huge achievement. Wangaree was a country estate in the grand manner. Even Gilgarra, though a top New England property, couldn't match it.

The fringing trees along the path kept the light a cool subdued green, even on this brilliant sunny day. His mother had kept a lovely garden, continuing to work in it even as she'd sickened. He remembered the delight she'd had in her roses. She'd adored the English roses in the walled garden. David Austin roses, he remembered, luxurious and wonderfully fragrant. Perfume had been a big priority with his mother. Her David Austin roses had done well for her. As a boy he had spent many hours helping her, doing what he had called the 'hard yakka', all the while drunk on perfume and contentment. He had an eye for beauty.

Cheryl, now, had no interest in gardens at all. Jewellery was her big thing. Chuck had shown a lot of spunk, demanding their father turn over to him their mother's engagement ring—a large emerald surrounded by diamonds. Their mother had always said it should go to her firstborn's bride. Whenever she'd said it she had always caught hold of Linc's hand, as if she had something else lined up especially for him. He thought it would have been her pearls, a gorgeous necklet her parents had given her for her twenty-first birthday. If he ever saw them around Cheryl's neck he thought he might die.

Gradually the stone path was narrowing—he supposed to enhance its secret quality. He had to bend his head beneath a glorious shower of blossoms from a free-standing iron arch that was wreathed in a delicate violet-blue vine. It might be easy passage for most people, but not those topping six feet. He could be following entirely the wrong path, but somehow he didn't think so. He fancied the spell that had been put on him was luring him on.

As he stepped inside the entrance to the walled garden, flanked by two huge matching urns spilling extravagant flowers, there she was: the only other one to find that enchanted glade.

He had followed in her footsteps. He didn't know whether to be troubled or amused by the fact he was utterly besotted with some aspect of her. Maybe when he got to know her it would pass. There was that cynical voice again. She was seated on a garlanded swing that was suspended from a sturdy tree branch. Wasn't that exactly where one might expect such a beautiful creature to be, in her berib-boned short dress? The dress was exactly the same colour as the flowers of the vine that grew so profusely up the swing's support chains, a porcelain pink.

He paused, looking towards her. 'You couldn't have found a more bewitching spot.'

'Hello,' she said simply. She didn't seem at all surprised to see him. 'You're right. How did you know where to find me?'

He gave a self-mocking smile. 'I just followed the magic petals. You *did* strew them for me, didn't you?'

'If that's how you want to interpret it.' Her glance held faint irony, as though she thought it wouldn't hurt him to be taken down a peg.

'It doesn't matter,' he said, moving over the daisy-flecked green turf towards her. 'I did find you.'

'You were looking.' It wasn't a question.

No point in denying it. He ran a hand through his shock of black hair, pushing back the unruly lock that had fallen forward onto his brow. 'I've been trying to get to your side for hours.'

She began to swing, very gently. 'How could you possibly fit me in between partners? You were never short of one.' The minute it was out of her mouth, Daniela regretted it. It sounded as if she had been keeping an eye on him. She hadn't been. Well, maybe she had directed a *few* glances.

'That thing actually works?' he asked, his gaze on the swing, wondering if it was safe. It looked more like a marvellous decorative element in the garden than functional.

'You can see it does.' She began to swing higher. 'The garlands are a lovely idea, don't you think? The flowers spring from these little planter boxes fixed to the base of the swing. See?' She slowed to point them out. 'It's the most amazing garden. I love it. I expect fairies with wonderful sparkling wings hold midnight parties here.'

He could feel the impact of her—her beauty and mystique—in every cell of his body. 'Do you suppose they ask mere mortals to join in? Why didn't you tell me you were coming to the wedding?'

She flew a little higher. 'It didn't seem to me we would meet again.'

'Oddly, I don't believe you.' A good thing she was a featherweight, but he was still getting anxious. He didn't want to see her fall.

Abruptly she slowed again. 'Perhaps you're too sure of yourself?' She knew she sounded touchy, prickly, but she couldn't seem to control it.

'And the idea upsets you? What sort of man do you like?' He moved, his hands reaching out for the flower-decked chains, testing them. They held very firm under pressure and he began to propel her forward.

'I'll recognise him if I ever find him!' she exclaimed, sounding a little breathless.

'Tell me. What's a young woman like you doing here all by yourself on a swing?'

'All by myself?' Briefly she met his eyes. 'I thought you were with me, pushing me?'

'Aren't I expected to in such a situation? Hold still for a moment,' he cautioned, as on a downward motion a thick green tendril sprang out from the vine and hooked into her hair.

Immediately her small high-arched feet in their pretty high-heeled gilded sandals anchored her to the ground.

He freed her. A small thing, but it hit him hard. She put up a hand to smooth her hair a mere second before he drew his away.

Skin on skin. He could have been wrong, but it seemed like an effort for *both* of them to pull away. Was he crazy? He wanted to pull her off that swing, pull her into his arms, make love to her there and then. Such was his physical turmoil.

Perhaps something of what he was feeling got through to her, because she gave him a look that came close to a plea. 'It's better if we return to the reception.'

'As you wish.' He inclined his head. 'Is there any particular reason you don't want to be alone with me, Daniela?'

His use of her name affected her. He had a good voice. A voice to listen to. Voices were important to her. She slid off the seat of the swing, then stood to face him. 'You flatter yourself, Mr Mastermann.'

'I think not,' he contradicted. 'And it's Linc. Or Carl, if you prefer.' His mother had been the only one to call him Carl. 'Lincoln was my mother's maiden name. It's something of a tradition within pastoral families to include the mother's maiden name among the baptismal names.'

She tilted her luminous head. 'I have heard of it, though I've never had the pleasure of mixing in such elevated circles. You say your friends call you Linc? I'll call you Carl.' She knew she was being perverse, but she felt a powerful warning to keep her feet very firmly on the ground. Linc Mastermann was a charmer, and a dangerous one. Not for a minute could she forget that. He wasn't an *easy* man, either. She had already taken soundings of his depths.

'So tell me about you?' he was asking as they moved out of the glade. 'All I know so far is you're Daniela Adami. You're home from London—your grandfather told me— where you were *sous chef* in a famous three Michelin star restaurant. Why did you come home, given you had such a great career going for you? Or do you plan to go back some time soon?'

She took her time answering. 'I'm here to see my family. I'd been missing them so much. Italian families are like that. They crave togetherness. Besides, I haven't had a vacation in quite some time.'

He wondered briefly, cynically, if his family were missing *him*. Chuck would be, but Chuck had found himself a girlfriend—Louise Martin. He couldn't have been more pleased for them. Louise was a great girl. 'You were born in Italy?' he asked.

She shook her head. 'I'm first-generation Australian. Everyone in my family loves Australia. We feel at home here, but my parents and my grandfather like to make a trip home to Italy at least every couple of years to see relatives.'

Again he had to bend his head beneath flowery boughs, while she passed beneath them unscathed. 'I spent a whole year in Italy after I finished university. Rome, mostly,' he told her.

'They do say all roads lead there.'

'*Ecco Roma!*' he exclaimed, falling back effortlessly into Italian.

She paused to look up at him. He was so very much taller she had to tilt her head back. 'Your accent is good.'

'I must have a good ear,' he said. 'At least that's what I was told. For someone born in Australia, you still retain a trace of your accent.'

'I know.' Just the merest flash of a smile. He all but missed it. 'We're bilingual as a family. Actually, I speak French as well. It's been a big help to me in my line of work.'

'As a chef?'

'Yes.'

'I'm surprised you don't speak fifteen languages.' He made an attempt to get a bigger smile from her. Longer. 'Sing, paint, play the piano, maybe even the harp? What you *don't* look like is you eat much of your own cooking!' he mocked gently. 'You're what? One hundred and two, one hundred and four pounds?' His downbent gaze lightly skimmed her petite figure.

He loved her dress, just a slip of a thing that left her golden arms and lovely legs bare. Low oval neck, short skirt—simplicity itself. Only what it was made of turned it into a work of art.

'Why are you looking at me like that?' she asked, turning her great dark eyes on him almost with censure.

'Actually, I was looking at your dress. What is it made of? Beribboned lace?'

She kept walking, twirling a perfumed pink blossom in her hand. 'If you must know it's embroidered crocheted cotton by a top designer.'

'Okay, I'm impressed.' He laughed in his throat.

'Thank you.' She coloured just a tiny bit. 'I bought it in London. It wasn't cheap.'

'Worth every penny, I'd say,' he said dryly. 'You should never take it off. So, how long is the vacation going to be?' How much time did he have? God, was he *mad*? This woman was drawing him deeper and deeper beneath her spell.

'I'm in no hurry to go back,' she said.

She couldn't tell him she feared to go back. She had told no one. Not even her family. Gerald Templeton, the only son of a very wealthy and influential upper-class family, a man about town in swinging London, had in a short period of time become obsessively attracted to her—to the extent he had turned into a stalker when she'd told him she no longer wanted to see him. It wasn't beyond him to follow her to Australia if he could track her down. All it took was a plane ticket.

He saw the shadow that crossed her face. 'Sounds like this vacation is more like an escape?' He was following a gut feeling. Chuck always did say he was good at interpreting vibes. Besides, one could learn crucial things through instinct and gut feelings.

She said nothing. She reached out to pick another flower, twirling it beneath her small straight nose. 'You told me you were interested in the Callaghan place—Briar's Ridge?' She changed the subject.

He nodded. 'Very much so. I have Alana's okay; now I have to get her brother's. I only met Kieran today, and we haven't had time to talk. I heard he's become a real someone in the art world, and I know Alex is involved. Guy and I went to the same school, where he was sort of like my mentor. Anyway, he kept me in check.'

'You were a bad boy?' She looked up into his undeniably handsome, charismatic face.

He gave a twisted smile, deepening those dimples. 'In some ways, yes.'

'I have observed your dark side,' she commented, pausing to admire a stone cupid. Someone had placed a mixed bouquet of flowers in the cupid's lap. A romantic touch.

'Now, how the heck did you manage to do that?' he asked wryly.

'A woman's instinct,' she said, turning to allow her eyes to roam his face.

'Maybe you would have made a good psychologist, had you followed that path.'

'Maybe I would. Do…do you have a girlfriend? Someone you care about?'

'Is this simple curiosity, Daniela?' His silvery green gaze, made even more startling against his darkly tanned skin, openly mocked her.

She walked on, picking up pace. 'All right, don't tell me.'

He caught her up easily. 'Like most guys, I've had plenty of girlfriends, but no one in particular. Tell me about the guy in London. The one you're on the run from.'

She felt a violent thrill of shock. 'I don't know what you're talking about.'

'It would explain why you're so wary.' He spoke tautly,

angry at the very thought some guy might have been hassling her.

'You're way off the mark.' She wasn't going to tell him he had scored a bullseye.

'Am I? You're a beautiful woman. A lot of beautiful women feed on their own self-regard. At least that's been my experience. You're not like that. You don't see your beauty as something special, more a danger. Am I right?'

What else had he learned about her? 'Maybe I'm beautiful only by *your* set of criteria?' she suggested evasively.

'Nonsense,' he clipped off. 'You'd warrant a double take anywhere. Unfortunately it's in some men's nature to hunt beautiful women.'

She stood looking up at him, trying to hide her emotions. 'Why are you speaking to me like this? You don't know anything about me.'

'You don't know anything about *me*,' he countered. 'Yet you said I have a dark side. I assure you, hunting beautiful women is not my style. So you can relax. I had a mother I adored. I would hate to throw a scare into any woman.'

She believed him. He would never do so deliberately. 'You said *had*?' She changed the subject again. 'Your mother is dead?'

'Breast cancer.' His tone, considering how he felt, was extraordinarily level—even matter-of-fact.

It didn't fool her. 'And after she died you didn't know how you were going to go on with life?' she suggested gently. 'You must have been a boy?'

There was definitely something between the two of them now. 'Are you deliberately turning the tables, Daniela? I was twelve, my brother Charles eighteen months older. Sad, sad times for both of us.'

She kept her eyes on him, fascinated and disturbed by

his dark good looks and magnetic presence. 'And your father? Was he able to offer much love and support? He, too, must have been devastated.'

'Oh, he was!' He could hear the cutting cynicism in his own voice. 'He remarried barely two years later.'

'A younger woman?' She felt his world of anger, pain and bitter resentment.

'Young women *are* nectar to older men,' he said with a twisted smile, 'but my dad's second wife, Valerie, was in the same age group. She'd been a long-time acquaintance of both my parents. Cheryl, on the other hand, is around Chuck's age.'

'I see,' she said quietly. 'It sounds like Cheryl is the wrong kind of woman?' The raven loop of hair had fallen forward on his tanned forehead again. She saw it annoyed him, but she thought it very dashing.

'It sounds like your womanly instincts are far too acute,' he drawled. 'Are you going to dance with me?'

She shook her head and walked on. Guests were spread out across the magnificent grounds, all laughing and talking, thoroughly enjoying their beautiful surroundings and the magic of the day. 'No.'

'Isn't that a bit harsh?'

'Maybe,' she said calmly. 'But I have serious reservations about becoming too friendly with you, Carl Mastermann.'

That didn't surprise him. He had concerns himself. 'Well, at least you don't fool around. You get right to the point. Is it because I have a dark side?'

Now she did smile at him. The first real smile he had received. It was so beautiful it took his breath away. 'Because you also have a *light* side,' she said. 'Maybe it's even brilliant on occasions. You're a mixture of both.'

'And this makes it impossible for us to be friends?'

'Is that what this is? *Friendship* that is passing between us?' she asked with a gentle air of melancholy.

'Maybe not.' Both of them seemed caught in a whirl-pool. 'But if I'm a mix, so are you.'

'No, no!' She shook her blond hair so the heavier side fell forward to hide her profile. 'I have always been a very happy person, much cared for by a loving family.'

'Only someone came along to change all that?'

It was a troubling challenge. He saw too much. 'Let's drop it, shall we?'

'Certainly,' he assented, 'as it clearly bothers you. Just one condition. You break your newly established set of rules and dance with me. It need only be one time.'

In an instant he knew she was going to consent.

CHAPTER THREE

THE day after the buying of Briar's Ridge was settled—
Kieran had been delighted by Linc's offer, and because he
had a substantial deposit and the bank on side, it took no
time at all—Linc drove into town. Not a single night had
he slept properly since his friend's wedding. If he wasn't
lying awake thinking about Daniela, how they had danced
together, the way she had let him hold her, she insinuated
herself into his dreams. He even felt her in his bed. He
woke with her fragrance on his skin.

You're crazy, Mastermann! His inner voice said in
disgust. *Give up while you've got a chance.*

He was so far gone he was indifferent to the voice.
There could be nothing remarkable about his calling in at
the bistro, he reasoned. Say hello, then ask her if she would
like to see over the property he had so very recently
acquired. He knew she was resisting him at one level, as
if she knew she *ought* to—wasn't he feeling something of
the same thing?—but they seemed to share a powerful
kinship. How was that so? In many ways she was a
mystery to him, yet he had been seduced on sight. Drawn
closer. He thought he recognised her soul. When they had
danced together at Guy's wedding he'd felt as though she

belonged to him. Even their bodies seemed to recognise one another.

That sort of thing didn't happen often. It had never happened to him, and he had held lots of pretty girls in his arms, made love to them, learned much. But he had never come close to a grand passion, the great enduring love lady novelists liked to write about. He remembered hearing his mother crying quietly during the nights his father was away from home. That had been when he was just a little kid, stealing along the hallway, checking on her but not wanting to intrude on her very private time. He couldn't have borne to humiliate her, but the sound still haunted him.

What had she been crying about? His old man's infidelities? The way he had turned from her when she'd first been diagnosed? Or how he never touched her after she had lost a breast and her glorious mane of hair? His dad had an irrational fear of sickness, but that didn't excuse his cruelty. Linc thanked God he had been around to console his mother. Even Chuck hadn't wanted to know how sick their mother was, though he'd been heartbroken and contrite afterwards.

Since leaving home, Linc had kept in regular touch with Chuck. Chuck sounded as if he was missing him like hell—especially in running the big sheep farm. But Chuck, good brother that he was, had been genuinely thrilled for him when he'd told him about Briar's Ridge.

'Man, I couldn't be more pleased for you. You always have to do things in your own way. And do them better than anyone else.'

'For the love of God don't tell Cheryl where I am.'

Chuck, who had eyes in his head that had been very uncomfortable with their stepmother's attraction to his younger brother, had assured him he wouldn't say a word.

'Dad still mad?'

'Filthy!' Chuck had crowed. 'Maybe he never told you—it would have killed him to do so—but he relied on you one hell of a lot. Come to that, so did I.'

'I'll keep in touch, Bro.'

At least Chuck would have his Louise. He wouldn't be a bit surprised if they didn't set a wedding date some time soon. And eventually Chuck would inherit half of Gilgarra; he would get the other half. His dad couldn't do anything about that. It had been Lincoln money, his mother's dowry, that had given their father his giant step-up. Never let that be forgotten. They were entitled. Linc wouldn't believe in Cheryl's providing their father with yet another heir until he held the baby in his own hands.

When he arrived at the bistro he found it crowded with happy customers. Aldo, a most genial man, caught sight of him and hurried towards him, beckoning. '*Buon giorno*, Linc. You want lunch? I can find you a table.' His dark eyes swiftly scanned the room for a spot to fit in a single table.

Linc smiled, looking around him. 'Everyone looks happy. Business is booming.'

'My darling Daniela must take the credit,' Aldo said, goodnaturedly leaning a hand on Linc's shoulder. 'She's running the kitchen. Word gets around. We're banked up Wednesday through Friday. We like her to relax at the weekend. She's a genius in the kitchen. She is teaching us all such a lot.'

'In that case, it's lunch.' He smiled. 'And I was hoping to speak to Daniela when she's not busy.'

'I don't see why not.' Aldo looked closely into Linc's eyes. 'You've bought the Callaghan farm?'

'All settled. I was hoping Daniela might like to take a look at the homestead. You, too, when it suits. It's good to have a woman's opinion on furnishings. Especially one with such style.'

Aldo blew a gentle breath. 'The man who wins my Daniela will be getting a goddess,' he said.

'Lovely thought!' Linc smiled back.

For the next hour Linc enjoyed food the gods might order. Aldo was right. His little Daniela was one hell of a chef. He didn't have to wonder why she had chosen that particular career. Her family had always been involved in restaurants, Aldo had told him. It had been a big upheaval coming to Australia, and they had arrived with little money, but in the end it had been well worth it.

Linc had found that eating and drinking was a national pastime in Italy, and that little bars, cafés and bistros were the mainstay of Italian life. He had loved the markets and all the wonderful fresh produce. Every city, every town, every village had at least one. He remembered how the women had appeared to spend a large part of their day— *every* day—going to the markets. Food and its preparation was a very serious business.

Daniela would have gravitated to a chef's career naturally. Not that what was on the menu here was solely Italian food. Definitely no pizzas. Linc started off with smoked eggplant with a marvellous crab sauce, followed by *abbacchio alla Romana,* which simply meant baby lamb, Roman-style. It melted in his mouth. He thought he couldn't fit in a dessert—he wasn't used to eating a big meal midday, or even stopping work a lot of the time—but a slice of the mascarpone sponge with a berry and rum sauce looked irresistible. A man could fall in love with Daniela for her cooking alone, though she *looked* as far away from being a chef as he could imagine.

Aldo beamed at him, staying to share a glass of wine,

treating him as a favourite customer. At least he was in favour with Daniela's grandad. The mother and father—the Adamis—were an exceptionally good-looking couple but, although charming, weren't quite so warmly welcoming as Aldo. Linc supposed they were wondering about him. Who he was. What he wanted. On the couple of occasions he had called in he must have betrayed his interest in their beautiful daughter.

He was lingering over his coffee when Daniela surprised him by coming to his table. Most of their customers had left by now, expressing very positive comments and indicating they would be coming back.

'You wanted to see me?'

That was the biggest understatement of all time, he thought, overtaken by dense emotion, fierce in its strength.

He stood up immediately, his heart wrenching yet again as he looked on her beautiful face. There was such grace about her, such refinement, sensitivity, the promise of passion. She was dressed very simply, in a crisp white shirt and black skirt, her lustrous hair clipped back behind her ears.

'I did, as a matter of fact,' he said. 'Could you join me for a minute?' He moved swiftly to hunt up another chair.

'I'm finished for the afternoon,' she said, sitting down and looking up at him—half expectantly, half what? He wasn't sure, but her great eyes glittered. 'So I take it the deal went through?'

He resumed his seat. 'It was settled yesterday. I am now the master of Briar's Ridge.'

'Now, why does that sound like Briar's Ridge is the first in a chain?' she asked.

He was a bit startled. 'I like a challenge.'

'I know you do.'

'More of that woman's intuition?' His eyes locked on

hers. 'Don't worry, I'm not knocking it. I have ambitions, Daniela. But you must know all about ambition. You've studied and worked hard. Le Cordon-Bleu, wasn't it, in Paris? Then London? You're rising to the top of your game. And you're what—twenty-four, twenty-five?'

'Does that matter?' She gave an expressive shrug of her delicate shoulders.

'Yes,' he answered bluntly. 'I can tell you I'm twenty-eight, so why can't—'

'Twenty-five,' she supplied. 'It is as you've said. I did have to study and work extremely hard to rise to the top in a very tough business. There was a time when I wanted other things.'

'Like what?' he asked, needing to know.

Her beautiful eyes were distant in thought. 'I wanted to go to university full-time. I was a good student. I could have got into any course I wanted. I was very interested in art history, psychology, the law—oh, lots of things. I wanted to stretch my wings. But there simply wasn't the money. I had to accept that. All of us have had to work hard. We've had to make a go of things. I was needed at home. It was actually an elderly relative who eventually became my benefactor and sent me to Paris. I had four years of schoolgirl French, which was a help. The deal was it had to be food. I was to become a chef.'

'Well, do you enjoy it?' His family had lacked lots of things, but not money.

Her lovely mouth curved in a smile. 'Of course I do. I'm Italian. I'm a woman. You could say my career was clear cut. My benefactor, for instance, wouldn't have advanced the money had I wanted to study Fine Arts.'

'How strange,' he said, thinking it was. 'But going on the reaction of your lunchtime customers you're a big hit. I was one of them, and what I had was superb.'

She gave a little laugh. 'I can do better. Lots better. I have to consider what our customers would like.'

'So you're telling me I don't know the best?'

'No, no.' She shook her head, looking embarrassed. 'I'm just saying…'

'I know.' He relented.

'You went to university?' She stared at him, unable to help herself. He was almost a stranger, yet she had a real sense of familiarity.

'I have a degree in Economics,' he told her. 'Not entirely useless.' Abruptly he caught hold of her fingertips. He hadn't meant to. It had just happened. 'Who's been cruel to you?'

She tried to withdraw her hand.

He held on. 'Well?' The tormented look on her face stopped him. He let her go.

'This is a mistake, Carl,' she said.

'Please don't go.' He was terrified she would. 'I'm sorry. I came to ask if you would like to see over Briar's Ridge.'

She paused uncertainly. 'What? Out of curiosity?'

'Not at all.' There was a brilliant sparkle in his light eyes, neither silver nor green, but a blend of both. 'There's another reason. I want a woman's opinion. *Your* opinion. You're a smart woman, a woman of taste. The homestead doesn't come with furnishings. I wouldn't want them in any case. I want to start out afresh. I want the place to be my own.'

She studied him strangely. 'How can that be, with *my* taste?'

'To be honest, I believe with you I can't go wrong. You have style. You've had time to acquire sophistication on top of your own inherent polish.'

'You flatter me,' she said. She put up a hand to remove a gold clasp from her hair, so one side went for a silken slide.

He watched in fascination. Everything about her was

just so damned romantic, even exotic. 'I don't think so. I'm certainly not trying to.'

'It's a bad time,' she announced, suddenly losing her composure.

'Not a bad time at all. Please—no more excuses, Daniela. Aldo told me you're always free at the weekend. Please say you'll come.'

Again she hesitated. 'You've asked me first?'

He frowned. She seemed to be making some point. 'Who else?'

'I really don't know.' She shook her head, looking as if she had concerns. 'You appeared to be getting along very well with Alana's cousins, Violette and Lilli.'

'So?' He gave her another puzzled frown.

'One of them might be perfect for you,' she said, really looking into his face. 'They come from your world—pastoral families, establishment, that kind of thing.'

He sat back, caught in a moment of empathy. 'I think I'm a lot wiser than that, Daniela. The people I most admire are those who make something of themselves, like you. You have ambition. You're a fighter. You're twenty-five. You haven't stepped back. You've stepped forward. I happen to know Violette and Lilli haven't done a day's work in their lives. In my book even rich girls have to *do* something.'

She began toying with one of the wine glasses. 'Sometimes I'd like to be rich,' she said with a brittle laugh.

'Would you do things differently?'

'What a question!' She stared away.

'Riches don't bring happiness, Daniela. A lot of the time money brings conflict. Anyway, a beautiful young woman like you would find it easy to attract a rich man. He need only *see* you. Maybe one of them did? Maybe he saw you often? It would be normal for you to have many admirers.'

'All these questions,' she said, returning her gaze to him.

'And no answers,' he said crisply. 'Will you come with me tomorrow? I'll pick you up.'

'I need to think about it.' The words implied she wasn't sure if she wanted to see him again. Only he knew differently.

'Okay, that's fine.' He sat back. 'I'm not doing anything in particular.'

She started to run a slender finger around the rim of the unused white wine glass, bringing a certain solemnity to it. 'Tomorrow afternoon,' she said at last.

'I'll pick you up at two?' His gaze pinned hers.

'Yes, two is fine.' She rose with faint agitation, as though if she stayed a moment longer she would change her mind.

At the same time he knew they couldn't get enough of each other.

Either something wonderful would come of it, or nothing good.

After breakfast at the truly excellent Hunter Valley motel where he was staying, Linc hopped in his car and drove out to Briar's Ridge.

A foreman, appointed by Guy, had been left in place to oversee the farm until he took over. Guy had told him he could, if he wished, take on this foreman, whose name was George Rankin. In his fifties George was a gentle giant, quiet but affable, who knew what he was about. George had lived in the valley all his life. He was well known and well liked. A bachelor—he said not by choice, that he had lost his sweetheart to someone else—he and his father had worked a small family property until his father had passed away a year before, after which the property had been sold. George had figured he didn't need much in the way of money, he had enough to see him out, but he quickly found he didn't like a lot of time on his hands. When Guy had offered him part-time work he had jumped at it, and Guy had subsequently shifted him across to Briar's Ridge to work the place until it was sold.

From what Linc had seen of George he did propose to keep him on. Full-time, if George were agreeable. George Rankin was a good man to have on the team. There was a bungalow he could have, so George could live on site as a young aboriginal lad did—Buddy. Alana had told him Buddy came with the place. There had been the sweetest plea in her eyes as she'd said it. It was Buddy's job to look after the stables complex—only two horses remained, but Linc would get more—and generally help out. What had endeared Buddy to Linc was the fact that the young man had taken it upon himself to look after the late Mrs Callaghan's rose garden. To Linc that seemed like an incredibly nice thing to do. For that reason alone he would have allowed Buddy to stay put, but he had also found Buddy to be hard working and reliable—in other words an asset.

Some of the stock had been sold off. The best of the flock—the remainder—came with the property. Linc had plans to expand every which way, and that was why he had taken on a mortgage: use the bank's money while he held on to a good part of his own. He would need it. The homestead—not big, but appealing, with a great view of the rural valley from the upstairs verandah—had to be furnished, and the surrounding gardens had been kept under control. But they needed a woman's hand to work their magic.

When Linc arrived, both George and Buddy were out mustering the woollies, to bring them down into the home paddock. As he looked up to the high ridges he could see their distant figures. The ridges were dominated by the eucalypts—the reason for the marvellous fragrance in the air, a combination of oils and all the dry aromatic scents of the bush. Briar's Ridge had once been one of the nation's premier sheep stations. The Denbys—Alana's family—had been around for ever, since early colonial days. Landed aristocracy with impeccable credentials. His own mother's side of the family, the Lincolns, were descendants of the old squattocracy too, but the Mastermanns, although highly regarded, hadn't been in that league. It had been a step up for his dad to marry a Lincoln. It had given him the seal of establishment approval.

Guy, as a Radcliffe, had always had it. The historic station he had inherited usually cleaned up all the competition in the wool sales. He had seen stacks of Grand Champion Fleece ribbons in Guy's study. Wangaree fleece was as white as snow and superfine. Everyone in the business knew the big overseas fashion houses showed enormous interest in it.

It was going to be tough for Linc. Sheep farming was a costly business, and the man on the land always had to contend with drought. Still, he knew he was up to it. It wouldn't be too long and he would be winning awards in his own right. He had won them for Gilgarra, of course. Chuck had helped, too, but their dad had taken all the credit. He'd have to get himself a couple of really good sheep dogs. A really good dog could work a couple of thousand sheep. He, like Alana, favoured Border Collies. Guy had pointed him in the right direction, but he would need to train them *his* way. He loved dogs. He loved animals. Sometimes he thought more than people.

It was very quiet, very peaceful, except for the birds flying through the air or diving ecstatically into the nectar-filled wilderness. This was the first time he had visited

Briar's Ridge on his own. Now it was *his*. It gave him a sense of accomplishment and fresh purpose. He hunted up the right key, unlocking the front door. Cleaners had been in. Everything was spick and span. Slowly he walked through the empty rooms, his mind already outlining what steps towards renovation he would take. Guy had given him the names of tradesmen who worked in the area—carpenters, painters, plasterers, tilers, electricians and so forth. This wasn't a grand house like Wangaree, and it didn't approach Gilgarra homestead either, but he was eager to put his own stamp on it. His boots were making quite a clatter on the polished floors—a bright yellow-gold, Queensland maple, he thought. He liked polished timber. It made a nice contrast with the pale walls. He would, however, need rugs…

He fancied his mother's presence went with him. Strangely, it was a lovely feeling instead of sad. She was never far away. He made a leisurely inspection of the ground floor, all the while with ideas flitting through his mind. He liked the proportions of the rooms. The kitchen probably needed a total make-over, but there was no real hurry. It was quite adequate as it was. Indeed, it was great to have absolute freedom and not have to dodge an over-sexed stepmother.

The golden timber staircase led to the second floor, where four of the bedrooms—there were five—were strung along the rear of the house, affording a splendid view of rolling hills and the broad valley. He walked out onto the verandah, resting his hands on the timber railing, drinking it in. The country wasn't as lush and green as he was used to in New England, close as it was to tropical Queensland, this area had the dryness of the bush. But there was a small creek that wound its way through the property. Its waters flashed silver in the brilliant sunlight. He wouldn't have much trouble adapting here.

He had asked Daniela because he wanted, *needed*, to see her. He hadn't the slightest doubt she would come up with ideas that would please him—that was if she was interested in pleasing him—but her presence was what he really wanted. He knew something about houses. He had always been interested in them. He wasn't about to change anything that didn't need changing—he needed to address its country feel—but he had already got a list going in his head.

Some time around ten he had a chat with George and Buddy. Both looked pleased to see him. He asked Buddy what he was planning to do that afternoon.

'Have fun, Boss!' Buddy gave his big engaging grin.

'Well, you'll be needing your wages, then,' Linc said, withdrawing two envelopes from his shirt pocket.

'That's okay, Boss.' Buddy threw up his hands. 'Mr Radcliffe paid us.'

George twitched the broad brim of his hat. 'That's right,' he agreed gruffly, his leathery face burning with what looked like embarrassment.

'Well, it's all official now,' Linc said. 'I'm the new owner. I'm paying you in advance.'

'Yeah?' Buddy gave a smile. 'That's great. I'm planning on having a big dinner in town. Maybe that Italian place. Everyone reckons it's tops.'

'What about you, George?' Linc asked, passing each of them an envelope.

'I'll just roam around.' George coloured hotly. 'Tonight I'm having dinner with some of my folks. My eldest sister Joyce and her husband. Joycie always tries to be kind.'

Should one have to *try*? Linc thought, divining the depth of the man's loneliness.

Buddy had opened his envelope. Now he was looking overjoyed. 'Did you check this, Boss?' he asked breathlessly, as though Linc might have made a mistake.

'I did, Buddy.' Linc nodded. 'You're on a man's wage from now on.'

'He earns it.' George gripped Buddy's shoulder tight. Buddy had been a big help that morning.

'Well, off you go, Buddy,' Linc said. 'Have a nice day.'

'You, too, Boss.' Buddy all but danced away. 'See yah, G!'

Linc gave an amused chuckle, then turned back to his foreman. 'I wanted to have a private word with you, George.'

George threw up his big weatherbeaten hands. 'That's okay—you got someone else.' He had leapt to the wrong conclusion.

Linc shook his head. 'That's not what I was going to say. I'd like to keep you on full-time, George, if you're agreeable. I even thought you might like to live on the property, like Buddy. There's that little bungalow near the creek that's standing vacant. I've had a look at it. A lick of paint, a few furnishings and it could be made very comfortable. What do you say?'

George took a deep breath, staring up at a flight of pink and pearl-grey galahs. He sighed heavily.

'No problem if you want to stay in town, George,' Linc said. 'I just thought it might make it easier all round?'

More silence. George took another deep breath, like a man in a haze. Linc was starting to think George couldn't quite believe what was being offered.

'If you'd like to think it over first…?' he suggested.

'Hell, no!' George came suddenly alive. 'It's very good of you to offer. The bungalow would suit me fine. I'd like that.'

'Hey, George, this will suit *me* as well as you,' Linc

pointed out with a smile. 'I'll open some accounts in town—the hardware store first up. You can buy all you need. Paint, brushes, whatever.'

George's eyes had turned inward. 'I've got plenty of furniture stored,' he announced, his dour face so bright he looked years younger.

'Then it's all settled.' Linc held out his hand. 'Better check your wages.'

'They'll be fine.' George slapped his thigh. His expression said it all. He liked and trusted Linc.

'Well, then…' Linc held out his hand. George took it.

'Welcome home, Mr Mastermann,' he said.

'Linc.' Linc waved the 'Mr Mastermann' away. 'Only my dad gets called Mr Mastermann, George. Though I don't mind Buddy calling me Boss. He gets a kick out of it, anyway.'

'He's a good lad. I can teach him a lot,' George said. 'Anything against my moving in by next weekend?' George wasn't going to admit it, but he found town life depressing.

'No problem.' Linc started to turn away. 'Oh, and Buddy might like to give you a hand with the bungalow?'

George was too jammed up with emotion to reply.

CHAPTER FOUR

HE DROVE her to Briar's Ridge and she hardly spoke a word for the first few minutes, looking out of the window as they made a smooth exit from town.

'This is a beautiful car,' she said appreciatively. 'It suits you.'

He gave an ironic laugh. 'You think so? I inherited the Lincoln passion for fast cars. My dad said it was a bad choice. He made it sound like *me*.'

'You and your father are not good friends, then?' she asked, turning her head to study his handsome, clean-cut profile.

'I don't think we ever were,' he muttered, almost to himself. 'It's always been a kind of confrontational relationship.'

'Your temperaments clash?'

His voice firmed. 'That's one form it takes.'

'What's another?'

He shrugged. 'My father is a tough, aggressive man, yet I seem to make him feel threatened. I don't know why that is. I've done nothing to make him feel like that. He gets on a whole lot better with Chuck—that's my brother, Charles. Dad abandoned the "Charles" very early in the peace. Chuck was named in honour of my grandfather—my maternal grandfather—a real gentleman of Guy Radcliffe's mould. Dad always tended to resent my mother's family as being a bit too grand when really they couldn't have been kinder or more generous.'

'Then how did your father win your mother's hand?'

He took a left, driving off the highway. In a grassy paddock two beautiful horses were racing each other around the perimeter, a bright chestnut and a glossy bay, manes and tails flying, a glorious sight. The car rode on seamlessly, as though it already knew the route by heart. A quarter of a mile on was the main thoroughfare that wound through the valley.

'Obviously I wasn't there at the time, but I think he played a loving role for as long as he had to. My mother was a beautiful woman—very gentle, very feminine. To be honest, I don't know *how* she got involved with my father. They didn't have a thing in common.'

'Outside sexual attraction?'

His laugh was dark-edged. 'That's the danger of sexual attraction, isn't it? If that's all you've got, a marriage mightn't have much of a chance. In time I guess passion banks. Maybe affection was always lacking? Disappointment and disillusionment were bound to set in.'

She looked at him in a searching way. 'My parents and my grandparents share much love.'

'Then you've been blessed,' he said shortly, his grip firming on the wheel as they took a sharp curve.

'I know.'

'You have no siblings?'

'I'm an only child. My parents wanted—prayed for more. But it was not to be.'

'Well, they got a one-off.' He glanced at her with a taut smile.

She was wearing a very pretty silk blouse, sunshine-yellow with little wings for sleeves, over cream linen trousers. The decorative gold buckle of her belt matched the half-dozen thin bracelets she wore on her right hand. She had a real feel for style. He was sure it was innate.

'As a child I missed not having a brother or sister,' she said. 'I had to deal with the question of identity as a first-generation Australian.'

He turned his head swiftly. 'You surely didn't have a bad time?'

'No.' She looked out at the surrounding countryside with its stands of banksia, urn-fruited peppermint and scribbly gums. 'A good time, really. Maybe at first there were difficulties. My family spoke a different first language, and I had acquired an accent, but I was bilingual. My grandmother to this day doesn't speak good English. And we looked different. We ate different food. We were Europeans, as opposed to the migrant families from the British Isles. They fitted in naturally. Most of the population is of British descent anyway. Those of us from the Mediterranean seemed to be cut off from the old home. But gradually I found my way and I became popular.'

'All you needed was to be yourself. I understand the difficulties,' he said. 'But I sense it has made you stronger. And there have been huge changes. You will have seen that yourself. Australia embraces its cultural mix.'

'Didn't someone say if you speak like an Aussie, you *are* an Aussie?'

He laughed quietly. 'Were you happier in London?'

She hesitated. 'I lived another sort of life there. London is a great city. It taught me much. But, like all ex-pats, I'm glad to be home.'

'You had problems there.'

It wasn't a question. She turned her lustrous head away, thinking he was too good at mind-reading. 'Don't we all have problems? I would have thought with your family background you would have wished to remain close to home. Yours is a working station—an important one, I understand. Or will your brother as the firstborn son inherit? You haven't spoken of any other family members?'

'That's because there's just Chuck and me. And of course Cheryl.' He had to struggle to keep out the derisive note. 'Dad is as fit as a fiddle—a big, strong, handsome man—but Gilgarra will eventually pass to both of us. The only reason for that is because Lincoln money really put Gilgarra on the map. I'm part of the deal. My mother looked after both her boys.'

'But you were the favourite?' She caught his silver-green eyes. 'There's always one.'

'If I was my mother didn't show it. At least I don't think she did. In any case, Dad favoured Chuck.'

'And who does your stepmother favour?'

'I hope you're not looking for an answer, Daniela?' He gave her a swift, sidelong glance, cool and sizzling at the same time.

She knew it was an incautious question, but she couldn't seem to help herself. 'So you thought striking out on your own was the best policy?'

'I should have done it years ago, but Dad really needed me. Gilgarra needed me.'

'Your father and Chuck can't do the job on their own?'

'They're going to have to,' he said. 'Are you finished with the questions?'

'For the time being,' she said lightly. Nothing could subdue the dangerous sense of excitement that shimmered between them.

She didn't see the homestead until they had broken out of the luminous green and gold speckled light beneath the crossed arms of sentinel trees. Then the broad circular driveway welcomed them, its fine gravel a dazzling white under the hot sun.

The word that immediately sprang to Daniela's mind for the homestead and its setting was an old one—picturesque. She sensed that for many years it had been a happy place. Alana had told her her mother had been killed in a tragic car crash with her father at the wheel. That would have been an awful lot of grief to contend with. Since then she had learned Alana's father had never thrown off an unwarranted sense of guilt. It appeared that guilt in the end had become too much for him.

She had taken for granted she was the only person Carl had invited, but a young woman was there before them. Lilli Denby. She was leaning back against the side of a silver Mercedes sports car, looking for all the world like a top model on a shoot. As they approached she made a move away from it, dropping her turquoise shoulder bag to the ground. It was impossible to tell if Lilli looked pleased Linc had a female with him. Lilli was wearing designer sunglasses with big black lenses, a stylish floppy-brimmed white hat on her blond head. A very trendy turquoise, black and white trapeze dress skimmed her ultra-slim body. Turquoise sandals were on her feet.

'It looks like your friend Lilli beat us to it.' Daniela spoke casually even though she was shrinking inside. She hadn't taken to two out of the three Denby sisters—Alana's cousins. Rose, the youngest, was by far the nicest, but Rose's two elder sisters had come across as incredibly snobbish. 'You might have told me she'd be here as well.'

'Oh, that?' he remarked dryly. 'The thing is Lilli neglected to tell *me*. You know perfectly well I didn't invite her.'

'That's okay. I believe you. You may well not have invited her *today*.' Going on what she had witnessed at the wedding, women threw themselves at him. It made her shiver. 'The wedding was obviously the start of a beautiful friendship.'

He glanced at her, a glint of amusement in his cool silver-green eyes. 'I promise she won't stay long.'

They all stood out in the dazzling sunlight. A flight of brilliantly plumaged lorikeets flew through the iridescent air, heading for the wealth of nectar-bearing grevilleas. 'Hello there, Lilli,' Linc called in his dark-timbred sexy voice. 'You're looking for me?'

'Who else?' she responded, with a sexy lilt of her own. 'I was on my way into town, so I thought I'd stop on the off-chance you were here.'

'You were lucky.' Linc smiled down at her, his deep dimples coming into play. 'The property was only settled yesterday.'

'I know.' She whipped off her sunglasses to give him an 'insider' smirk.

'Really? It wasn't exactly front-page news.'

Lilli's big blue eyes sparkled. 'We Denbys have our sources.'

He'd already learned that. The Denbys were an old family, but as far as he could gauge not terribly well liked. 'You know Daniela, of course.' Linc turned his head towards Daniela, standing so quietly.

Now Lilli's gaze held outright condescension. 'Didn't we meet at Guy's wedding?' She frowned, as though to place Daniela. 'Ah, yes! You work at your family's little bistro in town, don't you?'

'Let's just say I'm helping out,' Daniela answered with composure. Over the years she had met many women more arrogant than Lilli, and heaps further up the social scale.

'We must try to pop in some time,' Lilli said, as though the experience would amuse her. Immediately she turned back to Linc. 'Any chance of seeing through the house?' She twisted an arm through his.

'You're joking?' he scoffed. 'You must have been here countless times, what with Alana and Kieran being your cousins?'

Lilli gave a little grimace. 'Actually, while their dad was alive we stayed away. He wasn't the easiest man in the world. Quite the rough diamond, in fact. It was Alana's mother who was the Denby. Surely Guy told you?'

Daniela felt herself cringe at the snobbery and tried to disguise it.

Linc's answer was level enough. 'He didn't get into bloodlines, Lilli. It was Alana who told me you and your sisters are her first cousins. So how long is it since you've been here?'

Lilli hooted. 'Too long to tell. I'm sure you're going to want to do the place up?' She controlled a splutter of laughter, as though the homestead was all but falling down. 'Perhaps give a housewarming party? Is that why Ms Adami is here?'

Linc shook his curly raven head. 'Daniela is here at my invitation.'

Lilli picked up quickly on the steely note in his voice. 'Ouch!' She gave a tiny mock screech. 'No offence, Daniela.'

'None taken.' Daniela inclined her elegant head. 'I've handled many a housewarming party over the last few years.' She could have dropped a few world celebrity names, but she didn't. Her clients trusted her—and her discretion.

'Well, shall we go inside?' Linc put a good face on it. It was just impossible to get rid of Lilli, he thought. She had a remarkably thick skin. More than anything he had wanted Daniela to be the first one he showed over Briar's Ridge, but now Lilli had made her move. In a way she reminded him a bit of Cheryl. Cheryl, too, liked to take the initiative.

Lilli stayed perhaps thirty minutes, prodding Linc in the chest as she pointed out an endless list of things she considered had to be done. Not a room escaped criticism, nor he her little prods, accompanied by some sort of complicit grin. Daniela might not have been there for all Lilli included her in the conversation.

'Lilli, if you're interested you're going to leave me black and blue,' Linc said, not altogether in jest.

'A big strong guy like you?' She eyed him appreciatively from head to toe.

Lilli was definitely interested, Daniela thought. She would have found out all she needed to know about Linc Mastermann—a few comments from Guy, the rest on the pastoral grapevine. Neither Violette nor Lilli was currently in a steady relationship, she understood from Alana. She thought of Alana with nostalgia. She was a wonderful young woman, as lovely inside as out. So far as her cousins were concerned, Linc Mastermann must have appeared on the scene like God's gift to women.

'Can I give you a lift back into town, Daniela?' Lilli asked, suddenly remembering she was there. 'I can easily drop you off at the coffee shop.' Obviously she thought shoving Daniela down the social scale was the way to go.

'There are a few more things I want Daniela to see,' Linc intervened.

A lengthy pause. 'Okay,' Lilli managed, her sparkle

visibly dimmed. 'How long are you staying in town?' she asked Daniela. It wasn't conversation. She really wanted to know. 'A country town can't be much fun after London. Alana told me something about your career. You're a cook, aren't you?'

'Wake up, Lilli,' Linc drawled, thinking this had gone far enough, although Daniela didn't appear in the least bothered. 'The word is *chef.* Daniela has made it to the top of the tree.'

Lilli's laugh fell a little flat. 'It's great you're interested in such a career.' She made it sound an unacceptable one. 'I would have thought it would be very tough going, even dangerous, with all those sharp knives around and those volatile temperaments. I can't even boil an egg.'

'Why do eggs figure so largely on the "can't manage" list?' Daniela laughed. 'You'd soon learn if you didn't have someone to do things for you.'

'Actually, I've better things to do with my time,' Lilli trilled. 'Could you walk me out to my car, Linc?' she asked, training her blue eyes on him.

'Sure.' Lean cheeks creased in a smile.

Lilli interpreted that as a very good sign. She tethered herself to his arm.

No question—Lilli Denby had Linc Mastermann well and truly in her sights.

Left alone, Daniela brooded for a moment only. What am I doing here? she thought. I've fled one bad situation. I'd be crazy to walk into another.

Perhaps you're a little jealous of Lilli? asked a voice in her head.

She rejected that. She didn't blame Lilli for being so powerfully attracted to him. She was herself. But she wasn't going to let it go to her head. She had always prided herself on her common sense. Yet wasn't it true she'd been the last one to know Gerald Templeton had developed an intense fixation on her? In the early days she'd thought—if she'd bothered to think about it at all—that he fancied her.

It had been something of a joke with the other staff, but she had always kept her distance from customers—even when she and Tim, her talented offsider, had catered for the rich and famous. Besides, Gerald wasn't the only man who had endeavoured not only to chat her up but to ask her out. Eventually she had accepted one of Gerald's dinner invitations. It had gone well. He was good-looking, of good family, highly educated, clever. In short, a real catch. They had talked aimlessly and pleasantly about art, the theatre, books, people, travel, although she had steered clear of talking about his circle of friends who came frequently to the restaurant. Gerald was very much the man about town, with enviable connections.

Nothing dramatic had happened for quite a while. He'd taken her to lots of places, and she had even met his parents, at their beautiful country home—though not in a formal, girlfriend-meeting-the-parents sort of way. The young women of Gerald's circle always came from his own world. But what had started out in such a pleasant civilised fashion had turned into something else. It had grown darker and darker until she had fled.

'Daniela?'

Carl's voice pulled her out of her troubled thoughts. 'Carl?' Somehow Carl seemed more natural to her than *Linc*. She turned. 'Back again?'

He laughed briefly, something inside him tightening at the use of his real first name. He wasn't going to stop her. Maybe he even had a fierce necessity of the heart to hear his Christian name again? 'Do you think there was a damned thing Lilli *didn't* want to change? Next time she might come with a tape measure and take notes.'

'So there's going to *be* a next time?' She shot him a wry look.

He met those lustrous dark eyes. 'Tell me, is there a way to prevent it?' It was said with amusement, but a lick of bitterness escaped, too. It wasn't only men who did the chasing.

'I can only say Lilli appears to find you special.'

'Put it down to New Man in Town syndrome,' he returned.

'So modest? I think Lilli and her sister Violette meet plenty of men. They're on the social circuit, and both of them spend a lot of time in Sydney and Melbourne. Violette even implied she and Guy were once an item.'

'That must have been before Alana.' Linc spoke very dryly.

She nodded her strong agreement. 'I'd say so. I've never seen two people so much in love.'

They moved slowly into the large living area, with its pairs of French doors, shuttered on the outside, opening onto the wide covered verandah that offered refuge from the intensity of the sun.

'So how did you meet Alana?' he asked. 'Your face lights up when you talk about her.'

'I imagine a lot of people's faces light up around Alana,' Daniela said with a smile. 'She's a lovely person. Very endearing. No guile. No side. And she wears her beauty so gracefully.'

'As do you,' he said, allowing his eyes to feast on her.

She took in a deep, slow breath, not answering. The truth was she was feeling the intense heat of his masculinity—the height, the shape of him, the width of shoulder that tapered away to a narrow waist, lean hips, long legs. His aura was so magnetic she felt she had to stand a distance from him, just as she needed to stand a distance from her own emotions. She had never imagined anything so explosive as the effect Carl Mastermann was having on her.

'I think I need platforms around you.' She tried a joke, tilting her head as though it hurt her to look up at him.

He laughed, glancing down at her sandalled feet. 'I'd feel bad if you toppled over. So, how did you meet Alana?' he reminded her.

Daniela walked a few paces to the next set of doors, looking out. A bird was singing in the garden, its song plaintive but very sweet. She thought the sound came from an ornamental tree with a thick circle of pink flowers beneath it. 'She and her cousin Rose came into the bistro about a week after I arrived home. We got talking. You could say we were immediately drawn to each other. I like Rose as well—she has a sweeter nature than her sisters— but Alana is my clear favourite. We met up a number of times after that. And of course I had to meet her wonderful Guy. It was easy to see why Alana fell in love with him. Guy was very interested in the fact I had a couple of Cordon Bleu diplomas, and I'd worked in London's top restaurants. I've been to his Winery Restaurant and met the chef. He's extremely good. He'd get a top job anywhere. Guy was keen on sounding me out—whether I'd ever be interested in taking over the running of the Winery Restaurant at some time in the future. The money he was talking was certainly an inducement. I understand the chef has been there a good while and regularly gets tempting offers from all over—especially Hong Kong, where he has family. I got the impression there was a good chance he might move on.'

'Would you consider it if that happened?' Linc asked, his mind flying to what that would mean.

'I can't think that far ahead,' she said evasively, though in actuality she *had* thought about it.

'Really?' He had his own trip wire to the truth. 'It sounds to me like you've given Guy's offer a lot of thought. I could be wrong, but I don't think you have a mind to return to London any time soon. Did you quit your job?'

She continued to stare out at the shimmering dreamscape. The heat was like a pulsing white fire. A fountain would look lovely in the centre of the driveway, she thought. One always needed a fountain in this kind of dry heat.

'I've taken leave,' she said, not altogether truthfully.

'If you took the job at Guy's would you feel you had taken a step backwards in your career?' he asked, fully understanding that she might. 'After all, London is one of the great cities of the world—a far cry from the Hunter Valley.'

She turned to face him, a sudden flash in her dark eyes. 'You're forgetting I love my country. My family is here. I love everything about Australia—the peace and freedom, the friendliness, our whole way of life and for God's sake the *climate*! It's claimed not many Australians can settle in a cold, wet climate, and I believe it. Don't forget I'm also Italian.'

'I realised that right off.' He gave her his dimpled smile.

'Couldn't miss it.' She shrugged wryly. She would never hide her Italian heritage. She had no wish to. She was proud of it. 'What you mightn't be aware of is that Australia has some very important chefs, food writers and teachers. All of them have done stints in London and elsewhere. But in my view Australians can dine as well as anyone for a whole lot less, with the finest natural ingredients readily to hand, especially seafood.'

He admired her enthusiasm. 'So now we've got that sorted out. Anyway, I wasn't about to give you an argument. I've done my share of travelling.'

'But your roots are here?'

He extended his long arms as though to encompass his world. 'I have this amazing idea I'm going to start a dynasty of my own.'

She could see he was serious. 'Then I wish you every success. But you'll need a wife to bear your children, and before you marry you should consult your future wife about your plans for this dynasty. What did you have in mind? Twenty children, like Johann Sebastian Bach?'

He laughed. 'Four should be enough. And I think you'll find Herr Bach fathered all those children by two different women.'

'I knew that,' she replied, a tiny bit surprised that he did, too.

'So you want to marry, have children? Or are you a career woman?'

'I have to find a man I can love first,' she said, weaving her way elegantly around the living room.

'*Can* love? You sound a tad off men.'

'Good! You're learning that early,' she commented, moving into what would be the dining room.

'Okay, you're complicated. I understand complicated.'

They exchanged a brief glance. 'Both of us appear to have unresolved conflicts.' There was a brittle edge to Daniela's voice she couldn't control.

'Why do you want to keep yours secret?' He could see the struggle on her beautiful face.

'Carl, I don't know you.' She paused, her accent suddenly more pronounced. 'Not well, anyway. And I'm not the only one with secrets. There are things *you* don't want to talk about.'

'That's true.' He watched her stroke back a thick strand of hair that seemed to give off its own light. 'I like to keep a distance from my own emotions. Yours seem to be right there. I can't pretend I don't see your bruises.'

He had an uncanny knack to go to the heart of things. 'On my arms? Where?' She reacted sharply, turning out her slender arms, pretending to inspect her glowing golden skin. 'I see no bruises.'

'They're all inside. Okay—I can see it's necessary to change the subject, get onto something safe. Why don't we go through the house again now that Lilli has said her reluctant goodbyes?'

She stood framed by an open white timber archway. 'It seems a shame to waste her suggestions. Sorry, I didn't mean that.' She detested herself for sounding a touch cruel.

He laughed. 'I think really she wanted the house knocked down. I'm desperate to hear from *you*. I'm not going in for grandeur, like Wangaree. A laid-back style of living is what I have in mind. This is a country homestead.'

She nodded. 'But you'll want it to be comfortable and attractive, light and airy, a happy, welcoming place. I'd suggest a few unusual, possibly unique things. A light palette for the walls and furnishings. That should integrate the rooms. Thai furniture would work well, don't you think? Surely you brought things back from your travels?'

He studied her petite figure in an unabashedly sensual, brooding way. Being with her alone was making it hard to keep his attraction to her in check. 'As a matter of fact I did—especially from Southeast Asia. I've always been drawn to Balinese and Asian artifacts and antiques.'

'A touch of the exotic?' She smiled. It was a beautiful smile, glowing. That didn't make it easy for him either.

Did she have the faintest idea how much he wanted to kiss her? Only the last thing he needed was to fracture what was at the moment a fragile relationship. More to the point, he didn't want to spook her. He could see someone in her not too distant past had already done that. He found he hated the thought—hated the guy.

'I have quite a lot of stuff stored at Gilgarra. I can get Chuck to send it to me.'

'You don't want to go back and get it?' She, too, was picking up on the vibes.

'No,' he said briefly.

She walked towards the filmy curtains that had been left in place, putting out a hand to finger them. 'What about white interior shutters instead of curtains?' she suggested. 'They could look good—control the light—and you wouldn't have to worry about constantly getting the curtains washed. I love the polished floors. I love that dark honey colour. But you'll need rugs and a few paintings—prints, botanical or ornithological, whatever.'

'Your vision is pretty well the same as mine,' he said with satisfaction. 'Let's go upstairs,' he said, doing a slow turn and extending his arm. 'The master bedroom is a good size. I'll settle for that for myself.' He waited for her to precede him.

Neither of them spoke again until they were inside the spacious main bedroom. Daniela looked about her. 'I really like this room,' she said. 'It has a very serene feeling and the view is wonderfully soothing. You could easily fit in a huge bed—maybe Balinese, custom-made for your height. I see it already. Sofa, tub armchairs, low table, carved chest at the foot of the bed. And I'd change the ceiling fan to fit the décor you work out.'

She walked past him out onto the verandah, staring out at the marvellously peaceful view. Linc followed.

'This is magnificent!' She lifted a radiant face, breathing in the fragrant aromatic air. 'You have it first thing in the morning, last thing at night. Nothing and no one to spoil it. I love the smell of the eucalypts.'

'So do I,' Linc said. 'But we can never forget their fire danger. The oil is highly inflammable and it hangs in the air. Fires have broken out up there from time to time, so I'll be on high alert from now on in. I've always been strict on fire prevention methods. I'll be much stricter here than we ever were in the New England highlands.'

'So what do you intend to do?' Born and bred in Sydney, Daniela had little knowledge of rural life—apart from recognising that for all the rewards it was very tough, to the point of heartbreaking.

'Plough firebreaks around the perimeter of the property,' Linc told her. 'It mightn't be all that popular in some quarters, but with global warming!' He shrugged. 'Some superfine farmers don't like the dust in the air. It gets into the fleece and dirties the wool. I certainly don't want to do it—it will be one hell of a task, given the size of the place—but it has to be done. We've missed out on the spring rains, and last year the fire season started early in the Southern Highlands, around the Hawkesbury and the Hunter Valley regions. Major drought always brings the threat of severe bushfires. It's in everyone's minds. The end of last year—you wouldn't have been back in Australia then—bushfires raged in the Blue Mountains.'

'I did see some TV coverage,' she said. 'And I heard all about it from the family. The most horrifying aspect is that some of the fires were lit by arsonists.'

'They're murderers,' Linc said starkly. 'They seem to rejoice in death and destruction.' He reined his tone back. God help any pyromaniac who got onto *his* property. 'There's a great Rural Fire Service in the valley. I made it my business to meet up with them.'

'So you'll be well prepared?'

'As much as I can be,' he said. 'With bushfires, all the wildlife in the hills suffer. If the fires eventually sweep down into the valley we'll lose stock, but hopefully no lives.'

'There must be lots of wallabies and kangaroos up there?' She looked towards the rolling hills that stood watch over the station.

'Bound to be. Wallabies, kangaroos, possums, bandicoots, snakes and lizards, wedge-tailed and whistling eagles, lyrebirds and a phenomenal number of parrots. I plan on making a trek into the hill country some time soon. Want to come when I do?'

They were standing quite close. Too close. Hands spread on the balustrade, little fingers almost touching.

'Go up into the hills with you?' She felt a frisson of something like alarm. How could she possibly put herself in the way of temptation?

'No need to make it sound like a foreign country. You haven't been in hill country before?'

'I haven't been in the bush before,' she said wryly. 'I lived all my life in Sydney, forever drawn to the beach. The bird life here is wonderful, isn't it? They shriek, whistle, sing, and they're hardly invisible. I've never seen so many brilliant colours.' As she spoke another wave of rainbow lorikeets, flashing their showy plumage, dived into a blossoming stand of bauhinias. 'So many things in the garden are fruiting and flowering. I envy you, Carl. You can do such a lot with this place.'

'And I intend to do just that,' he said, pleased by her reactions. 'When we go up into the hills we'll have to get you a sleeping bag. You can discover the stars. In the wild bush they're so big and beautiful, so *close* they could be hanging from the branches of the trees. Can you ride?'

She shook her head with regret. 'The only horses I've been anywhere close to have been at the races.'

'You're not frightened of them?'

She laughed that away. 'No. Horses have to be the most beautiful of animals.'

'Then I can easily teach you.'

She was caught completely off guard. 'Why would you want to? Why do you want to take me with you up into the hill country?' She turned to face him fully.

'I think you know the answer to that,' he said. 'Shall we go through the other bedrooms?'

'Yes, of course.'

Whatever was between them, it was happening fast.

As soon as Lilli arrived home she went in search of her older sister. She was much closer to Violette than she was to Rose, who in any case was at work at the Radcliffe Estates Winery.

It rather amused the family that Rose was holding down a job. They were all in agreement that it was because it enabled her to come into daily contact with the young man she had long fancied herself in love with—Simon Radcliffe, Guy's cousin. That fact of his name alone ensured Simon was looked on favourably by the family. Simon had a dragon of a mother, but little butter-wouldn't-melt-in-her-mouth Rose seemed to be handling her surprisingly well.

Rose and Simon had been going steady for some time, and the family supposed they would soon announce their engagement. But Lilli and Violette were not getting any younger, and were no closer to finding suitable husbands. Both of them had had relationships, and Violette had seriously believed Guy would eventually get around to asking her to marry him—heritage families stuck together—but that had never happened. Alana had scooped the prize. Now Guy's friend, Linc Mastermann, had moved into the valley. Both she and Violette had been instantly attracted. This was one sexy guy. Better yet, on their social level.

She just *knew* Linc was going places. He had that air about him. Just as she knew that close sisters both being attracted to the same man might cause trouble. Privately she considered Linc had found *her* the more appealing. The last thing she had expected was to find someone else who might be ahead of them. She needed to alert Vi before a situation developed...

Violette was in her bedroom, trying on a new evening dress in her favourite shade of electric blue.

'What do you think?' Violette twirled for her sister's inspection.

'Gorgeous! You'll definitely score in that one.'

'And I know exactly *who* I have my eye on,' Violette chortled, running her hands caressingly down over her ultra slim hips.

'I have to tell you someone else has her eye on him,' she said bluntly, flopping down in an armchair.

'Who are we talking about, *exactly*?' Violette unzipped herself, at the same time aiming a piercing glance at her sister.

'Well, we're both keen on Linc...'

Violette gave a little inelegant snort. 'Darling, *you* should be so lucky! We both know he fancies *me*.'

'I don't know that at all.' Petulantly, Lilli swung a slender leg. Violette never let her forget who the big sister was.

'Yeah, well, I need to get married before *you*,' Violette reminded her. 'And Linc Mastermann is the only one I'd consider after Guy. He's drop-dead sexy.'

'Dreamy!' Lilli agreed. 'Only that Italian chick—the one from the bistro—thinks so, too.'

Violette looked dumbstruck. 'Italian chick? Should that mean something to me?'

Lilli gave a sly smirk. 'Ah, come off it! You know—the *bellissima* one at the wedding. Alana's latest friend.'

'Hell!' Violette pitched her evening gown onto her four-poster before swivelling towards her sister. 'How do you know? Anyway, isn't she a *chef* or something?' She made it sound like a kennel maid.

'She must be the only chef around who doesn't like food,' Lilli lamented. She and Violette had to work very hard to keep their admittedly great figures, while Miss Italy, who just *had* to be sampling what she turned out, was a perfect pocket Venus.

Violette pulled a white tank top down over her head, sounding thoroughly rattled. 'What would be the point of her getting interested in Linc when she's only here to see her family? She'll be back in London before we know it.'

'I don't know about that,' Lilli muttered doubtfully. 'I think she's a teeny weeny bit in love with him already. That could make a *huge* difference.'

'In love with him?' Violette questioned grimly.

'Are you going to repeat everything after me?' Lilli asked, quite crossly. 'Look, I don't *know*…but you know what Dad says: forewarned is forearmed. I was just passing Briar's Ridge—'

'You were *passing* Briar's Ridge?' Violette cried scornfully. 'You mean you went right out of your way. You've got to put a stop to going behind my back, Lilli,' she warned wrathfully.

Lilli cleared her throat. 'As far as I'm concerned, it's every man for himself. You know what they say, Vi. All's fair in love and war.'

'You get between me and Linc and I'll squeeze the life

out of you,' Violette said, making strangling motions with her long-fingered hands.

Lilli groaned in disgust. 'We're sisters, remember. *Family!*'

'To hell with that! You're not trying to tell me *she* was there?'

Lilli shrugged. 'I arrived first. They arrived about ten minutes later. He'd brought her out to show her around the place. He took us both on a tour.'

'Only he *invited* her,' said Violette, bitterly sarcastic. 'You invited yourself.'

'Unfair, isn't it?' Lilli sighed. 'And I have to say she looks really high class. I just thought I should let you know.'

'And maybe I'll get around to thanking you one of these days. No way I'm going to take this lying down.' Violette turned to stare at herself in a mirror, almost blinded by her own beauty. She was definitely the pick of the three beautiful Denby sisters.

'Maybe he thinks flirting is just a bit of a game?' Lilli suggested. 'At the wedding he seemed taken with both of *us*. Then again, maybe we were the ones doing the flirting. And he was just playing up to us. That's the trouble with sexy guys. They play up to us girls.'

Violette turned away from her self-adoration. She had already considered her move. 'What do you say we call in on this outsider at her place of business? Do lunch one day? Her aim is way off if she thinks she's got a chance of bagging Linc Mastermann.'

'If anyone can put her in her place, Vi, it's you,' Lilli said loyally, even though she had some private doubts.

'Easy-peasy.' Violette nodded a petulant agreement. 'And I think you mean *Violette*.'

CHAPTER FIVE

IN THE car, he was aware her lovely body was tense beside him. Tree branches above them loomed over the car like a shadowy canopy. Both of them had got under each other's skin. It was exciting, but not the most relaxed feeling in the world.

She looked sideways at him. 'Thank you, Carl, for asking me. I enjoyed that.'

'Then maybe you'll enjoy having dinner with me tonight?' he said, briefly pinning her dark gaze. 'And don't tell me you have to work, because I know you don't. I have your grandfather on side.'

'It would seem so,' she admitted wryly. 'But haven't we seen enough of each other for one day?'

He was quiet a while. 'You want to fight the attraction?'

'You're certain there *is* one?' There was a soft little ache in her voice.

'You are, too.'

By now she was resigned to it. 'But neither of us are relaxed about it.'

'No.' He answered without looking at her. He didn't feel he could absorb much more of her beauty before he stopped the car and reached for her. Could never get enough of her.

'Have you ever been in love? I mean *really* in love?' she asked, sounding to Linc's ears as though she actually cared. 'Putting someone above yourself?'

He took a moment to consider. 'Desire flares up suddenly, and often just as suddenly dies down. I've had some very pleasant relationships—and I certainly hope I haven't done any woman any harm—but I haven't had a relationship serious enough to study it in any depth.' Usually he deliberately shied away from getting serious, but he didn't tell her that. 'As a boy I was lost without my mother. I could never understand why such a beautiful, giving person should die so young. There was so much anger and grief trapped inside me sometimes I think I can still never get rid of it. Falling in love is delicious enough. *Loving* is something else again. Losing can be truly ruinous.'

She felt the truth of that. 'I just don't accept you haven't had women in love with you.' Take Lilli Denby, for instance. She also thought of her sister, Violette. Both of them were definitely looking forward to getting to know more of Linc Mastermann.

'That disturbs you?' he asked, exhilarated to think it might.

'The short answer? What I think about *you* is dangerous.' And *dazzling*.

'Perhaps I feel the same way,' he returned with a short laugh.

'I came home for a holiday.'

'Know what I think, Daniela?' He glanced at her sideways. Her beautiful hair was a halo around her honey-skinned face. 'You came home for some kind of respite. Maybe even to hide away.'

'Carry on, Herr Freud. That's very melodramatic.'

'You're that kind of woman.' He shrugged. 'Wherever

you are, you'd be the centre of male attention Some men soak up a woman's beauty like a sponge.'

'You're one of them,' she pointed out.

'I'd be the first to admit it,' he said, silvery green eyes sparkling, clear as crystal.

'Carl, I hardly know you. Surely *some* caution should prevail?'

He looked across at her without a smile. 'I understand your concerns. I share them in a way. But some things, like basic instincts, have a way of cutting through our best intentions. We could act conventionally, take months getting to know one another, but both of us are at a time in our lives when our instincts override caution. We're attracted to one another?'

'Yes.' She turned her head away, but openly acknowledged it. Their attraction had sprung fully formed.

'So, will you have dinner with me and forget your anxieties? I thought we could go to Guy's restaurant and do a little harmless criticising of his chef.'

That brought forth a real smile. 'We'd have our work cut out doing that. Anyway, as I understand it, it's always fully booked on a Saturday evening.'

'Well, very recklessly I booked a table,' he told her nonchalantly. 'It helps to be Guy's good friend. Please say you'll come.' He glanced at her, seeing how her long dark eyelashes were quivering against the golden bloom of her cheek. 'You know you want to.'

She nodded, but her expression was troubled. 'What I'm wondering is what *you* really want?' she said.

He reached out with his left hand and grasped the tips of her fingers.

It was like drowning in a sea of sensuality.

* * *

He picked her up at seven on the dot, found her waiting outside the bistro, sitting at one of the *al fresco* tables. Inside it was packed, so tables and chairs had been set strategically outside to accommodate the overflow. When she saw his car she stood up, gathered her little evening bag, said goodnight to the other people at the table, then walked towards him.

She looked a dream, he thought. Her beautiful dark blond hair, swinging free, caught all the light. He could feel ripple upon ripple of desire rush through his body. She wore a shade of green that suited her beautifully—apple-green, he thought. It was strapless, the bodice clinging to her delicate breasts, the skirt short and floaty. His eyes ran from her face down her body to her slender golden legs. She was wearing very high heels. That struck him as incredibly sexy.

'You look wonderful,' he said, taking her hand for a moment and carrying it to his lips. He was oblivious to the effect they were having on the couples at the tables until one guy gave a whistle so expressive it said it all. Devilment in his eyes, Linc returned the wave, before murmuring to Daniela, 'Let's go. It feels a bit like the red carpet out here.' He opened the passenger door for her.

A minute later they pulled away, to a few more appreciative cheers.

'Next time we won't make it so public,' he said dryly.

She smiled. 'We can face that when it comes.'

'You are staying with your family?' He had taken that for granted.

She glanced at his dark dynamic profile. If she had dressed up for him he had returned the compliment—or more probably he always dressed with style. Either way, he looked terrific.

'Actually, I'm renting an apartment while I'm here. There's not really enough room for me with the family, although everyone wanted me to stay. But I wasn't going to crowd them. I'm close by. That's the main thing.'

He was taken by surprise. 'So where's close by? Or is that a big secret?'

'View Point,' she said.

'I know it.'

'I thought you might.'

They drove down an avenue of palms, the headlights flickering over smooth green trunks and garden beds alight with tiny blossomed star jasmine used extensively as ground cover. Smoothly they turned into the car park. Cool with the air-conditioning flowing through the car, it proved much warmer out in the scented night air, redolent of flowers. With one hand barely grazing the smooth skin of her back he led her up the couple of stone steps to the restaurant. They could hear the humming of conversation even before they got inside.

Everything reflected light and glitter—the silver fire of wall mirrors, huge silver chandeliers suspended in the air, appropriately elegant furnishings, luxuriant golden canes in polished brass pots, delicate orchids taking wing in the centre of candle-lit tables, and floor-to-ceiling windows which by day gave a splendid view over the vineyards and by night showed a floodlit terrace, where antique garden carts overflowed with many varieties of colourful flowers, above them a sky full of stars.

The *maître d'*, smartly dressed in navy with a gold trim, greeted them like favoured customers, then led them to a window table.

'I love it here,' Daniela said when they were alone, her high cheekbones warmed with pleasure.

Linc looked around him appreciatively. 'Everything Guy does he does well. He's not only one of the top wool producers in the country, he's a wonderful businessman as well. He has a stake in lots of enterprises.'

'I'd say he'll make a wonderful husband, too,' Daniela smiled, her beautiful mouth tilting upwards.

'Would you give up your career to go off and get married?' he asked, watching her face in the candle glow.

She lifted her eyes to him. Her actual intention was, in time, to direct chefs working under her. 'Couldn't I have both?'

He leaned back in his chair, studying the flawless planes of her face. 'I don't see why not. But it could get difficult when children arrived.'

'Then I guess the career goes on hold for a while.'

'So you *do* want to get married?'

'Of course!' She made a little expressive gesture with her hands. 'What makes you think I wouldn't want to?'

He wanted to bombard her with lots of questions, though he knew he shouldn't. Not now. He wanted her to relax and enjoy herself. For himself, it was almost impossible to unwind. He wanted her as he had never wanted a woman before in his life. Desire at that level could be a tyranny.

'Just checking,' he said, giving her a smile.

The food, when it arrived, not only tasted wonderful, it looked like a work of art. Everything was perfect—the entrée of seafood, the roasted grain-fed lamb carved to perfection over creamed potatoes, with side dishes of perfect little baby vegetables so tender they melted in the mouth.

Daniela wanted to try the green tea crêpes served with mandarin sauce and a dash of orange liqueur.

'I'll have that as well,' Linc told the waiter, handing

back the menus. 'Our compliments to the chef. I haven't eaten better.'

'I won't take that as an insult,' Daniela joked a little later.

'Well, you know what I mean.' He shrugged. 'One has to leave the chef feeling happy. Besides, as you told me yourself, I have yet to try your specialties. I can't wait. Great food would cheer anyone up. It'll be a very lucky man who wins your hand, Daniela.'

Later, when they were lingering over coffee, a tall, striking young woman, in an eye-catching cobalt-blue dress, threaded her way rather recklessly through the tables towards them.

Daniela's face must have revealed a shadow of her dismay. She had an idea Violette had had a little too much to drink. The very last thing she needed was some sort of confrontation—such as the Denbys exerting their territorial rights…

'What is it?' Linc asked, turning slightly to follow her gaze. 'Oh-oh—it's Violette.'

Violette, swaying slightly, arrived at their table, smiling over her inner rage, blissfully unaware it was the smile of a tigress. She had spotted their arrival the minute they stood in the foyer, waiting for the *maître d'* to show them to their table. She hadn't been the only one interested. Any number of people—some with knife and fork halfway to their mouths—had broken off to stare politely. There was a trick to doing that. The only thing that had surprised her was that there hadn't been a scattering of applause.

She herself had broken into a sort of sarcastic quip about their entrance—she excelled at that kind of thing—but for once no one had paid attention. It had been bad enough suffering her cousin, Alana, but now there was this exotic

Italian creature. For the umpteenth time in her life Violette had felt a flood of jealousy. It was that which had caused her to over-indulge with the wine.

Linc rose to his impressive height at Violette's approach. He was seeing the funny side of it. Lilli in the morning, Violette at night.

'How are you, Violette?' He looked down at her.

For answer, she reached out and cupped one side of his face proprietorially with her hand. 'Exhausted,' she moaned. 'I had a few days in Sydney with friends. They ran me ragged.' She transferred her blue gaze to Daniela. 'Hello, there. We met at the wedding, remember?'

Daniela inclined her head gracefully. 'You and Lilli made beautiful bridesmaids.'

'Would you like to sit down for a moment, Violette?' Linc asked. Violette was reasonably steady on her feet, but one never knew. He looked towards a waiter, who surged forward with an extra chair.

'I must be quick,' Violette said, sinking very languidly into it. 'No one seems to say *anything* to each other if I'm not there. One of my roles in life is to be the life and soul of the party. Lilli tells me you showed her over your house?' She turned to Linc thinking he looked so at home, with his classy clothes and stunning good looks. She just loved his extraordinary eyes. They were like light-filled peridots in his darkly tanned face.

Linc smiled sardonically. 'I don't think it was to her taste.'

Violette gazed moved momentarily heavenward. 'You should have asked *me*. Lilli knows nothing about interior design, renovations—that kind of thing. *I* did a stint with a top-notch design firm some years back. I'd be only too happy to give you a few ideas.' A slow smile accompanied the *double entendre*. 'All it takes is to plan a date.'

'Then I'll let you know,' Linc responded, with a glint in his eyes.

A little more eye-rolling from Violette. This time in Daniela's direction. 'I love your dress. Who is the designer?' Unexpectedly she reached out and fingered the fabric of Daniela's skirt. 'Silk chiffon. It's so *you*!'

'Thank you,' Daniela said.

'It looks very, very expensive, but I suppose it wasn't?' She offered a little commiserating smile.

'Well, it all depends on what you'd call expensive,' Daniela said.

'I shouldn't say this...' Violette lowered her rather haughty voice '...but for me money isn't a problem. Now, I really should go back to my table. They'll be missing me.'

'Why don't I walk you back?' Linc suggested, already on his feet. He had calculated how far Violette might get before lurching into something.

'What a lovely idea!' Violette took his arm and held on as if the two of them were missing at sea. 'I want you to meet my friends. We're bound to be seeing a lot of each other.' She glanced back over her shoulder. 'Nice to see you, Donelda.'

If Violette had been trying to take a rise out of her, it didn't work. Daniela swallowed a laugh. She didn't envy the man caught between Violette and Lilli. And right now that was Linc.

They hardly spoke on the way back to town, their minds and bodies hooked on the powerful physical attraction that was binding them ever tighter. Linc had thought he would be returning her to the safety of the family home, a Mediterranean-style residence with white stucco and terracotta tiles on the outskirts of town. It was an attractive and well-kept house, but pint-sized when compared with what he was used to. He could well understand why Daniela had opted to give her family their space. But now everything had changed. Daniela had her own apartment. Thre was no way he could take her back to the motel, even if she consented to go. He was in no doubt she wouldn't, even if other young women of his acquaintance would have agreed without a second thought.

They turned into South Banksia Street, a fashionable part of town, dominated by the high-rise View Point apartments which he happened to know were expensive. He had looked over them when he had first arrived, but opted to go with the motel, which was situated farther into the valley. He pulled into a parking spot and cut the engine.

'Well, do I see you to your door?' He turned his head to her. He had often heard an expression—hell, he had even used it himself—when friends and acquaintances got caught up in relationships that screamed danger. *God, what gets into people?* He knew now. Desire for this woman had got into him. It was running through his body like flame.

Again a little hand gesture. 'Is that a good idea?'

He sighed, his light eyes burning over her. 'I can't think of a better one right at this moment. I want to make love to you, Daniela, as little or as much as you like.'

There—that was over and done with. You threw down the gauntlet.

She shook her head, almost sadly. 'Would it be all that easy to call a stop?'

He smiled, but there was an edgy down-curve to his mouth. 'I haven't actually had that experience, but I'm damned sure if a woman says no, I'll heed it.'

'And what if I don't wish to say no?' There was a slight break in her voice. 'So far what is between us I can control.'

With her admission he lost all thought. His hand flicked out and he caught her small-boned fingers. The trembling transferred itself to him like a sensual vibration. 'You must be doing a whole lot better than I. I wanted you from the moment I laid eyes on you.'

'And you feel this to be a unique experience?' she asked, as though she could see him tiring of her and moving on.

He laughed harshly. 'I told you once before, Daniela, you could have made it big as a shrink. Anyway, whatever you wish, I intend to see you safely to your door.'

'Very well, then.' She remained where she was until he came around to her side and opened the door.

As it happened no one was in the foyer or waiting for the lift. They rode it alone, both of them staring straight ahead. They had talked about many things over dinner, a man and a woman accepting each other as equals and enjoying the effortless flow of conversation. He had, in fact, told Daniela a number of things he had thought he had forgotten, perhaps they were better forgotten—and she had really listened. Needless to say he hadn't told her about Cheryl. He wouldn't, even if a suitable occasion arose. Cheryl had been doing her level best to make a nasty mess of all their lives. He knew himself to be blameless of any wrongdoing, but what man was mad enough to trust to the integrity of a scorned woman?

The lift door opened silently. They stepped out into the softly lit, thickly carpeted hallway. Three apartments to this floor. If apartment life suited, the View Point, looking out at the steeply rising blue ranges, was a good place to live.

At her door Daniela looked up at him with brilliant unfathomable eyes. 'I expect you'd like to see inside?'

God, alone! He tried to hold himself steady. How could he define what he was feeling? Love? Infatuation? Intoxication? A driving need to want a woman just for herself? And not just the here and now. It wasn't simple lust. It wasn't complex lust. What he felt was so much more than that. He had *found* her.

Yet when he spoke his voice was smooth, almost nonchalant. 'I'd like to know what sort of a home you've made for yourself.'

'Then please come in.'

Both of them were fighting hard to keep up their guard. Daniela was thinking herself on the point of disintegration. She ached for him to make love to her. Yet here in the quiet corridor, self-control reigned.

It gave way immediately once they were inside, the door shut tight against the outside world.

Daniela was standing small and slender, her back to him, her body as poised and alert as a dancer's, blazingly aware of what was to happen next.

Linc, too, felt that taut leap of fire. Of their own accord his hands found her bare shoulders, shaping them, gently exploring the delicate bones. She didn't move. He could smell her perfume, haunting but not pervasive, and beneath that the exquisite essence of *her*. He had made her a promise and he meant it, but he felt the dangerous frailty of his self-control. It was a wonder she couldn't hear his heavy heartbeats. Slowly, irresistibly, he lowered his head, letting his mouth and the tip of his tongue trail down beneath her ear to the silky column of her throat. The taste of her! She moved slightly, but it was back into him, her blond head falling against his shoulder. Now his arms moved to wrap her, to bind her to him. In a way the action betrayed him—because there was so much to betray.

The pressure grew. The tempo picked up.

When he turned her to him Daniela was so overwhelmed she didn't murmur or whisper one word of protest. Instead she let him kiss her with all the burning slowness he desired, until it became too much for her and she felt herself surrender completely.

'If you're going to stop me, it has to be *now*.' His strong, muscular arms were trembling. Even his voice sounded different—younger, shaken, husky in his throat. All the emotion locked up within him come to the boil. He was desperate to be a part of her, to make her a part of him. His hands had moved down over her small perfect breasts, full of passionate yearning. He had never felt like this before. The silk seemed to evaporate beneath his touch.

Her answer, when it came, was a soft, fluttery whisper. Like him, she sounded dazed. Her arms came up to encircle his neck. 'It's all right, Carl. I want you.'

The world spun.

He didn't speak, but picked her up.

It was almost three in the morning before Linc pulled into the motel, parking his car quietly, then letting himself into his room. He stood in the dark for long moments. Even the darkness seemed transformed. Without turning on the lights, he stripped off his clothes, laying them on a chair. His body ached for her even though they had made love until they were spent on splendour.

He knew every inch of her, nothing hidden. So tumultuous had been their hunger they had made love under bright lights, the bed a cool white field of cotton, scarcely aware of the illumination spilling over them because they couldn't stop or let go. Whatever he'd wanted, she had risen to meet him, the two of them physically, wondrously compatible. He had never known such intimacy existed. It had left him feeling exultant and a little unstrung. He sensed it was the same for her. It was almost as though for a few short hours they had forgotten everyone and everything—even their own identities. He hadn't wanted to get up and leave her. He just wanted to be with her for a thousand years.

You and me.

Always.

Or was that just a dream?

CHAPTER SIX

ALTHOUGH inside Cheryl Mastermann was screaming with boredom and frustration, she kept to her routine. Ben adored her, but she couldn't do a single thing out of the ordinary. She wouldn't have been a bit surprised to learn he kept tabs on her.

Most people in the district regarded her as the trophy wife—the *third* Mrs Ben Mastermann. She knew she wasn't liked. There had only ever been the one Mrs Mastermann so far as the district was concerned, and that had been the late Barbara. Wife Number Two—Valerie, socially well placed—hadn't gone the distance but had been reasonably well liked. In no way was she, Cheryl, an acceptable replacement for either—especially Barbara, the mother of Ben's two splendid sons. Barbara's premature death was universally regarded as a tragedy.

Cheryl had met him at a fundraiser on the Queensland Gold Coast, a holiday destination for anyone seeking the sun, the surf, the casino, and a frenzied night-life if you wanted it. As soon as she'd found out Ben Mastermann was loaded she had always managed to squeeze herself into the chair beside him. It hadn't been as easy as she'd thought to get him to sleep with her—most guys took advantage of that right off—but when she had, flattering him immensely, she'd had the multimillionaire all stitched up. Anyway, Ben was a fine-looking man—and plenty virile enough, as it turned out.

All might have gone along smoothly enough, only next she'd met his two sons. Chuck was a nice guy. No problem. She'd liked him right off. The other one, Linc, who really hadn't wanted to meet her—she understood from Ben he had been a mommy's boy—had shaken her to her very foundations. He looked dangerous—kind of *wild*. Nobody's idea of a mommy's boy, although it was certain he had loved his mother and continued to mourn her. Both brothers were tall, dark and handsome, but Linc made Chuck look dead ordinary. She would never forget the *lash* of his eyes—silvery green, sultry, brooding. It brought out her masochistic streak. So, instead of falling in love with the father—her husband—she had fallen violently in love with his younger son, when she hadn't believe she would ever genuinely fall in love with *anyone*. She was thirty-two years old—though she looked nothing like it—and it was no secret she'd played the field. When she was twenty she had even almost got married. Instead she had jilted Dean at the altar. Turned out she hadn't been pregnant after all. What a lucky break!

Though she had tried every way she knew how to find out where Linc had gone, all lips were sealed for her, and Ben refused point-blank to speak about his younger son, dubbing him 'a traitor'. Even she, who had no interest whatsoever in Gilgarra as a working station, knew as well as anybody that Linc was the driving force behind the whole operation. Chuck was just fine in the second chair, but everyone on the station was feeling Linc's absence. But she knew why Linc had had to leave, even if he had never spoken a word. He was secretly as nuts about her as she was about him.

Her mind had already begun the leap towards leaving Ben—though she wasn't such a fool she didn't recognise the danger. Ben was a proud man, and he regularly flew off the handle. Not with her—he wasn't that sort of man—but everyone knew Ben was furious with Linc for his defection. So where had Linc skedaddled to? No one disappeared into thin air. She could find out if she put her mind to it, but she had the dismal notion Ben might find out what she was doing, too. And, hell, if she got on the wrong side of him he might kick her out before she was ready. Ben was capable of anything. He had got her to sign a pre-nup agreement, which didn't say a lot about his trust in her.

There were a lot of things that frightened a girl. One was being left on her own. The other was being left broke.

Today she was on her way to a luncheon in town—another fundraiser for the local hospital. Whatever people secretly thought of her and said behind her back, as Ben Mastermann's wife, they were careful to include her on the important committees. Most committee women were older than she, and she knew they were green with jealousy over her youth and good looks. As always, she was done up to the nines. She wanted Ben to be proud of her even if she daydreamed of cleaning out his bank accounts and taking off to the South of France with Linc. She was struck by an image of him and groaned aloud.

It was as she was approaching Ben's study, her footsteps muffled by the long Persian runner, that she heard Chuck say, 'I don't need this, Dad. I work my butt off, you know that, but I'm not Linc.'

'Goddamned right, you're not. You're loyal. Your brother left us in the lurch. What the hell is he up to?'

'I thought you didn't want to know?'

'Son, I only have to lift my hand to the phone,' Ben growled. 'Where is he? Where did he go? What are his plans? His mother and his grandfather left him money.'

'And he has a half-share in Gilgarra, Dad, after you've gone.'

'After I'm gone?' Ben bellowed. 'I'm not planning on going anywhere real soon. For all you know Cheryl could bear me another son. We're working on it. If I had my way Linc would be cut out of everything. He doesn't deserve it.'

'Yes, he does,' Chuck answered flatly. 'You never tried at all with Linc, did you? You always favoured me.'

'On the other hand your mother favoured Linc over both of us,' Ben returned bitterly.

'It wasn't like that!' Chuck protested. 'Mum loved us all. But you didn't want to share her with anyone—even your own sons. Linc was right to go away. I shouldn't be telling you this, but he's bought a place of his own. And knowing Linc it won't take him long to make a name for himself in the industry.'

A moment of deadly quiet, then Ben snapped out, 'You mean he's been able to acquire a halfway decent property? Do I have to drag it out of you an inch at a time, boy? Where the hell is he?'

'All right, Dad, calm down,' Chuck begged swiftly. 'This flying into a rage can't be good for you. Just between the two of us, Linc has bought a place called Briar's Ridge. It's in a valley beyond the Hunter. The owner, a man called Alan Callaghan, died some time last year. Linc's friend Guy Radcliffe put in a word for him.'

'Radcliffe!' Ben let out another bellow. 'Ah, the rich, powerful Radcliffes—old family, old money. I just bet Guy was a big help. Probably came in as a backer.'

'No, Linc went in alone. I'd be grateful if you didn't tell Cheryl.'

'And why in the hell would I do that?' Ben yelled. 'Better yet, why would Cheryl want to know? She never said anything to me, and I never saw anything first hand, but Linc never did a damned thing to make her feel welcome in her own home. He resented her on account of your mother. I *never* discuss Linc with Cheryl. It's been mighty peaceful around here without him.'

'Then why are you missing him, Dad?' Chuck asked quietly, having the last word.

Cheryl backed up very quickly, her heart in her throat. Chuck could come out of the study at any time. She didn't want him to catch her eavesdropping as though her life depended on it. Little tears gathered in her eyes. Her prayers had been answered. Now she knew where Linc was. At the end of the month Ben and a group of wool producers had a trip to China lined up. As far as she knew he was expecting her to go with him. She would have to come up with a good excuse to stay home.

As Chuck strode into the entrance hall, on his way back to work, Cheryl appeared to be just coming down the stairs. 'Hi there, Chuck,' she called, giving him a bright, friendly smile. 'Man in a hurry?'

He nodded pleasantly enough. 'On your way out? You look great.' Even so, Chuck considered that in marrying Cheryl his father had made a horrendous mistake.

'Why, thank you!' Cheryl trilled. 'Your dad in the study? He always likes to see me dressed up.'

And *undressed*, Chuck thought bitterly, his nerves badly frayed. He had told Linc he wouldn't tell anybody. Now this! At least Cheryl wouldn't know. Chuck was sure his father would keep that piece of information to himself—

and thank God for that! He had the dismal notion that beneath the fluff Cheryl was a nasty piece of work.

In the weeks that followed Linc had the sense of living on a different plane. Whatever he was doing—and he was extremely busy—there simply weren't enough hours in the day, what with furnishing the house, stocking the property, putting on another man, meeting up with his fellow breeders, acquiring and training a pair of truly excellent, tireless sheep dogs. But Daniela kept insinuating herself into his mind. When he was with her all was right with the world. It was when he was away from her the feeling was especially strong—and that was most of the time, because she, too, was kept busy.

He was beginning to think he was falling for her, though he never let that out. Neither, for that matter, did *she* put words to her deepest feelings.

There had been no natural progression. Their passion had all the power and danger of driving his sports car at high speed, that was how big and fast it was. Their affair was virtually free of admissions, as though admissions carried a high degree of risk, and he sometimes felt the two of them were suspended in time. If their relationship continued they would reach a point where it wouldn't be safe *not* to face what was in them.

He wondered if her family—her mother, surely—knew the strength of their connection. Probably. Mothers had an infallible sense of such things. Though it was not as if he saw Daniela more than once or twice a week. Both of them, it seemed, were better than most people at hiding their true feelings, yet inside he felt as though a dam had burst, flooding his entire body with emotion. If she went away, went back to London, he wasn't sure how he would react. She had become the focus of his world. All he wanted, *needed* now, was to be near her.

Did he want her too much?

Was it possible to want a woman too much? All he knew was he couldn't take in the full extent of his hunger. He hadn't been prepared for it, for things happening over which a man had no control. He couldn't even control his hands when he was with her, holding her, kissing her, loving her. Even days after they made love he still felt the aftershocks.

Was it the same for her? He wanted to confront her with it. At the same time he knew confrontation at this stage of their love affair was potentially a danger. He was sure something had happened to Daniela in London. Something she wasn't comfortable with but wasn't about to confide. Maybe he had to talk first. Get Cheryl off his chest. He wouldn't put it past Cheryl to pop up out of the blue. Some women could twist anything around in their heads. Fantasise. Cheryl had acted as if they had shared an illicit passion. Maybe she truly believed it? Maybe she had reasoned the way he had shunned her only hid a fatal attraction? God knew what went on inside that airhead. All he knew was he didn't relish the idea of confronting his volatile dad, pointing a rifle at him. His dad was an 'act first and talk later' kind of guy...

Daniela was surprised when Violette and Lilli Denby made a reservation for lunch at the bistro.

'You're becoming famous, *cara mia*,' her grandfather told her. 'The word has gone out.'

Both sisters gave every appearance of enjoying the lightest lunch on the menu—scallops with watercress and a Vietnamese dressing, no entrée, no dessert—and they shared a chilled bottle of Cabernet Sauvignon. It was afterwards they got down to business, with Violette predictably taking the lead. Daniela privately thought Lilli would have developed better without Violette for a big sister. At least Rose had fought free.

Violette had requested a word, so Daniela finished off what she was doing, gave some instructions to her very capable mother, whipped off her big white apron and went out front. The bistro was slowly emptying, and as she threaded her way through to the Denby sisters' table she was repeatedly stopped by customers who wanted her to know how much they had enjoyed the whole experience of coming to the bistro. It might well be that the family would have to shift to bigger premises some time soon. Since she had been home she had passed on a lot of her expertise, and it showed. She had a dream of one day opening her own restaurant. She might employ her family—they worked closely and well together—but she had progressed much too far to settle for bistro dining.

As she approached the Denby table she had the sensation of two pairs of blue eyes burning over her, of blond heads inclined conspiratorially towards each other. As ever, both sisters were beautifully dressed, perhaps a touch overdressed, with not a gleaming hair out of place. She, on the other hand, had been working more or less flat out for hours, and could feel the heat of the kitchen in her cheeks.

Violette gave her a big smile, showing her perfect teeth, but her tone was brittle. 'Please sit down.' She gave a laugh.

Whatever did that laugh mean? Daniela reached for a chair at the adjoining table, now empty, turned it, then sat down. 'How can I help you?' she asked pleasantly, but didn't pick up on any wave of friendliness from the sisters.

Rather, they—and Violette in particular—appeared to be playing some sort of power game. Was it possible they were going to ask her to leave town? Such was their arrogance she wouldn't put it past them. The thought calmed and amused her.

'Great lunch, by the way,' Lilli told her with a note of surprise.

'I'm glad.' Daniela inclined her head. 'I do hope you'll come again, and perhaps bring your friends?'

'We'd love to,' Violette said. 'The thing is we're more or less committed to Guy's restaurant. Multi-award-winning, as I expect you know. But for a light lunch here is fine.'

'Is that what you wanted to tell me?' Daniela asked, her pleasant tone slipping a little.

Lilli responded swiftly, a little colour in her cheeks. 'No…well, yes… Tell her, Vi.'

Violette gave her sister an arctic smile. '*Violette*, dear.'

Lilli's trained answer was immediate. '*Violette*.'

'I'd be grateful if you would,' Daniela said, her calm returned. 'I still have some things to finish off.'

'Of course!' Violette sat back as if to say, *What do you have to do? What does it really matter?* 'I'm planning a dinner party for a few friends at the end of the month, on a Saturday night,' she said, as though announcing a meeting of the Commonwealth Heads of State. 'Just twenty of us in all—a small party. We'd like you to handle it. It would be a smart business move for you. If it goes well I'm sure you'll get plenty of spin-offs.'

So no written invitation, then? Business, not pleasure. 'Who do you usually use?' Daniela asked. Saturday was her night with Carl. She longed for Saturday every single day of the week.

Violette shrugged, her blue eyes shiny. 'Oh, one of the

chefs from Guy's restaurant. This time we thought we'd try you. The talk around the town is you're a marvellous cook.'

'I am,' Daniela said simply, no false modesty.

Violette laughed, as if success had gone to Daniela's head, but Lilli spoke up. 'Oh, please tell us you're interested,' she said. 'We'd want to see the menu, of course. Stuff like that.'

'And there's no need for budgeting,' said Violette, a woman who was only used to the finer things in life. 'Buy the best.'

'I always do,' Daniela said, giving a slight frown. 'I don't know, Violette…' She had an idea Violette could be just cruel enough to want to see her make a mess of things. Then again she might be overreacting. Violette would hardly wish to spoil her own dinner party.

'How can you knock me back?' Violette opened her eyes wide in amazement. 'What do you normally charge? Whatever it is, I'm prepared to go higher.'

Daniela immediately named a figure she was certain would put the Denby sisters off.

Lilli stared fixedly at the white tablecloth as if at an invoice. Violette was up for the challenge. 'Then we can rely on you?'

Well, she had no one to blame but herself. 'Certainly,' Daniela said in a businesslike voice. 'I'll prepare two menus, not interchangeable. Each dish on the set menu will complement the next. The final say is, of course, yours. The dinner party will be at your home?'

Violette nodded, her manner suggesting the guests would be royalty.

'I usually prepare the table,' Daniela said. The most gracious and aristocratic lady of her acquaintance had allowed her to do that—indeed, encouraged her. 'I choose the linen, bone china, silverware, crystal, flowers. All to complement the food. I imagine you have plenty to choose from?'

'Exquisite things!' Violette confirmed with her usual haughtiness, trying unsuccessfully to hide her shock. Who was this little upstart to take over the table setting and the flowers when *she* excelled at that sort of thing? But those great brooding dark eyes were on her, probing her motives. 'We'll leave it entirely up to you,' she said.

The truth was, Violette's great hope was that Daniela Adami would make a real mess of things. It might teach her a well-deserved lesson. Ms Adami had to learn she was way out of her class, and the sooner the better. If she thought for a moment she could snare Linc Mastermann then she was out of her tiny mind.

Daniela drove out of the canopy of trees and into the broad driveway. He was waiting for her up on the verandah, but as she slid into a parking spot in the shade he walked down the short flight of steps to join her.

'So what brings you here on a weekday afternoon?' Linc called, as if he hadn't seen her for weeks instead of a few days, his body and even his soul stirring. 'I thought you'd be working?'

'Forgive my weakness.' She smiled up at him, thrilled by his welcome, removing her sunglasses. She was wearing a summery white dress that showed off her flawless skin.

He gave in to his feelings. He pulled her to him, one-armed, and kissed her gently, then harder, tasting the peaches of her mouth. Or was it apricots? It was a marvellous feeling to have her here. Marvellous to kiss her in the blazing sunlight. It had been a magnificent day. Late afternoon was still hot.

'I'll forgive you anything,' he muttered. 'Just so long as it brings you to me.'

'Well, it has.' She lingered in his arms. 'I must be feeling perilous.'

'More perilous than usual?' He slipped an arm around her, leading her to the house.

'Let's forget I said that.' She had only just arrived, yet she was feeling the sizzle of excitement. At the same time she felt she belonged there. With him. It was a glorious feeling, yet in some ways it scared her.

'How long can you stay?' He looked down on her shining hair. It made a wonderful contrast with her dark eyes and golden skin.

'As long as you like. But I don't want to take you from your work. You've been quite a hit in the valley. Everyone seems enormously impressed.' Especially the female population. He would turn any woman's head.

'Oh, yes? Who told you this?'

He didn't sound in the least concerned. 'The word has gone around,' she said. 'People talk. You know that. It's a big valley with a small population. You've been the focus of all the attention of late. The Sextons come into the bistro at least once a week. They're very pleasant people. Tom thinks you're going to make your mark in the valley, and he and Grace already consider you a good neighbour. I don't know, but Tom said he once knew or knows of your father.'

'That would be "knows of ",' Linc said, with a sinking feeling, though it was no surprise that anyone in the pastoral world would know of the Mastermanns of Gilgarra. How the hell had he thought he was going to keep anything secret? If Chuck didn't spill it out in an unguarded moment, the news of his buying Briar's Ridge would inevitably leak back to his father.

And the ticking time bomb—Cheryl.

He would have to deal with that when it happened.

Inside the homestead, she turned to him with a gasp of pure pleasure. 'Good heavens, Carl! You've done wonders since I was last here.'

He was gratified by her expression. 'I wanted to surprise you. Chuck sent a lot of my stuff on.'

'I can see that.' She loved the Southeast Asian influence, a collection of artefacts, stone sculptures, tables, chairs and chests. The art on the walls was bold, modern, calling for one's own interpretation. 'You must be working twenty-four-seven,' she said, turning to look at him with unconcealed admiration. If he were, he was fairly blazing with energy.

'I've never had the opportunity of doing my own thing,' he said with satisfaction. 'Your coming into Sydney with me made a big difference. Because we were able to settle on most of the furniture there and then, I was happy to let the removalists put it all in place. Of course, I had to shift a few things around, but that was fun. I haven't touched the kitchen. It works at the moment. Like a cup of coffee? I bought the beans at the bistro, so they'll be good.'

'A cold drink would be even better,' she said, walking towards a seated gilt Buddha. It sat on top of a carved chest, flanked by two extraordinary silver lamps balancing on three legs.

'Sri Lankan,' he told her. 'They were originally altar lamps. Do you know what Sri Lanka means?'

'Beautiful island, isn't it?'

'Right in one. Guy and I stayed with family friends there. Both their sons were sent to our school and later on to uni. The family used to own a huge rubber plantation in the days when Sri Lanka was Ceylon. Now they have a tea plantation. They're an English-Australian family, but they'll never leave. They really love the place, and I have to say it's very beautiful. The chest with the Buddha on it comes from there, as do the ebony chairs. I like a mix.'

'Especially when it works as well as this.' She turned about. 'Did you paint that wall saffron?' It was spectacular against all the white.

'I did. It was well after midnight before I finished. The colour really sets off the big painting, don't you think?'

She nodded, studying the huge painting that might have been an abstract tapestry. 'All those blues!' She was forever seeing him in a new light.

'The bed arrived, by the way. Ready to deal with that?' His silvery green eyes glittered over her.

'Only if I want to forget the rest of the world for a few hours,' she said, a telling warmth rising to her cheeks.

'And don't you?'

'You're too good a lover, Carl,' she said, excitement flooding in on her.

'And you're a dream to make love to.'

She didn't betray what that admission did to her beyond the trembling in her hands.

Slowly she followed him into the kitchen, loving his lean, elegant frame, the width of his shoulder. His shirts and jackets always sat so beautifully. 'Violette and Lilli called in for lunch today,' she told him in a conversational voice.

'What a surprise!' His tone was ultra-dry. He bent to the refrigerator, withdrew two bottles of Coke. 'This okay?' He turned back to her, his skin giving off a wonderful bronze glow.

'Fine.' She really didn't care, as long as it was cold. 'They gave me quite a shock.'

'And more to come?' He hunted up one of the best glasses for her, intending to drink his from the bottle.

'As a matter of fact, yes. They've asked me to cater a

dinner party Violette is giving a few Saturdays from now. I didn't want to, so I made my asking price outrageously high, but it all rebounded on me, I'm afraid. Violette agreed. I'm not sure why exactly. Lilli kept her eyes glued to the tablecloth.'

'Probably as shocked as you were,' he said wryly.

'I think she knew better than to intervene. Violette is, without question, the boss.'

'She'll make a hell of a wife!' he said, pouring her Coke and placing it before her.

'Does that mean splendid, or what?'

'What do you think?' he asked with a rakish smile. 'The Denby sisters are very attractive to look at. One might ask the question why they're not married?'

She took a long sip of her cold drink. 'Well, Violette did carry the torch for Guy. She's since dropped it for *you*. The pity of it is, I think Lilli has the wild idea in her head that she can outmanoeuvre her big sister.'

'Should I be worried?' His tongue curled over his beautifully cut upper lip, tasting Coke.

'I think so. I'm betting Violette sends you a written invitation—or maybe she'll deliver it in person.'

He thrust back the unruly lock of hair that insisted on springing forward onto his forehead. 'She already has.' He waited for her reaction.

'She's a fast worker.' Daniela clasped her frosty glass to her. He hated that errant lock. She loved it. 'No doubt you accepted?'

He moved nearer her. 'There was a problem,' he said. 'As far as I'm concerned Saturday night means *you*. I'd back off dinner with every other woman alive for you.'

'But you accepted Violette's invitation?' She was surprised how cool and collected she sounded.

He didn't say anything but continued moving towards her, blocking the sunlight streaming through the windows, blocking her entire vision of the world. Though it thrilled her, she didn't really know how to deal with it. Gently he placed his hands on her shoulders. The fingertips were callused from hard work, but she didn't mind that in the least. It only served to make his hands on her soft skin even more erotic. 'The thing is,' he said, looking down at her wryly, 'the party is for *me*.'

'*Wh-a-t?*' Shock and a lick of anger shook her voice. Instantly she regretted it. What they had, no matter how deep and elemental, wasn't any sort of a commitment. Neither of them, even in the throes of passion, had cried out the dreaded L word.

He curled a hand around her nape, beneath the thick silky bell of her hair. 'It's supposed to be a "welcome to the valley" sort of thing. A "neighbourly thing" was how Violette described it. She and Lilli want me to meet their friends.'

'So you couldn't possibly refuse?'

'Daniela,' he said gently, 'that would have been very churlish. I know you understand that. I never even asked her if you would be invited—'

'Me?' She shook herself free. 'I could hardly be classed as a friend. Alana made things smooth for me. Easy. But Violette and her sister are out to make things very difficult indeed. One doesn't need an instinctive mind to sense that.'

'Okay, they're jealous,' he agreed. 'Can you blame them? They fear you. You're a beautiful woman. Not only that, you've cut out a career for yourself working with the world's elite chefs in what must be a male-dominated world. You have talent, strength and ambition. Violette and Lilli have been near ruined by their money.'

'And I pity them.' She knew she shouldn't give in to her

anger and her deep sense of hurt—it *would* have been very difficult for him to refuse, a newcomer to the valley, dependent on valley goodwill—but she knew she was failing to do so. Restraint had always been her way. Now that restraint was crumbling beyond repair. 'The real question is *why* did they ask me to do the catering?'

'The answer is simple. You're the hot new chef in town. You have winning credentials. In fact, you've made so much of an impression I hear one has to book well in advance to get into the bistro. All *we* need to do is move Saturday to Sunday. There's a big plus going here. You'll be in a position to showcase your culinary skills to people who do a lot of entertaining.'

'You mean the old families?' she asked, with a tinge of sarcasm.

'I suppose. Anyway, *I'll* be proud of you.'

She turned away quickly. 'Violette didn't mention to you she was going to ask me to do the catering?'

'I would have told you right off.'

'Really?' She turned back, her great dark eyes flashing. 'So, tell me—you don't trust me?'

The question, the sombre way it was put, took her by surprise. 'I'm sorry. I apologize.'

'Yet irrationally some part of you thinks I've failed you?'

She recognised the truth of it. 'We have no commitment, Carl.'

Looking at her, hearing what she said, brought out the weakness in his defences. He threw out an arm beyond him and gathered her in. 'That's funny? No commitment?'

She saw the hard edge to his handsome features. She dropped her eyes.

'Look at me, Daniela,' he ordered. 'I want you so much it scares me, and I know every inch of your beautiful body, but you won't let me get close to you. Something happened to you when you were in London. I want to know but I'm afraid to push it. I don't even know if you intend to go back there.'

'It's personal,' she said, her own weakness causing her to rest against him, her arms of their own accord going around his waist.

'Important?' He ignored the pain in her voice. 'I assume it's some guy?'

She sought his eyes. 'Carl, I wish I could talk about it, but I can't. I want to put the whole thing out of my mind.'

'So you were in love with him?' he asked, very quietly. How could she still be in love with some guy in London and be as she was with *him*?

'No.' Violently she shook her head. 'He was—is—a bit unstable.'

'You mean crazy?' he replied, his tone perplexed and a little bitter. He didn't believe her.

'No, not that at all. I can only explain it as an obsessive nature.' She grew cold at the thought of it.

'Is that so unusual?' he retorted. 'Most men would turn obsessive over *you*. So you had a passionate affair that didn't work out?'

She withdrew her arms, but he didn't let her go. 'No affair,' she said tightly. 'You don't get it. And I don't want to talk about it.'

Abruptly he relented. 'Daniela, if you're frightened of someone, frightened this man will follow you here, I promise you I'll take good care of you. No one will ever hurt you while I'm around.'

She searched his face, knowing he had a very protective attitude towards women. No doubt his great love for his mother was a big factor in that. She knew he was tough. She knew he was strong. She knew he would be ruthless if he had to be. She thought, all things being equal, Gerald Templeton wouldn't have a chance against him. It all came down to whether Gerald had forgotten her or not.

Or perhaps nothing would stop him? In his own way he tortured her.

She leaned her head back against Carl's chest and closed her eyes. Gerald, for all his threatening behaviour, had never had such power over her.

'Come upstairs,' he murmured very quietly into her scented, silky hair. 'I can't be alone with you without wanting to make love to you, Daniela.'

Later, she couldn't even remember walking back through the silent house and up the stairs with him. All was fluid motion and miraculous excitement. She remembered it was he who threw himself down on the splendid carved bed that looked as if it could easily accommodate three or four people. He who lifted his arms to her as she stepped closer, her breath coming fast over her wildly beating heart.

'Come here to me,' he said, his shimmering eyes a mix of hunger, tenderness and an odd compassion.

She leaned over him and kissed him, holding nothing back, one hand flat against his lean cheek, her blond hair falling forward around her face.

He pulled her onto the bed, as easily and as gently as if she were a piece of porcelain.

This was their escape route to ecstasy.

CHAPTER SEVEN

WHAT really got under Gerald's skin was the fact none of Daniela's colleagues—indeed no one who had ever worked with her—would level with him about where she had gone. That rankled badly, although he took good care not to show it. He kept his enquiries to the seemingly casual. A few of the people close to her might have known they had been seeing quite a bit of each other, though he had never been able to get her into his bed. They were taking care to keep what conversation there was to the usual pleasantries. The fellow who worked with her when she did her party catering, Peter, told him in confidence he was pretty sure she had gone back to Italy.

'Danni told me once she ached for Italy. I expect that's where she headed. We all expect a postcard from Rome sooner or later.'

If she had gone to Rome it had proved surprisingly difficult to track her down. But Gerald was not to know he had been deliberately led astray. What Daniela had actually confided to Peter was that she ached for *Australia*.

Templeton's own crowd, the top-notch people, had no idea where she'd gone, couldn't care less although quite a few said it was a pity she had gone because she really was a terrific chef. Oddly enough, Gerald had objected very strongly to her working in kitchens. Such busy, noisy places—all hands working at a frantic pace. Why ever had she chosen such a career? His views on the matter he'd decided to keep to himself—at least for a time. She was maddeningly beautiful and fine company. She even spoke well, with a faint and intriguing Italian accent, but he had never for a moment thought of her as suitable to be his wife. His mother, a woman to be reckoned with, had the right girl in mind—Lady Laurella Marks. He would go along with that. Laurella was a good sort, with a cool, down-to-earth streak and no consuming libido—which was a relief. He could find passion elsewhere. Laurella had missed out a bit in the looks department, but she had dignity and elegance and she could be relied upon to keep a stiff upper lip. Best of all, she had money of her own. And there was, of course, the family name. What he had in mind for Daniela was the role of mistress. He thought in time she would come round to it. She was a working girl, after all. One he rather suspected—or all her beauty—had come from humble roots. Society these days sanctioned mistresses, especially those as beautiful as Daniela.

Imagine his shock—he still hadn't recovered—when she had told him she found his suggestions not only highly objectionable but nauseating.

'And I thought you were a gentleman!'

'I am—and I can do better than that. I'm a real catch.'

'For some women, I suppose. Not for me.'

It was a few weeks after that when he had begun to stalk her. No use hiding it. His fascination with her had turned him into a different man. Either that or it had brought out the worst in him. He phoned her. He e-mailed her, keeping the messages ambiguous. He waited for her wherever she went. Once, she had approached him and told him she would go to the police.

'My dear Daniela, sadly no one will listen to you. I'll have a different story to tell. People know me. They know my family. What are you, after all?'

And now, though it was the last thing he had intended, he had driven her out of London. Obviously she had made a run for it. But sooner or later he would find her. When he least expected it would be the time he would get a break…

It was on a flight home from Zurich that he found himself seated beside Malcolm McIver, an acquaintance, big in advertising. They talked easily enough most of the flight back, though they would never make friends. It wasn't until they were told to fasten their seatbelts for the landing that McIver turned to him and asked, 'Whatever happened to that gorgeous little Italian girl you used to have on your arm?'

'Oh, that was just to annoy Laurella.' He shrugged it off, man to man.

'Lady Laurella Marks, you mean?' McIver looked at him rather hard.

'Of course. Just a matter of time before we walk down the aisle.'

McIver's expression hardened. 'Wouldn't having an affair with another woman give you a bad name and upset Laurella dreadfully? No wonder—Daniela, wasn't it?— headed off for Australia. I never thought she'd stay with you anyway. Too good, in my opinion.'

Gerald decided to keep that insult very much in mind. If ever he got the opportunity to hurt McIver in business he wouldn't hesitate to sink the boot in. Yet shouldn't he be thanking the man? He had never thought about Australia. To his mind Australia was an absolute backwater. It was *huge*, he knew that, but hardly packed with people.

His eyes lit up with a malevolent gleam. He would find her. As the saying went, persistence would win the day.

Daniela surveyed the Denby formal dining room with satisfaction. She had gone to a lot of trouble and it had paid off. The table looked spectacularly well. It helped that the room was beautiful and spacious, of perfect dimensions, with a lovely high ceiling, moulded and delicately coloured in a design of various fruits. A magnificent antique chandelier hung over the centre of the long table which, when fully extended, could comfortably seat twenty guests and certainly a few more.

With so much to choose from she hadn't had the slightest difficulty deciding on the right napery, the bone china, the silver, the crystal. The Denbys were collectors, and over the long years they had collected many fine things. In every drawer, cupboard and cabinet she had found silver, silverware and a dozen fine bone china dinner sets: Aynsley, Royal Doulton, Wedgwood, Coalport, Mikasa. Deep drawers contained a wealth of fine table linen, including some beautiful Irish linens, both single and double damask, in white and cream.

She felt relief that Mr and Mrs Denby would not be present. They were staying at their Sydney Harbourside apartment, where they would remain for at least a week.

Gary, her number two at Aldo's, had helped her with the placement of the settings, commenting on the exquisite gold-rimmed crystal wine glasses, three at each setting. Gary and Jules, a determined and remarkably capable seventeen-year-old apprentice Aldo's Bistro had taken on, would be on hand to help her.

The Denby kitchen was the workplace of a serious cook.

It was huge, ultra-modern, and fitted with every conceivable appliance, a cooking island, and loads of bench space.

It had been Daniela's idea to use a beautiful almost life-size silver swan that had been stored away at the back of a cabinet as a centrepiece. One of the Denby maids had polished it to perfection, and now it gleamed, its hollow back filled with a profusion of delicate ferns and lovely white orchids with cerise throats. The right flowers were very important—no heavy scent, a full arrangement, but low so the dinner guests could easily see one another across the table. Eight matching silver candlesticks, four to each side of the swan, were spaced down the table. She had deliberated over beautiful lace-trimmed placemats versus a near floor-length Irish linen cloth, a chrysanthemum double damask she fell in love with, and in the end went for that. For a touch of colour she had wound tiny Thai orchids of an incredible shade of purple-blue with trails of gypsophila around the base of the candlesticks. It was a nice touch. The table needed a little colour, and the deep blue was picked up in the rim of the beautiful white bone china.

At first Violette, slowly orbiting the table, wanted to find something glaringly wrong. The fact that it was all so *perfect* gave her quite a jolt. That silver swan had been stuck at the back of a cabinet for years on end, although she seemed to remember her grandmother using it a lot for her flower arrangements. Never on the dining table, however. The arrangements had always graced the library table in the entrance hall as far as she could remember.

Of course Lilli couldn't be counted on to stay aloof. She had gone up to the outsider and taken her hand, swinging it gently.

'It's *wonderful*, Daniela. You're a true artist.'

Violette wanted to silence her with a good hard slap,

like when they were kids. Instead she pursed her lips. 'I think I would have preferred table mats—and those little orchids could be a touch too vibrant...' She dragged one a little higher.

Daniela shook her head, thinking she would have to fix it back. 'I don't think so, Violette. So much white needs enlivening.'

Lilli tapped her taller sister playfully on the shoulder. 'Come on, Vi. This is really beautiful. Even Mum hasn't done better.'

Violette glanced at her sister, her finely chiselled nose wrinkling ever so slightly. 'Excuse me, Lilli,' she drawled, 'Mother is famous for her exquisite table settings and her roses. I expected *you* to use roses, Daniela.' She sounded disappointed at Daniela's choice.

'Roses would have been lovely,' Daniela conceded, keeping her sighs to herself. 'But this is a little different, don't you think?'

For her answer Violette made a 'tsk' noise and reached forward to minutely adjust a finely penned placecard. 'I have an infallible eye,' she explained. 'That didn't sit straight.'

Lilli chortled. 'You've just *got* to change something, Vi.'

'God, Lilli—how many times do I have to tell you it's *Violette*. I detest Vi.'

'I wouldn't worry if you called me Lil,' Lilli retorted.

'Why don't we just concentrate on the table?' Violette said. 'Now, let's see. Maybe we should move Zoe a little farther down. There is a pecking order, after all.' She switched a card that said Selina Morris for one that said Zoe Baker. I'm at the head of the table, of course.'

Another eye-roll from Lilli. 'Of *course*!'

'Linc, as guest of honour, is to my right. Did I tell you

Linc Mastermann will be coming, Daniela?' Violette said, with a happy flourish.

'You must have. Daniela wrote up the placecards,' Lilli reminded her, winking at Daniela.

Daniela thought it time to intervene. 'And you've settled on Menu Two?' She had to double-check. Although even if Violette abruptly changed her mind Menu Two would still have to go ahead. 'All the food had been bought in.'

'Just let me check again,' Violette said, as though she suddenly saw Menu Two through different eyes.

Lilli rolled her blue orbs heavenwards. 'We've already settled on Menu Two, Vi. We can't mess Daniela around.'

'That's true.' Daniela smiled pleasantly. Why did Violette set out to be so odious? Lilli seemed to be coming around. There was hope for *her*. 'I think you've come up with the right choice,' she said, putting approval into her voice.

A chef's palate was his or her most crucial faculty. What separated a good cook from a chef was the understanding of food, the ability to bring together complex flavours and bring those flavours to a new dimension. An important part of her job was constantly tasting, refining, adjusting, innovating. It was this that years before had brought her to the attention of a famous French chef—that and her calm and careful temperament in a volatile environment. And it was the nod from that famous chef that had helped her jump a few rungs. Everything took time and concentration. She knew this menu worked. It might have been fun to try out some of the new 'molecular gastronomy', but the tried and true had its advantages—especially first-off.

'Menu Two' featured a tartare of ocean trout, served with fresh goat's cheese as an entrée; Sansho peppered chicken breasts with poached baby vegetables, shitake mushrooms and *foie gras velouté* as the main course, that was safe, followed by a fresh lime curd tart with a *crème fraîche* sorbet. She had even picked the wines to go with each course. The Denbys kept a fine cellar.

'Well…please don't do anything wrong, Daniela,' Violette warned as though terrible things might happen to her if she did. 'I'd be *most* unhappy if we had slip-ups.'

'Nothing at all will go wrong,' Daniela told her, with a confidence she didn't really feel. She couldn't rid herself of the idea that Violette had the whole thing rigged. But surely that was absurd?

'All the toffs have arrived,' Jules told them gleefully, as he swung back into the kitchen. He was relishing the occasion. 'Dressed to kill, the lot of 'em. Nothing like a party to make people shine. I've never worn a tux in my life. One guy out there looks exactly like James Bond—except our guy's got light eyes. Cat's eyes, I reckon. Hell, he looks good! The ladies think so, too.'

It wasn't difficult to guess who that was.

'Well, don't just stand there, boyo!' Gary broke in. 'It's all hands on deck.'

'Right you are, matey!' Jules, a handsome young man with thick flaxen hair gelled into the latest style and bright blue eyes, gave an impish grin.

Jules was to help Gary with the serving. Though young, Jules was a great mover, with nerves of steel and an enviable self-confidence. Daniela had refused Violette's request that she do the serving herself, saying that in all honesty her place was in the kitchen. No doubt Violette had had a little accident in mind, like landing a main dish in someone's lap. It was Daniela's practice, however, to make a brief appearance at the very end of the meal—minus her protective clothing—to ensure all had gone well.

Gary and Jules were dressed alike, in narrow black trousers and snowy white shirts, collarless and pintucked. They looked good. An A-grade student, Jules had disappointed his parents with his choice of a career. It had upset their plans. They knew nothing about the food industry—and had wanted him to study law. Jules just wanted to become a cook.

Twenty minutes after it had been agreed that the guests would be seated at the dinner table, ready to be served the entrée, they were all still congregated in the drawing room, where they had been enjoying pre-dinner drinks. Daniela could feel herself getting upset. It wasn't easy to keep food at its peak. It needed to be served right on time.

'Are you sure everyone has arrived?' she double-checked with Gary. On rare occasions it happened that a guest was unavoidably late. Not everything went as planned.

'Did a head count,' Gary confirmed. 'All present and accounted for.'

'Have a quiet word in Violette's ear,' she told him, after another ten minutes had elapsed.

'She'd slap him if he got that close.' Jules gave another bad-boy grin.

'Do it all the same.'

To no avail. Instinctively Daniela *knew* Violette was counting on getting her out of the kitchen and into the drawing room, to do the reminding herself. Anything to cause a bit of embarrassment or, in Violette's view, bring her down a peg. Her most distinguished clients back in London, always the most considerate, would never have done this to her. Their guests would have been gently shepherded into the dining room.

'Damn it!' Gary was getting angry now. 'I'm starting to think this is deliberate. The woman wants us to fall on our faces.'

'Try her one more time,' Daniela advised. 'Tell her very quietly that if she and her guests don't go to the table now, she might well be doing the serving herself.'

'Good for you, Danni—call her bluff,' Jules egged her on. 'Better yet, let *me* do it.'

Daniela waved that risky suggestion away, shifting her attention to the food. She had made the final touches to the entrée a good twenty minutes before, but as it was a cold dish it could stand for a while before it was ready to be eaten. Even so the ocean trout mixture that had been packed so gently within baking rings might lose its precise shape.

The seasoned chicken breasts, sealed in a hot frying pan, had been transferred to a pre-heated oven. The poached baby vegetables could be kept warm in the stock they were cooked in. She could whiz the sauce a couple of times to keep it light and frothy.

Violette heeded the warning, and they got through the rest of the meal without incident.

Coffee and liqueurs had just been served, along with some tiny dark chocolate confections Daniela had made especially, when Jules glided back into the kitchen, wearing an expression of concern. 'What's the matter with the flowers?' he asked.

Daniela stared at him. 'They're all right, aren't they?' What *could* go wrong with them?

'They've really wilted,' he said, drumming his fingers rather nervously on a benchtop. 'You didn't forget about the water?'

'Don't be stupid, Jules.' Gary reprimanded the boy without wanting to cause him too much discomfort. Jules had performed extremely well tonight, validating their confidence in him. He might easily have been in the business for years instead of six months.

Jules shook his trendily coiffed head. 'All I know is the ferns and the orchids in the swan have kind of keeled over through dinner. I'd say it won't be long before they're *dead*. One of the guests—the sweet little redhead, Zoe—' Jules's face momentarily lit '—was trying to fix them with her fingers. It was a sort of talking point. *Madam* looked very put out. Personally, I think Violette Denby looks wicked.'

Daniela felt herself go cold. 'The tiny orchids and the baby's breath around the candlesticks. Are they okay?'

'Spry as ever,' Jules nodded. 'And they don't have *any* water. Anyone would think someone had poured some bleach into the swan.'

Gary glanced across at Daniela. 'Maybe *that's* her game?' he asked, his eyebrows coming together in anger and concern.

'Would *you* do such a thing at your own dinner party?' Daniela retorted.

Gary shrugged. 'Leave it to a jealous woman every time. She's giving that Mastermann guy the full treatment—matter of fact, all evening she's looked like she wanted to eat him, forget the menu. Or that's how I see it.'

Danielle barely heard. She was reflecting that she was the outsider here. Violette was on her home ground. She was a stunning-looking woman and she knew how to be charming when it suited her. The knowledge lay coiled like a snake in Daniela's chest.

Daniela made her brief appearance a short time later, in her little black dress. She wasn't sure what she'd expected, but the guests greeted her with much interest, enthusiasm, and lots of plaudits on the beautiful food and its presentation.

Carl, looking fantastically handsome in his evening clothes, came to her side, lowering his voice for her ears alone. 'Dinner was wonderful, Daniela,' he said warmly, looking smilingly into her eyes. 'Rest happy. As for the flowers in the swan…I'm not sure Violette hasn't been up to a few tricks.'

'It would certainly explain it,' Daniela murmured, immensely grateful he had made a point of coming to her.

'Such a pity about the orchids,' Zoe, the pretty redhead, came up to say. 'I expect the heat got to them.' Her voice conveyed nothing but sympathy and friendliness, no guile.

'I've never had such a thing happen before,' Daniela said regretfully, her eyes on the wilted arrangement, so cruelly robbed of its beauty. So much for any *heat*—a lovely breeze was coming in through the open French doors. The delicate white petals almost looked as if they'd been *burned*.

'Don't let it put you off,' Zoe whispered behind her hand. 'You won't be waiting long for the phone to ring. *Everyone* will want you. You're marvellous! Please don't go back to London early.'

Violette, her high-cheekboned face taut with anger, had no qualms at all about taking Daniela to task. The last of her guests had departed, and she clearly felt free to raise her voice.

Daniela felt a preparatory charge of adrenaline. This wasn't going to be pleasant.

'I hope you're not expecting the full amount of your exorbitant fee?' was Violette's opening salvo. She seized hold of a piece of notepaper, shredding it violently as though it was the cheque Daniela was expecting.

Daniela gave her a very straight look, thinking how dumb she had been taking the job in the first place. 'I certainly am. My fee was agreed. All the guests I spoke to were perfectly happy with dinner.'

'Okay, so they were too kind to point out that the centrepiece was a disaster,' Violette said, her voice vindictive.

'And I can't quite fathom why. Perhaps it's time for you to tell me what *you* put in the water?' Why should she put up with this? Daniela thought. This strange young woman had gone out of her way to humiliate her.

For answer Violette flapped her hands wildly in the air, as though swatting a plague of flies. 'Are you mad?'

'Are *you*?' Daniela countered, thinking Violette might have brought herself to a new low. 'You were prepared to spoil your own dinner party to make *me* look bad. If that's not mad, please tell me what is?'

Violette's blue eyes flared with shock. She was about to reply, only there was a knock on the kitchen door.

Gary put his head around it. 'I'm off, Danni. Everything okay?' His eyes went from the petite Daniela to the tall Violette, who for all her stunning good looks, seemed ready to kill.

'Fine.' Daniela gave him a reassuring smile. 'Ms Denby is just complimenting us on a splendid effort.'

Gary's round pleasant face looked highly dubious. 'Okay, then. I'll say goodnight.'

''Night, Gary.'

Violette shooed him off, her mood explosive.

'Actually, if you don't mind, I'll take a sample of the flower water and have it analysed,' Daniela said. 'I'm sure a chemist will do it for me.' It was an empty threat. She had no intention of doing any such thing, even if a chemist would oblige. But Violette must have believed her, because her haughty expression wavered.

'No, no—you'll do no such thing!' She placed her hands on her slim hips, standing tall. 'I'd like you out of here.'

Daniela gave a wry laugh, sitting down firmly on the

nearest chair. 'Then we both want the same thing. But I'm not going anywhere without my cheque. Tell me, is there *sport* in doing what you do, Violette?' she asked, genuinely curious.

'I can't for the life of me think what you mean.' Violette's voice was so tight it had trouble making it out of her throat.

'Now who's kidding who? You were prepared to let the food go cold, and you sabotaged the arrangement—all as a way of embarrassing me. It didn't work. Though I hate to see those beautiful flowers deliberately ruined. Plus, they were very expensive.'

Violette didn't cave in. Not for a moment. 'Who would care?' she snapped, then swept out of the room, returning moments later, cheque in hand. 'You should be very grateful I'm giving you this,' she said, ice chunks for eyes.

'I'm not, particularly.' Daniela took the cheque, studying it as though it might be a dud. Violette couldn't be childish enough to stop payment, could she? 'I did my very best for you, Violette. Your guests went off happy. A few of them, however, might go home wondering what *really* happened to the orchids. What did you put in them, and when?'

Black storm clouds scudded across Violette's patrician face. 'I was as dismayed as everybody else. Certainly *Linc* thought you had slipped up somewhere. But I bet this isn't the first time you've messed up,' she said through clenched teeth.

Daniela nodded, refusing to believe Carl had thought— or said—any such thing. 'Sure, I've made mistakes. Who hasn't? But you're the one who had better pray no one finds out about your little trick. They might find it all too possible to believe.'

* * *

Linc sat in the darkness, in his parked car, sheltered by trees and blossoming shrubs. He was waiting for Daniela to appear. It seemed as if he had been waiting for her all his life. And now that she had come he would never let her go. Daniela Adami had become central to his plans. He not only desired her madly, he admired her immensely—not simply for her beauty and her intelligence, but for her driving force, her will to succeed. She had done so very, very well—for herself and for her family, who were rightfully proud of her. He was proud himself.

He had seen all the other guests leaving, followed some time later by the tall young fellow, Jules, who had served the truly memorable dinner like a pro, and then Gary. Just as he was wondering—and it had to be admitted worrying—what was taking Daniela so long, she came down the steps of the homestead, carrying a fairly large basket.

His heart flipped at the very sight of her. The familiar excitement gripped him. She could literally bring a man to his knees. She had made an appearance at the end of the evening in a little black dress, looking impeccable and, as far as he was concerned, putting every other woman in the shade. The more he thought about that business with the centerpiece, the clearer it became. The Denby sisters were escalating their campaign. Violette had only hired Daniela to find some way to embarrass her. He had the dismal feeling *he* was at the bottom of things, as the latest eligible male in the valley. There were a lot more unstable people around than one would think. Violette could well turn out to be one of them...

He hopped out of his car, lengthening his stride to get to Daniela. 'Here—let me take that.' He reached for the white basket filled with various items she had needed for the night. The weight meant nothing to him, but it was probably heavy for her. 'I was getting worried.' He glanced down on her. Even at night the bell of her hair shone.

'I didn't think you would stay,' she said, enormously gratified he had.

'What, and not follow you safely home? Something's the matter, isn't it?' His eyes never left her. He was so attuned to her he could read her body language even in the dark.

'No, everything's okay.' They had reached her small car now, and Daniela was trying to organise her chaotic thoughts. She opened the boot and Linc swung the basket in.

'It's no use telling me that, Daniela.' His voice was openly sceptical.

'You can read me like a book?' She looked up at him. He had taken off his dinner jacket and his white shirt gleamed in the indigo darkness. Superbly tall and lean, he was, to her, the epitome of male power and grace.

But he laughed harshly. 'Not entirely. I do have an idea you and Violette might have had words. I mean, she deliberately held up dinner. I wasn't the only one to notice. That Zoe is a sharp little thing, and a few of the others. Then there was the business with the flowers. God knows when she picked her moment.'

'All in a day's work,' she said calmly, but in the next instant her temper spurted. 'I was a plain fool accepting the job. At least I know she'll never call on me again.'

'I'm pretty sure none of her friends will join her,' he said dryly. 'Everyone enjoyed dinner immensely. Let's get out of here,' he said. 'Someone is looking through the curtain. I think it's Lilli. I saw her give her sister a few hard looks. There are a lot of similarities, but Lilli has the potential to be a whole lot nicer free of her sister's influence.'

It was Daniela's opinion as well. 'Nevertheless, she's

keeping an eye on you now, with a view to reporting back to Violette. *You'd better get over here. She's talking to Linc.*'

'Mightn't that work for us?' he asked swiftly. 'Their seeing us together? Neither of them mean anything to me, Daniela.'

'That's sad when they both want you.'

He could hardly deny it. Linc drew in a deep slow breath. 'I'm sure I haven't given either of them the slightest encouragement, beyond a bit of tomfoolery at Guy's wedding. Certainly no serious business. A lot of women hanker after what they can't get.'

She responded sharply to the note in his voice. 'You're speaking from experience?'

'I'm just laying it on the line,' he answered, his voice terse.

She moved to the front of her car, ready to unlock the door on the driver's side. 'It would hardly surprise me to hear a lot of women have hankered after you.'

He gave a laugh, a sardonic glint in his eyes. 'What does a man do to avoid them?'

That gave her pause. Hadn't she done everything in her power to avoid Gerald Templeton, without success? 'Look, it's one o'clock in the morning,' she said, determined not to be the kind of woman ripe for the plucking. 'You don't have to follow me, Carl. Fly away home. I'm fine.'

He rested his hand over hers, tightening it slightly, stirring up all her senses to something like anguish. 'You're really not. Come back with me. Please.'

She could feel herself starting to tremble. In all other things she could keep her emotions under restraint. With him she was demonstratively passionate. He was the one who had unlocked her sensuality. 'I don't want to do that,' she said, knowing how half-hearted it sounded.

'It's odd, but I don't believe you. That's *exactly* what you want to do.'

She rounded on him with unconscious seductiveness. 'You're so sure of yourself, aren't you?'

'You'll have to do better than that, Daniela.' He rested his hands on her delicate shoulders. Every part of her body was lovely—her hands and her feet. He wondered for the very first time what a child of theirs would look like. A little girl, with her mother's wondrous beauty and spirit. 'If you're upset—and you are—I really want to hear about it. And afterwards I want to make it up to you.'

'In bed?' Her honeyed voice bit, though her yearning was sharp.

'Can you think of a better way?' he retorted, wanting to pull her into his arms, but aware that Lilli was probably still watching from upstairs, believing herself unobserved. 'Don't let's argue,' he said, looking down at her intently. 'Come back with me—if only for a little while.' Very gently he touched her cheek, letting his finger trail down to her swanlike neck.

Their eyes met. He lowered his dark head, nuzzling the side of that neck softly. She tilted her head so as to better accept his caressing mouth. It was impossible not to surrender to the spell.

Believing herself screened by the curtain, Lilli continued to look down into the drive, her stomach tied in knots. The exterior lights were still on, so she could see their dusky silhouettes. She couldn't have moved even if she had wanted to. She was caught up in what was happening down there.

The death of her dreams, she thought dramatically, though in her heart of hearts she had known she had no chance.

The exterior lights hit their figures obliquely. He was facing the house, towering over the petite Daniela, his white shirt gleaming. She saw him take Daniela's shoulders. She saw the way he lowered his head to kiss her cheek, or her throat—she couldn't quite make out which, but she wished to God it was happening to *her*. Linc Mastermann was the kind of guy to drive a girl wild.

Moments later both of them got into their cars, Daniela leaving first. Lilli slowly dropped her hand from the curtain. She had a vivid image of them together. *Naked*. In bed. She knew the way he would make love would be unforgettable.

'What the devil are you doing?'

Violette's loud voice startled her so much she jumped.

'For crying out loud, what are you trying to do? Shatter glass? What does it look like?' Lilli croaked, made to feel like a sneak by someone who had made sneakiness an art form. '*He* waited for her.'

Violette's rage overflowed. 'He *wh-a-t*?' She broke off, speechless, stalking to the window. 'There's no one there.' She turned on Lilli, as though Lilli were delusional.

'They've gone.' Lilli stood a distance away, a beautiful, sadly disappointed young woman in her lovely lilac satin dress. 'You've yet to learn how to play it smart, Vi,' she said with regret in her voice. 'That bit with the flowers was just plain dumb. What did you spray them with? I can just see you ransacking the kitchen cupboard.'

'Don't be so ridiculous,' Violette shot back savagely. It was Violette's way to deny everything she didn't want to face.

Despite her wretched disappointment Lilli laughed. 'Hey, it's *me*, remember? Your sister. The last person in the world to trust you. Hell, I remember the tricks you used to play on Alana. That didn't stop her from landing Guy. Now you want to play your little tricks on Daniela.'

'And what evidence do you have to support this?' Violette demanded in her most crushing Big-Sister voice.

'The evidence of our whole lives flashing before our

eyes,' Lilli answered quietly. 'Remember that girl—the scholarship girl—Fiona Scott at school? Poor old Fiona! Didn't you cause *her* some grief! You've been a bad influence on me, Vi. You've made me do a whole lot of things I didn't want to do. I've been gutless. Too easily led. Okay, I took a real shine to Linc. What girl wouldn't? He's gorgeous. You felt the same. Only *one* problem—and it's huge. Daniela is the one he's interested in.'

'Daniela who's going back to London, or have you forgotten?' Violette retorted, absolutely seething at her sister's disloyalty.

'I'll believe that when it happens,' Lilli replied. 'My advice is save yourself for another guy. There must be someone out there who doesn't know or hasn't heard you're so horrid. I'm going back to Sydney tomorrow.'

'Good!' Violette responded hotly. 'Then we might be able to get a bit of peace around here.'

CHAPTER EIGHT

A COUPLE of weeks later Daniela took a call from Florence, the birthplace of the Renaissance. It was Alana, sounding absolutely on top of the world, her voice as clear as if she was ringing from Sydney. Daniela had received two post-cards from the honeymooners, one from Paris, another from Rome, and now she was delighted to take the call.

The two young women chatted for a few minutes, with Alana filling her in on all the wonderful sights she had seen. She raved about the Uffizi, one of the world's most splendid art galleries, and said the food was to die for. Their honeymoon was the experience of a lifetime. But Guy wanted to talk to Daniela. Alana handed over the phone.

Guy's smooth cultured voice came on the line. They talked for a little while, and then Guy sprang his big surprise. His chef, Lee, at the Winery Restaurant, needed to return home to Hong Kong as soon as possible. His father, who had been in poor health for some time, was declining and his ageing mother needed him to be on hand. He estimated he would need to be away a month, maybe a little longer. Would Daniela be interested in taking over the position of Executive Chef in his absence? There were two chefs under Lee, and they would be remaining in place. They could handle most weekdays. It was the Friday and Saturday nights Guy was most concerned with. He named a figure no chef would turn down, but didn't expect Daniela to consent on the spot. He would give her another day to decide.

The offer was very tempting. At the Winery Restaurant she could go beyond the norm, which was to say the menus could be far more creative than what she was currently planning at the family bistro. She immediately thought of French-Japanese combinations, or her own interpretation of Japanese food. Her style was drawn from French origins—after all, she had received her training in Paris—and she understood the French kitchen. Although even Japanese chefs described themselves as French chefs.

The Winery had a full client list. If one wanted a table a reservation had to be made well in advance. It would be a challenge, but first she would have to speak to her parents, who were pretty much relying on her to come up with the kind of dishes that kept customers flowing into the bistro. Then again, she could overcome that problem by formulating written menus and instructions without actually doing the cooking herself. Her parents had been amazingly quick to pick up on her techniques. Whatever she had asked, they had done very well—if not the first time, then certainly the second. The *sous chefs* at the Winery had to be first class, with a high level of technique, and the chances that she could do a lot of directing those without actually having to demonstrate were excellent.

It wasn't her habit to write things down, but she could easily make a start. When Guy rang late the following afternoon she said what he was hoping to hear—yes.

Gerald had hired a car in Sydney, then followed the route to the Hunter Valley—which he had to admit was beautiful. So much so, he made a stop overnight to sample the best of the food and the wine. Surprisingly good. This was his first trip to Australia—the far end of the world. They had the climate and Sydney Harbour, but he had not been prepared for just how much more Australia offered. Sydney was a flourishing metropolis, a world-class city, blessed with the magnificent harbour and glorious beaches within easy reach. He had even been impressed by the massive Sydney Harbour Bridge and the Opera House that occupied a prominent harbourside position. He'd had an excellent view from his luxury hotel.

Nevertheless it was beyond bizarre that his Daniela would want to bury herself not in the metropolis, but in the sticks. This Wangaree Valley, his destination, was still farther on from the Hunter. Who in their right mind would leave London and all it had to offer for a rural valley on the other side of the world, no matter how beautiful and prosperous? There was no logic to it. Rome he might have believed. Not some place called Wangaree Valley, which he had been told was something of a stronghold for the descendants of Australia's sheep barons.

He had led this conversation at Reception, and the very attractive brunette behind the desk had been most forthcoming with information. He had always had a way with women. She had even named a prominent family in the area, the Radcliffes. For a sickening moment his mind had jumped to a connection between Daniela and a Radcliffe, only in the next breath the brunette had told him Guy Radcliffe, the current owner of Wangaree Station, had recently married a girl called Alana Caulfield... Calloway—something like that.

It should be very easy to find her. For the past couple of months he had been unable to think of anything but finding Daniela. One couldn't lose a woman like that without feeling a tremendous jolt. In his thirty-two years of life he had never experienced anything like what he felt for Daniela. He had even come around to the idea of marrying her, if that was what she wanted. His frame of mind hadn't lent itself to his work. He wasn't raking in the usual commissions. Finally the head of the firm, who just happened to be his uncle Philip, had told him to take a break.

'I can't let you handle anything of significance, Gerald. There's something on your mind. Go ahead and sort yourself out.'

Some part of him registered he had treated Daniela badly. Obviously she had become deeply disturbed by his habit of turning up wherever she was, and by the silent phone calls. There was nothing he could do about all that. It had happened. What he had to do now was convince her he had changed. That she had the chance of a wonderful life with him on a grander scale than anything she could possibly aspire to. Offer marriage. Even his difficult to impress mother had commented on how truly beautiful Daniela was. *And such an air!* Daniela should ask herself this question: where would she find better?

After his mother had died so tragically young, Linc had doubted he would ever find true happiness again, find that wonderful contentment he had felt as a boy when he was with his mother. She had been so lovely, so sunny-natured, so full of fun and understanding. Such women were unforgettable. His mother had been taken from him and Chuck, and after her death their father had rarely spoken her name. His dad was one of those men who had to do the macho thing and have little flutters on the side, but he had genuinely loved his wife. That was until her illness had robbed her of her health and her beauty.

Linc was sure his dad didn't love Cheryl. What he felt for Cheryl was lust, pure and simple—plus there was the bonus of having a glamorous young wife on his arm. That meant something to his dad and men like him. Maybe they felt driven to prove something? Either way, he didn't admire his dad. He wished he did, but he didn't. End of story.

His own relationship with Daniela had changed everything. Suddenly he was feeling on top of the world. Full of zest, full of plans. Both of them were working extremely hard—he at Briar's Ridge, where he slogged until his body ached. He had taken on a middling enterprise. He intended to make it big. And Daniela had taken on the job of Executive Chef at Guy's Winery Restaurant. She was pulling in even bigger crowds, some coming from as far away as Sydney. She had spoken to him about it before giving Guy her answer. Her family hadn't wanted to spoil her chances. Neither did he. The only problem was they had less and less time together, so what they did have was doubly precious.

Tonight he was driving into town to her apartment. A quiet dinner; just the two of them. *Perfect*. His heart literally danced in his chest, pulses thrumming like guitars in his ears. They would talk about all that had been happening to them—both of them took a great interest in what the other was doing—and afterwards they would make love. He had never thought of sex as being as addictive as a powerful drug but he was sure what he and Daniela shared together must be on that level. The natural progression from that, in his view, was marriage. He didn't just want to share a table and a bed with her. He wanted to share his entire life. He wanted her to be the mother of his children.

Their children would be a mix of them. They would love them to bits and bring them up right.

He knew in his heart his mother would approve his choice. But neither he nor Daniela had discussed the future, so he decided it was high time to prepare the way. He wasn't going to rush her. There were still some of his questions she wouldn't answer, but he truly believed there was a future for them. How could he let go of this miracle in his life?

He had his own key to her apartment. Even if there were times she was late arriving home, he could always let himself in.

Carl usually arrived right on time. Tonight he was a good twenty minutes early. She didn't mind in the least. She couldn't wait to see him. There were so many things she wanted to tell him. Get everything out in the open. No secrets between them. Instinct told her there was something in his relationship with his stepmother she needed reassuring about. She knew how certain people could scar you. Maybe, like herself, Carl had put himself out of reach of a person who could hurt him.

Swiftly she removed the apron that protected her pretty dress and hurried out into the small foyer, responding to his knock. Clearly he was having trouble finding his keys. She threw open the door, a lovely welcoming smile on her face.

Instantly she lost it. The past had reached out and caught up with her.

Gerald Templeton stood outside her door—handsome, debonair, immaculately dressed, dark wavy hair barbered to perfection, an answering smile on his face. He was carrying a sheaf of long-stemmed red roses which he tried to urge into her nerveless arms.

'Gerald, go away!' she cried in a low throbbing tone. 'I

don't want this. I have absolutely nothing to say to you.'
Hadn't she left London feeling emotionally stripped?

His chiselled face and the soft upper-class voice were
full of pleading. 'Daniela, listen—*please!*'

'No way.' After the way he had persecuted her? She
went to shut the door, but he forcibly held it open.

'I know this is a tremendous surprise,' he said quickly,
a lot of emotions struggling in his good-looking face.
'Please don't send me away. I should have let you know I
was coming. I'm in Australia on business and I thought it
might be better this way—face to face. How are you? You
look more beautiful than ever. Please let me in for a
moment. Is that so much to ask? Please, Daniela, *please*.
Can't we talk?'

Life returned to her limbs. 'I don't know how you found
me, Gerald,' she responded tautly, 'but it should have
become obvious, even to you, that I didn't want to be
found. I'll ask you again to go away.'

He tried a smile, as though this might calm her down.
'Good lord, you wouldn't want to get rid of me so easily,
would you? I've come all this way—mostly to apologise
for what an insensitive brute I was. I have no excuse except
to say I was temporarily off my head. I couldn't bear for
our relationship to end, especially the way it did. All I'm
asking is a few minutes of your time. I think you'll find it
worth your while.'

Now the familiar arrogance was back in play. 'Believe
that and you'll believe anything, Gerald,' she said. 'I accept
your apology. Your behaviour *was* both appalling and
threatening. Now I'd like you to go. I have a guest who will
be arriving at any minute.'

'You're cooking dinner?' Despite himself, he couldn't
keep the lash of jealousy out of his voice. He could smell

the delicious aromas, but that gave him no pleasure. Of course she was cooking dinner. For a *man*. There would always be a man.

She turned her head briefly over her shoulder. 'Yes. So—'

She got no further.

He pushed his way in, casting the beautiful, fragrant roses aside and grasping her arm, compelling her into the living room.

'Get away from me!' Daniela cried, breaking free, horrified by his actions.

'Daniela, calm down—please calm down,' he begged, his expression imploring. 'The last thing in the world I would do is hurt you. How could you think that? I'm here to ask you to marry me.'

'Oh, my God!'

His dark eyes lit. He stared back at her, waiting. Even to his own ears the offer was mind-blowing. She was probably swept off her feet. 'You know you're very fond of me. What we had was good. Given a little time, I know I can make you love me.'

She knew she was under threat. Gerald might look as respectable as they came, but he was unstable. 'You must be insane,' she said. 'You can't *make* me do anything. What about your fiancée? Lady Laurella? Or have you lost her as well?'

Gerald studied her, told her to sit down. Daniela remained on her feet. 'Laurella had my parents' backing,' he said. 'I thought I needed her, but I find I don't. I was trying to please the parents. I've thought this through and through, Daniela. I'm here to beg you to forgive me. I want you to come back with me. We're meant to be together.'

He reached for her, but Daniela's temper, that she had

spent her lifetime keeping under control, flared out of bounds. She wasn't frightened any more. Carl would come. Carl would take care of Gerald Templeton. Everything would be all right.

Linc left in plenty of time to make the drive into town. He was halfway there when he came on an accident. A small car had run off the road and hit a tree. A 4WD was parked on the opposite side of the road. The occupants, he guessed, were the middle-aged couple several feet from the crashed car. He picked up the scene in his headlights. There was no way he could glide past.

He stopped on the steep verge and applied the hand-brake. 'Has an ambulance been called?' He moved swiftly to look inside the car. He checked the ignition was off. A young fellow was slumped against the wheel, mercifully alive, but moaning in pain. There was blood on his face, his head, and down the front of his shirt. He didn't respond when Linc spoke to him, asking how badly he thought he was hurt. To make matters worse Linc had no difficulty picking up the reek of alcohol.

The woman came up to Linc, a sensible-looking coun-trywoman. 'We rang the ambulance right away. He's hardly more than a child. Been drinking, it seems. He must have been speeding and lost control of the wheel. You're the new owner of Briar's Ridge, aren't you?'

'That's right, ma'am. Linc Mastermann.'

'Marjorie Beecham.' She introduced her husband, Alan, who had joined them. The husband, much older, looked very shaken. 'We were just on our way back home,' he said. 'We saw it happen.'

'I don't think we should move him,' Linc said, thinking there could be internal injuries, at least a broken rib.

'That's what we thought,' Mrs Beecham replied. 'Might do more harm than good.'

As they were speaking the ambulance arrived, making a U-turn and then parking in front of Linc's car. A weight of anxiety was taken off their minds. They stayed until the young man had been checked over, then put into the ambulance. The ambulance driver sketched a salute, hopped in the vehicle, then moved off.

The upshot was that Linc was late arriving at Daniela's apartment. He locked his car, then took a step back, glancing up at her floor. The balcony lights were on, flooding over an array of plants and a prolifically flowering white bougainvillaea in a glossy ceramic pot. He would let himself in.

Impetuously he bounded in and out of the empty lift, filled with a wonderful sense of wellbeing. He moved fast down the corridor, his body language expressing a real sense of purpose and his urgency to see her. He wanted to hold her face in his hands. He wanted to kiss her until she was swooning in his arms.

He tapped on the door first to alert her of his arrival, then unlocked it, calling, 'It's me.' Almost at once he knew something was wrong. 'Daniela?'

She usually hurried out to greet him. His eyes fell on a sheaf of red roses that looked as if they had been tossed on the floor. The head of a rose had broken off, to roll a short distance away. Now, that was distinctly odd.

'Daniela?' At once he was as tense as a jungle cat, his muscles coiled to spring.

'It's all right, Carl.'

Sudden relief swept through him. Her voice had come from the bedroom.

'You scared me,' he called, walking down the passage-

way. 'You shouldn't do that.' Even as he moved, he tried
to think it through. Her voice had sounded different…
strained? Then there were the roses. One would hardly
leave roses lying on the floor. That bothered him.

The bedroom door was half shut. He pushed it open, at
the same time keeping well back against the wall. Two
people were in the room. Daniela was standing at the far side
of the room, arms wrapped protectively around herself; a tall,
suavely handsome guy stood immobilised opposite her. The
bed was fully made up with a gold silk brocade quilt and an
array of silk cushions. It was the only barrier between them.

'What the hell?' Linc asked discordantly. He felt stupe-
fied for a moment, none too certain what was going on.

Daniela moved very quickly around the bed, rushing to
his side. She was very pale, her dark eyes huge in her face.
'I knew you'd come.'

He seized her with one arm around her waist, holding her
to him. He could feel the trembling that ran right through
her body. All the while he kept staring at the other man. 'So
who are *you*?' He addressed himself directly to Daniela's
visitor, a guy who looked absolutely trustworthy, though it
was abundantly clear Daniela didn't trust him at all.

The man cleared his throat. 'Gerald Templeton.' He
identified himself as though his name must be distinguished enough to allay anyone's fears. He glanced down
at his watch. 'I expect I should be on my way. I had an appointment fifteen minutes ago.'

Daniela drew even closer to Linc.

'What's he doing here, Daniela?' Linc asked tightly, deliberately blocking Templeton's exit. He needed to find out
what this was all about. Templeton looked fit, around six
feet, a few years older than him by the look of it, but Linc
knew he was strong enough to defend himself if necessary.

'Easily explained,' Templeton broke in, aware the other man, impressively tall and in wonderful shape, was on trigger alert. 'I'm in Sydney on business. I thought as I was so close I'd call on Daniela. We saw quite a bit of each other in London.'

Realisation slotted in. 'So you're the guy who was harassing her?' Linc asked, silver-green eyes narrowing with menace.

Templeton responded to the implied threat. His head fell, not in contrition, more as an indication of deep betrayal. 'Is that what she's been telling you?'

'Come on.' Linc threw him a disgusted, challenging look. 'You were giving her a lot of trouble.'

Templeton looked up, his mouth twisting in a grimace. 'Sorry—it was the other way around. Look, I don't want to say any more. It will only make matters worse. I just came here to ask Daniela to marry me.'

'And you were going to make yourself comfortable in the bedroom while you were doing the asking?' Linc's eyes fairly blazed in his face. He was trying his best to understand, but he was having more trouble than he thought. Clearly this guy was genuinely in love with Daniela.

Templeton appeared to be bracing himself against all insult. 'When Daniela left London she knew things weren't over between us.'

'And you were giving her a little breathing space? Is that it?' Linc was still searching the other man's face in an effort to divine what was really going on.

Daniela shook her head frantically. 'Carl—please.'

Both men ignored her.

'The answer is yes!' Templeton's voice rang with sincerity. 'I love her and she loves me.'

'If she only knew it.' Linc's laugh was harsh, his fists

clenching of their own volition. The anger and confusion that was in him was cresting. Daniela had never fully explained her relationship with this man who had so inopportunely turned up. He looked civilised enough, only Daniela's reactions were telling him something was very wrong.

Now Templeton appealed to Daniela—full of passion and turmoil. 'Aren't you going to say something, darling?' he begged. 'Tell your…friend here, every word I've spoken is the truth. I *did* come here to ask you to marry me?'

'Why don't you just go, Gerald?' Daniela said, her voice dropping to a whisper as she was overcome by a spasm of weakness. Carl had arrived not a moment too soon.

Incredibly, there were tears in Templeton's dark eyes. 'You won't come back with me? You're upset now. I can come again tomorrow.'

'Don't even think about it,' Linc warned, gripping Daniela tighter. 'There have been some big changes around here, Gerald.' He glanced down at Daniela, oddly silent within the curve of his arm. 'I take it you haven't told him?'

'Told me what?' Templeton's eyes riveted themselves to Daniela's face.

'Think, man,' Linc said crisply. 'How can Daniela accept your proposal when she's already accepted mine?'

There was a stunned silence, then Templeton burst out in rage. 'How could you do this to me?' he cried. 'Leading me a fine dance.' He was boiling with fury. 'Coming to Australia was just a stunt to get me to follow you, wasn't it? You wanted to bring me to heel.' His eyes shot to Linc. 'This is one sick girl,' he said, his voice packed with warning and the bitterest disappointment. 'She keeps it hidden, but you'll find out soon enough.'

Linc's face showed no emotion whatsoever, so tight was his self-control. 'How did you get here, Templeton?' he asked.

'I drove—what else?' Templeton thrust a hand violently through his thick dark hair.

'So your car's in the street?'

Templeton nodded, looking like a man who had been dealt a mortal blow. 'Even after everything you've done to me I can't hate you,' he said, his eyes settling once more on Daniela's beautiful face as though mesmerised.

'Why don't I see you to your car?' Linc suggested in a voice that brooked no refusal. 'I have a few questions.'

'And I'll answer them, so help me God!' Templeton let out a strangled breath. 'My beautiful Daniela! I would have given you the world!' He made a visible attempt to pull himself together. 'At least I might be able to stop someone else from putting himself through the same hell I went through.'

'That's not the way it was, Gerald,' Daniela said, raising her head.

'I loved you with my whole heart and soul.' Templeton took several steps towards her, the set of his handsome features ennobled in grief.

'Done. You're done now.' Linc stopped him in his tracks by putting out an arm and steering him backwards. 'I've heard more than enough. You have to leave. *Now.*' He extended an imperative arm to shepherd the other man from the room.

As far as Linc was concerned the evening seemed to have shape-shifted itself into a disaster. What had they been doing talking in the bedroom anyway? Why not the living room? What would it have taken for Templeton to get her into bed? Okay, that made no sense at all. Daniela had known he would be arriving. What she hadn't known was that Templeton was going to ask her to marry him. He'd seen the guy—the smooth, handsome image—heard his voice. English upper class. Social background meant a lot to them. Was it possible Daniela had been hanging out for marriage, as Templeton had claimed? Was Daniela a witch who lived to put men under her spell? He couldn't sustain a thought like that. It was so disloyal.

Sunk in despair, her nerves jangling, Daniela began to put food back in the refrigerator. She covered the salad and mustard seed dressing. The escalopes of tuna to be served with mushrooms and witlof had only to be put under the grill. And Carl loved lime tart, so she had used a classic recipe. But who could eat in this state? She could just imagine what Gerald would be telling Carl. How would he know what were lies and what was real? Gerald was very convincing…

It was to have been a wonderful night. She had realised finally she had to tell Carl the truth about what had happened to drive her to find sanctuary back home. Gerald Templeton had been her worst nightmare. His handsome façade had hidden deep character flaws she had come to find repellent. Until Carl had arrived tonight she had been truly frightened. When Gerald had forced her to go with him to the bedroom her very scalp had crawled. What had he intended to do? She had repeated vehemently that she had a guest arriving. Yes, a *man*, she'd confirmed. A superbly fit young man, who would never permit her to be harmed. It was *he* who should be worried. Yet Gerald hadn't appeared fully capable of taking that in. Or had he thought he could deal with any male guest simply by opening the door and telling him to go away? Gerald's arrogance was unbelievable. She couldn't shake the sense he had intended to use force if need be to get her to agree to what he wanted. What he wanted was *her*.

She gulped down the rest of the glass of Riesling she had been sipping while preparing the meal. It had gone off the chill. She knew Gerald would spread his lies, doing everything in his power to convince Carl she had worked her way into his life, seduced him into falling in love with her and then, when he didn't immediately offer marriage, she had thrown down an ultimatum by fleeing to Australia. Gerald was clever, highly plausible. A by-product of his privileged life was the belief that he could have anything he wanted.

When Carl returned her heart flipped a double beat. 'He's gone?'

Carl, looking grim, threw himself onto a sofa, his expression dark. 'God!' he said soberly. 'How long did you know this guy?'

'A few months.'

'Please…don't hold back.' His extraordinary eyes were aglitter.

She slid down into an armchair, thinking her legs were about to give way on her. 'I'm guessing he said longer?'

'He said you were together a year.'

'He was *lying*!' The words burst from her. She might feel like it, but she wasn't about to dissolve in tears. 'We were *never* together in the way he wanted. And I didn't sleep with him, if that's what you want to know?'

'*Were* you waiting for him to propose marriage?' Was that possible? Linc stared across at her. She was wearing a dress new to him, in a shade of red that was perfect with her golden complexion. He didn't think any man could want a woman more. 'It's a ploy that's worked since Anne Boleyn,' he suggested, with a sardonic shrug.

She shook her head sadly. 'I thought you knew me better than that. There's a devil in Gerald. I missed it completely when we first met. He was—well, you saw him. Gerald looks the quintessential English gentleman. We had dinner a number of times. We went to concerts, the theatre, art galleries. He took me down to his parents' country home, a very impressive place.'

'Sounds like he wanted you to meet them.' Linc watched the play of emotions on her beautiful face. Her stress was palpable. And because of the strength of his feeling for her his sexual jealousy had been unleashed.

'Not at all. A party was going on, and I was aware Gerald's parents had a suitable bride lined up for him—a Lady Laurella Marks, one of his own circle. What Gerald had in mind for me was the role of mistress. Let's see— mistresses were invented long before Anne Boleyn, weren't they?' Now her soft, honeyed voice held a trace of bitterness.

'He said you were lovers.' Not long after that he had hit Templeton's sneering, abruptly coarse mouth.

'Don't you think I would have told you if we were?' Her dark eyes were brilliant with unshed tears.

'Daniela, you haven't told me much at all.' He sighed. 'How does a man get to be obsessed with a woman when he hasn't even made love to her?'

Colour flamed in her cheeks. 'I didn't say he hadn't made love to me. It stopped short of sex.'

'Were you teasing him? Goading him?' There were so many images in his mind.

That hurt like an open wound. 'No. I was becoming increasingly uneasy about him. It got to the point he was ringing me—checking up on me—sometimes twelve times a day. He once accused me of starting an affair with a friend of his. He couldn't have been more wrong. It didn't seem to mean anything to him that his friend was married—happily married, I might add. To Gerald there was a certain cachet in having a loving wife and an exhilarating mistress. Why are you so angry anyway? You appear to have fallen for his lies.'

His eyes glinted. 'Not at all, but I'm feeling a little lost, and I have to admit jealous. Anyway it's becoming plain he was trying to poison *our* relationship.'

'Which is?' she asked quietly.

'Well, we *are* sleeping together.' He found himself responding to the turbulence in the air.

That hurt, too. 'Tell me about your stepmother?' she retaliated. *He* was the one who had opened the envelope. See how *he* reacted. 'Or are you afraid to?'

Linc thumped a hand on the arm of the sofa. 'Don't be ridiculous.' A muscle twitched along his taut jawline.

'You're not fond of her? *Too* fond of her?' *I mustn't do this. It's crazy!*

'I loathe her,' Linc muttered between his fine white teeth.

'But she doesn't loathe you?' Jealousy appeared to be driving them both.

That upset Linc. He had done everything in his power to give Cheryl a wide berth. 'Why talk about Cheryl? She isn't a part of this. Perhaps I ought to go?' He stood up, knowing the evening had been ruined but somehow unable to save it. Templeton had said things that had really got under his skin. No wonder his temper had got the better of him.

'Please yourself.' Daniela rose as well, her surface antagonism hiding a wealth of hurt feelings. Gerald had afflicted them both with his venom. 'But go and you don't come back,' she said, in the full bloom of upset.

For a moment he didn't answer, and then he came slowly towards her. 'You know, I think you're really, *really* clever.'

She threw up her chin, her dark eyes brilliant with anger. 'What do you mean?'

'These ultimatums,' he said.

'You don't trust me?'

Why the hell didn't he confirm his trust in her? Jealousy was such a dangerous thing. It made a man say things he shouldn't. 'You're *my* witch,' he said. 'Why not Templeton's? Besides, you obviously don't trust *me*.'

'Then mightn't it be a good time to call it a day?' Sadness suddenly enveloped her like a cloud. Men stuck together. Woman was the temptress of choice.

She stared away and Linc took her by the shoulders, overwhelmed by her closeness and hating what was happening. 'Is that what you want? Talk to me, Daniela,' he pleaded. 'I'm crazy about you. You know that. But you confuse me.'

She threw up her head, tears in her eyes.

'Why do you cry? *Why?*' The hunger in him surged out of bounds. He could feel it all through his body, his heart, his lungs and his chest.

'I'm *not* crying,' she said, setting her delicate jaw. 'How can you possibly care about me and yet be ready to believe an unstable man like Gerald Templeton?' she accused him. 'I fled a great job, friends, to come home and escape him. He made my life a nightmare. He rang my phone endlessly and never spoke. He was somewhere there, wherever I was. Across the street, in the same building, in shops, parked in the street where I lived. You can't know what it was like!' She drew a long shuddering breath as disturbing memories hit her afresh.

A vertical line split Linc's black brows. 'You could have got a restraining order,' he said reasonably.

'You think that would have kept him away? His name

carries weight in the City. Who was *I*? Besides, unstable people follow rules of their own. Do you know how many wives, girlfriends have taken out restraining orders only to be beaten up or killed? Some men are brutes. Don't for a minute think the upper classes are excluded. Gerald was brought up to believe he could have anything he liked. Certainly any woman. He wasn't a womaniser, but he wanted *me*. I desperately wanted to be left alone. That's why I had to move away. He could come back, for all I know.'

A truly daunting expression crossed Linc's face. 'He *won't* be coming back.' He spoke emphatically. 'Men like Templeton see women as helpless victims, easy marks. Essentially they're bullies on some sort of power kick. Templeton won't want to stick around here while I'm on the scene. You can be sure of that.'

'You told him you'd proposed to me.' She didn't look at him as she said it. She didn't know where they were any more.

'I did.' Linc nodded briskly. 'And I told him it really wouldn't be worth his while if he ever came near you again. I honestly think he paid attention.'

She had to force herself to move away. 'I feel sick, Linc. I think you should go.'

He grieved for the friction between them. He certainly wasn't about to leave her. 'Sorry. I'm staying here,' he said quietly. 'I won't bother you in any way. I can sleep on the couch. I just want you to know I'm here with you.' He was silent for a moment, then he burst out, 'Hell, I'm hungry. Let me put something together for you. It might make you feel better. I was so looking forward to tonight.'

'So was I.' Her gaze went to the roses that Gerald had pitched to the floor. 'Now it's destroyed.'

'I won't let you say that!' Linc's voice was full of intensity. 'Men like Templeton set out to be destroyers. They can't achieve their aims if you don't let them. Let's settle down, Daniela. *Please*. I could do with a drink. Let me get you one, too.'

Linc took a long time going to sleep. It wasn't just that his tall frame was way too long for the sofa—it sure was. It was more that he was wound up so tight it was damned near impossible to unwind. How could he when he was desperately trying to subdue what Daniela might see as the brute or the beast in him? No getting away from it—some of the male of the species had a brutal streak.

He could have kissed her, to the point where her own sexual needs were too driving to be refused. He knew he could have done that. On the other hand he knew he wouldn't. That would make him no better than Templeton, with his sick fantasies. The sooner it was morning the better. Maybe both of them needed to take a step away. Or maybe—he groaned—they needed to get closer. He only had to walk down the corridor, but he loved her too much.

Loved her?

Isn't that it, Mastermann? You love her. Nothing can change that.

He awoke with a start, his body tensed up. 'Daniela!' He wrenched himself halfway up, abs and chest tight. 'Are you okay?'

She was bending over him, her hand on his shoulder. 'I couldn't sleep,' she said, in her soft, mellifluous voice.

God, the *sweetness* of her! She had come to him. Felt the need. That thrilled him to the core.

She started to crawl over him, her hands seeking his face, the ridges of his cheekbones, the line of his jaw, then slipping down to his chest, clawing on a whorl of hair. Her touch was electric. Impulses were shooting all over his body. He could no longer hold off. He hauled her onto his lap, tilting her head back over his arm and burying his face against her throat. The flavour of her skin was exquisite. She was wearing a nightgown, a mist of a thing, and his seeking hands, desperate to touch her all over, told him she wore nothing beneath it.

'I w-want you so much,' he stammered, his strong hands trembling with emotion. 'I'm sorry about earlier. I over-reacted. I—'

'Hush!' She pulled his head down to her, pressing her mouth against his as though there had been enough words. Desire was rocketing through him, made all the more powerful because he felt the matching desire in her. His body was so heated it was as if he was about to burst into flames. He manoeuvred his arms beneath her with the greatest care, lifting them both clear of the sofa while she clung to him, yielding so magically he moaned with the pleasure.

There were no words beyond that. Just breathtaking intensity, ecstasy to come.

Whatever the future held, they would face it together.

CHAPTER NINE

VIOLETTE DENBY drove into town, her driving fast and confident, matching her personality—or so she thought. Violette, in actual fact, drove as if no one else was on the road, or indeed had any right to be. Hairy for those coming the other way and finding Violette's car holding centre line.

Violette Danby had never been known to give ground or acknowledge that courtesy from anyone else. Violette Denby was incredibly smug. She was angry, too, and feeling betrayed. Lilli, who had followed her in all things since they were bits of kids, had gone back to Sydney with a parting shot.

'You've always been your own worst enemy, Vi! You know what I'm saying? You're a loser. I don't want to be one.'

She had been stunned by her sister's insubordination. It had struck her as bitterly cruel. Today she had a lunch appointment with the most sycophantic of her circle, Pammy Moreton. She needed soothing, and Pammy was the one to do it. It didn't strike her as odd that she had chosen Aldo's Bistro for the lunch venue. Quite simply, it offered the best food in the town. It was a Friday, so she knew the *Outsider* wouldn't be there. She had taken over the management of Guy's restaurant while the resident chef was in Hong Kong. Violette had shut her ears to all the good things she was hearing about the new chef. Okay, the *Outsider* knew her way around a restaurant kitchen. She could cook. She could manage staff. So what if she hadn't even found her way into a kitchen yet? Cooking was not in her repertoire.

She was early for the appointment. For one thing she had a few errands to run. Things she usually got Lilli to do. The town was abuzz with people. Friday was a busy day. She acknowledged those worth saying hello to and walked determinedly past the rest.

Those stuck-up Denbys. Just about everyone hoped one day Violette Denby, the worst offender, would trip over something on the pavement and fall flat on her face.

Violette, blissfully unaware and uncaring anyway of the general disgust, was coming out of the local pharmacy when her attention was arrested by the sight of a stranger in town—a very glamorous blonde in her early thirties. Maybe she was a little bit too curvy—Violette was totally against *too* much curve—but she watched with interest as the blonde stepped away from a swish coupé, bleeping it locked over her shoulder.

Ah, one of us!

Violette licked her top lip. The big question was, who was she? What was she doing here? Most tourists spent their time in the Hunter Valley. Those whose big interest was good food and wine found their way farther on to Wangaree. Guy's restaurant had received extravagant praise from the food critics. Even she couldn't fail to notice what had been said about the current chef in the newspapers. She had brooded a whole day over that. What was so good about *tori shisomaki*—whatever that was? She'd sooner a duck mousse any day.

The blond woman—as a natural blonde herself, Violette unerringly spotted a great dye job—walked to the pavement, looking around her rather hesitantly. Am I really going to go up to her? Violette thought. Yes, I am. It wasn't the sort of thing she did with strangers, but something told her this woman was in town for a purpose. That thought stirred up memories. Hadn't Ben Mastermann, Linc's father and a prominent wool producer like her own father, remarried a few years ago? It was all coming back to her now. She was sure she had seen a photograph somewhere of the latest Mrs Mastermann—a great deal younger than her husband, and an eye-catching platinum blonde.

At the last count, two and two still made four! Now, this could be really juicy. Violette almost sprinted towards her. She might even invite Mrs Mastermann—she had a powerful perception that was who she was—to join her and Pammy for lunch. She couldn't stand Pammy's gushing *all* the time anyway. She had a little bet with herself that the glamorous Mrs Mastermann was here to pay her drop-dead sexy stepson a visit. Linc Mastermann would make any woman's sense of decency and caution twirl in the air before taking a nosedive.

Violette fixed a brilliant smile to her face. She elbowed a fellow pedestrian rudely out of the way and moved towards the other woman.

'Hello, there! You look lost.'

The woman looked back at Violette, saw a tall, equally glamorous young woman and smiled back. 'Don't I know it! I'm looking for a property called Briar's Ridge. Do you happen to know it?'

'I certainly do!'

Double whammy!

* * *

Daniela thought about leaving her mail until the following day. There was probably nothing important. It had been a long night. She'd had to break in a new assistant who was lacking confidence and she was tired. She knew it was because she was going all out to make an impression. She greatly admired Guy's resident chef, but she had her own ideas about everything. The glowing review in the papers hadn't hurt. The food writers had made big mention of her 'brilliant application of both French and Japanese cuisine'. As Carl had predicted, this stand-in time was proving her showcase.

No one was around. She parked her car on the drive and made a dash for the rows of letterboxes, key in hand. She unlocked hers quickly, then withdrew half a dozen letters and a postcard from California. That would be from an old friend who had scored a great job there.

Back in her car, she used the remote to open the huge security gates, then drove in to the basement car park. It wasn't until she was inside her apartment that she bothered to check the other mail. Two bills, one letter from Gerald—she knew his handwriting—plus another minus a postage stamp, with her name and address printed, one might have thought, by a child's hand. Wasn't that standard for an anonymous letter?

Her mind sprang to something bad. Her premonitions always had been very sharp. Should she open it? Would it matter if she tore it up? Gerald's letter bore a stamp. Then there was his fine handwriting. Not a follow-up from Gerald, then? Not Gerald's style. It saddened her that with so much going for him Gerald Templeton was only handsome and presentable on the outside. She ran a fingernail beneath the flap. There was a photograph tucked inside a sheet of notepaper—very ordinary notepaper that one could buy at any supermarket. The photograph fell to the floor. She bent to pick it up, standing motionless while she studied it.

She had never seen the woman before, and she would remember her. Once seen, it was unlikely anyone would forget this women and her showgirl beauty. She was an eye-catching platinum blonde, quite shapely, expensively and very glamorously dressed. She was standing beside a car, a Mercedes. Daniela had no difficulty recognising the main street of the town.

This was no joke, and she couldn't pretend it was. The photograph had been sent with only one purpose in mind. To upset her. Daniela released a jagged sigh. The anonymity of it all was appalling, gutless. She hated it. People who couldn't put their name to something were always up to no good. It appeared she attracted such people.

She opened out the sheet of notepaper, stomach muscles clenching.

Don't you think your boyfriend should have told you about Stepmama? From what I hear they are way too close for comfort.

Daniela's skin tingled with shock. She was riveted by the horribleness of it all. The truly sickening thing was some part of her had been waiting for something like this. Her hand crunched up the sheet of paper in disgust before she tossed it from her. Reluctantly she took another look at the photograph, feeling as if her whole world was imploding.

She had a pretty good idea who had sent it. Violette Denby was one combative character and she emerged the clear favourite—though Daniela knew she could never prove it. The subject of the photograph just had to be Carl's stepmother.

Lover?

No way! Daniela took a deep breath, regaining her composure.

From all that had passed between them Daniela was totally convinced Carl was a moral man. What could the sender of the photograph know to back up this sick claim? It wasn't as though Carl had been deceptive about the situation. He hadn't lied. It was more he hadn't told her the truth. Was it remotely possible this woman had been involved with both father and son?

No! Her whole being screamed rejection. The man she realised she had come to love had far too much integrity. She firmly believed that.

Or did being deeply in love with someone automatically ensure trust and a fierce loyalty?

The voice in her head required a response. What had happened to Carl to drive him away from his own home and family? He had told her since his father's latest marriage he and his brother had been virtually running the family property, one of the finest and most productive sheep stations in the country. Why would he turn his back on such family heritage and go in search of a new life? She had gathered his father had been very angry with him, seeing his moving away as a betrayal. She had tried to question him about his stepmother but he had cut her off, as though his stepmother had absolutely nothing to do with anything. She had seen the pent-up exasperation on his face at the very mention of her.

Which brought her to the question of seduction. Some women boasted with good reason of their powers to seduce. A man might find it difficult to hold out against a campaign of temptation. Could Cheryl Mastermann have constituted such a threat? And Carl had seen getting as far away from home as possible as the only way out?

Hadn't she done the same thing?

Yet here was Cheryl Mastermann, surfacing in a big way.

It didn't matter who you were, Daniela thought bleakly, or of what station in life. It was possible to be victimised. All one had to do was cross the path of one wrong person. Such people operated on an entirely different moral plane. The normal restraints most people abided by simply weren't there. The idea made her sick to her stomach.

Determined not to freak out, she ripped open Gerald's letter. If there were any more little scares in store for her, she might as well confront them. She couldn't turn away from all this. She had to get it out in the open.

It seemed there were no further threats from Gerald. Only spleen. Whatever Carl had threatened Gerald with it must have been bad, she thought wryly. A psychiatrist really should see this. It was Gerald at his very worst—or, then again, his best. Impossible as it was to believe, Gerald had convinced himself his behaviour all along had been entirely honourable. *She* was the one who should look for forgiveness. He cited a long list of her sins that went on like a criminal history. Daniela winced at the viciousness of it all. To her, it was testimony to Gerald's instability.

> *I hope that Aussie fool you've got yourself involved with gives you as much hell as you've given me.*

For some reason that made her laugh. If Gerald didn't like the tough Australian male he should get out of this country as soon as possible.

Weekends didn't really mean a thing for the man on the land. There was always work to be done. Linc had spent the morning at the extreme end of the property, repairing a fence with Buddy. It was actually Buddy who had knocked it down when Linc had given him a go on the tractor, ploughing a fire break. Thank God *that* job was over. He and George had worked day and night getting the job done. Not that it was ever really done. Constant maintenance had to be carried out in case of cave-ins.

Spring had swung into summer, and it was getting hotter by the day—still no rain, but lots of dry storms, with spectacular cloud build-up raising hopes that were soon dashed. He had rid the property of any areas of tall grass and dried brush that could act as tinder. The homestead and all the outbuildings were well cleared. But the constant worry was that there could be someone driving through the valley who thought nothing of pitching a cigarette butt out of the window. Even in the heat the paddocks were embroidered with daisies and wildflowers and now he and Buddy rode companionably back towards the homestead, where he planned to give the shearing sheds extra attention. Buddy had the afternoon off to play cricket. From all accounts Buddy was developing into a top spinner. The Australian Cricket team was an inspiration to him, and millions of other Australian youngsters. Linc was pleased with Buddy. He was a good worker, ready to take on anything, and he was great with the horses—shoeing no problem. George Rankin had proved a fine mentor, too. Best of all, George had had a lot of experience classing superfine wool. Years before, he had topped his own wool-classing course. Linc was very comfortable in the knowledge that he and George could handle their own clip without bringing in another experienced wool-classer.

The creek, a natural fuel brake, glittered metallic in the hot sun. He parted company with Buddy and rode on. Nearing the homestead, he saw a sleek car turn into the gravelled drive. At first his mind sprang to one of the Denby sisters, but as he drew closer, familiar with luxury cars, he recognised the late-model coupé. He thought the driver was a woman. If that were the case, there was no question who it was. It had to be Cheryl, in her new toy.

He was stunned at her audacity. Unless she had his dad with her? He began to pray that was the case. Only his dad never let a woman do the driving for him, even his 'angel'! Some *angel*. He could ride away in the opposite direction, only he knew whenever he returned she would be sitting waiting for him. Cheryl didn't have angels' wings. They were more like a bird of prey's.

From her vantage point in the cool of the wide verandah, Cheryl watched for Linc to round the side of the homestead. Freshly painted, with a thick border of agapanthus lining either side of the short flight of front steps, the homestead was amazingly attractive, she thought. She could even live here. If only she had met Linc before she'd met his father! There was no justice in life. Thank God husbands could be pushed aside.

Cheryl had no idea that trying to push Ben Mastermann aside would be like trying to sidestep a charging rhino.

And here was Linc! She was hungry for the sight of him, and not ashamed to admit it. If the person who had first said 'out of sight out of mind' had met Linc Mastermann they might have changed their idea—especially if that person had been a woman. A broad-brimmed akubra covered his glossy crow-black head. It was tilted at a rakish angle. He wore a blue and white checked shirt, tight-fitting jeans, dusty boots on his feet. Inside the neck of his shirt he had wound a red bandanna, to protect his nape from the burning sun. Even his walk was so sexy she had to catch her breath.

She stood up at his approach, smoothing her tight skirt. She knew this was going to be awkward, but she thought she could handle it. She knew she looked gorgeous. One guy had once told her there were just no words to describe how gorgeous she was. Her looks, even more embellished since Linc had last seen her, always gave her a huge boost in confidence. She could coax her dear husband out of his blackest moods.

Linc spoke first. 'What the hell are you doing here, Cheryl?' he asked flatly. It was all he could do not to tell her to clear off the property and not come back. 'Where's Dad?'

At the daunting expression on her stepson's striking face Cheryl's heart began driving like a piston. His polished bronze skin was sheened with sweat. His muscular arms were grained with fine dust. God, it made her *hot*! She had never wanted a man so badly in her life.

'Is that any way to greet me?' she cooed, making her voice as sweetly innocent as she could. No mean feat, considering she was an experienced woman of the world. 'I got lonely. Your dad is in China, of all places,' she jeered.

'China is Australia's major trading partner, Cheryl,' he told her shortly, coming up the steps with that amazing easy grace. 'They're the biggest buyers of our wool and one of their most prominent new buildings is being constructed from Australian steel from the Pilbara. It might pay you to bone up.'

Cheryl dipped her platinum head. She had had her hair recoloured before she came, so she was certain of pristine roots. 'I always thought it was damaging to a woman to be too smart,' she quipped, fixing her big blue orbs on him. 'Look, I know you have every right to be angry at me, Linc,' she started quietly, just as she had rehearsed. 'My behaviour was inexcusable. I just misunderstood—'

'You certainly did.' He cut her off before she could finish her rehearsed spiel. 'Are you such a fool you could think Dad would tolerate your looking sideways at another man, let alone infidelity? You know all about his temper. He mightn't have unleashed it on you yet, but ask anyone who knows him. I'd hate to think of a bloke getting shot over you, Cheryl. You've taken a big risk even coming here. Does Chuck know?'

Again she looked at him with feigned innocence. 'No, he doesn't. I told Chuck I was spending the weekend on the Gold Coast, looking up old friends.'

'Old customers?' he asked contemptuously, pulling off the akubra and shaking his head.

Sweat had made his hair curl in tight clusters. He still wore it long on the nape. He had great hair. Something told her not to stare at him too much. Difficult when she was presented with the splendour of him. He smelt hot and spicy, but clean.

'*Girl*friends,' she corrected, pursing her full lips. She had a luscious mouth. No worries there. And she'd had all her front teeth capped. Not that there'd been anything wrong with them before, but now they were perfect. 'Could we go in? I'd love a cup of coffee.'

'Why didn't you get one in town?' he returned smartly.

'Look, Linc.' It was time to plead. 'I want us to start over.'

'Really?'

He stared her down with those shimmering silvery green eyes. She had never, ever seen eyes that exact colour. 'You must believe me. The last thing I want is to cause a rift in the family. Your father loves you. He misses you. Chuck does. So do I. We're family! We should all be friends.'

'So why didn't you tell Dad and Chuck you were going to pay me a visit?' He tossed his hat onto a planter's chair.

'A drink of cold water, then?' she pleaded, putting a perfectly manicured hand to her temple. 'The heat is making me a little sick.'

'Not pregnant, are we?' he asked satirically.

'I like to think one day I will be.' She gave him a valiant smile, though she had no intention of ever coming off the pill. She had heard that childbirth was a million times worse than root canal, never mind having a tooth capped.

'Then you better get a move on,' Linc returned harshly, having been exposed to Cheryl's little games for too long. 'Come in. I need to take a shower. I'll show you the kitchen. Maybe you can make us both a cup of coffee?'

She visibly relaxed. 'Sure!' She gave him a great big smile. She could well afford to. She knew it wouldn't be easy, but somehow she was going to get him to talk. Open up. After a while he might ease up on that spring-loaded tension which only served to make her desire him more. She was going to be a whole lot smarter this time. Jumping the gun had been her one big mistake. Usually men just rolled over when offered sex. Not Linc. She needed to get to him at a really weak moment. Maybe drunk? What she so desperately needed from him could wait a little while.

Daniela planned to be at the restaurant until around five. She liked to be early, making sure everything was in order. Saturday was their biggest night, and they had a full house. She liked to run a relaxed kitchen. Not easy, but it could be done. The team she had under her had had years of experience in top restaurants. They were highly trained, with a passion for cooking and experimentation, and they had understood immediately what she was trying to do, passionately interested in getting the formula right.

That note and the accompanying photograph had put a

lot of pressure on her. She couldn't get it out of her mind. Hating what she was doing—ashamed of it, really—she rang the top hotel in the valley to ask if a Mrs Cheryl Mastermann was staying there. Surprise, surprise! They said Mrs Mastermann most certainly was, with a fair bit of gush. Unfortunately they couldn't put her through to Mrs Mastermann's suite—though she hadn't actually asked for them to do that—because the concierge had Mrs Mastermann's car ready for her. Mrs Mastermann had told them she was going out for the afternoon.

You bet she was going out for the afternoon, Daniela thought dismally. She'd have a plan. And she just bet the hotel staff had bent their heads together over *that* one. Mrs Cheryl Mastermann, and Linc Mastermann already making a name for himself in the valley. What was the connection? One thing was certain—their guest surely wasn't his *mum*.

By two o'clock Daniela knew what she was going to do. She was going to drive out to Briar's Ridge and see Carl. No reason why she shouldn't. With everything that was between them it was the normal thing to do. He wouldn't know she was coming. Ordinarily she would ring, but today she didn't.

Why, Daniela? her inner voice asked. *What's the motivation here, girl?*

It isn't a crime, is it, to be a little bit suspicious?

The trouble was, she couldn't help thinking it might be. She wanted—needed—to push her love for Carl to its outer limits. Love relied heavily on trust, didn't it? Otherwise every wife in the country would be demanding her husband fill in a daily logbook to be pored over at his return. Carl had convinced her he trusted her over what had happened with Gerald. Why couldn't she do the same for him? She could readily believe his stepmother—only a handful of years older—would be attracted to him. Carl had a powerful sexual aura. They had lived together in the same house. Probably they had gone for long rides together.

It was all her fault. Just so had Adam rounded on Eve.

Get out there to Briar's Ridge! Her inner voice told her. *Stop beating yourself up.*

The closer she drew to Briar's Ridge, the worse Daniela felt. He would hate her checking up on him. She didn't blame him. On the other hand, he didn't know anything about the 'anonymous' letter sent to her by Violette Denby. Probably Violette thought anonymous letters were just quaint little customs. Something thought up by the do-gooders of this world. If his stepmother wasn't there Daniela supposed she could say she was in the area to expand her knowledge on the valley's hot air ballooning, for example—no harm done. And Carl would conclude she couldn't wait until later tonight to see him.

If Cheryl Mastermann *was* there, what was she doing to do? She was too civilised to give in to primitive urges like pulling hair. She had a certain view of herself. Was there such a thing as an innocent visit? Of course there was.

You're talking about a blond bombshell here, girl!

Innocent herself, Daniela felt very guilty.

It was a brilliantly fine day. Too fine and too hot, with a north-westerly blowing up. People in rural areas in times of drought feared the north and north-westerlies, she had been told. The deep blue sky had an odd metallic glint, the sun beating down like an anvil. Daniela drove down the cool avenue of trees, then turned into the circular drive, the gravel almost blindingly white.

Push off again. Don't stop.

A very expensive-looking car was parked in the coolest

spot beneath the overhanging grevilleas so brilliant with golden and dark pink colour.

Her inner voice suddenly chipped in. *Fight for your man. Don't you think you should?*

Daniela switched off the ignition and lifted her knuckles to her mouth. Restraint was what she did best. For all her Italian heritage, she was no simmering volcano.

This man is worth everything you've got. You want him, don't you?

She wanted *him* all right. Him and his children. Mere seconds later Daniela had transported herself to the verandah, knocking on the open door. 'Carl?'

There was a long silence. Where were they? She didn't feel up to barging in. She couldn't believe Carl might be double-crossing her, but if she found them together she might well throw up. She called out again, louder this time. Was there any such thing as lasting love, lasting fidelity?

Of course there is, girl! Think of your parents, your grandparents.

True, they had been blessed in that way. But they had been essentially good people, who'd held family very close. Carl had been brought up in a highly dysfunctional family. Sometimes people in that situation turned out very differently. His dad didn't sound like much of a role model.

What the hell? She might as well go and get it over. She was ready to *marry* him. She had even been thinking about her wedding gown. It would be glorious. She had just the style in mind. And she had begun thinking about brides-maids. Alana, who had been so warm and welcoming, would be matron of honour, and then her first cousin Sarina, and Lyndsey, her long-time friend from their schooldays and lovely Sondra in California if she could make it. If she were honest, she would have to admit she was well into the whole wedding thing, like a woman who had finally found her way.

Just as she was moving purposefully into the living room a blond woman suddenly appeared from the rear of the house. On sighting Daniela she frowned in apparent shock, and with more than a touch of indignation. 'Can I help you?' she asked sharply, regarding Daniela from head to toe.

Indeed, to Daniela's eyes it looked very much as if she was shortly to be asked to provide ID. 'I'm sorry if I startled you,' she said pleasantly. 'You didn't hear my knock?' Best to answer question with question. 'I called out a couple of times. I'm Daniela Adami. I'm a friend of Carl's. Would he be at home?'

The woman replied with great reluctance. 'He's not right now,' she said, with an upward toss of her platinum head. She was dressed in a beautiful pink chiffon shirt with a ruby sequin trim, and a figure-hugging skirt with tiny ruby-coloured spots. Not normal dress for the country, but then she was the sort of woman who could cause city traffic jams, Daniela thought. Glitzy as they come.

'So where is he?' Daniela asked, still keeping her tone non-confrontational. Wasn't the best way to get through life to be civil? *Oh, quit being so damned polite, Daniela*, the voice in her head broke in disgustedly. 'And *you* are?' she responded to that voice, her tone picking up a brisk notch.

'I'm Cheryl Mastermann,' the woman replied, as though it was none of Daniela's damned business.

'Ah, yes.' Daniela nodded gently. 'You're Carl's step-mother. I do hope you're going to tell me his father is here? I'm so looking forward to meeting him.'

'My husband is in China,' Cheryl clipped off, not at all happy with this turn of events. The last thing she had

expected was another blonde to blow her out of the water.
Not that Cheryl was a blonde, actually. But it hadn't been
until she'd turned blonde that her love life had really taken
off. The fact that Linc's visitor was a true blonde as
opposed to bleached blonde, with contrasting large velvety
dark eyes, only compounded her chagrin.

'So is that why you waited to visit Carl?' Daniela asked.

It was a totally unexpected broadside. This woman
didn't look remotely as if she got into broadsides. 'What?'
Cheryl placed her hands belligerently on her curvy hips.
'What's that supposed to mean?'

'I suppose it means exactly what you think it means,
Mrs Mastermann,' Daniela said. 'Where is Carl?'

'Don't you mean Linc? Everyone calls him Linc.' Cheryl
eyed Daniela with a mixture of outrage and perplexity.

'Yes, I understand that,' Daniela said. 'It's just that Carl
came more naturally to me.'

'You're saying you *have* to be different?' Cheryl glared.

'No. I'm saying I have to be myself. Are you
staying or are you going straight back into town, Mrs
Mastermann?'

Cheryl looked taken aback. In fact she was genuinely perplexed. 'That's up to Linc,' she said. 'I've only just arrived.'

'You were planning to stay the night?'

'Look, my dear, why don't you shut the hell up?' Cheryl
suddenly snapped. 'What Linc and I do is our business.
This has gone far enough. I have to tell you Linc has never
mentioned *you*.'

'I know someone who has!' was Daniela's instant retort.
'Violette Denby. She must have spotted you in town.'

'We had lunch, as a matter of fact,' Cheryl freely admitted. 'I liked her. She's very clued up on what's happening in the district.'

'And you told her the reason you were in the valley?'

'Of course. Listen, this is getting ridiculous. I don't have to answer to *you*.' That Cheryl was fast losing confidence, despite herself.

'You've made a mistake there, Mrs Mastermann,' Daniela told her quietly. 'Carl and I are on the point of getting engaged. Matrimony not too far behind. Neither of us can wait.'

Cheryl was poleaxed. Linc getting *married*? Hell, he hadn't even had time to settle in, let alone find a bride. Cheryl dropped all pretence of a feminine pose, even her carefully cultivated accent. 'What are you saying?' she yelled, her clear skin blotching fiercely. 'I don't believe it!'

'True.' Daniela confirmed, inclining her head. 'Surely you didn't cast yourself as in with a chance? I understand your husband is a very aggressive man. Wouldn't you find it a tad difficult trying to get away from him, even if Carl had been thinking along your lines? Death by shooting your husband might find too tame.'

Cheryl abruptly bent over, as if pain was jack-knifing through her body. Here she was thinking divorce, when Linc was thinking marriage. It couldn't be true.

Daniela made a quick move towards her. 'Mrs Mastermann, are you all right?' she asked in automatic concern.

Cheryl snapped bolt upright, eyes afire. 'You're sleeping together?' she gritted through perfect white teeth.

'Does that shock you?' Daniela spoke almost kindly.

'You realise he was sleeping with me?'

Here it is, girl. Your trust in the man you love is on the line.

'Then you'll know all about the unusual birthmark on his left flank?' Daniela said.

Cheryl hooted, surveying Daniela with scorn. 'Of course I do. For your information, I didn't mean to fall in love with

Linc. I dedicated myself to acting with the utmost propriety. You've no idea how difficult it has been, trying to cauterise my emotions. It *tortured* me, living in the same house.'

'So Linc made the first move?' Daniela pressed her for an answer.

Cheryl's hard blue eyes suddenly swam with tears. 'Do you think he didn't fight it?'

'It must have been a very grim situation,' Daniela said, implying sympathy. 'So what brought it to a head? What happened to drive him away to seek a new life?'

'What do you *think*?' Cheryl cried with magnificent abandon. 'He was trying to do the honourable thing. So was I.'

'But you still want him?'

'And he stills wants me.' Cheryl pressed the back of her hand against her hot cheek. Her colour had come up so fast it looked near life-threatening. 'If you're telling the truth about an engagement, it will never work. Linc is trying to forget me, but I'm in his blood.'

'Why don't we sort that out right now?' Daniela suggested. 'Just tell me where he went. If he truly loves you, it stands to reason I can't marry him.'

'Well put! I can readily understand that,' Cheryl said, at once part of the sisterhood. 'Why demean yourself by asking him, though? Why don't you simply break up with him?'

'I would like to give a reason,' Daniela said. 'Where did he go?'

Cheryl became agitated. 'I have no idea!' Her face beneath the immaculate make-up turned abruptly from scarlet to pale as paper. 'Some rough-head, a leathery yokel called George, came to the door. They talked a while, then Linc took off.'

'Don't worry. I'll find him,' Daniela said.

* * *

Walking back to the homestead with one eye on the sky—
it looked as though another dry storm was not too far off—
Linc thought how fortunate he was having George. It was
George's day to visit his sister in town, but he had opted
to stay put. Like Linc and the rest of the valley, the north-
westerlies had made George uneasy.

Rounding the side of the house, he saw to his surprise
Daniela's little runabout parked a few feet from Cheryl's
car. An uncontrollable anger flared through him. Cheryl
was the sort of woman who believed she could have any
man she wanted if only she schemed hard enough. She had
landed his dad, and his dad wouldn't have been a push-
over. He didn't have the slightest doubt that on meeting
Daniela Cheryl would be hell-bent on convincing her the
two of them had shared an illicit relationship. It might be
a fantasy played out in Cheryl's head, but did Cheryl care
about that?

Amazing things happened to people who thought
positive. He had been hoping Cheryl would be gone by the
time he arrived back. He had certainly told her that was the
way to go. But Cheryl, the inveterate schemer, had held on.
He hadn't been expecting Daniela until late that night,
when she had finished at the restaurant. Ordinarily he
would have been thrilled she had called in to see him—only
Cheryl was a dangerous as a hammerhead shark.

Linc picked up pace, near running up the front steps just
as Daniela was coming out of the house. 'Hi! This is a
surprise.' His eyes embraced her, even as they sought to
detect her mood.

'I was just coming to find you.' She sounded just the
faintest bit shaken out of her natural calm. 'I've met Cheryl.'

Linc held up a darkly tanned callused hand. 'Then I have

only one thing to say. It's all lies. Cheryl is having a mid-life crisis.'

Overhearing such a charge, Cheryl stalked onto the verandah, striking a familiar pose, hands on hips. 'What the hell are you talking about, Linc? Mid-life crisis? I'm only thirty-two.'

Linc slammed a hand down on the railing. 'Some people's birthdays go up. Others go down.' He turned his face to Daniela, his whole body thrumming with tension. 'She told you we were having an affair, right?'

Daniela could see the look in his glittering eyes 'It's all right, Carl, settle down. We just had a quiet talk. Cheryl was about to leave. Weren't you, Cheryl?' She offered the woman a way out, at least with some dignity.

Cheryl decided not to take it. 'Why shouldn't she know about us?' she cried angrily. 'She tells me the two of you are getting married. Don't you think you should level with her, Linc? If you don't you're running the risk she will find out about us from someone else.'

Linc made a sudden move, looking so tall and daunting both women jumped back. Cheryl into the entrance hall, Daniela barring Linc's way. 'Don't—don't.' Daniela shook her head vehemently. 'Just let her go.'

'I'd prefer to *throw* her out,' Linc gritted. 'God, however was my dad fool enough to marry *you*, Cheryl? If I told him about you, your marriage would be over.'

'Only you daren't tell him,' Cheryl cried, breathing hard. She had reached the stage where she thought if she couldn't have Linc she'd be damned if another woman could.

Daniela acted fast. She seized the towering, magnificently fit Linc by his two arms, applying maximum force. It was pitiful under the circumstances—he was unbelievably strong—but a symbolic gesture. 'Get your bag and go, Cheryl,' she threw over her shoulder. 'And you'd better hurry!'

'*Go!*' Linc bellowed, so loudly Cheryl yelped.

Moments later Cheryl took off, optimising all her powerful car's horse power, tyres momentarily loose in the gravel, spraying it everywhere.

'So what was the long talk about?' Linc asked, his eyes searching, grave. Cheryl's car had long since disappeared into the tunnel of trees.

'As though I can remember so far back.' Daniela tried for lightness even though she heard the hard edge in his voice. She knew he hated being forced to declare his innocence. She recognised and understood his upset.

'I know you're trying to make light of it, Daniela,' he said. 'But I *know* Cheryl. You'd better tell me.'

Daniela shook her head, trying to control her own agitation. 'I'd rather forget it. She won't be bothering you any more.'

He bit back a harsh laugh. 'Cheryl isn't famous for her IQ. And there's another worrying thing. She doesn't know my dad. I wouldn't want to be the one to try to make a fool of *him*.'

Daniela looked into his eyes, a quality of pleading in hers. 'I thought I'd put a stop to it by telling her we were getting married.' Her voice broke a little.

His heart leapt. He wanted to take hold of her and kiss her in a way that would make her completely his. Of *course* they were getting married. The sooner the better so far as he was concerned. This afternoon, if she liked.

He wasn't at all sure why he didn't cry that aloud. Instead, he asked with black humour, 'And how did she take that?' He bitterly resented Cheryl's pouring lies into Daniela's ears.

'She bent double.' Daniela opted for the truth. 'The poor woman is mad about you.'

Linc burned with the heat of impotent rage. 'She's not so much mad about *me*,' he said tersely. 'Cheryl is just plain mad. Chuck and I knew the moment we set eyes on her she was nothing but a gold-digger. If only you had known our beautiful mother!'

'If only I had,' Daniela said very gently. 'But Cheryl *is* stunning in her way.' She knew the instant she said it, it was all wrong.

Carl's eyes fairly blazed. 'Well, *I* didn't lust after her, if that's what you're implying.'

'No, no. I wasn't implying that at all.' Daniela felt her own powerful wash of anger. This was so unfair. There was a lot Carl must have to say, but he wasn't saying any of it. Was this going to develop into a fight? And all over an un-scrupulous woman. So much for Carl's secret birthmark—the mark Cheryl claimed she had seen. Carl didn't have a mark on him.

Anger only seemed to ratchet up Linc's desire. This was the most captivating woman in the world. He loved the look of tenderness that was so much part of her beauty, the sheer mystery of her. He reached for her, pulling her into his arms. He could see he had made her angry, and that cut into him.

'I hate these people who try to come between us. *You're* the one I want,' he muttered with great urgency. 'I want to be inside your body. Inside your head. Behind your beau-tiful eyes.'

He could feel the powerful drive to make love to her. He lowered his head, taking her mouth, kissing her harder and harder, desperately wanting to wipe all memory of devious Cheryl and what she had said away. He kissed her mouth, her eyes, her neck, all over her face. Her mouth always tasted like the most delicious piece of fruit. His hands moved over her, but somewhere along the way she stopped him, her head jerking back.

'Carl!' She couldn't contain this emotional level. Though it filled her with excitement, other emotions were caving in on her.

Instantly he pulled back, his breath rasping in his throat. He felt lost and desperate. He half turned away in something like despair. Events of the past always had a hold on you.

'We're both upset,' Daniela said, coming quickly behind him and touching a tentative hand to his shoulder.

'Whatever she said, there wasn't a sliver of truth to it,' he bit off.

'I know that.' She knew he was hurting, and there didn't seem to be a thing she could do about it.

'But there were a few minutes when you doubted?' He swung back to stare down at her with brilliant, piercing eyes.

Daniela couldn't answer for a few seconds. She was a fool to feel so weak. 'Weren't there moments when *you* doubted me?' she quietly countered. They had been equally wronged.

He nodded an admission. 'But I soon got over it. You had some kind of a relationship with Templeton, however brief, and I accept his feelings became obsessive and caused you grief. Cheryl has caused *me* grief, and I had *nothing* to do with the woman. That's the thing. *Nothing!* It was all in her head. I despise her. But mud sticks.'

'Not in this case,' Daniela said, hoping the deep sincerity of her tone would calm him. 'I understand it was all untrue. Sometimes we have no control over what is happening in our lives, Carl. A lot of people could tell you about someone they've met who turned out to be destructive.'

Still the tension between them was strung out like a live wire.

Daniela sighed and dropped her hand. Maybe it was all the intensity that was in him that made him such a splendid lover. 'Anyway, she's gone and I must go, too. There are a lot of things I have to attend to before tonight.'

He shrugged, his handsome face shut tight. 'I'll walk you to your car.'

Somehow she didn't expect him to ask if she was coming back to him tonight. He didn't. That filled her with sadness. Linc Mastermann was a fine man, way out of the ordinary. He was also a complex, difficult man.

CHAPTER TEN

THE storm broke late afternoon, after hours of eerie silence. In the mood he was in, Linc had found the silence sinister. Now jagged flashes of lightning lit up a sky that was a dramatic study in silver-black, purple-black, with livid streaks of green. Great booms of thunder followed, causing squadrons of birds to take wing and head for shelter. Another dry electrical storm? Or maybe the valley would get some rain?

He continued to stand, hands clenched on the white timber banister, looking up at the sentinel hills. Fast-moving cumulus clouds scudded across the vast bowl of the sky. There was a telling smell of ozone in the air that gave some hope. On the downside, a dry wind—hot like the blast from a furnace—had picked up, stripping leaves from the trees lining the long drive and sending them into whirling spirals mixed up with the colourful kaleidoscope of spent blossom.

He felt very uneasy, and he couldn't break out of it. He knew most of it was a result of the way he and Daniela had parted. Sometimes he couldn't understand himself at all. Was he frightened of loving her so much? Was that it? Although he had always been popular enough with women, hadn't he always deliberately kept his distance? God knew he had learned the hardest lesson of all, and learned it young. Loving meant loss. Hadn't he suppressed his capacity for loving since his mother died?

He and Chuck had watched their mother grow worse and worse, then die. Their father, although profoundly affected, had survived by shutting it all out. Maybe he had a bit of his father in him? How could you love a woman as he loved Daniela yet shut her out? It didn't make a lot of sense. Sex was one thing; love was another. He had taken Daniela deeply into his heart, yet bizarrely he found himself acting as if it was just the opposite. But at least he was coming to recognise his feelings for what they were.

Fear is at the root of it, pal! his inner voice said. *Your problems hark back to your childhood.*

He felt like ringing Daniela, making contact, apologising, telling her how much he loved her and asking her if she would come back to him tonight. Only the knowledge she would be too busy to take private calls kept him from doing it. He fully intended making things right between them, but that wasn't the way life worked. No time was absolutely perfect. First there had been Templeton and then Cheryl. Linc's biggest mistake was letting such people get between him and the woman he loved.

She had gone off so sad-faced. His beautiful Daniela. He had messed up yet again. From now on in he had to focus on getting things right. To lose Daniela would break his heart.

The rain came down briefly thirty minutes later—no more than a shower bath and then the tap turned off. He was witness to a spectacular fork of lightning spearing into the hillside. Clearly it had hit a tree. Moments later he saw the upward spiral of grey smoke, an orange tint at its highest point, tapering to a dense dark grey.

There wasn't a moment to lose. He knew fires could run through open hillsides for hours before being brought under control. He had long since committed the phone number of the rural fire unit to memory, and the sooner they got here the quicker they could stop the spread of flames. He knew there was a helicopter in service. The community had raised the money to buy it with a big donation from Guy. The helicopter could drop a big payload of water and pink-coloured fire retardant on that hill. Fire travelled faster and burnt more intensely uphill than downhill.

The homestead, standing on a gentle slope within a well cleared area, was as ready as ever he and George could make it. He looked out of the open French doors in time to see George just as much on the alert as he, huffing and puffing up the front steps. Linc made the call. Smoke had turned to flame.

The minute Russ, his twenty-two-year-old assistant, raced into the Winery kitchen Daniela could tell something was wrong.

'There've been lightning strikes all over the valley,' he told them, tugging frantically at the quiff of his sandy hair. 'Those poor firies must be having a time of it. I reckon it's time for me to join up as a volunteer.' His gaze had shifted around them all. It moved from Paul, the *sous chef*, to Daniela, who had visibly paled. 'That friend of yours, Daniela—the new guy, Linc Mastermann—his property was the first to take a hit.'

'And?' she prompted, fear swelling up in her at a tremendous rate.

'That's all I can tell you.' He shrugged helplessly. 'I know the chopper's up. I saw it on the way in. The fire unit was pretty slick off the mark. I reckon if we hadn't had that heavy shower things could be a whole lot worse.'

'So the main valley road is open?' Daniela knew Russ would have had to come to work that way.

Russ slid onto a high stool, dangling his long legs. 'No problems there. The hits were on the open hillsides.'

Paul, an intensely sympathetic man, saw Daniela's distress. He and Daniela had formed a quick bond. She had met his wife, Robyn, and his two teenage girls, who had taken to her just as much as he had. Daniela was a lovely person. He regarded her not only as a colleague but a personal friend. Though Daniela didn't talk freely about her relationship with Linc Mastermann she had confided in him and Robyn that she had been seeing quite a bit of him. And Robyn, who had a sure instinct in these matters, had told him afterwards she was certain Daniela had fallen very deeply in love.

Now Daniela turned to him, the panic she was trying to hold down mirrored in her beautiful dark eyes. That tugged at him. 'Look, Paul, I know I'm asking a lot,' she said, 'but could you take over for me tonight? Everything is sorted. You're just as capable as I am.'

It wasn't strictly true, but Paul found himself nodding. 'Only one thing, Danni. You don't really know the situation. Mightn't you be putting yourself in danger?'

At that moment she didn't care. She had to get to Carl. She had to know he was safe. She had driven off with distance between them. That was terrible. She knew she didn't want to face life without him.

'Let me make a few phone calls,' Paul said, whipping out his mobile. 'If there's real trouble the restaurant won't be doing much business anyway.'

Daniela turned away to hunt up her own mobile. Carl wasn't answering. Her call went to his message bank. It struck her then how very vulnerable life was.

Small grass fires had broken out along her route, but nothing that the volunteer firefighters, ordinary valley people, couldn't cope with. Probably the grass fires had been lit by flying embers from the hills. Clouds of smoke were in the air, and the smell of burning leaves would have been wonderful had its presence not been so starkly serious. Paul had told her a house near where he and his family lived had been struck not once but twice, and had burned fiercely to the ground despite all efforts to save it. Once fire caught, it could be virtually impossible to stop.

She doubted anyone would turn up at the restaurant tonight anyway. People would stay at home to guard their properties and their precious stock.

She made the turn-off to Briar's Ridge, then drove fast down its long avenue of trees. Her very real fears began to ease. She knew just how much back-breaking work Carl and his foreman George had put in, ploughing and harrowing and clearing wide areas all around the property. She knew the creek that meandered through the property was a natural fire break.

But didn't fire skip creeks?

As she swept into the driveway she gave thanks aloud. The homestead and all the outbuildings remained untouched. It was hard to see up into the hills. Dusk had fallen and the hills were shrouded in smoke. She didn't, however, see flames. The fire unit must have arrived just in time. She parked the car right at the foot of the steps. It wasn't her imagination. The wind that drove fire had not only dropped marginally, it had dropped a lot, now blowing away from Briar's Ridge. That was a great blessing.

It was only when she stood on the verandah that she saw fire devouring a slope farther to the west. She thought that might be Narooma, the McDermott place. Her heart bled for them if it was. How did people survive the loss of everything they had worked for?

The front door was open, but Carl was nowhere around. She knew once his own property was safe he would have gone to help any neighbour in trouble. That was how the bush worked. Bred to the city, she had had no experience of fire herself, but she had seen terrible fires on television, agonised over the tragic loss of life. When Carl came home—and he *had* to come home—she would be here waiting for him. She would wait for him as long as she had to.

For ever.

It was almost midnight before he got back, driving the tractor right up to the front steps.

Danaiela flew down them, keening little cries of relief issuing from her throat. Another minute and she'd let the tears out. 'Oh, thank God, Carl! Thank God! I was so worried. Are you all right?'

Her need was so great she reached for him, not keeping in her love for him, but pouring it out.

'Easy, my love,' he breathed, as she threw herself against him. 'I'm covered in grime. You'll get it all over you.'

'As if I care!' He was indeed a mess, but Daniela was nearly dancing in an ecstasy of relief. 'Oh, Carl!' She couldn't help herself. She burst into tears, her arms coming up to lock around his neck. 'Are you hurt anywhere?' she asked, thought there was nothing she could see. He was covered in dust and grime, and darn near black, but could there be burns beneath? 'You must be sick from all the smoke you've inhaled?'

'I'm fine.' He was now, but there were some odd throbs in his exhausted body. He could handle it. He drew her back against him, vowing to never let her go. Life was a journey—not all of it good—and he had found his safe haven. When he had seen his Daniela running out of the house towards him it had fulfilled a cherished dream of coming home.

Home was this woman.

'The Gregsons have lost everything,' he told her sadly. 'Their house went up before a fire unit could get to them. The McDermotts were lucky. They've lost a lot of fencing, but no stock. We brought it all down into holding yards. Sheep will have to be put down in the Wilcox area, but the losses were minimal—considering. All property owners have been right on the ball. None of us can adequately express our gratitude to the firefighters. They're a marvellous team—so damned brave. We have to do something to raise more money for them. But right now I have to take a long shower to wash all this grime off me. Thank you for coming, Daniela,' he said, his heart bursting with love for her.

'Shh!' She placed a gentle finger against his parched lips. 'There's nowhere else I would want to be.' Her tone was exquisitely tender, like some miraculous balm.

His underlying fear of love and loss suddenly ceased to exist. Her words were like the most beautiful music he had ever heard.

Love reigned.

Arms entwined, they moved into the house. 'You're going to stay?'

She allowed herself her first laugh of the night. 'I haven't got my nightie.'

His arm tightened around her narrow waist. His woman. His soon-to-be wife. 'You won't be needing it,' he said.

For those fortunate enough to find a soul mate in life, dreams really did come true.

EPILOGUE

IN ACCORDANCE with tradition, the engagement party for Daniela and Linc would be hosted by Daniela's parents, Marc and Lucia. Linc had formally asked Marc for his daughter's hand in marriage as a mark of respect, and it was one Daniela's parents found both charming and affecting. In fact, in the weeks preceding the engagement party, Linc endeared himself to the entire Adami family. As far as they were concerned their Daniela had got things just right. This was a fine young man—one they were full of enthusiasm to make an important member of their family.

It was an excited Lucia who came up with the idea of a theme for the engagement party, only she was a little tentative about how they would take it. She had thought herself it would be glorious fun, and would give the young women in particular a great opportunity to dress up.

Twenty young couples had been decided upon, and the party would take the form of a banquet, catered by the family and celebrated at their new restaurant. They had become so popular, especially since Daniela had returned home, that they had desperately needed bigger and better premises. They had retained the name Aldo's, but the new restaurant was almost three times as big, and much better situated, with a lovely view of the town park. Its décor showed the family's Italian background. They had even imported from Italy six beautiful hanging light fittings like great starbursts. They had set them back quite a bit, but had proved well worth the money. These light fittings had been the inspiration for Lucia's plan.

'I thought Renaissance?' She launched into this plan one Sunday night, over a family dinner, examining each face in turn. 'Beautiful long floating dresses for the young women, lots of sparkle, gem-encrusted bodices, costume jewellery, perhaps an elaborate hairdo. Some licence for the young men, who mightn't fancy the idea of wearing tights and tunics?' A quick sideways glance at Linc. 'Maybe a very fancy flounced shirt, fitted black trousers? Perhaps a velvet cap?'

Silence around the table. Aldo rolled his bottom lip over his top one, considering.

'Of course it's only an idea,' she said hurriedly. 'I thought a theme would be nice. Maybe the great lovers of history, literature, grand opera?' she suggested. 'I so want this great occasion to be truly memorable for you both.'

'It's brilliant!' Linc suddenly declared, with Daniela not far behind. How could he pass up the opportunity of seeing his Daniela as a ravishing Renaissance promised bride? He didn't know if he could manage the tights but, hell, there was nothing wrong with his legs—and Lucia *had* given the guys an out.

As it turned out, the engagement party was a night to be remembered by everyone who attended. The young men had entered fully into the spirit of the occasion, hiring costumes that, even if they weren't absolutely Renaissance, certainly allowed them to cut dashing figures. In fact they looked amazing! This added greatly to the general excitement. And the twenty young women—a group that included Alana Radcliffe, who had finally returned from her honeymoon—looked ravishing. Lyrical figures from the past. All of them had taken great care, searching for just such a costume that would make them appear at their most magical. The results were truly wonderful, and the gala evening was given an extra charge.

It was an engagement party to dream of. The food was superb, and the wine, the music. The room had the fragrance of roses. Roses for love. The marvellous glass light fittings above the tables lent young faces and flesh a most tender bloom.

Daniela, wearing a seriously beautiful and extravagant long dress in gold silk with a train, moved a hand over her beautiful engagement ring, letting it still over the dome of the central diamond, a large flawless stone flanked by more diamonds of a carat and more. She thought it the most beautiful ring she had ever seen.

Linc, who was getting enormous pleasure out of seeing her constantly doing this, bent his face to her, a smile in his brilliantly glimmering eyes. 'I'm thrilled you love your ring, my love. Other precious stones are lovely, but to me the diamond is the jewel of jewels! As you are mine.'

Very gently, exquisitely, their lips met. 'It's perfect,' she murmured, gazing lovingly into his eyes.

'And I've never seen you looking more beautiful,' Linc spoke again, piercingly aware he had never felt happier in his life.

'All for you,' Daniela whispered back. 'Mamma's idea was a *coup*. Everyone looks so marvellous. Ordinary evening dress couldn't have made such a spectacle. I almost

feel like I'm back in the Renaissance. I'm so proud of
what my family have done for us tonight.'

'My family, too, now,' Linc said, happy it was true.
'You look ravishing.'

At the naked look of love and desire in his eyes she let
her blond head, piled into an elaborate coiffure set with
jewels, fall gently onto his shoulder. Tonight he wore an
ornate velvet jacket, sleeveless, ruby-coloured, heavily
embroidered in gold, over a splendid white flounced shirt
with black moleskins. Not for one moment had he appeared uncomfortable in such flamboyant garb. He looked
stunning.

Beautiful—all beautiful! Daniela thought. She couldn't
wait until she and her father were walking up the aisle, with
her beloved Carl waiting for her at the altar. His brother
Charles, who was to be their best man, was here tonight with
his sweet-faced companion, a lovely young woman called
Louise. And a wedding invitation had been sent to Carl's
father which naturally had had to include Cheryl. They had
readily accepted. No doubt Cheryl had convinced herself her
trip to Briar's Ridge had been a harmless piece of fun,
Daniela thought. But none of that mattered any more. They
had invited Rose Denby and her Simon to the party, but
Rose's two older sisters had made things easy by removing
themselves to Sydney. Daniela was on Cloud Nine with
happiness, and wished everyone in the world well.

'Love…' Linc's wine-scented breath caressed her cheek.
'It's the doorway to heaven,' he pronounced.

He was right, of course.

CATTLE RANCHER,
SECRET SON

PROLOGUE

FATE, Destiny, Chance: call it what you will, it has a hand in everything.

Gina Romano, a young woman of twenty-four, whose classical bone structure, golden skin, lustrous dark eyes and hair richly proclaimed her Italian heritage, was walking to her friend Tanya's front gate. It had been a lovely relaxing afternoon with Tanya and her beautiful new baby, Lily-Anne.

Tanya, cradling tiny Lily-Anne, naturally the most beautiful baby in the world, was standing at the front door, waving Gina off: Gina's hand was on the wrought-iron gate making sure it was closed securely after her, when she felt a tingle like an icy finger on her nape. It alerted her, bringing on a familiar feeling of alarm. Every time she felt that icy finger, and she had felt it many times in her life, she took it as a signal *something* was about to happen.

She pulled away from the gate, moving swiftly out onto the pavement, hands shaking, legs shaking, head humming as if it were filled with high tension wires. She was no clairvoyant but she had come to accept she had an extra sense most people either didn't have or didn't get to develop. It was a gift, simultaneously a curse; an inheritance handed down through the maternal line of her family as other families claimed the second sight.

The *noise* came first. One minute the leafy suburban street was drowsing under a turquoise sky, the next, a range of things happened. An early model car with its engine roaring and trailing grey-black clouds of exhaust fumes turned into the street without slowing at the corner. Gina watched the driver correct the skid, only to gun the engine even though the left front wheel was wobbling. Gina estimated he was doing a good fifteen to twenty kilometres over the fifty kilometre speed limit.

From the property directly opposite, the real estate agent overseeing the forthcoming auction, camera in hand, strode out onto the pavement on the way to his car. He stopped, took in the situation and cried out. Simultaneously a flame-haired cherub called Cameron from the house next door to Tanya's came bounding down his unfenced driveway and ran pell-mell onto the street without so much as a glance in either direction. He was totally oblivious to danger, his mind was set solely on retrieving his blue beach ball, which was fast bouncing away from him into the opposite gutter.

The estate agent, a man of sixty, to his everlasting horror was assailed by such a terrible feeling of helplessness he simply *froze,* but Gina, who didn't even hear Tanya yelling frantically so focused was she on the child, reacted like an Olympic sprinter coming off the blocks. Adrenaline poured into her body, causing a surge of power. She *flew* after the little boy, at one point her long legs fully extended front and back as she rose in an extravagant leap. Or so it appeared to the neighbours alerted by Tanya's screaming and the awful din set up by the smoking bomb. As one of them later confided to the television reporter, "It was the coolest thing I've ever seen. The young lady was moving so *impossibly* fast she was all but airborne. Ought to make the headlines!"

So this then was much more than a simple good deed. It was seen to be on the heroic scale. But Gina herself felt no sense of valour. She did what she thought anyone would have done in the circumstances. A child's life was on the line. What option did she have but to attempt to save it? Her very humanity demanded she act and act *fast*.

Heart almost bursting through her rib cage, she scooped up the child in the bare nick of time, her body sparkly all over as though wired, and then flew on to the safety of the grassy verge thinking there was no way she could avoid taking an awful fall or being pulverized by Tanya's formidable brick and wrought-iron fence. She had a vision of herself lying on the grass, moaning because of broken bones, maybe even covered in blood. But for now, her main thought was how to cushion the child whose vulnerable little head was buried against her breast.

Please, God…please, God! Every atom in her body braced in case He didn't hear her.

She needn't have worried. It had been decided all would be well. What could so easily have been a tragedy—glittering metal pulverising two tender bodies—turned into a feel-good human-interest story. A workman built like a double-door refrigerator but as light on his feet as a ballet dancer in his prime appeared out of nowhere to gather Gina and child in like it was a set piece of choreography. Little Cameron, now the drama was over, broke into frightened howls of *"Mum-eee! Mum-eee! Mum-eee!"* the *ees* mounting ever higher.

A distraught young woman, with orange locks that refused to lie down, was running to him, calling repeatedly, "My darling, my darling, my baby!" Gina, her own body trembling in after-shock handed Cameron over to his mother to an outpouring of thanks. Cameron, for some reason common to children, stopped his heart-wrenching wailing and began to laugh merrily. He reached into the pocket of his little blue shorts to hand Gina a couple of jelly beans he hadn't touched, presumably as a reward.

Incredibly it was all over in a matter of seconds, only now

there was a small crowd surrounding them who burst into spontaneous applause as though they had witnessed a great piece of stunt work. The battered car, scruffy young man at the wheel, didn't stop or even slow though he did flash a nonchalant hand out of the open window, obviously taking the philosophical view "all's well that ends well."

Angry fists were raised in his direction, cries of condemnation. A silver-haired old lady added a few words one would have thought she wouldn't even know, much less use, but he accelerated away, apparently with a clear conscience, mobile now glued to his ear. He would later be picked up by the police who were delighted to have his licence number handed to them on a plate. There was also the matter of a stack of parking fines he had completely ignored.

Praise shifted to the real estate agent. Belatedly, he had done something right. Momentarily transfixed by horror he might have been, but he had immediately swung into action on witnessing Gina's spectacular transformation into "Wonder Woman you'd have to call her! Used to love that show!" He was ready for a laugh now. Hadn't he snapped out of his sick panic to get "the whole blessed thing" on film?

Thus it was, Gina Romano found herself an unwilling heroine and would remain so for some time. Cameron's immensely grateful parents later went on television to say they would never forget what Ms Romano had done. In fact, viewers got the decided impression Gina was now part of the family. Tanya took the welcome opportunity to show off her beautiful baby to the larger world, added her own little bit. "Gina's so brave! Why only a few months back she saved Cameron from a big black dog."

"Let's hope there won't be a *third* time for wee Cameron!" the woman reporter joshed, smiling brilliantly into the camera.

Gina, the heroine of all this, prayed inwardly: *Don't let anyone recognise me.*

But recognised she was. By her colleagues and friends, just about everyone who knew her at her local shopping centre, the inhabitants of the small North Queensland sugar town a thousand miles away where she had been born and raised, and most crucially by the last person on earth she wanted to see her captured image; the man she had fallen hopelessly, madly, irrevocably in love with four years before. The man Fate had denied her. The man she had so carefully hidden herself away from. Not even her closest friends even suspected she knew him. Or *had* known him. *Intimately.*

Gina never discussed her former life, her secrets and her haunted past. She had a good life now for which she was very grateful. It had all the trappings of normality. She had an attractive apartment in a safe area with importantly a lovely little park nearby with a kiddies' play area. She had a well-paid job with a stockbroking firm who valued her services. She had men friends who admired and desired her. At least two of them definitely had marriage on their minds if mentioning it meant anything. Men, generally speaking, had to be helped along in these matters.

She couldn't commit. And she knew why. Hardly a day went by that she didn't think of the man who had taken her: body, mind and soul. Trying to forget him hadn't just been one long struggle: It was a battle she had come to accept she was doomed to lose.

CHAPTER ONE

Coronation Hill Station
The Northern Territory

FROM the crest of Crown Ridge, tumbled with smooth, near perfectly round boulders like a giant's marbles, Cal sat his magnificent silver-grey stallion, watching a section of the lowing herd being driven towards the holding yards at Yering Springs. From this incomparable vantage point on top of the ancient sandstone escarpment, the whole of Jabiru Valley was revealed to him. Silver billabongs lined by willowy melaleucas and groves of pandanus wound away to the left and right, the sun flashing off surfaces as smooth as glass. He could see the flocks of magpie geese and whistling ducks congregated around the banks and exploding from the reed beds. Wildlife was abundant in the Valley: native mammals, reptiles, trillions of insects and above all, the *birds*. The gloriously coloured parrots, the cockatoos, galahs, rosellas and lorikeets, countless other species, the beautiful water birds and, at the top of the chain, the reigning jabiru. It was the great numbers of jabirus, the country's only stork, fishing the billabongs and lagoons that had given the Valley its name.

The Territory was still a wild paradise with a mystical feel about it that he firmly believed derived from the aboriginal culture. The *Dreaming*. The spirit ancestors had fashioned this ancient land, creating everything in it. Where he now sat on his horse had provided natural art galleries in its numerous caves and rock shelters. Many of the walls were covered in ancient rock paintings, art treasures fiercely protected by the indigenous people and generations of McKendricks who had taken over the land.

In whatever direction he looked, the landscape was potent with beauty. He supposed he would have made a good pagan with his nature worship. Certainly he was very much in touch with the natural world. He even knew, like the aboriginals on the station, the places where great *energy* resided, certain sandstone monuments, special caves, rock pools and particular trees. The lily-covered lagoons on Coronation Hill were filled with magnificent waterlilies of many colours: pink, red, white, yellow, cream. His favourite was the sacred Blue Lotus. Underneath those gorgeous carpets it had to be mentioned, glided the odd man-eating croc or two. They had learned to take crocs in their stride. Crocodiles were a fact of life in the Territory. Don't bother them. They won't bother you.

God it was hot! He could feel trickles of sweat run down his nape and onto his back. He lifted a hand to angle his wide brimmed Akubra lower on his head, thinking his hair was getting much too long. It was curling up at the back like a girl's. He would have to get it cut when he found time. The mob had been on the move since the relative cool of dawn but now the heat was intense. The world of sky above him was stunningly clear of clouds, an infinity of burning blue. He loved his home with a passion. He loved the colours of the land. They weren't the furnace-reds of the Centre's deserts but cool blues and silvers, the deeper cobalts and amethysts. Instead of the rolling red sand dunes of the central part of the Territory, in the tropical north, the entire landscape was covered in every conceivable shade of lustrous green.

And flowers! Extraordinary flowers abounded in the Valley. The grevilleas, the banksias, the hakeas, the native hibiscus and the gardenias everyone knew, but there were countless other species unique to the far-away regions that had never been named. No one had ever had the time to get around to it. Australia was a dry, dry continent but oddly produced the most marvellous wildflowers that were becoming world renowned. Everywhere he looked exquisite flowers unfurled themselves on trees and shrubs, others rode the waving tops of the savannah grasses that could grow after the Wet a good four feet over his head and he was six feet two.

It was here in the mid-1860s, that his ancestor, the Scot, Alexander Campbell-McKendrick swore an oath to found his own dynasty in the savage wilderness of the Australian Outback. It was quite an ambition and a far, far, cry from his own ancestral home in the Borders region of Scotland. But as it stood, a second son, denied inheritance of the family estates by the existence of an elder brother, Alexander McKendrick, an adventurer and a visionary at heart, found an excellent option in travelling halfway across the world to seek his own fortune in the Great South Land, where handsome, well-educated young Scotsmen from distinguished families were thin on the ground. McKendrick had been very favourably received, immediately gaining the patronage of the Governor of the then self-governing colony of New South Wales.

The great quest had begun.

It had started in the colony of New South Wales, but was to finish far away in the Northern Territory, the wildest of wild frontiers, where a man could preside over a cattle run bigger than many a European country. This was the mysterious Top End of the great continent, deeply hostile country, peopled with a nation collectively called the *Kakadu*.

McKendrick had been undaunted. It was from this very escarpment he had named on the spot Crown Ridge because of its curious resemblance to an ancient crown. He had looked out over a limitless lushly grassed valley and he had recorded as "knowing in his heart" this was the place where the Australian dynasty of the Campbell-McKendrick family would put down roots. Land was the meaning of life. The land endured when mighty monuments and buildings collapsed and dissolved into dust.

So that was my great-great-great-great-grandfather, Cal thought with the familiar thrill of pride. *Some guy! And there is my inheritance spread out before me.* The McKendricks—they had abandoned their double barrel name by the turn of the twentieth century—were among the great pioneers of the Interior.

By late afternoon he was back at the homestead, dog-tired, bones aching after a long, hard day in the saddle. It was truly amazing the amount of punishment a young man's body could take. His father, Ewan, so recently a dynamo had slowed down considerably this past year. Ewan McKendrick was a legendary cattleman like the McKendricks before him. There had only been one black sheep in the family, the third heir, Duncan, the supposed *quiet* one, whose exploits when he came to power got him killed by an unerring aboriginal spear, the terrible consequence of ill-treating the black people on the station. It was a crime no McKendrick had committed before him and none ever did again.

Cal found his mother and father and his widower uncle Edward, his father's brother, in the library enjoying a gin and tonic and talking horses, a never-ending topic of conversation in the family. Their faces lit up at his arrival as if he had just returned from an arduous trek to the South Pole.

"Ah, there you are, darling," cried his mother, Jocelyn, extending an arm.

He went to her and put his hands lightly on her thin shoulders. A beautiful woman was his mother. She had made a great wife to his father, a fine mistress of Coronation Hill but she had never been a particularly good mother. For one thing she was absurdly wrapped up in him when sadly, she had spent little time or attention on her daughter, his younger sister, Meredith.

"Settle this for me, will you, son?" His father immediately drew him into an argument he and Ed were having about blood lines. The McKendricks had a passion for horses. Coronation Hill, named at the time of settlement in honour of the British queen, Victoria, was very serious about its breeding and training programme, not just for their own prized stockhorses, horses capable of dominating not only rodeos, gymkhanas and cross country events, but the racehorses on the bush circuit. Bush race meets were enormously popular, drawing people from all over the far-flung Outback.

Ewan clapped gleefully as Cal confirmed what he had been maintaining was correct. "Sorry, Uncle Ed." Cal slanted his gentle uncle a smile. "You were probably thinking of 'Highlander.' *He* was a son of 'Charlie's Pride.'"

"Of course." Edward nodded his head several times. Edward had never been known to best his elder brother. Though the family resemblance between the brothers was strong, Edward had always been outshone by Ewan in all departments, except Cal thought, in sensitivity and the wonderful ability to communicate with children and people far less fortunate than the grand McKendricks.

"Thanks for arriving just in time," his father crowed, giving his loud hearty laugh and stabbing a triumphant finger at his brother. "Fancy a cold beer, son? I know G&T's aren't your tipple."

"I'll go and get cleaned up first, Dad," Cal replied, quietly dismayed at how much pleasure his father took in putting his brother down.

"Did you sack young Fletcher?" Ewan grunted, shooting his son a startling, blue glance.

Cal shook his head, not prepared to alter his decision. "I've decided to give him another chance. He's young. He's learning. He takes the pain."

"Very well," was all his father said with a rough shake of his handsome head, when once he would have barked "You're not running Coronation yet, son."

Except these days he was, or close enough. It was, after all, his heritage. Irresistibly, Cal's gaze went to the series of tall arched stained-glass windows that dominated the library. The sinking sun was starting to stream through the glass, turning the interior of the huge room into a dazzling kaleidoscope of colour; ruby, emerald, sapphire, gold. Ceiling-high mahogany book-cases in colonnaded bays were built into the walls on three sides of the library housing a very valuable collection of books of all kinds: literature, world history, ancient and modern, mythology, science, valuable early maps, family documents, colonial history. It was a splendid collection that desperately needed cataloguing and maybe even re-housing. When his time came he would make it his business to hire someone well qualified to carry out this long-needed important work. Sadly neither his grandparents nor his father and mother had felt impelled to have the arduous task begun. Uncle Edward knew better than to interfere. Since he had tragically lost his wife to breast cancer ten years before, Ed had lived with the family.

Cal had no family of his own yet. No woman to share his life, ease the burden. Kym Harrison was the girl he was supposed to have married. He had been briefly engaged to her a couple of years back. He was still marvelling at how he had allowed it to happen. Of course, his mother had never let up on him to "tie the knot." But it hadn't been right for him and Kym deserved better.

Six months the engagement had lasted. Six months of fighting something too powerful to be overcome. Passion for another woman. One who had betrayed him. Every loving word that had fallen from her beautiful mouth had been a *lie*.

How could he have been so blindly mistaken? Even at near twenty-five he'd been no naive young fool. He was supposed to be, then as now, one of the most eligible bachelors in the country. He had to know it. The women's magazines kept him constantly in their lists. But there had been no serious attachment since. Just a few pain-free encounters, pain-free exits. Not that there was any such thing as safe sex. Someone always got hurt. It wasn't just a question of taking his time, either, of being *sure*. It was more a battle to exorcise those memories so vivid, they denied him the power to move on with his life. Yet he had tried.

He had known Kym since they were children. They connected on many levels. But compatibility, similar backgrounds, close family ties, weren't enough. Not for him anyway. Their relationship lacked what he had learned, to his cost, truly existed. *Passion*. Wild and ravishing; emotion that took you to the heavens then when it was ruthlessly withdrawn dropped you into your own pit in hell.

Hadn't he wanted her from the very first minute? The memory surfaced.

"Good morning, sir. Another glorious day!"

No shy dip of the head, but a calm, smiling, near-regal greeting, as if she were a princess in disguise. A princess, moreover, of uncommon beauty, even if she did happen to be folding towels.

He had stood there transfixed, desire pouring into him like burning lava. And it wasn't desire alone. He honestly felt he had no other choice but to fall madly in love with her. It was his fate. He hadn't been looking for any holiday fling; certainly not with a member of the island staff. Yet he had wanted this woman to have and to hold. *His woman*. God, in his secret heart she still remained *his woman.* What an agony love was! It forced itself on you, never to let go.

Gina!

How could he remain faithful if only in mind to a woman who had utterly deceived him? Kym had been his parents' choice almost from the cradle. Kym was the daughter of his mother's best friend, Beth Harrison. The Harrisons were their nearest neighbours on Lakefield. A marriage between them was a fantasy both mothers had harboured. His mother who had told him all his life she adored him—his mother was the classic type who doted upon the son—was still trying to come to terms with the split up. He had spent most of his childhood fighting off his mother's possessiveness, so it had been almost a relief to go away to boarding school even if it meant leaving his beloved Coronation Hill. How differently his mother had treated Meredith! Not unkindly, heavens no, she loved Meredith in her way, but rather as though daughters didn't matter all that much in the scheme of things. His mother's special love had been directed to *him.*

No little girl child should have to suffer that, he thought. When he married and children came along he would make sure any daughter of his would be treasured. Kym, an only child, enjoyed full parental love. It had been lavished on her. No son had come along in the Harrison family so Kym would inherit Lakefield. "You couldn't find a better match, my darling," his mother always told him. "No other woman could love you more than Kym does. Outside me, of course." This with a bright laugh. "Kym is perfect for you."

His mother didn't know about Gina unless his aunt Lorinda had told her. Lorinda had sworn she wouldn't. Lorinda, his mother's only sibling had helped him in a remarkable way back then. He was very grateful to her for her kindness and empathy. She always had been enormously supportive. It had to be true about Kym's really caring for him. They were still friends, despite everything. Or maybe Kym was just hanging in there until such time he realised she really was his best choice. Maybe compatibility could be made to work. Obsession after all, was a disaster. He gave a small shake of his head, warding his visions off. How could a man keep a woman's image burning bright when it was all of four years since her desertion? He had taken Gina's betrayal not just hard. It had near crushed the life out of him when up to then he had shown no fear of anything.

He had hated her at first. He had thought hate was a way out. But hate hadn't worked. Having loved her, he found it was less corrosive to hate himself. That's when he had allowed himself to become engaged to Kym, convincing himself Kym was the path to healing. That hadn't worked, either. It was just as impossible to remove Gina from his bloodstream as live without a heart.

He was passing his father's study when Meredith called to him, "Got a minute, Cal?"

"Sure." He walked into the room, his eyes ranging over her face. Usually his sister had a welcoming smile for him, but this afternoon she looked serious, even sad.

"Hey there, what's up?" His voice echoed his concern. Meredith was three years his junior. They were the best of friends. In fact, he would have to think really hard to remember a cross word between them. Their isolated upbringing had forged strong personal loyalties between them. He had always looked out for his little sister, though, like all the McKendricks Meredith had grown tall with the slim, lithe build of the athlete she was.

She was a marvellous horsewoman. She had won many cups and ribbons over the years, nearly as many as he had but no one had thought to display them as they did his. Once when they were kids, he had pinned her ribbons and rosettes all over her and taken pictures of her, both on and off her horse. He had hung on to those early photographs, too. The best one he'd had enlarged and framed. It sat on the desk in his bedroom along with a few other family portraits of them both. Great shots all of them.

He had to admit all his family were exceptionally good-looking. Genes were responsible for that. Meredith was beautiful but she made no effort to play up her looks. Rather she seemed to work at playing them down. She wore no make-up, just sunscreen and a touch of lipstick, jeans, neat little cotton shirts, her rich brown hair bleached gold at the temples by the sun, pulled back into a section of thick plait that ended in a loose ponytail. Even without her making the slightest effort, men turned to look at her.

There were lots of things he wished for his sister—a fuller more rewarding life, a man she could love and who loved her, marriage, children, but none of this was happening. For *either* of them. His father had frightened most of Meredith's serious suitors off. Their dad could be a very intimidating man. Although, it wasn't as if Meredith was the apple of his eye as any-one might expect with an only daughter. Meredith came well down the line when she should have been right up there. But that's the way it was. Nothing he nor Meredith could do about it. He was eternally grateful she had never blamed him. There had been no sibling rivalry, no wrenching jealousy. It had been bred into Meredith that sons not daughters were the ones who counted. As for suitors, most guys knew not to apply unless they could come up to scratch, and McKendricks' scratch was a very hard call.

"Take a look at this," Meredith was saying, breaking into his reverie. She laid a sheet of newspaper flat on the massive partner's desk, smoothing the crumpled surface. Such graceful hands, he thought, but regretfully getting knocked about with hard work. His sister did a lot more than pull her weight. She handled most things so quietly and effortlessly her capabilities tended to be overlooked or at the very least taken for granted. Meredith was not only beautiful but she had brains to spare. She would make some lucky guy a brilliant partner.

"What is it?" He rounded the desk, to stand beside her, topping her easily. "Oh, my God!" He felt the ground open up beneath his feet....

Watching him keenly, Meredith's face filled with anxiety. "Look, I'm sorry if I've done the wrong thing, Cal. But something inside told me you'd want to see this."

Physically and mentally reeling, he still managed to put a reassuring hand on her arm. "That's okay, I do."

"I thought so," Meredith breathed more easily. "You really loved her, didn't you?" She glanced at her brother's strong profile, registering his shock, and the way the muscles had bunched along his strong jawline.

"It's been a job trying to hate her," he answered, trying to control the grating harshness of his tone. He stared down at the beautiful unsmiling face of the girl in the newspaper photograph. "I always knew this day would come."

"I think I did, too," Meredith murmured quietly.

"How did you get a hold of it?" He glanced at the top of the page, seeing it was a Queensland newspaper. The State of Queensland adjoined the Northern Territory. They didn't take this newspaper.

"It came wrapped around some supplies Dad ordered," she said. "I almost screwed it up and threw it away. Something stopped me." Meredith paused, involuntary tears welling into her deep blue eyes. "She's still as beautiful as ever. More so now she's a woman. The first time I saw her back on the island I thought she looked like a very young Roman goddess. Full of grace, but there she was beavering away as a domestic. She had such a *look* about her."

"Enough to stop your breath." His mouth had turned so dry it was difficult to speak.

"I so liked her," Meredith lamented, even now wondering how she could have been so mistaken in Gina. "She seemed as beautiful inside as out."

"Error of judgement," he said with a humourless laugh. "I just couldn't believe it when Lorinda told me Gina had gone." Cal made a big effort to shove the old agony away. "She didn't even bother to give notice. She just took off."

Meredith recalled it well, her own shock and dismay, as Cal continued speaking. "The odd thing was Management didn't seem perturbed about it, when anyone would have thought they would be angry at the way she'd left them in the lurch. I could never figure it out."

"Aunt Lorinda would have had a private word with them," Meredith said quietly, "or her pal did. Ian Haig owned the island. Still does. Obviously to avoid further upsetting you, they dropped it."

"I guess so," Cal said, nodding. How did one learn to shut down on images that persisted? In his mind's eye, he saw Gina lying back on the white sand, the sea breeze all around them, him bending over her, ready to claim that lovely, moulded mouth. "We've been there, Mere." He sighed. "No one is going to take the ground from under my feet again. No point in going over it. Whatever the full story, Lorinda tried to help in any way she could."

"Not much use, was she?"

Cal's mahogany head, sun streaked like his sister's, jerked towards her in surprise. "What is that supposed to mean?"

"Well, she could have persuaded Gina to at least attempt to explain herself to you," Meredith said. "I would have, but Gina didn't confide in me. As for Aunt Lorinda, I haven't exactly forgiven her for interfering in my pitiful fling with Jake Ellory."

Cal grunted, "Ellory wasn't half good enough for you, Mere." He lay a sympathetic hand on her shoulder.

"Okay." She had to acknowledge that. "Point is I was able to see that for myself. I know Aunt Lorinda means well. She dotes on you, always has. She's very nice to me, too, but she's a master manipulator just like Mum. They're as thick as thieves. The facts were she was all in favour of Kym. Kym was the blue-eyed girl. Gina was the seductress. I guess we're never going to know exactly what happened. I could have sworn Gina was as madly in love with you as you were with her. The *feeling* that was generated between you two turned the air electric!"

"That wasn't electricity, my dear, that was hot air," Cal said flatly, his handsome features grown taut. "Gina didn't have the guts to tell me what she told Lorinda. What she had going was a great holiday fling. The reality was, she already had her serious boyfriend back home. Italian descent just like her. Marrying him was obviously very important in her family."

Meredith could accept that as true. Italian and Greek communities were very close. "Well, it was a sad, sad business. That's all I can say. But how does someone who readily puts her life on the line for a child act in a spineless manner? It doesn't make sense. Look at her face. It's not just a beautiful face, it's a *brave* face. I'm not surprised she did something like this. I can see her doing it, can't you? Why then didn't she try to explain herself? Why did she allow herself to get in so deep in the first place, given she was virtually promised to someone else? Perhaps she was frightened of her dad? I got the impression from something she let drop, he was super strict. I know all about strict dads."

Cal, re-reading the article, turned his remarkable gaze back on her.

A McKendrick in every other respect, the height, the splendid physique, the handsomely chiselled features, Cal had inherited his emerald-green eyes from their mother. Devil-green one of Meredith's girlfriends called them, always trying to capture Cal's attention with her bold, sexy glances.

"I'm going after her," he announced.

"You are?" Somehow that didn't shock her. She even wondered if she hadn't deliberately set it up. She could have thrown away the article. Instead she had kept it for him. Was it possible this time he and Gina could make it work? Gina's wedding plans with her Italian boyfriend hadn't come off it seemed.

"You bet!" Cal rasped, radiating determination. "How come she didn't marry that guy? It says here, Gina Romano." He stabbed the paper with a tanned forefinger. "That's her maiden name, not Gina Falconi, or Marente or whatever. Another guy she left with a broken heart. She's still unmarried. I want to know *why.*" Cal threw up his head, unable to control the thoughts of revenge.

Meredith made no attempt to dissuade him. Cal had the bit between his teeth. When Cal decided to do something, it was done and pretty damned quick. She knew Gina had broken his heart. She knew he had been trying to forget her ever since. He deserved the chance to find out once and for all if Gina Romano simply wasn't worth all his pain. Cal was approaching thirty. He had to move on. Their parents were desperate for him to get married. They needed Cal to produce an heir, give them their first grandchild. Needless to say they would be hoping for a boy.

"What are you going to tell Mum and Dad?" she asked. "You run the station. You can't just vanish."

"I'm going to tell 'em I'm in need of a short break," he answered tersely. "Steve can hold the fort while I'm gone. He's well capable of it. He carries his old man's genes, even if Lancaster won't acknowledge him." Everyone in the Outback knew Gavin Lancaster, Channel Country cattle baron, was Steve Lockhart's biological father. Steve might as well have had *Lancaster* stamped on his forehead. "Even Dad concedes Steve has turned out just fine when initially he was against taking him on. Didn't want to get on the wrong side of Lancaster I suppose. Lancaster's one mean man."

Meredith's expression was wry. "They call Dad a son of a bitch behind his back," she reminded him.

"Maybe. But he's not *mean*. Mostly he's generous. Steve is shaping up to be the best overseer we've ever had. Had he been granted a bit of Lancaster money he could have bought a property of his own and worked it up."

"Well, that's not going to happen," Meredith spoke briskly, hoping the heat she felt in her veins didn't show in her cheeks. "Gavin Lancaster will go to his grave refusing to acknowledge Steve. One wonders why. His wife is dead. His other son doesn't measure up from all accounts. One can only feel sorry for him. Ah, well!" Meredith threw the issue off with a shrug. Usually she kept her thoughts about Steve Lockhart under wraps. She had learned the hard way to feign indifference to any man who attracted her, a man, moreover, who was a McKendrick employee and Gavin Lancaster's illegitimate son to boot. As far as her parents were concerned there was a *huge* gulf between family and staff. She found life easier if she kept up a pretence. No one was to know what went on inside her.

"I'll take this," Cal was saying, folding the sheet of newspaper so it fitted into the back pocket of his jeans.

"Be my guest. I suppose this just *could* be a mistake, Cal," she offered gently, feeling a sudden obligation to warn this brother she so loved and respected.

"That's just a chance I'm going to have to take." Cal started to move off, his stride swift and purposeful. At the door he turned to give her his heart-stopping smile. It was a smile Meredith shared, though she wasn't fully aware of it.

"It's been four years?"

"It only seems like yesterday."

Meredith blinked rapidly at the expression in his eyes. She knew the struggle he was having trying to keep his passionate emotions in check. The newspaper clipping had come as a revelation. "What are you going to do when you find her?" She realised she actually *wanted* Gina Romano back in their lives. Her memories of Gina were of a beautiful young woman strong but gentle with a great sense of humour and highly intelligent. The sort of young woman she would have treasured as a friend. She knew she couldn't speak for her mother and father. She had the sinking feeling they would be strongly against someone like Gina. Gina wasn't a PLU. It was the snob thing, PLU meaning People Like Us.

Cal took a moment to reply. "I'm going to demand she tell me to my face why she *lied*."

The words were delivered with chilling force.

CHAPTER TWO

GINA parked outside "Aunt" Rosa's modest bungalow made beautiful by the garden Rosa lavished such love and attention on. Taking the myriad scents of the garden deep into her lungs, Gina walked slowly up the stone-paved path to the front porch decorated with flower-filled hanging baskets. When Rosa had bought the bungalow three years back, Gina had helped greatly with the clean-up operation, cajoling a few of her sturdy male friends to join in, especially when it came to hauling in the rocks Rosa had used as natural features. In those days there was *no* garden, a few straggly plants, but Rosa had turned the allotment into a private garden paradise. The stone paths led through a wealth of flowering shrubs, camellias, azaleas, peonies, hydrangeas, through cascading archways of roses, all strongly fragrant, the floribunda wisteria, "Alba" and groves of lush ferns. There was always something happening in Rosa's garden, something to lift the heart.

Rosa was her godmother, her mother's bridesmaid at her first disastrous marriage which had produced Sandro and her. The great tragedy of her life was the disappearance of Sandro, her brother. Two years her senior he had run off at the age of sixteen after a violent argument with their father, the most difficult and demanding of men. Sandro had not only run off, he had vanished from the face of the earth. How did one do that? Gina had asked herself that question countless times. How did one lose one's identity? How did one go about obtaining a driving licence? What about credit cards, a Medicare card? Could Sandro be dead? Something inside her told her, no, though he had never contacted her or their mother to tell her he was safe, not a single phone call or a postcard. His disappearance had almost killed their mother and caused her, his loving sister, deep grief that continued right up to the present day.

Rosa knew all about her family's deeply troubled past. Rosa had been there. "One day, *cara,* Sandro will return to us. You'll see. It was just that he could no longer live with your father." What Rosa felt Gina's father to be was always delivered in impassioned Italian. Rosa was a woman of volatile temperament.

Yet their father had worshipped her, his daughter. She could do no wrong. She was his shining star. She might have been marked down for future canonisation. *"My beautiful Gianina!"* Until the night she confessed she was pregnant. Then her virgin image had been well and truly shattered.

Rosa had always kept in touch with her. Indeed, Rosa had offered to take her in, after her father had literally thrown her, the fallen idol, out. It had truly been the never-darken-my-door-again situation she had hitherto thought only existed in novels. But the last thing she had wanted was to bring down trouble on Rosa's head even though her godmother had sworn she could handle the likes of Ugo Romano.

"He's a great big bully, you know!"

When Primo, Rosa's husband, died at the early age of fifty-four Rosa sold the old sugar farm and travelled to Brisbane to be near her goddaughter. Rosa, a warm, generous woman had not been blessed with children, a great sorrow to her. *"Poor Primo, he couldn't manage it."* Otherwise Primo had been a good, good man. Everyone in the community had agreed on that.

"Someone has to look after you!" Rosa announced when she arrived on Gina's doorstep, followed by a torrent of curses aimed at Gina's father. At least one of them must have worked because Gina's father barely eighteen months later had bounced off a country road, the old farm utility turning over a few times before landing in a ditch killing him in the process.

"God has spoken," Rosa, never short of an explanation, pronounced at the funeral. *"Now everyone is safe. My poor Lucia, maybe, might find herself another husband. One to cherish her. I see Vince Gambaro over there."*

Gina's mother, Lucia, was pardoned by both her daughter and Rosa. Though desperately unhappy in her arranged marriage, she had been too cowed by her husband to leave him though the friends who cared for her had begged her to do so.

"Sometimes poison isn't all that bad!" muttered Rosa, with black humour.

Before Gina was even at the door, painted cobalt-blue and flanked by matching glazed pots bearing a wealth of pink camellias, Rosa, unconventionally, but eye-catchingly dressed in her own creations, was out on the porch, smiling a welcome.

"He just loves this cartoon," she said. "Lots of giggles, clapping, singing, dancing, peals of laughter. Such a beautiful sound, a child's laughter! I think the video is nearly through."

"Has he been a good boy?" Gina bent to kiss her godmother's satin-smooth cheek. Rosa was a striking-looking woman with a passionate, lived-in kind of face. She was also very queenly in a gypsy fashion. And she had admirers. Rosa had always had admirers, though she had never once succumbed to temptation in all the years of her marriage. One admirer was very much in the picture, a well-to-do widower, a retired bank manager. Gina had met him on several occasions, thinking him a nice man but lacking Rosa's broad cultural interests.

"Always a good boy! Impossible not to love him." Rosa was stroking Gina's arm, showing the depth of her affection. Her god-daughter had filled a vacuum in Rosa's life, but nothing could erase the sorrow of not having children and grandchildren of her own. Gina and Roberto came somewhere in between.

"Mummy!" Now Robbie was at the door, holding up his arms.

Gina picked him up and hugged him to her while he covered her cheeks in kisses. "Hello, my darling," she said, her heart melt-ing with love. "So what happened at preschool today?"

"I learnt lots of things," he told her proudly, then frowned. "I think I've forgotten now."

"No matter. It will all come back."

"Are you coming in?" Rosa asked, standing back from the door.

"For ten minutes," Gina smiled. "I've got something for you."

"For me, too?" Robbie asked hopefully.

"Something for you *both*," Gina said setting her son down. Goodness he was getting heavy and he was tall for his age.

"I hope mine comes in a bottle," Rosa flashed another dark-eyed grin. Rosa was a wonderful cook and something of a wine expert, partial to a really good red, preferably a Shiraz.

"It got highly rated," Gina told her

"Bellisimo!" Rosa cried, throwing up her arms and going into a spirited little dance that made the gold hoops in her ears sway and Robbie laugh. Rosa was far more of a grandmother to Robbie than ever his real grandmother was, now living far away on a New Guinea coffee plantation.

They walked through to the kitchen, Robbie running ahead. Modest from the outside, inside the bungalow was a reflection of Rosa's exuberant, artistic nature. The walls of the house were covered in her paintings. The warmly welcoming yellow-and-white kitchen was dominated by a large painting of a wicker basket filled to overflowing with yellow lemons and their lustrous leaves, the leaves spilling on to a white tablecloth. Gina loved it. Rosa had given her several of her paintings to decorate the apartment.

They were home in less than ten minutes. She settled Robbie in front of the television in the living room so he could watch the end of the video while she went through to her bedroom to change out of her smart business clothes. Inside the walk-in wardrobe she reached for a comfortable caftan that was still rather glamorous, fuchsia silk with a gold trim. She'd been out to a business lunch, which she thought should carry her through dinnertime. Maybe a light salad? Robbie wanted his all-time favourite which she allowed him once a week—sausages and mash. She always bought the best quality pork sausages, wrapped them in bacon, which he liked and let him have tomato sauce, which surprise, surprise, had turned out to be one of the dwindling number of things good for everyone. Once a very fussy eater, Robbie now enjoyed his food, eating the healthiest food for most of the time. The great news was she now had him eating banana porridge before he went off to school. He refused point-blank to eat cereal or eggs. *Yuck!*

She was passing through the hallway when a knock on the apartment door startled her. Visitors had to buzz through to her video-intercom and identify themselves before being allowed through the security door. It had to be Dee from the Body Corporate Management. If parcels arrived and couldn't be delivered because she was at work, Dee usually took care of them. Dee was a good sort, ever helpful, kind and gentle with Robbie. And why not? Her beautiful little son was a gorgeous child with the sunniest of natures. Everyone loved him.

She didn't open the door immediately. She checked through the peephole but could only see someone holding up a large bouquet of yellow roses. They looked like her favourite, *Pal Joey*. Nat Goldman, a very nice guy she worked with, had taken to sending her roses, but they were usually red. Shaking back the long tumble of her hair, she threw back the door, a smile on her face.

And there was Calvin McKendrick; the power elite!

There had been no icy tingle this time to warn her. Her powers had deserted her. Or his powers were stronger. The blood roared in her ears and she wrapped her arms tightly around herself as if the action could prevent her from falling. No trace of her smile remained.

Four years were as *nothing*. His presence was as vividly familiar to her as if their separation had only been fleeting moments. Yet she stood rooted to the spot, unable to move, unable to speak, struck dumb with wonderment. Then very gradually her entire body began to react. She felt an unbearable urge to throw herself into his arms, feel them close powerfully around her. She wanted to inhale his marvellous male scent. She wanted to kiss his beautiful mouth. She wanted to *taste* him. Hadn't she suffered grievously these past years? Instead she took a long, deep breath, widening her eyes in surprise.

"Cal!"

"Ah, you've remembered!" he said suavely. "Do please go on." There was a dangerous edge to the civility of his tone. It matched the glitter in his remarkable eyes, as green as emeralds, and as cold.

"Go on?" She groped for the door behind her so she could close it. He couldn't be allowed to see Robbie. She had to keep him from it. She was too frighteningly vulnerable, now as then. He could take her beloved son off her, or curtail her time with him. That prospect she couldn't bear. The McKendricks were powerful people with an army of lawyers at their disposal and limitless funds. That alone inspired fear.

"Well, surely you're going to add you're surprised to see me?" The voice she had so loved, was filled with mockery.

"I am, *very!*" Even to her own ears her voice sounded strangled. She was trembling all over, her heart kicking against her ribs. "How did you find me?"

He tut-tutted. "And you, the heroine?"

Of course. The newspaper story that had even made it onto the television. People still pointed at her in the street. Some even came up to her, congratulating her on her bravery.

What can I do? She couldn't get her head around the dilemma that now faced her. It was imperative she pull herself together.

"Have you someone with you?" he asked, seeing the agitation that was written all over her. His eyes went beyond her to the entrance hall; a small console, a striking oil painting above it, two Victorian lustres, emerald-green glass, decorated with tiny white flowers and gold leaves; all very pretty.

Gina scrambled to nod her head, though she felt dazzled and dazed.

"Are you asking me to come back another time?" Perversely he found his eyes consuming her. She was a wonderful-looking woman; more beautiful than ever, if that were possible. Her classical features were more clearly defined, her eyes, deep, dark bottomless pools. Her masses of hair, neither straight nor curly, fell in thick sinuous coils halfway down her back. Desire over which he had no control streamed through his blood, like a river in full spate. He was a greater fool than even he had thought.

"Please don't come back, Cal," Gina begged, spinning very quickly as she heard Robbie, his programme over, moving to join her. "There's absolutely nothing we could have to say to one another after all this time." Galvanised, she tried to shut the door but Cal deliberately blocked her efforts with one foot against it.

No, Robbie! The voice inside her shrieked.

But Robbie came on, dead-set on finding out who his mother was talking to. Robbie had great social skills. He loved visitors. Just as she feared, he rounded the partition that divided the entrance hall from the living area, running to Gina and grasping her around the hips. "Hello!" he said brightly, addressing Cal. "Are you a friend of Mummy's?" He gave an engaging little chuckle, looking at Cal with the greatest interest.

But Cal for once in his life was literally struck dumb. He stood pulverized by shock. Whatever scenarios he had considered on his long trip here, it was never this! He found himself rocking back on his heels as the truth came roaring for him like an express train.

God! There was nothing irreverent about his silent oath. Recognition shot simultaneously to his heart and his brain. This was his child. This was his son! There could be no mistake. The child resembled him too closely.

He dragged his eyes away from the beautiful little boy, to pin Gina's treacherous, dark gaze. She looked frightened, utterly wretched, as well she might! "I'd like to come in, if I may." He fought to keep the tight rein on his voice, for the child's sake. "It seems, Gina, we have things to discuss." He put out his hand to his son: dark copper curls like petals, framing an angelic little face. In adolescence those dark copper curls would turn a rich mahogany like his. He had the McKendrick features, but even more tellingly the black-lashed eyes so brilliant a green, they were often described as emerald. There was the McKendrick cleft in his chin, not deep like his father's, more shallow like his. Uncle Ed had a cleft chin. Meredith had a distinctive dimple.

"Hello there, Robbie." Cal showed the child all the gentleness and warmth he denied the mother. "I'm Cal. Calvin McKendrick.

I am an old friend of your mother's. I'm so very pleased to meet you at long last, though I think I would have known you anywhere." Anywhere on this earth, he thought, trying to come to grips with Gina's treachery.

"And I'm pleased to meet *you*," Robbie responded, sweetly, unlocking his grasp on his mother and extended his hand as he'd been taught.

Cal thrust the beautiful yellow roses into Gina's rigid arms before taking the child's hand. "So, Robert?"

"*Robbie*. I've been watching my favourite cartoon."

"Really?" Cal spoke normally, though naked shock was showing in his eyes.

"You can see my video if you like," Robbie offered graciously.

"That's very nice of you, Robbie," Cal said.

"Have you got time now?" the little boy asked hopefully, obviously having taken an immediate liking to Cal.

"Darling," Gina interrupted, "Cal only called in for a minute." She drew Robbie back against her, giving Cal a pleading look.

It had no effect on Cal whatsoever. "No, that's okay!" He shrugged a rangy shoulder. "I wasn't going anywhere special. Do you mind, Robbie, if I come in?" Cal gave his son an utterly winning smile.

"Oh, *please*, Mummy, can he?" Robbie stared up into his mother's face, a highly intelligent child, trying to puzzle out the atmosphere. "I haven't had my tea yet," he told Cal. "It's bangers and mash. Would you like some?"

"If there's any to spare." Cal twisted Gina a hard, challenging smile. He was absolutely certain he wouldn't be able to eat anything, but he definitely wasn't going away.

"Oh, goody!" Robbie put out his hand to take Cal's. "Oh, your hands are rough inside!" he burst out in surprise, as baby soft three-year-old fingers met up with hard calluses.

"That's because I'm a cattleman," Cal explained.

"What's that, a cattleman?" Robbie asked with great interest, beginning to pull Cal through the door. "Do you own cattle, cows and things?"

Cal nodded. "One day I'll show you."

"Promise?" Robbie's big beautiful eyes lit up.

"Let's shake on it."

"You're a very nice man," Robbie pronounced, taking the handshake as a promise.

"Thank you," Cal replied. "It must be getting along to your bedtime soon?" he asked, desperate to have it out with this woman who had so betrayed him.

"Seven o'clock." Robbie lifted his head to scan the face of this tall man he seemed to know somehow, but couldn't understand why. "That's when I go to preschool. I can stay up a little later at the week-end. Will you be here when I go to sleep?"

"Bound to be," Cal said.

Somehow they kept up a reasonable pretence until Robbie went to bed. His mother kissed him as she always did when she tucked him in. "Good night, my darling."

"'Night, Mummy."

"Sleep tight."

"Don't let the bed bugs bite." Robbie giggled as he finished off the nightly ritual, then he put out a hand to Cal.

"You're going to come back and see us, aren't you, Cal?" he asked hopefully.

"Count on it."

Gina watched Cal lean down and touch her little boy's cheek with the most exquisite tenderness.

"That's good. I really like you," Robbie said, the glow from the bedside lamp turning his eyes to jewels.

"As it happens I really like you." Cal smiled, watching his son sigh contentedly, then close his eyes, dark lashes heavy on apricot cheeks.

They returned in a fraught silence to the living room. Gina was amazed tears weren't streaming down her cheeks. She had never seen Robbie respond to anyone like he had to Cal.

Blood will out!

Carefully, she shut the door that led down the corridor to the bedrooms, grateful Robbie slept very soundly, especially when he was overexcited as he was tonight.

"You hate me," Gina said. His face was a taut mask.

"Who in hell would blame me?" Cal replied in a tone so contemptuous it cut deep. "Why did you do it?" He went to her and seized her arms with controlled fury. "So you ran back to your boyfriend! Why didn't you make a fool of him like you made a fool of me? When you realised it was my child you were carrying, why didn't you try to pass it off as his? Didn't think you'd be able to pull if off, eh? Worried he might kill you when he eventually found out? Where did the green eyes come from, the copper curls? Robert is the image of me when I was his age. I have stacks of photographs to prove it, as though we *need* proof." He released her so abruptly, Gina stumbled and had to clutch at the back of an armchair to stay upright.

"I'm sorry if you feel hurt, Cal," she said, tonelessly. "At least it proves you're human."

"Human? What the hell are you talking about? And you're *sorry?* God!" He began to pace the carpet like a caged tiger. "Is that all you can say, sorry? I had a right to *know.* Robert is three years old. Just think what I've missed! Or haven't you any heart at all? For three years I've had a son I didn't even know existed. I wasn't there when he was born, when he took his first steps, when he started to say his first words. I've missed his birthdays.

I've missed loving him. I've missed the joy of having him love me. What's wrong with you? How could you do that to me?" He fell down on the sofa, throwing back his head and covering his eyes with his hands. "What the hell were you thinking about? Dear God, Gina, are you devoid of all conscience?"

She stared back at him, trying hard not to burst into tears. "Don't, please *don't!* I had to cope any way I could."

He flung up his handsome head, tension making his features more hawklike than ever. "And that meant absenting me from your life?" He stared about him at the large room, decorated with style and care, the furnishings, the art works, the fresh flowers. "You live here?"

"Of course I live here." She thrust the heavy fall of her hair over her shoulder.

"Alone with Robert?" He shot her a challenging glace.

"Yes." She dared not add "As if it's any of your business." He was furious, shocked, a pallor beneath his dark tan. She was frightened of him; of what he might do. She just knew something was going to come of that newspaper article.

"You work?" The question was terse. "Sit down, why don't you?"

Demolished she took a seat opposite him. Her heart was beating so fast she thought she might be sick. Low voiced, she named her firm of stockbrokers.

"It must be a darn good job!" He let his eyes move insolently around the attractively furnished room.

"It is," she answered shortly, regaining her breath. "All you see here is mine."

"Bravo!" he crowed.

"What do you want, Cal?" She cut across him, the room thick with tension.

"Who looks after Robert until you get home?" His eyes lanced.

She hated this interrogation, even as she knew she had to endure it. "My godmother, Rosa. She's a wonderful woman. Roberto loves her."

"What's the wonderful Rosa doing down here in Brisbane, or is *everything* you told me a pack of lies?"

"No!" she protested, shaking her head. "When Rosa's husband died she sold the farm to be near me. She takes her responsibilities as godmother very seriously."

"Her prayers couldn't prevent you becoming an inveterate liar," he countered bitterly.

"I never lied to you."

He laughed harshly. "God, you're lying *now*. You were the one who told me you loved me. You told me you never dreamed there could be such happiness. You told me you wanted to be with me always. If they weren't lies, may I ask what in hell *were* they?"

Fearful only a moment before, Gina's magnificent dark eyes flashed. "Why weren't *you* truthful with me?" she demanded, the pain of the past as raw as yesterday. "You had a girl back home you were expected to marry. I even know her name, Kym Harrison. Don't look so shocked. Men are notoriously unfaithful. I saw a photograph of you together in a magazine. You were at the Melbourne Cup. Calvin McKendrick and his lovely fiancée, Kym Harrison. I still have the clipping somewhere to remind me of your treachery. Why didn't you tell me about your Kym?"

He couldn't answer for a minute so taken aback was he by her use of the word *treachery*. "Why are you drawing Kym into this?" he retaliated, heavily frowning. "As soon as I met you there *was* no other woman. No Kym. You were everything I wanted. *My* woman. Getting engaged to Kym came after. It shames me to say it, it certainly wasn't my finest moment, but I became engaged to Kym to forget *you!*"

She stared at him, this man who had haunted her, the father of her child. "It didn't work?" Her tone was deeply hostile. She was out to wound as he was wounding her.

"No more than your relationship with your Italian boyfriend," he countered, sending her a glittering glance that would have crushed her, only she was too startled by his mention of a boyfriend.

"I beg your pardon?" she said, disdainfully, lifting her chin.

He laughed at the hauteur. "Oh, come off it! How easily you assume the regal demeanour. Sure there's not a Contessa or two in the background?"

"I wish!" There was a curl of her moulded lips. Those lips he had kissed so often. "I had *no* Italian boyfriend if that's your idea of an excuse. My father frowned on boyfriends. I was a virgin when I met you. You *know* that."

Colour mounted to his prominent cheekbones. "Yes," he admitted, "but we did use protection."

"One time we didn't."

He buried his head in his hands. "Then my responsibility was far greater than yours. You were just a girl. I was mad about you. Absolutely crazy with love and longing. The last thing I wanted to do was hurt you."

"Am I supposed to believe that?" Her tongue lashed him. "You *did* hurt me. More than you will ever know. I've suffered, but I have my beautiful Roberto."

"And Robert is a McKendrick family name. I recall telling you that."

"Maybe you did—" she shrugged "—but I named him after my brother, Alessandro. Roberto is his middle name." She didn't tell him both factors had influenced her.

Cal studied her with a frown, suddenly remembering how she had told him an older brother had defected from home. "You're talking about the Sandro who went missing when he was sixteen?"

"Aah! You actually remember something!" Her voice throbbed with scorn.

"I remember *everything!*" he corrected her harshly. "He's never contacted you?"

She shook her head, sadness replacing the scorn. There was a long, long list of Missing Persons. "He could be dead for all we know."

Even through his shock and anger, her obvious sorrow reached him.

Gina swallowed on a dry throat. Before her she saw a man who had matured a good deal since she had last seen him. He looked every inch a man of power and authority. The sweetness, however, that had been so much part of his expression had disappeared.

The fear returned. "Please, Cal. Can you reassure me you wouldn't be so cruel as to try to take Robbie from me. I adore him. He's my son."

"He's *my* son, too, Gina," he said curtly, rising to his feet and looming over her. "Tonight I claim him. Fortune has at long last decided to turn my way. I have every intention of taking him back to Coronation Hill. He's a McKendrick. Coronation is his home. It's his heritage. He's my heir."

Anger and fear boiled together in her great dark eyes. "He's my heir, too, I remind you! Romano blood runs in my son's veins. Just when do you think you could take him? Go on, tell me that. And what about me? Do you really think I'm going to stand back and let you take Roberto from me? You'd have to kill me first."

His expression, unlike hers, was astoundingly cool. He took hold of her wrist, letting her feel just a touch of his vastly superior strength. "No need to kill you, Gina," he drawled. "*Marrying* you suits me better."

For a moment she thought she would faint. "Because I have

your child?" she cried passionately. "I wasn't good enough for you before." She pulled away violently, rubbing her wrist. "Marriage between us would never work."

He went down on his haunches before her. "Listen and listen carefully." He spoke softly but his demeanour conveyed forceful determination. "I want my son to have a proper upbringing. No broken home. I want him to have a mother and father. That's the two of us. Are you going to tell me there's someone else on the horizon? Someone prepared to take on another man's child? Not that he would have to. I'm intent on getting custody of Robert. I don't think the court would look too *favourably* on you and your deceit. Your brother, Sandro, isn't the only one in your family who likes to disappear. Tell me this? How can a woman who put her own life on the line to save a child, lack the guts to come forward? To stand up and be counted. Or were you overcome with guilt?"

She kept her head lowered, not daring to look into his mesmeric eyes. She was overwhelmingly conscious their faces were mere inches away. "Even when you were making love to me, making our baby, you were lying," she said wretchedly.

He made a sound of the greatest impatience. He caught her chin sharply, holding a hard thumb to it to keep it up. "You could get any acting job. You're great!" he scoffed. "It's the Italian thing. You know how to exploit emotion. I told you I loved you. I never meant anything more in my life. That part of it is over. I can never trust you again. These past four years I've learned to *hate!*"

"And I have hated, as well. A nice basis for a marriage!" Gina looked him right in the eye, her tone inflammatory. Damn him, damn him! Being so close to him was tearing her in all directions. "And what about your so lofty family?" she demanded. "They wouldn't have accepted me then, why now? Although I don't include your sister, Meredith, in this!"

He stood up, rigid with disgust. "Lord, what a fake you are, Gina. Don't try to drag my family into this. Why don't you just admit it? I was your last big fling before you settled down and became a good little Italian wife. You were going home to marry your boyfriend, the one *Papa and Mamma* had picked out for you." Unforgivably he parodied an Italian accent.

"You were the one going home to marry your Kym." Her great eyes flashed. "So you see, liars on both sides." Suddenly she saw clearly her version of events would clash with his own. She had had her knowledge from his aunt, but at this point she didn't want to draw his aunt into the whole tragic mess because it would only serve to further anger and alienate him.

"Well, we got our just reward," he said with deep irony. "My engagement didn't work. Your marriage prospects were doomed to failure. It's the old story, isn't it? Damaged goods. Hate that expression myself. I have to say motherhood has done wonders for you." He made it sound like she'd once been an ugly duckling. "The dewy girl has turned into a woman. You didn't answer me about your current love life? Not that it matters a damn whatever you're going to say."

She stared across at him, feeling a tightness in her chest. She had loved him as much as she was capable of loving anyone outside her son. *Their son.* "You're serious, then? You're going to force a marriage on me?"

"You bet!"

The hard light in his eyes swallowed all her breath.

"I seem to recall your telling me your parents' marriage was arranged?"

"And it was desperately unhappy as any marriage between us would be." Remembrance of her unhappy family life shadowed her face.

"You omitted to tell me that. I suppose another lie?"

"So, I'm an accomplished actress and an inveterate liar?" She gave him a scathing glance.

"Maybe the two sometimes go together! And how are the Romanos?" He used his suavest tone.

She was racked by a little convulsive shiver. "My father is dead. My mother has remarried. She and her husband live in New Guinea now. I rarely see her."

He lifted supercilious black brows. "She didn't waste much time?"

"She's trying to make up for the lost years," Gina said crisply. "My father had a very difficult temperament."

"I'm sorry to hear it. I suppose that's why Sandro took off?"

"My father was very hard on him. Not at all kind."

"Yet you gave me the strong impression he adored you?"

Adored her? When she exactly matched his vision of her. She sometimes thought her father couldn't have coped with a pregnant daughter, in or out of wedlock.

"What no answer?" He stared across at her, so wanting to pull her into his arms he had to grip the sides of his chair.

"I'm not going to allow you to question me further," she said angrily. "You McKendricks are cruel people."

That stung him. "Don't you think you should wait to meet them before you decide that?'

"I've met *you*." Her great dark eyes dominated her face. "Let me say again. A marriage between us couldn't work."

He steepled his lean hands, as though considering. "Given you're the mother of my son," he said finally, "I suggest you try to make it work. Or sit it out."

"Sit it out?" she gasped. "I would never, never choose to sit my life out. I want what every woman wants—a man to love her, children, a happy home. We have nothing in common."

"Apart from our son. Never forget that. And unless I'm very

much mistaken we're still physically attracted to one another. We could still have the sex. That might keep us pinned together. The sex hasn't gone away, has it?"

She could never deny it. But she *did*. "Oh, stop that!" she said sharply. "Sex is out of the question."

"But I've never forgotten it. You were terrific, Gina. I wanted you to the point of madness. Pathetic how you made me feel! You made me so weak with longing I couldn't see straight. I used to go around all the time my body aching with pain and desire. I was *nuts* about you." He could barely contain his hostility.

"But that was it, wasn't it?" she retorted. "You just loved having sex with me."

"Why not? Sex with you was Heaven. And so disastrous!"

"Some relationship!" she muttered bitterly. "Well, I paid for it."

"Not just *you!*" His expression hardened into granite. "If you can spare a thought for me, who was never told he was a father. How long will it take you to get yourself organised?" he asked crisply. "I assume you'll have to give notice to your firm. You'd better make it as short as you can. There'll be no difficulty taking Robert out of play school or whatever it is."

She put a hand to her pounding temples. "I can't do this," she near wailed. "You're quite mad."

"My dear Gina, I've never been saner." He leaned back in the armchair, the picture of nonchalance. "If you fight me I promise you, you'll lose. Your best course—indeed, your only course—is to try to make a go of this. *I'm* prepared to."

His arrogance made her livid. "*You're* prepared to!" She totally forgot herself and shouted.

"Keep it down," he warned, turning his head towards the bedroom area.

"Don't tell me what I should do in my own home," she hissed, saturated in hot feeling. "I can see you've grown ruthless."

"If I have it's because of you," he retorted on the instant. "If it makes you more comfortable I give you my solemn promise I won't touch you until you're ready."

"And what makes you think I'll *ever* be ready?" She stared at him coldly.

"Let's have a little test run, shall we?"

He confounded her by rising from his chair.

An unbelievable thrill shot through her. "No test runs!"

He hauled her to her feet, holding her so she had no chance of getting away. "Not so easy to run now, is it, *Gianina?*"

Passion came boiling to the surface. Will subservient to the flesh. Past merged into present. "Don't accuse me of running one more time," she gritted. She hadn't run. She'd been persuaded it was the only thing she could do. The honourable thing.

"Or you'll do what?" His eyes rested compulsively on her full mouth. "Don't try playing the innocent victim with me, Gina. It won't wash. You're a born seductress. You don't have to do anything but look at a man. *Kiss* me."

"Too many kisses," she said, yet her whole being was thrown into a sensual upheaval. No one touched her like he did. She tried to call on her pride and her sense of self-esteem. It would have been easier to call up thunder and lightning. "Damn you to hell!" she cried weakly as his grip tightened.

"I've been there." He spoke with great bitterness, sweeping her fully into his arms. There he held her as though that was where she belonged and nowhere else. She wondered how, after so much pain, her body could respond so brilliantly to his touch; but shamefully it did. It was no mock-up test kiss. It was incredibly turbulent, profoundly vengeful. Deeply suppressed emotions erupted as if at the touch of a detonator.

When they finally broke apart, both were breathing heavily. Cal waited only a speechless moment before he pulled her against him again. "So it's not all over then?" His emerald eyes glittered as though he had won an important battle.

How could she find the words to deny it anyway? He had ruined her utterly for other men. "You said it yourself. All we've got is sex."

"And it's *good*," he ground out harshly, before covering her mouth again.

Hungrily his hand sought her breast, shaped it, his fingers taking hold of the erect nipple, tightening *exquisitely*. She couldn't help her quick gasps that he muffled with his lips. There was a hot gush of feelings inside of her as powerful chemicals were released into her bloodstream.

Surely it was a type of cruelty this power he had over her? she thought fiercely. Would she never be safe from him, safe from herself?

It wasn't just Cal's strong arms that were holding her hostage. Gina could deny it all she liked, but it was her own heart.

Hours after he had gone back to his hotel, Gina lay in bed sobbing as she hadn't sobbed for years. All the suffering came back to haunt her. Her parents' unhappy marriage; her mother's inability to stand up for herself or for her children, in particular Sandro; her father's periodic rages and she the only one they were rarely directed at; Sandro's disappearance after that last dreadful fight. Later the miracle of the island that had touched her with such radiance, then left her an outcast. The terrifying discovery she was pregnant; her own banishment from the family home, the all pervading sense of loss. Just seeing Cal again brought it all rushing back like the incoming tide to the shore.

She could never have survived on her own without the small stash of money her mother had secreted from her father and stuffed inside a pocket of her suitcase, all the while crying broken-heartedly, without the courage to intervene. More financial help had come from Rosa and Primo; and all through, Rosa's tremendous support. Gina had known the background of her baby son's father, scion of a rich and powerful family, but she had never considered contacting him. She didn't need to be paid off. She had her pride to sustain her. The love she had felt for Cal McKendrick, the ruling passion that had altered the course of her life, was soured by betrayal.

In the last couple of years she had found her feet, but the memory of him had shadowed her life, making it near impossible for her to embark on another relationship. Now he had marched right back into her life, filled with a violent outrage she had kept the existence of his son from him. She tried to block out the harshness and devastation that had been in his voice. Did she really deserve such condemnation? Perhaps she did. She understood his pain even as she feared his power and influence. The time had come for him to assert his rights; to claim his son and as a consequence his son's mother.

"This time you're not getting away, Gina. You're going to do exactly what I tell you."

She rose from the bed to change her tear-drenched pillows, turning her head to look at her bedside clock. 2:10 a.m. She reminded herself she had to get up early in the morning. She had to shower and dress, wake Robbie, get his breakfast, then ready him for preschool, drop him off, then continue on into work where she had to do what he had instructed her to do. Hand in her notice.

CHAPTER THREE

YARDING up had gone on all day. Steve was closing the gates on the portable steel yard when she rode up on him. He knew even before he turned his head it was Meredith. That's how sensitised he was to her presence. She had helped out all day on a tough job. Too tough for a woman, he thought, but there was no dissuading her. She was a McKendrick. Most of the young guys on the station were in love with her. Fat lot of good it would do them, the only daughter of the "Duke and Duchess" Ewan and Jocelyn McKendrick.

"I think I can say it's been quite a day!" she sighed lustily from behind him.

"You did more than your fair share," he said as he turned, using a matter-of-fact voice. It was the usual way they talked to one another. Keep it businesslike. "Any news of Cal?"

She dismounted, and he took the reins from her, knotting them around a rung of the fence. "Plenty." She was dressed like he was, in jeans and a cotton shirt. He had a bold red bandana around his throat. Hers was blue to match her shirt, but the colour paled into insignificance against the sapphire of her eyes. Both of them wore cream felt Akubras low over their eyes. Even the late-afternoon sun had a real bite to it.

"Big secret, is it?"

She didn't smile and she had the most beautiful smile in the world. Lovely white teeth, finely cut mouth. An aristocrat yet with no vanity or ostentation. "I guess you're going to know about it soon enough," she said, "but I'd like you to keep it to yourself."

"Sure."

She nodded, knowing he was as close lipped as she was and very loyal. "Let's walk down to the creek, shall we?"

He dared not speak. What could he say? I'd walk to the ends of the earth with you? He'd been on Coronation Hill the best part of two years with hardly a day when she hadn't been stuck in his head. Truth be known he was well and truly smitten with Ms Meredith McKendrick. Enormous effrontery but he'd learned from early childhood how to cover up his feelings. The men, never slow to catch on, hadn't a clue, though Tom, the retiring overseer, had muttered to him just before he left: "Reckon you could handle McKendrick, son. Why don't you have a go?"

He would, too, only he had precious little to offer a woman like Meredith McKendrick. He couldn't even offer her a clean name. All because of Lancaster! It had been tough growing up, as he had, in a family with various shades of blond hair when his was as black as a crow's wing. His eyes instead of being the Lockhart's azure-blue were more gold than brown. Eyes were a dead give-away. They showed one's ancestry. Meredith, for instance, had the McKendrick eyes. They were so blue in some lights they looked purple. Cal had his mother's eyes—dark green with a jewel-like quality. Steve was barely ten when he discovered his "foreign" colouring didn't come from his mother's side of the family as she had always claimed. His colouring came directly from Gavin Lancaster.

He remembered hiding out on the verandah, listening to his mother crying in the bedroom until her tears must have blinded her. He remembered Jim Lockhart berating her, full of an impotent rage now the secret was out. No one could touch Gavin Lancaster. He was too powerful. But Gavin Lancaster could make life very hard for a stockman like Jim Lockhart and his family. He had two half brothers and a half sister. All of them, including his mother, had long since packed up and moved to New Zealand, putting the Tasman between them. The Outback was Lancaster's territory. A man needed to be frightened of Gavin Lancaster and his vengeance.

All except him. He sure as hell wasn't frightened. He had remained. No one was going to separate him from the land he loved. Certainly not the man who had sired him.

He followed Meredith's lead down to the bubbling stream, a small tributary of a much larger billabong, their boots bruising hundreds of tiny wildflowers he thought were native violets.

"Let's sit here," she said, sinking wearily onto the pale golden sand and throwing off her wide-brimmed hat. She had beautiful hair…long and thick and gleaming, burnished at the temples with streaks the colour of champagne. He would love to see it out, streaming over her shoulders. A dream?

Slowly, he lowered his long length beside her—he was six-three—relishing the moment but keeping a respectful distance. "Problems?" he asked, slanting her a glance. No one would have known he was suffocating inside, just to be near her. The two of them alone together. It rarely happened. He calmed himself, feeling the slick of sweat on his brow.

Meredith stared across the creek that could swell to a river in the Wet. The late-afternoon sun was flooding the area with light, throwing rose-gold bands across the rippling surface of the water. "I'm telling you this, Steven, because I trust you. Cal does, too."

She was the only one to ever call him Steven. He loved his own name on her lips. "You know anything you tell me remains private."

She nodded. "It will all come out eventually."

"It can't be that bad if it has to do with Cal?"

"I'm hoping with all my heart it will be good," she burst out emotionally. "This all has to do with a woman."

"Most things do." He sounded solemn.

"The only woman for Cal," Meredith said. "It started four years ago. Some of the family took a long holiday on a Barrier Reef island, a small privately run luxury resort. A friend of my aunt's owns it. Our group, extended family and friends took over the island. It only caters to around thirty. On the island was a very beautiful young woman called Gina. She was working in the university vacation as a domestic, waitress, whatever was required. Cal fell madly in love with her and I could have sworn she fell madly in love with him. It was really something to see them together."

"Sounds like it ended badly?" he said, feeling truly sorry. How could anything end badly with a guy like Cal McKendrick who had everything?

"Very badly," Meredith said. "Gina left the island without saying a word to Cal. He was devastated. She didn't say anything to me, either, though we quickly got to be friends. She did, however, speak to my aunt."

Aaah, Steve thought, gazing off to the opposite bank where graceful sprays of crimson flowers were blossoming amid the trees. The uppity Aunt Lorinda. A fearful snob like the rest of them except Cal and Meredith who were totally devoid of that defect.

"Gina told my aunt it was just a mad fling," Meredith said quietly. "It didn't look like it at the time. Anyway, Cal has never forgiven or forgotten her."

"Yet he got himself engaged to Kym Harrison?"

Meredith ran a finger down her flushed cheek. "I know. But it was a big mistake. There's always been a lot of pressure on Cal."

"His shoulders are plenty wide enough," Steve said admiringly.

She turned her face to him, surreptitiously studying his profile. Steven Lockhart was a great-looking guy, the golden eyes, the inky-black hair, the strong, regular features. He had an inherent authority to him. The Lancaster Legacy, though he'd bust anyone in the nose for saying it. "Cal thinks a lot of you, too."

"That's good," he reacted with dry amusement. "I always get the impression your dad would like to see me move on."

What could she say? *I don't know why my father is as he is?* Maybe her father had intercepted one of her stray looks in their overseer's direction. "That won't happen while Cal's around," she assured him. "Cal is running the station as you know. Dad has more or less semiretired. Cal's very happy with you. Didn't he leave you in charge?"

He turned his sleek black head to look smilingly into her eyes. "I thought *you* were?"

"Me?" She gave a bittersweet little laugh that nevertheless was music to his ears. "I'm not in charge of anything. No, that isn't true. I run the office. I do lots of things."

"Too smoothly," Steve said, unconsciously echoing Cal. "You make the job look too easy. People take the super-efficient for granted. Anyway go on. I want to hear this story. I've sensed, underneath, Cal is far from happy on the personal front."

"Who is?" she asked, suddenly serious. "Are *you* happy, Steven?"

I've been happier than I've ever been in my life since I met you.

He couldn't tell her that, instead he managed casually, "I'm happy sitting here with you. Or aren't I supposed to say that?"

She caught the metallic glint. "You've got a big chip on your shoulder, Steven Lockhart."

"I've got a big chip on *both* shoulders," he commented. "That's why I'm so well balanced. So this trip of Cal's is connected to Gina?"

"It's all about Gina. He's dead-set on bringing her home."

"What, here to Coronation?" That stopped him in his tracks. "This *is* his home."

"So they've reconciled after all this time?" he asked more quietly.

"There's more."

"Of course there's more." He picked up a pebble and sent it skittering across the ruffled surface of the water. "There's *always* more."

Meredith could still feel the shock of her brother's revelation. "Gina had a child, a little boy," she said simply. "His name is Robert, Robbie."

"And the child is Cal's," Steve finished for her.

Meredith released a pent-up breath. "Apparently he's the image of Cal at the same age, even to the green eyes. He's convinced Gina they should get married."

Steve gave a little grunt. "So marriage it will be, knowing Cal. What do your parents think?" He knew perfectly well the McKendricks still had their hopes set on Kym Harrison who was a nice enough down-to-earth person, but no match for Cal.

"They don't know anything about it as yet," Meredith told him, her tone tinged with worry. "It's going to come as an enormous shock and they don't like shocks. Cal rang me to tell me the news. Cal and I are very close."

"I know that." He picked up another pebble. He had to do something with his hands. "How do you feel about it? I mean, you have a nephew you didn't know about."

With a sigh she fell back against the sand, looking up at the luminous sky that was filling with birds homing into their nests. "And I can't wait to meet him. It will be wonderful to have a little nephew to love. I want to love Gina, too. I know Cal has never stopped loving her. Cal feels very deeply. I could tell he was shocked out of his mind to find he had a son but I could hear the joy, as well. This is what he truly wants."

Steve put a hand to his head, painfully aware of the length of her slender body beside his; the swell of her breasts, the curve of her hips, her lithe thighs and long legs. He got a tight rein on his feelings. *Man, don't let go or you'll go straight to hell!* But didn't she realise the way she was lying back like that presented a danger? He felt he was teetering on the brink. Relaxed around women, he was like a cat on a hot tin roof with Meredith. To counteract it he said almost sternly, "Why didn't she tell him? I can't see Cal turning his back on her, or his child!" The likes of Lancaster certainly, but not Cal McKendrick. "I don't think I could forgive a woman for doing that to me. Just think what he's missed out on. The boy must be…three?"

"They'll have to work it out, Steven," she said, and her voice wobbled a little. "Gina is from a migrant family. Italian. They had a sugar farm in North Queensland. Her heritage shows. She's very beautiful."

"More beautiful than you?" Now, why the hell had he said that? He never got too personal. It was taboo.

"Most certainly," she said, flashes of excitement heating her body. She was deeply attracted to Steven Lockhart. She'd known that for a long time. Just as she knew his prime concern had to be survival. At twenty-eight he'd made overseer on one of the nation's premier beef-producing stations, which was no mean feat. He was well paid, lots of perks. He had a future, providing he didn't get on the wrong side of her father. An adverse word from Ewan McKendrick could harm him in the industry. There was *no* future as Gavin Lancaster's illegitimate son. Lancaster refused to acknowledge him.

She shut her eyes, so now Steve was free to look down at her beautiful face. She had lovely clear skin, with a healthy gloss to it. He loved the soft dimple in her chin. He loved her finely cut mouth. He wanted to kiss it. *So badly.* He wanted to pull her long thick hair out of its plait. He wanted to arrange it the way he had often imagined himself arranging it around her face. "Don't you want to hear you're beautiful?" he asked, unable to keep some of the spiralling sensuality out of his voice.

Meredith's dark blue eyes flew open. The very air was trembling.

"Not from *you*, Steven," she said, swift and low.

He pulled back. Looked away. "Right! I get it. I'm out of line." Some part of him wanted to teach her a lesson. One she wouldn't forget. He wanted to reach for her and haul her into his arms. He could feel the dark force in him, the driving male need. Managed to get it under control, but hell, did it have some power!

"I'm not sure you *do* get it," she said, swinging up into a sitting position. "I didn't mean to offend you, Steven. I know that came out badly. I'm sorry. We're rarely alone together. I'm nervous. What I was trying to say is, *we* can't go anywhere."

His golden eyes had sparkles of light in them. "I didn't think we could, actually," he returned, his tone as cutting as a blade.

She put out a shaking, conciliatory hand; let it hover. She was frightened to touch him. She was frightened what touching him might do to her. She could see the lick of sweat on his darkly tanned skin. She wanted to put her tongue to it. "I've hurt you."

"*Never,* I hope." He flashed her an upbraiding look. "Relax, Meredith. I've put the man back in the box. I'm the dumb employee again So when are they arriving?" Crisply, he changed the subject.

The snap in his voice stung. "Cal is coming home Saturday. Gina and Robbie will follow at a later date."

And the Duke and Duchess didn't know? Only Cal McKendrick could pull that off.

"Well, I hope with all my heart it comes off." And he meant it. Cal McKendrick was not only his boss but a good friend, a supporter.

"That's very nice of you, Steven," she said softly, feeling, inexplicably about to cry. And she *never* cried. She had learned early not to.

"I'm a sweet guy," he said with an ironic twist to his truly sexy mouth.

"No, you're not." A little laugh escaped her. "You're a good person but that's not the same thing. You're a very complex man. You're carrying a lot of baggage."

"And you're not?" His black brows shot up in challenge. "Now, aren't I being outspoken today?" Extreme sarcasm charged his expression.

She stared back at him, wanting for a long time to know all about his life, aware of his deep reserve. "It must have been tough for you growing up?" she asked gently. "When did you find out about Lancaster?" The question should come as no surprise. Everyone knew the story.

He was silent for so long she didn't think he was going to answer. "I'm sorry if I'm intruding on a private grief. You don't want to talk about it?"

"I'm surprised you want to hear," he said, his mind spinning, as all of a sudden picturing himself having a child with her.

"No, you're not!" She surprised him by saying. "You know I want to hear. I like you, Steven."

"How very gracious of you, Ms McKendrick." He didn't hold the sarcasm back.

"Does it help to mock me?" she asked, turning her eyes on him.

"It does actually." He shrugged. "The difficulties of our situation and so forth. To answer your question I found out that Lancaster had fathered me when I was around ten. The man I thought was my father, Jim Lockhart, had always been a bit uncertain of me. My mother explained away my colouring as being on her side of the family. She was a honey-blond. I was the black crow among all the white feathered cockatoos. Lancaster, strangely no great womaniser, took a fancy to my mother—she was, probably still is, a very pretty woman. She said he raped her." He laughed harshly. "You can bet your life it was a lie. That was just a story to serve up to poor old Jim. Even he wasn't fooled. Lancaster didn't have to rape any woman. He could have any woman he wanted. Mum loved Jim, the father of three of her children. But sleeping with Lancaster was like sleeping with a god. A wicked one at that. She wasn't supposed to get pregnant."

"But it happened."

"It must have. *I'm* here. I'm so much like him we don't need any DNA. They took off for New Zealand where Lockhart had family. I hear from them from time to time. Jim could never take to me, especially after, but he did his best."

"So when was this? When were you on your own?" Sadness jolted her heart.

"Fourteen. I couldn't go with them, too difficult for Jim my mother explained, too destructive to the marriage. I was sent to boarding school for the next three years. They must have had to dig deep. It was a top school. My friends came from Outback properties all over Queensland. That's how I finished up as a station hand."

"Who very quickly rose to the top," she reminded him. "Have you ever spoken a word to Lancaster?"

"I couldn't trust myself to speak to him," Steve said, tasting violent anger at the back of his throat. "I despise the man. He's supposed to be Gavin Lancaster, the big man, the cattle baron! He's a spineless, gutless, wimp. One day we're going to come face-to-face. One day—"

He broke off, his expression so dark, Meredith caught a glimpse of his inner demons. "You don't need him, Steven. You're going to make your mark on your own."

"I intend to," he said. Somehow he knew he was capable of extraordinary things. "You know I've got half brothers everywhere. A Lancaster, two Lockhart's. A half sister—she was a sweet little thing—yet I feel connected to no one. Cal comes the closest."

Meredith's tender heart smote her. She saw in her mind's eye a vision of the fourteen-year-old left all alone while his family started a fresh life in another country. "Give me your hand," she said very gently, reaching out to him.

His tall, powerful body went taut. "I don't think that's a good idea," he warned, knuckles clenched white, obviously agitated when he was usually so in command.

"I want you to think of me as your friend." It seemed very important to her he did. "*Please,* Steven. I told you. I like you. I…"

She never got to finish that hopelessly inadequate sentence. With an explosive oath, he lifted her forcibly, effortlessly into his arms, so she was lying across his chest, staring up into a face brilliant with a passion he couldn't control.

"You can't try the teasing, Meredith. Not with me, you can't!"

Teasing? She had no thought of teasing in her head. "But, Steven, it's not like that!" She was so agitated she had difficulty speaking.

"Then you should be more careful," he rasped, lowering his head with such a look of hunger it overwhelmed her. Heartbeats shook her body. She was aware of an acute sense of trepidation. She had imagined something like this happening, though she had held it a secret deep within her. What if the reality fell far short of those imaginings? What if…

He kissed her until she was swooning in his arms, the excitement breathtaking. His beard was slightly rough against her soft skin, grazing it, yet it was so wonderful! He was cradling her, covering her face and neck with kisses, as if only she could make his hunger and pain go away. His hands closed around her face as he kept returning to her yielding mouth, over and over, his tongue slipping around the moist interior, exploring it and the shape of her teeth.

It was astonishing as though it were all happening in the most voluptuous slow motion. Meredith didn't see how it could go on without their shedding their clothes, rolling naked on the sand. Her shirt was already off one shoulder. She was crushed against him, the pressure of her breasts against the hard wall of his chest, going along with this tumultuous tide, with not a thought in her head of fighting it. She could smell him, the wonderful male scent of him, something *warm* and intoxicating like the smell of fine leather and warm spices.

"Do you know how beautiful you are?" he muttered. "No, stay there." He had unloosened her thick plait, now her hair was swirling all around them releasing the herbal scents of her shampoo. He took a handful of it, kissed a lock, then her cheek, inhaling her skin. She'd been working all day yet she was so fresh. Always was.

Meredith had never felt so weak in her life. Her body had turned boneless. She didn't think she could possibly stand up or find her balance if she did. She was making no attempt to block his moving hands. She didn't want to. It was all too thrilling. Now his hand was reaching into the neck of her shirt, moving down to her breast; long strong fingers reaching further down, seeking the nipple, already erect.

How could she stand it? She was unravelling like a bolt of silk. She had to do something. God, what? This was *ecstasy*. She'd had little of that. She wasn't a virgin—a few, mostly pleasant experiences—but she'd never known anything like this or felt so remotely close to someone. And they were only kissing. *Only!* His fingers had reached her nipple, stimulating it further, setting her off wildly. Sensation was spreading down to her groin. She had to squeeze her legs together, when she wanted to throw them wide apart. Her heart was pumping madly She didn't know it but her nails were sinking into his back. Stars exploded behind her tightly shut eyelids, a kaleidoscope of colours.

Easier to put out a fire before it reaches a conflagration.

The warning voice in her head tried to call a stop, but she was too caught up in sensation. Calling a halt was so totally against her desire.

Meredith, you're losing yourself. Stop now. The voice came again. This time it had the power of a scream! She could so easily fall pregnant. It was a long time since she had taken the Pill.

Somehow she stayed his hand, though the effort nearly split her open. "*Please,* Steven." Her voice was no more than a ragged sob.

For a moment, an eternity, she thought he couldn't or wouldn't heed her plea. She was unsurprised. She should never have let him go so far. But, oh, it was ravishing, electric! And she had learned a few things about herself she had never known. She was electric only for *him.*

Steve's anguished groan came from way down deep in his throat. How was he supposed to let go of her after that? Didn't women understand a man couldn't just shut down at the flick of a switch? He didn't know how to protect himself from the pain. He buried his face in her sweetly scented neck, his hands breaking off caressing her. He could have howled aloud. "I don't know what to say," he muttered, as much to himself as her.

"You don't have to say anything," she tried to comfort him, feeling as if they were sealed off from the rest of the world.

"I frightened you for a moment, didn't I?" He threw his head back to stare into her eyes, his own glowing.

"Maybe," she whispered, not hiding from the truth. "I frightened myself, too."

He gave a strange laugh. "See what happens when you ask to hold my hand?"

"It's been coming a long time. But you know what they say? Forewarned, is forearmed." She tried to joke, when she had never felt so emotional, allowing her forehead to rest against his. "I care about you, Steven. I don't simply like you. I really care."

He accepted that now. All that wild passion wasn't only on his side. The tremors that shook her had been real. For long moments there he had thought she would let him do anything he liked with her. Let him peel off her clothes, run his tongue over every inch of her satiny body, find every little secret crevice. "If someone saw us and reported to your dad I'd be out of here this same afternoon," he said wryly, thinking it would have been well worth it. "Even Cal couldn't save me."

She felt bolder, stronger, than she had ever felt in her life. "*I'd* save you," she said, planting a kiss near the corner of his eye. "My father has played the heavy in too many of my relationships. God knows why. It's a puzzle. Cal is the one my parents love and adore. Not me."

"They must be mad," he muttered thickly and with disgust. "A wonderful daughter like you to fill their lives?"

She gave him another sweet kiss, this time on the cheek. "I must get up. Go home, Steven." Life went on. Reality replaced rapture. She had to make a big decision. She had to decide what she really wanted out of life. She had to decide if the emotion that had ripped through her like a hurricane could move on from a powerful sexual attraction to something deeper, stronger, more permanent. She realised she expected it with a man like Steven Lockhart. There were deep waters beneath that calm, controlled exterior, deep surging passions.

A kiss can be life changing. Strange but true.

With her hair undone it was blowing this way and that in the late-afternoon breeze. "You've wrecked my hair," she said, smiling down at him, the warm flush in her cheeks highlighting the burning blue of her eyes.

"You wouldn't say that if you could see yourself. A woman's hair truly is her crowning glory." He sat looking at her, his heart ravished, as she rebuttoned her shirt, then set about re-plaiting the gleaming masses. "How is it going to be from now on, Meredith?" he asked, his tone very serious. "I couldn't have made it more obvious how I feel about you. Now everything has changed. How do we handle that?"

She flicked her thick plait over her shoulder, making the de-cision to speak the truth. "I want…I want *you,* Steven."

He nodded as though she had revealed something very impor-tant. Then, "Talk around the station is, your parents want you to marry that McDermott guy. Are you going to do it?"

She began to brush sand off her clothes. "Nope."

"He's got a lot to offer," he persisted. The McDermotts were a wealthy pastoral family and McDermott was a likeable guy, a great polo player.

"I suppose. Everything but love." She didn't tell him Shane McDermott had already proposed to her. Twice.

"So where are you leading me, Heaven, or Hell?" He stood up; looming over her, a superbly fit young man, his golden-brown eyes searching her face.

"What about the stars?" she suggested softly, wishing the two of them could stay like this for ever.

"I'd snatch them down for you if I could." He pulled her tight…tighter.

"I'll remember that." She leaned back against his arm.

They stayed like that for long moments staring into one another's eyes, then he released her. She turned away to pick up her hat, settling it jauntily on her head. It was very difficult trying to return to normal again. Steven was right. Every second of their explosive lovemaking had brought them closer and closer together. Everything had, indeed, changed. Her desires, her longings, her hopes had been dredged up from some deep quarry inside her. She had to start thinking about wanting *more* instead of settling into a pattern of accepting *less*.

"Let's move slowly," she said, blue eyes going back to him, seeking his understanding. "One day at a time." She knew opposition from her parents would be fierce if she came out with her feelings for Steven Lockhart. "Okay?" She sought some gesture of agreement. "I don't care if we're seen together often. I'm past pretence." She waited nervously for his answer, frightened he might move back from the brink, seeing himself as a man with a lot to lose and probably nothing to win.

He inclined his raven head. "Whatever you say." How he wished he had more to offer her. Right *now*. He knew he could get it, but it would take time. "I guess your family will have enough on its hands welcoming Gina and their little grandson."

She sighed in agreement. "You'll be hearing about it." She held his gaze, wanting to make sure he understood the opened lines of communication between them really mattered. Changes came through making decisions and carrying them through. If she wanted Steven Lockhart—and she realised she did—she knew she would have to give up her ingrained reticence and *reach* for him. He had suffered too much rejection and he was a man of pride.

To her relief he gave her a little salute. "At the end of the day, this is going to affect us all."

It was only after she rode away that the voice in his head began. It whispered words of caution that dropped, heavy as a pile of stones.

Remember who she is, Steve.

Yet she had come willingly and without resistance into his

arms. She was as powerfully attracted to him as he was to her. That much he knew. Or had they both simply surrendered to an overwhelming temptation? And what about the McKendrick rules? Cal had broken them. Even for him it hadn't been simple. How much more difficult for Meredith?

When Meredith went downstairs some fifteen minutes before dinner—which was always at 7:00 p.m. on the dot, dress please, no jeans, slacking not accepted—her mother called to her the moment she saw her.

"There you are, dear," Jocelyn spoke brightly. "Join me for a moment, would you?" She beckoned Meredith to follow her down to the library, leaving behind her a light trail of her very expensive signature perfume.

"Anything wrong, Mum?" Meredith asked when they were inside the room. It was huge, but wonderfully atmospheric and welcoming despite the size. She loved books. Couldn't live without them. For years she had wanted to make a start on cataloguing the library—Uncle Ed had been keen to join her—but they both realised they were going to be refused the project.

Don't bother me now, Meredith. When I decide the time's right I'll call in a professional. Someone who knows what he's about.

He. That was her father, the quintessential chauvinist.

The ambience of the library settled her slightly when, truth be known, she was a bundle of nerves what with Cal's affairs and hers. Cal couldn't come home soon enough so far as his sister was concerned.

Jocelyn turned about, delicate brows raised like wings. "Why should anything be wrong, dear? No, no, I was planning on asking Kym to stay for the week-end." She settled herself gracefully into a deep comfortable chair, upholstered in a rich paisley, indicating to Meredith to take the one opposite. "I thought you

might like to ask Shane. Make up a foursome." She gave her
daughter an encouraging smile. "You're getting on, my dear.
Time to settle down. One should have one's children young. Your
father and I did."

"I'm not twenty-six yet, Mum," Meredith said thinking sub-
tlety often eluded her mother.

"Twenty-six is getting on," Jocelyn said, her voice firm.

"Not what anyone else would call over the hill," Meredith
murmured dryly. "And aren't you forgetting something, Mum?"

"Remind me." She put a hand to her triple string of large,
lustrous pearls. She was rarely seen without them even if they
were half hidden by collars or under sweaters and the like. They
were a wedding present from her husband and very valuable.

"Dad has made an art form of scaring off my admirers," Meredith
pointed out. As if her mother didn't know! And often condoned.

"Don't be ridiculous!" Jocelyn now studied her slim ankles.
She had kept her tiny waist and youthful figure and was very proud
of it. "Only the fortune hunters, dear. Shane isn't one of those."

"No, indeed, he's *one of us,*" Meredith lightly mocked, thinking in some respects her mother was a throwback to far less
egalitarian times. "Shane and I aren't going anywhere, Mum.
Sorry to disappoint you. I like him. I value him as a friend, but
I'm not and never will be in love with him."

Jocelyn's equable temper suddenly flared, putting diamond
chips into her glass-green eyes. Jocelyn thoroughly disliked having
her plans thwarted. "Who said anything about love?" she demanded
to know. "There are far more important things than love in a marriage, my girl. Love can fly out the window as fast as it flew in. You
have to consider more lasting qualities. Similar backgrounds,
shared interests, liking and respect. Friendship is very important.
Friendship between the families, as well. I'd like you to know—"

"Did you love Dad when you married him?" Meredith interrupted the flow, wondering if her authoritarian father had ever been a lovable person.

Jocelyn did effrontery exceedingly well. "Of course I loved your father. How could you ask? We are *still* in love."

Meredith supposed they were in their own way.

"And we're excellent friends. Your father and I see eye to eye. We've been greatly blessed. We have our wonderful son. A better son no parent could ask for. And we have you. You're a beautiful young woman, Meredith. Or you could be if you ever decided to do something about yourself. You could take a leaf out of Kym's book there. She's always marvellously turned out. All I ever see you in is jeans with your hair scraped back. It's scraped back even now."

Meredith put a hand to the loose curls that lay along her cheeks. "And here I was thinking I had prettied it up. Could the fact I do a lot of work around the station, as well as in the office have anything to do with the way I dress, do you suppose? It might come as a surprise to you, but Kym has often told me she'd give anything to look as good as I do in jeans."

Jocelyn lifted a porcelain ornament—eighteenth-century Meissen—off the small circular table beside her, then put it down again gently. "Well, she is a bit pear shaped," she conceded with a smile. "So what about it? We ask them both, Kym and Shane. Give the poor boy a chance, dear. You won't have any trouble with your father. I've already spoken to him. We like Shane."

Meredith clasped her hands together. Looking down at them she was sure she should be taking more care of them. Especially now when she had never felt more a woman. Bring on the hand cream! "Be that as it may, Mum, you're wasting your time. I don't think this week-end is a good time to invite anyone. Cal won't want to come home to find Kym here. Do you never stop hoping?" Meredith looked at her mother with pitying eyes.

Jocelyn had gone through life getting what she wanted. Maybe that was why she couldn't seem to give up on Kym. After all, she and Beth Harrison had dreamed of a marriage, uniting the two families and eventually uniting the two stations.

"Never!" Jocelyn gave a shake of her beautifully groomed head, dark hair swept back off a high brow. "Kym suits Cal perfectly."

"Kym suits *you* perfectly, Mum," Meredith corrected. "There's a big difference. The engagement didn't work. It's never going to work. Please don't ask Kym over. It won't be any nice surprise for Cal, believe me. He may have a few surprises of his own."

Jocelyn, who had settled back, sat up straight, her unlined forehead suddenly furrowed. "Meaning what? Are you trying to tell me something, Meredith? If you are, I'd advise you to be out with it. You surely can't be inferring Cal has someone hidden away?" She looked aghast at the very idea.

"Why don't you wait until he comes home," Meredith advised, and went to stand hesitantly by her mother.

"What is it, Meredith?" Jocelyn looked up to meet her daughter's gaze directly. "You know I hate surprises. I like to know *exactly* what's going on."

Meredith let her hand rest on her mother's shoulder. "Cal does have some news, Mum, but it's not my news to tell. He'll be home on Saturday. You'll have to be patient until then."

CHAPTER FOUR

THEY were all gathered around the long mahogany table in the formal dining room listening to Cal deliver his momentous news. It was an elaborate setting, Meredith thought. The table, for instance, had always reminded her of the deck of an aircraft carrier. Around it were ranged Georgian chairs, tied with elaborate silk tassels, convex gilded mirrors on the walls, a magnificent Dutch still life over the sideboard—fruit, vegetables, game birds. Only one of the great chandeliers was on. Even then the light was dazzling. The room was only used for gala occasions—but it seemed as good a place as any for her brother to tell his extraordinary story.

Cal told it simply, but movingly. He had to convey to them how powerfully Gina Romano had affected him from the very first moment he saw her. He had wanted no other woman. No way could he tell them in bringing Gina here he was bending her to his will. He had to stick to the charade. He must have been convincing, because Meredith's expression was soft and tender. She looked thrilled.

And thrilled Meredith was. If Steven could feel the same way about her as Cal did about his Gina, what a priceless gift that would be! The rest of the family greeted Cal's news with a ringing silence.

This was never meant to happen!

Meredith's eyes flew to her brother's, renewing her support. Still, the family continued to sit there as if they'd been turned to stone; or Cal had spoken in an unfamiliar tongue and they were struggling to decipher it. Meredith gritted her teeth, her throat aching with tension.

Their father, for once, was plainly at a loss. Nothing in response. He started to speak, then stopped. Their mother held her fingers to her temples as though she had suddenly developed an appalling headache, which, indeed, she had. Uncle Ed continued to stare down at the gleaming surface of the table as though amazed at the shine.

"I don't believe this," Jocelyn finally burst out, in evident anger and confusion. It tore at her, making her blind to anyone else's feelings but her own. "This is the most appalling news. This Gina doesn't sound the sort of girl you would bring home. Let alone *marry.*"

Meredith winced, hardly daring to look at her brother to gauge his reaction. "Mum, *please!*" she begged, excruciatingly embarrassed by her mother's outburst.

Jocelyn ignored her, beginning to cry, but Cal's handsome features showed no softening. They hardened to granite. He thrust back his chair and then stood up, addressing his mother. "How did you get to be such an appalling snob, Mother?" he asked, his voice tight. "I'm sure the Queen of England wouldn't carry on like you. You've gone on with your PLU nonsense ever since I can remember. There has to be an end to it."

He sounded so disgusted that Jocelyn, who was used to the greatest respect from her son, started to pull herself together. "Lorinda did warn me," she said, in that moment of stress letting the cat out of the bag. "She was most concerned."

Cal's heart tightened up like a fist. "When was this?"

Jocelyn didn't answer. Instead she made a small agitated flourish with her hand.

"Are you saying you knew back then?" Suddenly Cal had to confront the fact Lorinda, the aunt he had always trusted, had deceived him.

"Of course we knew, son." Ewan McKendrick reached out to take his wife's shaking hand. "And she had your child?" The question ended upwards in a kind of wonderment.

"Your grandson, Dad," Cal told him, strong emotions etched on his face. "It's just as I told you. I never knew."

"I'm certain you didn't," Ewan responded on the instant. "You're a man of honour."

"Honour short of *marriage,* you mean, Dad?" Cal asked bitterly. "Provide for her and the boy. Sweep it under the carpet. Get on with life. I'm afraid that's not on. I'm going to marry Gina. I'm going to bring her and my son home."

Jocelyn blew her nose exceedingly hard when she was always so dainty about such things. "But how can you love her after all she's done to you?" she cried. "She's a heartless woman. Not worth knowing. You probably wouldn't look at her now," she added, though it didn't make a lot of sense.

Meredith rushed to support her brother. "Gina is a beautiful person, Mum. Anyone would be proud to welcome her into the family."

Jocelyn burst into fresh tears. She had no desire whatever to meet this Gina person. But Gina's son? That was a matter of great concern to her. The boy was Cal's heir.

"Let me repeat I'm going to bring Gina and our son home." Cal didn't know it but he looked colder and harder than his father ever had.

"And is he going to be page boy at the wedding?" Jocelyn stopped her tears, to enquire with great sarcasm. "Where is this wedding going to be held, may I ask? Not here. I won't be humiliated in front of the world. I couldn't bear it." She followed up that announcement with an exaggerated shudder.

"Steady on, Jocelyn." Ewan held up a warning hand. He knew his son if Jocelyn didn't. No way could he allow his son to take leave of the family. Ewan knew Cal would, if pushed.

"What do you think, Uncle Ed?" Cal looked across the table at his uncle who had remained silent throughout as though being seen was one thing, heard another. Not that anyone could get a word in with Jocelyn.

Ed spread his hands. His sister-in-law was behaving in a disastrous fashion but he was living in the family home. Hell, he had a right to it come to that! "Anything that makes you happy, makes me happy, Cal." He said with obvious sincerity. "I'm sure your Gina is as beautiful as Merri says. I can see you're stunned, but your mother and Lorinda have always been as thick as thieves."

Jocelyn gasped. "Shame, shame, shame, Ed McKendrick. Lorinda is a loyal sister and she *adores* Cal," she rebuked him. "Lorinda acted on the highest motivation, love and concern. It was your Gina who ran off, Cal, back to her own world. Is that how to love someone, deceiving them then running away? Utterly spineless I say."

Cal strove to keep the fury and confusion he was feeling out of his voice. "I think the less you say, the better, Mum. This is a fait accompli. I've found the mother of my son. I'm finally going to bring them home. Her and Robert."

Jocelyn's green eyes gushed afresh. "Damn it, damn it, damn it!" she cried, her whole body trembling under the force of her shock and anger. "No wonder you didn't want Kym over, Meredith." She turned on her daughter as though she were greatly to blame. "Kym will be devastated when she hears about this."

"For God's sake, my dear, you're flogging a dead horse,"

Ewan McKendrick groaned, raising a hand to stay his wife. "I have told you."

Jocelyn stared back at her husband, feeling greatly undermined. "The point is *you* wanted Kym, too, Ewan. She was *our* choice. Not some young woman who won't belong. Had Cal and Kym married, in time Lakefield would have been added to the McKendrick chain. It was all so suitable."

"Business is business and PLU is PLU, eh, Mum?" Meredith couldn't resist the dig.

Her father turned cold blue eyes on her. "Please don't speak to your mother like that, Meredith."

"I'm only stating an evident truth, Dad. Why don't you stop treating me like a child?"

Jocelyn broke in irritably. "I don't think I'll ever forgive you for not warning me, Meredith. I've suffered a betrayal. I'm terribly, terribly wounded."

"Then I'm sorry, Mum. But as I pointed out at the time, it was Cal's story to tell."

"Exactly! I told Meredith to leave it to me," Cal confirmed in a clipped voice.

"What, keep the truth from me, Calvin?" Jocelyn asked piteously.

Ewan wasn't attending to anything being said. "I haven't met my grandson and he's three years of age," he murmured, very poignantly for him. "Who does he look like?" He turned beseeching eyes on his son.

Cal sat down again, sighing heavily. "Like you, Dad, like me. He's a McKendrick, but he has Mum's green eyes."

"My green eyes!" Jocelyn spluttered, as though only one other person in the world was entitled to them. "You're the one with my green eyes, Calvin. It's impossible, I tell you. She can't come here." Jocelyn's small face started to crease up again. "I won't be grooming a total stranger, to take over from me. Not that she could," she added scathingly. She stared back at her son. No adoration there, only anger and condemnation.

"If Gina isn't welcome here, *I* don't stay." Cal laid down the ultimatum, looking grimly resolute.

There was no question in at least three people's minds he meant it. "I can wait it out until it's my time to inherit. You don't own Coronation Hill, Dad. You're the custodian. Just as I will be for *my* son, my son Robert."

But Ewan McKendrick was way ahead of them all. "As though I would ask you to go," he cried, exhibiting great dismay, and not looking at his wife. "When is it you want to bring Gina and the boy home?"

Oh, thank God, thank God! Meredith gave silent praises. When the chips were down, their father always chose the smartest course.

Cal shot a wry glance at his sister, reading her mind. "By the end of this month. This house is big enough to swallow up the lot of us. We wouldn't have to see one another if we didn't want to," he added satirically, though it was perfectly true.

"Good God, son, we don't want you to go into hiding!" Ewan exclaimed. "Dear me, no. What's happened, has happened. Now we must move forward. The sooner the better."

"Thanks for that, Dad," Cal said, the severe tension in him easing fractionally. "In view of what I've just heard I need to have a talk with Aunt Lorinda." Anger and disillusionment flinted from his brilliant eyes.

"Well, you'll just have to wait now, won't you!" Jocelyn cried in a kind of triumph. "She's in Europe."

"She'll be back," Cal answered shortly. It was important he get to the bottom of the matter. Gina hadn't said anything that implicated Lorinda in her decision to flee the island, but the fact his aunt and his mother had discussed their blossoming romance had suddenly opened up a Pandora's Box.

"So when do you plan to take your marriage vows?" Ewan was asking, busy looking at the situation from all its angles in his head. Wouldn't even make a nine day wonder he shouldn't be surprised. Times had changed dramatically, if only Jocelyn could see it!

"I'm not entirely sure." Cal glanced across at his sister. What better sister could a man have? Yet he couldn't tell her Gina wasn't exactly ecstatic about marrying him. He was forcing her into it. He wasn't happy about that, but he was determined on his course. Robert was a McKendrick. His place was on Coronation Hill. Robert needed his parents together, not apart, two people to love and raise him. He couldn't risk Gina marrying someone else, providing an alternative father to *his* son.

"If you're going to go ahead with this it will be better if you marry her at some register office. Brisbane, Sydney, Adelaide, whatever," Jocelyn said bitterly. "I'm sure your sister will be delighted to act as a witness."

"Absolutely! I'd be honoured," Meredith said. "I think it's a miracle Cal and Gina have come together again."

"With *your* help!" Jocelyn bitterly accused her daughter, so often the scapegoat.

"No register office," Ewan broke in, his stern glance silencing his daughter who was about to respond to her mother. "The wedding will be here on Coronation."

Jocelyn looked at her husband with betrayal in her reddened eyes. "You can't mean it, Ewan."

"All the McKendricks have been married from here," he answered, with blunt force. "Including you, Ed. We've all had huge weddings, great celebrations. We're going to do things right."

"And if I refuse to be here?" Jocelyn threw down the challenge.

Ewan reached out to pat her shoulder. "But you won't refuse, will you, my dear? You've always been an excellent wife." He turned his arrogant, handsome head towards his son. "Would you like that, Cal?"

"That's what I want, Dad," Cal said. "But nothing big."

"Frankly I don't see how we can avoid it." For the first time Ewan smiled. "You've been through a tough time."

"*Gina* has been through a tough time," Cal said, mustering up his most caring tone.

"That's absurd." His mother might have seen through him she gave such a scoffing laugh.

"She must be a strong person." Ewan cut in, frowning on his wife. Ewan McKendrick was every inch the diplomat whenever an occasion demanding diplomacy arose. "Bring Gina home, son. We'll make her welcome." He ignored his wife's bitter exclamation, but turned on her a rare, cold eye. "I can't wait to meet my grandson. Especially if he looks like me."

Would a little granddaughter have fared so well, I wonder? Meredith thought, then immediately chided herself for being so mean.

"Thank God that's over," she said an hour later, after she and Cal made their escape to the garden. "It was a bit of a surprise learning Aunt Lorinda was busy informing Mum of everything that went on at the island. Do you suppose she had anything to do with Gina's abrupt departure? Now that I think about it, I wouldn't put it past her, though she was always sweet to Gina."

"Yes, she was." Cal was forced to admit it, but inside he was hurting badly. He had blamed Gina for years, when it now seemed he didn't know the full story.

"Gina didn't explain why she left?" Meredith read his mind.

"She certainly didn't say Lorinda made any decision for her."

"So what was Gina's decision based on?" Meredith frowned. "Wouldn't she say?"

Cal stared up at the brilliant clusters of stars. "Merri, Gina made it quite plain she wants to shut the door on the past. She refused to get into any discussion, but I gathered she thought at the time she wasn't good enough for me. Pretty damned silly, I know. But I suppose looking at it from her side she was made aware there was plenty of money being splashed around. She came from an ordinary family with I imagine little money to spare on luxury holidays. Perhaps she felt overwhelmed. People do. You know that."

"But Gina gave no sign of it," Meredith said. "Her manner couldn't have been more natural. Gina could take her place anywhere."

"She was so *young*," Cal said. "Maybe that accounts for it. She got frightened off."

"Did you ever mention Kym to her?" Meredith persisted. "The fact Mum and Dad cherished hopes the two of you would marry?"

"God, no!" Cal protested violently. "I never gave Kym a thought. There was only Gina. But she found out later about Kym. She saw a photo of us in some magazine. Kym and I were engaged at the time."

"Oh!" Meredith gave a little anguished moan. "Do you suppose Aunt Lorinda might have told her about Kym? She saw a grand love affair unfolding right under her nose. Time to put a stop to it. We now know she contacted Mum."

"I'll get to the bottom of it, don't you worry," Cal said with quiet menace. "Gina had her opportunity to denounce Lorinda. If there was anything to denounce. She didn't."

Meredith pondered it all in silence. "So what happened to Gina's boyfriend? I imagine the marriage was well and truly off when Gina discovered she was pregnant?"

"Now *that's* the strange thing. Gina claims there was no boy-friend," Cal answered. "She must have gone into denial. I'm fairly sure she was frightened of her father. He's dead, by the way." He held back a curling palm frond from his sister's face. "Did you get around to telling Steve any of this?"

She nodded, grateful for the cloak of darkness. "You said I could. He was very sympathetic. Steve's on your side. He's had a hard life. He understands a great deal."

"You like him, don't you?" Cal spoke directly.

She felt the heat rush into her skin. "I do." Meredith was beyond pretence. She had to get a life. "He's quite a guy. But can you imagine if *I'd* told Mum and Dad tonight I was pregnant and Steve was the father, what their reaction would have been? Krakatoa! Do you really think Dad would have jumped in to say we must be married on Coronation? The crazy ironies of life, brother. We live by a different set of rules."

"They're not *my* rules, Merri," Cal said, with the greatest regret, knowing her assertion to be true. "Dad and Mum—especially Mum—have to lighten up." He broke off to stare down at her. "Say, you're not telling me in a roundabout way you *are* pregnant?"

"What would be your reaction?" she asked, confident she knew what it would be.

They kept walking. "If he loved you and you loved him I could only be happy for you, Merri. Love is all that matters."

"Tell that to Mum," Meredith replied. "No, I'm not pregnant, though Mum has recently told me I'm leaving it almost too late to have kids. She wanted to invite Shane over this weekend. Shane *and* Kym."

"Struth!" Cal exclaimed wryly. "I just hope Mum hasn't been giving Kym false encouragement. That would be too cruel."

"I don't think Kym needed anyone's encouragement,"

Meredith said. "I think she has just been waiting for you to come to your senses as it were."

"Some people are just one-track. I'm sorry if Mum's going to take it out on you, Merri. It's too bad the way she does that."

"It does tend to fray the nerves," Meredith admitted, "but I'm here for you, brother." She tucked her arm through his, as though anchoring him to the moment.

"And I'm here for you, Merri. Never forget that."

Gina didn't put her apartment on the market. There was no way she could tell if a marriage between herself and Cal would work out. But what real alternative did she have but to try? There was no way she could risk not having her beloved Robbie with her all the time. A custody battle would be costly, time-consuming and in the end she would be the loser, forced into, at best, sharing custody with Robbie's father and his family, all locked away in their private stronghold. No wonder she had simply folded like a pack of cards.

She didn't dare look deep inside her heart. Except sometimes at night.

"You're still in love with him. You are and always will be."

Always the inner voice to never let her escape.

Cal McKendrick was and remained her incurable addiction. Maybe they would have a chance if he were an ordinary man, a colleague like Nat Goldman. She had met Nat's family. They would have been delighted if the friendship between her and Nat had become more serious. She remembered Cal's beautiful sister, Meredith, on the island. Meredith had always been so friendly yet she had the sense there was a considerable gulf between them. Such wealth as the McKendrick family had, was quite outside her experience. She had never witnessed anything like it. She hadn't started the affair with Cal. An affair had never occurred to her. She had been too much aware of her position on the island to offer any male guest the slightest encouragement, let alone *him*. She had been hired as a domestic/waitress, whatever was needed. She certainly needed the money to help her through her final semester. She was the first in her family ever to attend university. That in itself had been a great source of pride to her father. She had scored the highest rating. At university she had once been voted the girl with the three *B*'s. Brilliance. Beauty. Brains. Just a fun thing. No one had mentioned anything about Luck.

Her family had had little money to spare, however hard her father had toiled. Theirs had been a small sugar farm not a plantation. There was no way she would have embarked on what in the end turned out to be the most momentous, the most unforgettable, the most painful course of her life.

Cal McKendrick had been her lost love.

Until now.

When she told Rosa about Cal's re-entry into her life, Rosa had barely been able to contain herself.

"What's he want this time?" she asked, her voice, as always, fiercely protective.

Even Rosa had been silenced when Gina told her what Cal McKendrick wanted was marriage.

"You still love him?"

"I can't help it." No point in covering up from Rosa. Rosa would see through it.

"Gran Dio!" In response, Rosa balled up a rock melon and pitched it through the open kitchen window into the backyard where it narrowly missed a visiting cat who took off shrieking for safer territory. "Tell him I come with you for a week or so, perhaps a month. We face this family together. You and Roberto are *my* family. I am Aunt Rosa. You cannot do without my support."

When Cal phoned, Gina passed on Rosa's message, which was more or less an ultimatum. If she had expected some kind of sarcastic comment, even downright opposition, he had only laughed. "That's nice!" Cal phoned often. Probably checking on her whereabouts, if he didn't already have someone on the job. She had even started to check if there were any strange cars parked for any length of time in front of her apartment block. No way was she going to be allowed to abscond with his son.

Then there was Robbie. She had spent a good deal of time pondering what she would tell him, but if she had agonised over what to say: that the man Robbie had met only a short while ago, the man he had taken such a liking to, was in reality, his father, Robbie wonder of wonders took it near effortlessly on board.

"He's my daddy?" he asked, his eyes full of amazement and a dawning delight. "Where is he right now?"

"Are you listening to me, Robbie? Cal's your *father.*" She hadn't expected it to be this easy. She was worried he didn't fully understand. Bright as he was he was still very young.

"Yes, Mummy." Robbie replied blithely, "but where *is* he?"

She had swallowed the hard knot in her throat. "He's back home, Robbie. His family is what is known as cattle barons. That means they own vast properties in the Outback they call *stations.*"

"Like train stations?" Robbie nodded knowledgeably.

"No, darling. A train station is a stopping place where passengers get on and off," she explained. Robbie had never been, in fact, on a train. He had always travelled by car. "In Australia we call really huge farms with lots and lots of land, *stations.* There are cattle stations and sheep stations and sometimes sheep and cattle together. The McKendrick holdings—they have a number of what they call *outstations*—are cattle stations. You must have heard cowboys in the videos you watch call them *ranches.* That's the American word. We say stations."

"Wow! So Cal's a cowboy?" Robbie asked in such delight his greatest ambition might have been to be one.

"Well, a cattleman like he said."

"That's *wild!*" Robbie breathed. "Cal said he was going to show me some time." So at the tender age of three, Robbie was taking in his stride what might have shocked an older child or cast him into a state of panic.

"The time's almost here, Robbie," Gina said. "Your father is coming for us at the end of the month. Not long to go now. We have to leave Queensland and live in the Northern Territory. I'll show you on the map where it is. It borders Queensland, but it's a long, long way from here."

"How do we get there…by train? Gosh, I hope so." The excitement showed. "The great big long one on the TV. The Ghan, they call it. It travels through all that red desert with no one in it."

Gina shook her head. "I'm sure we'll travel on the Ghan one day but your father will be picking us up in the family plane."

Robbie's eyes went as round as saucers. "My daddy flies a plane?" Seated on a chair facing his mother he suddenly dropped to his knees, staring up at her and squeezing her hands.

"It's not a great big plane like you've seen at the airport," Gina hastened to tell him. "It's much smaller."

Robbie dramatically collapsed on the carpet. "He must be very rich!"

"Sort of." Gina didn't want to stress that side of it. "Your father and I are going to get married. How do you feel about that, my darling boy?" She gazed down earnestly into his beautiful little face.

Now all of a sudden Robbie looked deeply flustered. "I don't know. Do you *have* to?"

She couldn't begin to imagine what she would do if he suddenly burst into tears. "Your father wants us to be a family,

Robbie," she explained very gently. "I will become Mrs McKendrick. You will become Robert McKendrick. We take your father's name."

Robbie rolled onto his stomach. "It sounds very nice," he said after a few seconds of consideration. "He likes to call me Robert, doesn't he?"

"Yes, he does like I often call you Roberto. I don't want you to forget your Italian heritage. That's why Rosa and I speak Italian to you, as well as English."

Robbie gave a perky little nod. "My friend Connie speaks Italian just like me. Jonathon speaks Greek and Rani speaks Vietnamese. We think it's fun being able to speak another language."

"And so it is. So the answer's yes, Robbie?" she asked. "Your father and I will be getting married."

Robbie jumped to his feet, and then threw himself into his mother's arms. "I guess it's all right. But what is going to happen to Aunt Rosa?"

Gina silently applauded her son's caring nature. "Rosa is going to come with us." Her arms closed around her precious son, while a tear slid down her cheek. "At least for a little while to help us settle in."

"Goody, hurray!" Robbie lifted his head from her shoulder to give her a beatific smile. "I'd hate to leave Aunt Rosa behind."

"We'll never lose Aunt Rosa," Gina said.

It was a solemn promise.

CHAPTER FIVE

TEN minutes before the plane was due in, many of Coronation's considerable complement of staff began to assemble. They lined the airstrip in front of the giant hangar. This was a day of celebration. Cal was bringing his family home, the young woman soon to be his wife and their three-year-old son. Everyone had been told an aunt of Cal's fiancée was to accompany them. Whatever the lovers' star-crossed past, everything was set to be put right. A big bar-b-que had been planned for the staff starting around seven. The latest addition to the McKendrick clan would probably be tucked up in bed fast asleep, but the family was expected to look in on proceedings at some part of the evening.

Whatever Gina had expected, it wasn't a welcoming party. As they came in to land she could see all the people assembled on the ground. Even Rosa who had determined on being unimpressed, rolled her eyes and gestured with her hands. "Like something out of a movie!"

It was true. The aerial view of the great station complex was fantastic. It looked like an isolated settlement set down in the middle of a vast empty landscape that stretched away in every direction as far as the eye could see. Gina remembered reading somewhere the Northern Territory had less than one percent of the population of Texas in the U.S.A although it was twice the size. So there was a long way to go in the Territory's development. It was still frontier country and perhaps because of it wildly exciting.

She couldn't begin to count the number of buildings. The homestead had to be the building that stood apart from the rest, set within an oasis of green. It appeared to be enormous if the roof was any indication. The airstrip was at a fair distance from the homestead. It was easy to pick out from the huge hangar that had a logo painted on the silver glinting roof. It appeared to be a stylised crown. Beside the hangar stood a tall mast with the Australian flag flying from it. Farther away she could see holding yards jam-packed with cattle, three circular dams, probably bores. Beyond the complex lay the vast wilderness.

Some areas of it resembled jungle, other areas were almost parkland. Dotted all over the landscape were winding streams and smaller tributaries she supposed were the billabongs. They were quite distinct in character from the huge lagoons mostly circular and oval, where palms and pandanus grew in profusion. She could see a huge mob of horses running down there. Wild horses by the look of them, the Outback's famous brumbies.

Robbie, who had been alight with excitement at his very first plane trip, had actually slept for most of the flight. Now he was wide-awake and raring to go.

They were dropping altitude, coming in to land. Her stomach muscles clenched in anticipation, though it had been a remarkably smooth flight with Cal, a seasoned pilot, at the controls. He gave every appearance of a man who thoroughly enjoyed flying. With great distances to be covered, she began to appreciate how private aircraft in the Outback would seem more a necessity than a luxury, although she knew this particular plane cost a good deal more than one million dollars.

"Steady on, matey!" Robbie cried out in gleeful excitement, clapping his hands together. This was the adventure of a lifetime.

"Sit still now, little darling." Gina placed a calming hand on him.

"Who are all those people down there?" he asked in wonderment.

"Station staff," Gina whispered back.

That thrilled Robbie and made him laugh. More people appeared as if they had been hiding in the hangar.

"Big, *big!*" Rosa exclaimed, gesticulating with evident awe.

It was big all right!

The tyres gave a couple of gentle thumps on the tarmac, the brakes screeched, then Cal cut back to idle as they taxied towards the hangar. There he cut the engines, making his afterchecks. A few minutes later they were walking down the steps into the brilliant Territory sunlight.

"These are *our* people, Robbie," Cal explained, swooping his son high in his arms.

"Why? Are you a prince or something, Daddy?" Robbie asked, touching his father's face and staring into his eyes as though Cal was the font of all wisdom and authority. Robbie had learned all about the Queen and the royal family at nursery school. There was a picture of the Queen in a beautiful yellow dress in his old classroom. The teacher had told them a famous Australian artist called Sir William Dargie had painted it.

"A prince? No way!" Cal laughed. "I'm just an ordinary person."

That had to be the understatement of the year, Gina thought, trying to calm her own jittering nerves. Robbie had taken to calling Cal "Daddy" in the blink of an eye. No working up to it. It was as though her little son had longed to use the word. Both of them, man and boy, appeared to be going on instinct. Cal and his son had reached a place from the outset where the relationship was set. She was proud of the fact Robbie had found enormous security with her, his mother, but there was no denying the very special role of a father. It was as Cal had said. Robbie needed *both* his parents. Their son was revelling in the family wholeness.

"Other kids have a mummy and daddy. Now so do I!"

That observation had been delivered with tremendous satisfaction. Why had she ever thought him too small to notice her single-parent status?

With Rosa standing excitedly at her shoulder, Gina watched as a tall, very slender young woman—it had to be Meredith—broke ranks and rushed towards them.

"Welcome, welcome," Meredith was crying happily.

Gina was enveloped in a hug. "I've thought of you so often, Gina," Meredith said. "It's wonderful you're here."

"It's wonderful you're here to meet me." Gina was unable to prevent the emotional tears from springing to her eyes. "Meredith, I'd like you to meet my aunt Rosa. She has always been a great support to me."

"Lovely to meet you, Rosa." Meredith smiled warmly, both women taking to each other on sight. Meredith had been expecting a "motherly type" figure but Aunt Rosa was a striking, very sexy-looking woman with remarkably good skin.

"Lovely to meet *you,* my dear." Rosa well satisfied with what she saw, put her arms around Meredith and hugged her back.

Meredith turned excitedly to her brother and the little boy in his arms. "Well, I recognise *you,* young man," she said, laying a gentle, faintly trembling hand on Robbie's flushed cheek. "You're the image of your daddy." Her brilliant eyes went to her brother's. "This is truly marvellous, Cal."

His triumphant smile flashed back at her. "Isn't it just? This is your aunty Meredith, Robbie." He introduced them with pride. "I told you all about her, remember? Meredith is my sister."

"Merri," Robbie said. "You called her Merri, like Merry Christmas."

"Merri it is," Meredith said, shaking the little hand Robbie gave her. "Do you want to come and meet the rest of the welcoming party?" she asked. "They're longing to meet you."

"Oh, yes, please," Robbie said, wriggling to get down.

"We're right behind you." Cal set his son down, watching him catch hold of Meredith's hand with the utmost trust and confidence. He was an amazingly friendly little fellow, remarkably self-possessed for his age. It was easy to see from his general behaviour and his advanced social skills Gina had raised him with a tender, loving hand. He also spoke very well and gave every appearance of being highly intelligent. He was a little son to be proud of.

A group of children had materialised—they had been kept in the shade of the hangar—making Robbie even more excited. They were the children of Coronation's staff, educated until the age of the ten at the small one-teacher schoolhouse on the station. All in all, it took some twenty emotion-packed minutes before the welcoming party broke up with another round of cheers led by the station's overseer, a very dashing young man called Steve Lockhart, before Cal was able to drive them to the homestead.

"That was the greatest thing ever!" Robbie exclaimed with satisfaction. "Everybody likes me."

"And why wouldn't they?" Meredith laughed, looking over Robbie's glossy head into his mother's eyes. "You're a great little boy!"

Time enough to see if Cal's parents like me, was Gina's thought. It didn't strike her as odd that Cal's parents hadn't come down to the airstrip to greet them. She supposed they might be people like the aunt Lorinda she well remembered. Cal had carried off the introductions with marvellous aplomb. No one looking at them both would have suspected things weren't as they seemed. As they had walked down the receiving line he had kept an arm lightly at her back, an expression of pride in her etched on his dynamic face. Steve Lockhart she recalled, had been observing them closely behind the charming welcoming smile. There was some strong connection between Meredith and Steve. She felt it keenly. But she also felt as far as the senior McKendricks were concerned staff would be expected to keep their distance. How then would that affect any friendship between Meredith and the station's impressive overseer? Gina recognised the quality in him.

They were received in the library. Good heavens, what a room! Gina thought. She could have fitted her entire apartment into the huge space. And *received* was the only way to put it. Cal's mother, a beautiful, well-preserved woman, dressed as though she were going to an important luncheon minus her hat and bag—glorious pearls—was seated in a wing chair. Cal's father, a very handsome man with piercing blue eyes was standing behind her. Another man, also standing, a few feet away, and bearing a close resemblance to Cal's father had to be Uncle Edward. Uncle Edward for a mercy looked kind and approachable. He was smiling, a lovely warm smile. Gina returned it with gratitude. This was certainly one good-looking family! But that was okay! The Romanos hadn't been behind the door when good looks were handed out. Rosa, too, was immensely attractive. Uncle Edward certainly appeared to think so going on his expression as his eyes came to rest on her.

Rosa, for her part, wasn't worried about the McKendricks. She could take them in her stride. What she was worried about, was how they would respond to her goddaughter. Looking after Gina was the reason Rosa was here.

Cal took the direct approach, making introductions. His

mother remained seated. They were all obliged to go to her. Gina could feel the little waves of resistance that emanated from the seated figure though Jocelyn spoke the right words as though she had learned them from a script. *Obviously she believes I've brought disruption and disgrace to the family,* Gina thought, shaking Jocelyn's unenthusiastic hand. There was no question of a hug much less a kiss. The handshake was as much as Gina could expect to get.

Cal's father, Ewan, after an initial moment of what appeared to be shock was quite genial by comparison. Gina caught him giving his wife a sharp, rebuking glance. She must have got the message because the charged atmosphere lightened somewhat. Friendly and outgoing as Robbie was, he had been half hiding behind his mother. Now Cal picked him up in his arms.

"This is your grandmother and grandfather, Robert. And that gentleman over there is my uncle Ed, your great-uncle. Say hello."

"Hello, everybody," Robbie piped up sweetly, looking around them all. Even at three he could recognise family going on appearance alone.

There were two spots of colour high up on Jocelyn's cheeks. Her green eyes that had appeared unfocused suddenly rested with great clarity on the little boy. "What a beautiful child you are!" she now exclaimed. "Come give Grandma a kiss." She held out her hand.

"Why he's the living image of you, Cal!" Ewan McKendrick burst out in triumph, his eyes settling with approval on the beautiful, self-composed young woman his son had brought home with him. This Gina, who he and Jocelyn had worried had no background at all, looked magnificent! He was quite taken aback. But what a blessing! "I want you to know, Gina, you're most welcome to the family. Most welcome."

Gina made no answer, but graciously inclined her head, unaware how very regal it appeared.

"And how good of you to accompany her, *signora*." Ewan's blue glance swept on to Gina's decidedly attractive companion. She was a damned sexy-looking woman. "May I call you Rosa?"

"But of course!" Rosa replied graciously.

"What, not going to shake hands with your grandfather, young man?" Ewan asked the little boy jovially, absolutely thrilled the boy was so clearly a McKendrick. What a plus!

Robbie went to him immediately. "I'm happy to meet you, Granddad."

Jocelyn chose that precise moment to burst into tears motivating Ed to jump into the void. "You must all want to rest after such a long flight?" he suggested, his eyes alighting more or less compulsively now on Rosa. She positively radiated life and vitality! Things couldn't get any better.

"Long but very smooth," Rosa assured him, meeting his gaze straight-on. There was a natural voluptuousness running like a ribbon through the accent Rosa had never lost. Now she took to studying with equal interest this tall, gentlemanly man with the blue, blue eyes and chivalrous expression. A widower she had been told. There was a strong attraction already between them. Could there be a little love for her around the corner? It was astonishing when and where love turned up.

Meredith who had been busy watching proceedings, spoke up. "One of the men will have taken your luggage to your rooms. I'll come up with you…help you settle in." It would give her mother time to compose herself, she thought.

"That will be lovely." Gina bestowed on her a grateful smile.

"You're coming, too, Daddy?" Robbie asked, looking back to his father with a melting smile.

"You bet I am," Cal assured him, though he remained where he was, a bracing hand on his mother's shoulder. "I'll be with you in a minute."

"Didn't you promise me you were going to teach me to ride a horse?" Robbie asked as though they might start the lessons now.

"A *pony,* Robert. I'll get one in especially for you."

"Oh, bravo!" Ewan McKendrick cried heartily. "It's only natural you have the love of horses in your blood, Robbie." My word, this was turning out well, Ewan thought. Jocelyn would just have to pull herself into line.

"Make this work, Mum." Cal bent to murmur in his mother's ear.

"Who said I haven't?" she replied haughtily, when the party were out of earshot. "At least she's beautiful." Even as she acknowledged the fact, Jocelyn felt a fierce stab of jealousy. She had always been Number One in her son's life. She had expected to remain Number One even if he had married the amenable Kym. This Gina was something else again. It wasn't easy to be supplanted. "As for the other one!" She threw up her hands.

Now it was Ed's turn to stun them. "Spellbinding, wasn't she? I just might ask her to marry me."

His handsome face wore a wide grin.

"You're joking of course!" Jocelyn looked at her brother-in-law with extreme disfavour.

Wasn't he?

Jocelyn, who had hardly eaten anything at dinner said good-night early and withdrew. Ewan, who couldn't completely disguise his anger with his wife, made his departure some time after.

Count on it. There would be words upstairs, Cal thought, angry and disappointed with his mother. He had never seen her so stiff and ungracious, even if he recognised her nose was out of joint. Both Gina and Rosa had that ineffable thing—glamour.

"You can stand in for me, Cal, at the party," Ewan said over his shoulder. "All they want is to see more of *you,* and Gina, not me!"

An overtired, overexcited Robbie had long since been tucked up in bed.

Rosa and Ed who had hit it off extremely well over dinner, the attraction continuing apace, had talked art among other things, Ed all the while staring at her in admiration. Now they expressed the desire to go along with the young ones to join the bar-b-que, which was in full swing judging by the sound of country-and-western music filling the air. Rosa who had wisely taken a short nap to look her best, showed no sign whatever of fatigue. Meredith, looking really beautiful, was also eager to join the party.

Cal detained Gina as the others moved off, chatting happily like old friends. "Let's go out on the terrace," he suggested. He needed privacy as two members of staff continued to hover in the dining room, checking that everything would be left just so.

"As you wish." Gina let him take her arm, unable to control her body's response to his touch. It made her feel extraordinarily vulnerable.

"Well, we lived through that," he offered dryly when they were out in the gardenia-scented night air. Inwardly, he was wondering if his father was going to throttle his mother.

"Your father is trying," Gina answered. "And Meredith and your uncle Ed are so kind, but it's just as I expected. Your mother doesn't and never will, like me."

My mother is jealous, Cal thought but couldn't bring himself to say it. "My mother is used to being in total control of the situation," he said by way of explanation. "This time she isn't. Don't let her bother you too much, Gina. She'll come around."

"If only for Robbie's sake." Gina took a calming breath. Inside love and hate were battling for her soul. "It's as well he looks like you. He'd have had no chance had he looked like me."

Cal glanced down at her, trying unsuccessfully to numb his own strong feelings. He had been watching her all night. She wore her hair the way he liked it. Loose, centre parted, flowing over her shoulders. Her dress was short and lacy, gold in colour. The low neckline showed her beautiful bosom to advantage, the skirt-length revealed her long sexy legs. "It so happens I'm praying for a daughter who looks just like you."

"You may have a long wait," she said coolly.

"Then I'll just have to seduce you all over again. That's what you think I did, isn't it? Seduce you? Because, you know, I thought the attraction was mutual?"

"I don't remember." She turned her face away.

"Liar." He led her down the short flight of stone steps. "Ed seems to have taken quite a shine to Rosa?" There was amusement and surprise in his voice.

"Sometimes you just never know what people are capable of," Gina said. "Your uncle has been alone a long time?"

"Ten years. His wife, Aunt Jenny, was a lovely person. I remember Meredith crying her heart out at the funeral. I wanted to, but couldn't. Men don't cry and all that. I had to bite my lip until I drew blood."

"So you do have a heart after all?"

It wasn't a tease. She sounded serious. "Oh ,well, while we're at it, where have you stowed yours?"

She tossed back a long sable lock. "I have Robbie. My son is everything in life to me. That's the only way you got me here, Cal. You gave me no option but—"

"To stage a battle you'd very likely lose," he finished for her. "Now, what about if we call a truce while we're on show. Remember, we're supposed to be lovers, cruelly separated for so long now to be gloriously reunited in marriage."

She laughed though her heart was beating like a drum. "Don't think I'm taking off on any honeymoon," she warned. "And don't think we're going to finish up in the same bed."

"*Gianina, mia,* it's not as though I've actually asked you to have sex," he mocked. "But never fear. I will get around to it." His voice grew more serious. "I thought we might defer the honeymoon until Robert is more used to the family. Or we could take him with us?"

She stopped moving, visibly agitated. "Where on earth are you thinking?"

"Need you ask, the island?" Now, what was the matter with him, baiting her like that, because she reacted like that was the cruellest thing he could have said.

"You must be mad."

He shrugged. "That's the sad thing. You *made* me mad. Good and mad. Tell me what happened on the island, Gina. You can make it brief if it pains you to speak."

She glanced up at the twinkling fairy lights strung through the trees. Their glow swept the grass and illuminated the garden beds that were filled with rich tropical flowers, the fragrance intoxicating in the warm air. "What are you trying to trap me into saying? I told you I don't want to discuss the past. Suffice to say I fell in love unwisely but too well."

"You jumped right in."

"So did you."

"I shared your reckless streak," he freely admitted. "You were my Juliet. The girl I thought I could die for."

"No tragedy, a farce."

"We have Robert, don't we?" he said in a low voice.

"Yes," she answered quietly.

"I should tell you I intend to have a long talk with my aunt when she gets back home. I have an idea she had more to do with events than I'd realised."

"The past is ancient history. I'm determined to move forwards.

So where is your aunt? Does she take off on her broom stick now and again?"

It was said with such scorn, he stopped in his tracks. "Where did that come from all of a sudden?"

Immediately she made a rueful face. "That was a slip. I withdraw it." She had to close a door on the past now that this new door had opened. His aunt would always remain family. She would always be around. "I would never go back to the island," she said, changing the subject. "It was another time."

"I wouldn't go back, either," he said crisply.

"You were just being cruel then?"

"I feel cruel towards you once in a while."

She felt her heart contract. "Small wonder I'm scared of you."

"I should think you would be," he replied, glancing down at her.

They walked on through the tropical night, the path overshadowed by magnificent broad-domed shade trees. "I don't want any big wedding, Cal," she said nervously.

"So why don't you make a list of a few close friends?" he suggested in a suave tone. "I don't want any big wedding, either."

"I have no intention of dressing like a bride, either."

"What?" He brought them to a halt. "When you'll make a *glorious* bride?"

She bit her lip, her body aching at his closeness, her mind bent on running away. "I'm the mother of a three-year-old boy."

"High time you got married then," he commented. "I have to insist you dress the part. I'm not going to be denied my trophy wife. That's part of the deal."

They moved on. "Would you like me to ask your Kym to be a bridesmaid?" she asked silkily.

"You'd have to be really crazy to do that."

"Stranger things have happened. I know someone who invited all his old girlfriends to his wedding."

"You were one of them?"

"Never! I'm a one-man woman at heart." Damn why had she said that?

"I'll disregard that. The only man you'll ever be allowed to get romantic over is *me*."

"That's not going to be a lot of fun."

"Why are you working so hard to hate me?"

She gave a brittle laugh. "That's a lot of question, Cal. Loving you turned out to be very, very painful."

"Surely you made me pay keeping Robert from me." His hurt, his sorrow, his impotent rage burst through his lips.

Gina reacted fiercely. So fiercely Cal was forced to pull her to him, silencing any tempestuous outburst of hers by covering her mouth with his own. "People can see us," he muttered, against her gritted teeth.

How very stupid of her! An anguished moan escaped her throat. People, of course. She had to keep her wits about her, yet every time she was alone with him she thought them sealed off from the rest of the world. Ever so slowly she managed to pull herself together. Even that wildly discordant kiss had made her knees buckle.

"You shouldn't say things like that to me," she censured him, shaking back the silky hair that was spilling around her hot face.

"I'll let you go when you say sorry."

She could hear the taunt in his voice. "You'll let me go *now*. I'm just mad enough to scream. Besides, I can't run away."

"That's right," he agreed. "You can't. You look beautiful. Did I tell you? I love that dress."

"I thought you might like it," she said, tartly.

"Oh, I do. It shows off your beautiful figure. Your mouth tastes of peaches and champagne."

"I've had both," she pointed out. "Shall we walk on?"

"Why not?" he agreed suavely. "Arm in arm like a happily married couple."

"And just how long do you think this marriage will last?"

"Well, let's see now. It's the start of the twenty-first century," he said musingly. "Hopefully we'll have a good fifty years, probably more. The thing is, when you said yes to marrying me, Gina, in my book that means *for ever.*"

The expression on his handsome face looked a lot more like ruthless than loving.

Steven had reached the stage where he thought she wasn't going to make an appearance that night. The evening was a great success. No effort had been spared to ensure Coronation's staff would find it memorable. The food was great—as always—Coronation's premier beef, numerous side dishes, hot and cold, salads galore. Icy-cold beer was on tap to stimulate the appetite, soft drinks and fruit juices for the children—they were still running around—wine for the ladies. The dessert table—a mecca for anyone with a sweet tooth—was a long trestle covered with a white linen cloth. It was laden with dishes that looked like they had been prepared by a master chef dedicated to that sort of thing. He circulated constantly—it was part of his job—still, she didn't come.

Then he saw her.

His mood lifted to the skies. She was walking with Gina's aunt Rosa and Edward McKendrick. He really liked Ed, who was vastly more approachable than his elder brother. Gina's aunt, he realised, was an unconventional dresser but he thought she looked great in her vividly coloured outfit. It was sort of gypsy-ish, embroidered with something glinting. From the body language Ed seemed to think she looked fantastic. Good for you, Ed, Steven thought. It was a tragedy what had happened to Ed's wife—a lovely woman from all accounts—but eventually one had to get on with life.

Meredith stopped his breath. She wore a dress, a beautiful deep blue dress. He had seldom seen her in a dress, not even at the polo matches or informal functions Coronation hosted from time to time. She mostly wore jeans or tailored pants. Why not? Hers was the ideal figure to show them off. But tonight she wore something filmy and to him desperately romantic. Romance his soul craved. Did women realise men were every bit as romantic as they were? The fabric of her floaty skirt wrapped itself around her lithe body as she moved. Her wonderful hair was loose, falling in a shiny waterfall down her back.

Ed came towards him, extending his hand. "Everything going well, Steve?"

"Everyone's having a great time, Mr McKendrick." Steve returned the smile and the handshake, shifting his gaze to Meredith and Aunt Rosa. "Good evening, ladies. May I say how beautiful you both look?"

"Certainly you may!" Rosa nodded her dark head, her thick hair short and expertly cut. "I think there is something a little bit dangerous about you, Steven." She waved a finger.

"No worries." Steve smiled back at her. "It's just that I like women. Are Cal and Gina coming?" He glanced towards the main path.

"Right behind us," Meredith said, surprising herself greatly by going to him and taking his arm. Never once had she done that. "I think I'd like a cold drink. What about you?" Her gaze moved from Rosa to her uncle, who overnight looked ten years younger with a renewed zest for life.

"You two go on ahead," Ed answered in a relaxed voice, "Rosa and I will stroll for a bit."

Rosa took Ed's arm companionably. "You must tell me everything I need to know about your magnificent gardens, Edward."

Her intriguing accent made not two but three sensuous syllables of *Ed-ah-ward*. "I'm longing to explore them by daylight."

"And I'd be delighted to show you," Ed responded gallantly. "That wonderfully exotic fragrance on the air is from the many, many beds of yellow-throated Asian lilies, the pinks, the whites and the creams."

"Why, yes, I can see them glowing in the dark," Rosa said. "I would love to paint them."

"Then you must have your chance."

"Why is it I think Ed has taken a great liking to Gina's aunt Rosa?" Steve asked as Ed and Rosa moved away across the grass.

"She's an extremely attractive woman and a woman of culture." Meredith smiled. "She and Ed got into a discussion on art at the dinner table. Both of them are well informed, but I could see Dad was rather bored. He and Ed look very much alike but their personalities are completely different."

"How did the little dinner party go?" Steve asked. "Are your parents going to make an appearance tonight?"

Meredith shook her head, mightily relieved. "Mum retired early. Dad followed. I expect they might have a few words when they're alone. Mum scarcely pretended a veneer of charm over dinner."

"That's awful." Steve winced. "I would have thought your parents would be delighted to have such a beautiful woman for a daughter-in-law. And Robbie is a great little kid, full of life and so well spoken for his age. Mother and son made a really good impression with the staff. So did Rosa. Everyone on the station is full of praise for them and delight for Cal. That's why the evening is going so wonderfully well. Everyone's happy."

"Are *you* happy, Steven?" She stared up at him, the bronze of his skin in striking contrast to the snowy white shirt he wore with his tight fitting jeans. For herself, she was glowing inside, certain now she was in love.

"I am now you're here," he said softly, gazing down at her. "I was beginning to get worried you mightn't make an appearance."

"Nothing would have kept me away." She gripped his arm tighter, a gesture Steve found utterly enchanting. It was all he could do not to turn her into his arms. Alas, there were too many people around. "I meant it when I said you look beautiful. You dazzle me. You're a *dream* in a dress, especially one that floats all around you."

"Why thank you, Steven." She smiled, stars in her eyes.

He bent his head to her urgently. "I want to kiss you."

"I want to kiss you back."

Only voices intervened. *"Hi, Steve! Good evening, Ms McKendrick!"*

"Hello there!" Meredith responded brightly, lifting her hand to return the greetings.

"Can't we go somewhere *quiet?*" Even as he said it Steve couldn't help laughing. They would have to get right out of the home compound to find silence. Someone had turned the music up louder. Someone else toned it down a little. People were dancing.

"Not tonight I'm afraid." She sighed with deep regret. "Cal and Gina will be along soon. Why don't we join in the dancing?"

"Do you think that's wise?"

"It's too late to talk about being wise now, Steven," she said, yearning to be in his arms.

Steven came back to himself for a minute. "I don't want to put you into any stressful situation. Your happiness is very important to me, Meredith."

"So you're *not* going to dance with me?" She tilted her head to one side.

"Are you asking me if I'm game?" he responded to the challenge.

"Something like that, Steven Lockhart."

His smile faltered slightly. "But I'm not a Lockhart, am I? I'm not a Lancaster, either. What *am* I to you, Meredith?"

She reached up to gently touch his mouth, tracing the outline of his lower lip, beautifully cut and undeniably sensual. "You're too touchy."

"I want to touch *you*," he said, his voice mesmerizing. "I want to very gently unwrap you from your beautiful clothes. You can't be wearing a bra, not in that dress?" His golden-brown eyes moved over the tiny bodice with its thin straps, cut to reveal her décolletage.

"There's one built into the dress," she explained, aware her voice shook. It felt like he was stroking her. Featherlike strokes that ranged over her throat and down to the upward curves of her breasts.

The music had changed to a ballad.

He took her into his arms. Wasn't this what he had been longing for all night?

Other couples were dancing beneath the trees, some were twirling down the paths. Some were just having fun. Others were intent on each other.

He was a beautiful mover. She knew that from the way he walked.

They were perfectly quiet. There was no need for words. The intense communication came from the sizzling proximity of their bodies. She was falling fathoms deep into a bottomless lagoon of sexual hunger. It surpassed anything she had felt before. She had to go further, much further than kisses. She let him steer her this way and that, her heart beating madly. If only they didn't have to stop. She wasn't even sure she *could* stop.

"Meredith!" Somewhere a little distance off, amid the babble of laughter and music, her father's voice cracked out.

"God, it's your dad," Steve muttered, "and he's heading this way."

He didn't release her, however. He made no move to. "I

thought he was supposed to have retired for the night?" he asked, the merest thread of humour in a dead calm voice.

"I thought he had."

Still, he held her.

"Good evening, Mr McKendrick," Steve greeted his boss smoothly. "We weren't certain if we were going to have the pleasure of your company this evening."

Ewan McKendrick stopped right in front of them. "So you took advantage of the situation by thinking you could dance with my daughter?" he retorted in an insufferably arrogant tone.

Steve kept a tight rein on his temper and his tone low. People were starting to look their way, aware things weren't quite right. "Excuse me, sir, is there a law against that?" There was no trace of insolence in his voice, just a simple question requiring a simple answer.

Meredith's nerves were fluttering badly. "Please, Dad! You're drawing attention to us."

Her father ignored her. Fresh from a humdinger of an argument with his wife, he was ready for blood. "Would you mind letting my daughter go?" he said thickly, reaching out to shove Steve away, but Steve, a good thirty years younger and superbly fit, didn't budge. He did, however, drop his hands not wanting to further inflame an already inflammable situation.

Some distance away Gina felt that warning finger on her nape. She began to walk faster.

"It's good you're so eager to join the party." Cal laughed, stepping it out with her.

"Something is wrong up ahead," she told him, sounding serious. "I feel you should be there."

Cal didn't ask her what she meant. He had seen in Gina a lot of things beyond her physical beauty.

It was as she said. Cal saw with dismay his father give Steve Lockhart a hard shove in the shoulder. It had no effect so far as he could see on Steve, but it told him all he needed to know. A head-to-head confrontation was already in place. Meredith's body language spoke of embarrassment and anguish. Poor Merri! She looked so beautiful tonight. She didn't have to take this sort of thing. Their father was as dictatorial a man as he had ever met, whereas Steve had earned his trust and deserved respect.

"Your parents would do well to step into the twenty-first century," Gina murmured, shaking her head. It was inevitable she would be on Steve's side.

"I can't help but agree," Cal gritted, increasing his pace. "They run Coronation Hill like their own kingdom." It wasn't something he was proud of. He glanced down at Gina, not wanting to draw her into it. "You might like to stay here."

She shook her head. "I'll come with you."

"It might get sticky."

"I have no doubt you can handle it."

They closed in on the trio fast. "Hey, everything okay here?" he called, the heavy tension in the atmosphere coming at them in a wave.

Ewan McKendrick rounded on his son. "You *can't* be talking to *me!*"

"Actually, yes, Dad," Cal said, coolly quiet.

Out of the corner of her eye Gina saw people moving quickly away from what looked like shaping up to be a war zone. Most of the staff would have taken note of the fact their very popular overseer was dancing with the boss's daughter. Not only that, but *how* they were dancing. Hadn't she divined an involvement between Meredith and Steve Lockhart, within the first few minutes?

"You're upset, Dad," Cal spoke to his father soothingly, knowing·words had most likely passed between his parents. "Why don't I accompany you back to the house?"

"What am I supposed to make of this?" Ewan demanded of his son. "I come out for a breath of air and to make an appearance and what should I be confronted by but my daughter snuggling up to this fella here." He stabbed a condemnatory finger in Steve's direction. "Didn't you see what was going on?"

"Dancing, Dad. All quite respectable," Cal answered reasonably. "You've overreacted. Merri can dance with whomever she pleases."

"Not while she's under *my* roof," Ewan returned furiously.

"Your roof, certainly," Cal agreed. "My roof, Mum's roof, Merri's roof, Ed's roof."

"No need whatever to include me!" Gina broke in ironically, vividly reminded of how her own father had tyrannized her male friends.

"Gina, darling," Cal stressed, "You and Robbie go with *me*." He returned his attention to his father. "Let's go, Dad. Don't spoil what has been a pleasant evening. I think you owe Steve an apology. He's done no wrong."

Ewan's handsome face reddened. "He hasn't, eh? I gave you more credit, Calvin. Lockhart here has a larger purpose than being our overseer. Mark my words. He has designs on my daughter, *your* sister, I might remind you."

"You're absolutely right, sir," Steve broke in, "I do think the world of Meredith."

"Indeed!" Ewan thundered, now totally enraged. "You just keep away from her, fella. I have in mind someone from a fine family for my only daughter. Not a no-one like you!"

They were all startled by his tone, swept with vehemence.

"That's it, Dad!" Cal got a firm grip on his father before Steve lost it. He was about to, judging from his expression. "It would help a lot if you come away."

Ewan McKendrick shook his head several times as if to clear it. "The fella's a bastard!" he ground out heavily. "No way could you ever be good enough for my daughter. You're fired, Lockhart. Don't try to go against me, Cal. I'm still in charge of Coronation and don't you forget it."

"I'm not forgetting it, Dad," Cal said very quietly, yet his voice carried an effortless authority. "But I'm relying on you to regain your common sense. Steve is very good at what he does. You can't expect me to carry the burden without him. Come along now. Your blood pressure was up the last time the doctor took a look at you."

"Why wouldn't it be up in this family?" Ewan McKendrick glowered, but he allowed himself to be led away.

Gina reacted first. She reached out a hand to the distressed Meredith, who clasped it tightly. "My father used to interfere in all my friendships, Meredith," she lamented. "I was never allowed to bring a boy home. Only girlfriends were allowed. As I got older no one was good enough for me. I was my father's 'shining star.' He always called me that. When I fell pregnant he literally threw me out."

Meredith and Steve were so shocked by that admission they momentarily forgot their own outraged feelings. "Gina, how dreadful!" Meredith was aghast. "I never thought—"

"I've never spoken about it," Gina said. "My mother gave me whatever money she had spirited away. Somehow I was able to finish my degree. I didn't show until the seventh month, which helped a lot. I didn't tell anyone. Only Rosa knew. I couldn't have done without Rosa. She's been an enormous support to me and wonderful to Robbie. You can't allow your father to run your life, Meredith. Please don't think *I* am now interfering in your personal affairs. I do so out of my own experience and concern for you."

"I know that, Gina." Meredith shook her head utterly dismayed. "Does Cal know this?"

Gina smiled sadly. "One day I'll tell him."

"You should tell him now."

Gina shook her head. "There are still a few issues we have to work through. I'll know the time."

"Of course you will." Meredith backed off. "How mortifying this all is. What must you think of us?"

Gina spoke directly. "Your mother doesn't like me, Meredith. I doubt she ever will. Your father will try. But I'm not sure I can live under the same roof as a mother-in-law who so clearly doesn't approve of me."

"What are you saying, Gina?" Meredith's voice rose in alarm.

"I'm saying if I'm not happy here I mightn't be able to stay." Gina's beautiful face took on an adamant cast. Gina had had more than her share of dysfunctional families.

"You've told Cal how you feel?" Steve asked. He was still fuming inside, having come very close to punching McKendrick in the nose. Cal had known it. That was why he had spirited his father away.

"No, but I will if it becomes necessary," Gina said, with a note of resolve in her voice. She knew if Meredith and Steve didn't, Cal wasn't about to let her leave. For *any* reason. By the same token she knew he wasn't going to allow his mother to continue on her present course. She looked back into two distressed faces, as much for her as themselves, she realised with gratitude. "I was surprised and very touched by my welcoming party when we arrived," she told them. "I'd like you to know that. I suppose it's normal enough for your mother, Meredith, to have difficulties accepting me. I'm not the daughter-in-law she wanted. Kym, wasn't it? Your aunt, Lorinda, told me all about her." In the stress of the moment that withheld piece of information spilled out.

"So it had to be when we were on the island?" Meredith's face darkened with a frown.

Immediately Gina made a little dismissive gesture with her hands. "Sorry. I've said too much already. Cal doesn't know. I'd prefer the past to stay in the past, Meredith. It will do no good to rake it all up. Now, if you'll excuse me, I'll carry out Cal's wishes and mingle with the staff for a while. I expect he'll be back soon."

Meredith looked at Steven in sharp dismay. She could see he shared her feelings. "Please remember Cal needs you desperately, Gina."

Gina didn't answer but turned away with an enigmatic little smile.

Cal needs his *son* desperately, Gina amended in her own mind.

Left alone, Meredith put a conciliatory hand on Steve's arm.

"Careful," he warned, his lean body taut.

"Please don't be like that, Steven," she begged. "I am so sorry, but it's not my fault.'

Or maybe it *is,* she thought wretchedly. She should have protected-Steven. That meant leaving him well alone.

"It would have given me a great deal of pleasure to have punched your father in the nose," he said tightly.

"I think we all knew that, Steven. My father can be unbelievably arrogant. In some ways my parents don't know a lot about *real* life."

"They're too protected by their wealth," Steve diagnosed accurately. "But I suppose it's not all that surprising. Isn't God a McKendrick?"

His tone cut. "He *can't* fire you."

"He *can* fire me," Steve corrected, his attractive voice oddly harsh.

"Cal will speak to him. He'll listen."

"You think so?" Steve threw up his hands. "I think it more

likely you'll disappear overseas. Join your gadfly aunt who appears to have done some mischief whether Gina wants to keep her out of it or not. As for you, you'll come home and marry your father's nominee. None of your family will accept me, Meredith, outside of Cal and Gina. And that would only make it hard for them both."

Anger came, swift and unexpected. "Shouldn't you be worrying more about whether *I'll* accept you?" she cried.

That settled it for Steve. "I'll be out of here by midday tomorrow, okay?" he said curtly. "Maybe sooner. It's been great knowing you, Meredith. Tell Gina if she wants a normal life then she sure picked the wrong family."

She ran after him, mortified. "Steven, please don't go." She made an effort to catch his shirt, and almost lost her footing on the exposed root of a tree.

He didn't notice and kept going, taking swift, powerful strides away from her.

Meredith gave up. Her father had made sure of it calling Steven a bastard. How dare he?

See what you've gone and done? the voice in her head taunted. *You should have left him alone. You knew what was going to happen. You fool you! Getting to think things might be different. Nothing will ever change around here. Not until it's Cal's turn to reign.*

Steven, she knew, had been sitting pretty as Coronation's overseer, a position of trust and responsibility. He had security and earned good money. It would be highly unlikely he could find a comparable position in the near future. She wasn't even sure if Cal could persuade her father to relent even if Steven agreed to stay. And that didn't look like it was happening. Not from the way he had stormed off.

Meredith returned to the house feeling sick to her soul.

CHAPTER SIX

READY for bed, Gina looked in on Robbie, whose bedroom was just across the hallway from hers. She opened the door very quietly, widening the opening so a golden ray of light fell across his face. She had left a small night-light burning in any case. It was possible he could awake some time during the night and feel disorientated in a strange house. She didn't really expect him to. It was Robbie's practice to fall asleep as soon as his head hit the pillow, sleeping right through until she woke him by pulling the lobe of his ear very gently in the morning. It was a trick that always worked.

Just as she thought, he was fast asleep, clutching his favourite teddy bear. Her face softened into an expression of the utmost maternal tenderness. Robbie wouldn't go anywhere without that bear. His father had promised him the room would be redecorated in any way he liked. Maybe a few lighter touches here and there, but it was a beautiful big airy room with French doors leading out onto a broad verandah. It was a full moon outside; the big copper moon of the tropics. She had to say it affected her.

She wanted Cal. She wanted him to come to her. She wanted to hear his voice.

How could you love a man so passionately when he had broken your heart?

Gently, she closed Robbie's door. His room had a different view from hers, overlooking the extensive gardens that led to the large stables complex at the rear of the house. Coronation Hill's homestead was very impressive, she thought. A huge substantial house, it had evolved, so Cal had told her, from the original single-storey stone colonial cottage. One would never have known it. Today it was a lofty two-storey structure with the central section linking two long wings. Obviously the generations of McKendricks had spared no expense developing a homestead that befitted their station.

She returned to her own room, feeling bruised, emotionally and spiritually. How could this possibly work out? Even Meredith's developing relationship with the extremely attractive Steven Lockhart seemed heading for a shipwreck.

"Damn!" she said out loud, giving one of the pillows several good thumps.

"Bad as that, is it?"

She looked up to see Cal standing in the open doorway. His handsome face wore a brooding expression. It was obvious he, too, was deeply disturbed.

"Need you ask?" Another minute and she would have shut her door. Would he have knocked?

He sighed in a way that told her the events of the evening had well and truly taken their toll. "May I come in?"

She shrugged. "Shut the door after you. Robbie's asleep. So tell me what's happening about Steve? Did you manage to persuade your father to change his mind about sacking him?"

"I can handle my father," said Cal, thrusting a hand through his thick mahogany hair. "It's Steve I'm worried about. Meredith has come back to the house in a hell of a state. Sometimes I think there's not a guy in the world who would pass first base with Dad."

"Meredith can't live her whole life being dictated to."

Cal shrugged. "Of course she can't. But I don't think there's been anyone who really mattered to her up to this date. No one to really push for. Steve would seem to be different. She said he told her he was leaving in the morning."

"Oh, no!" Gina looked back at him in dismay. "Have you spoken to him?"

"I'm giving him some space. Hoping he'll cool off. He can't get anywhere until the freight plane gets in around noon."

"And Meredith?"

"What about her?" His jewel-like eyes moved over her, studying her hungrily. The muscles of his thighs tensed as his body stirred. No make-up, long hair tied back at the nape, a shell-pink satin robe sashed tightly at the waist, slippers on her feet. She still looked glorious, he thought with a hot burn of desire that was exposed in his eyes.

"Is she going to give in without a fight?" Gina's breathing started to come rather fast. Labour as she might, she still couldn't keep her physical yearning for him under control. Just to look at him triggered a response.

"*We* did, didn't we?" He suddenly flung himself down on the end of her huge four poster bed, falling backwards with a groan.

Ohhh! Gina didn't feel she was any way near strong enough for such temptations. "Why was your father so horrible to Steve?" Autocrat or not Ewan McKendrick's reaction had seemed excessive.

"Because Dad can be bloody horrible sometimes." Cal addressed the ornately plastered ceiling. "For a man like my father, a family liaison with a staff member is *verboten*."

Gina moved well away from the bed. Hadn't her liaison with him been forbidden? "*Mein Gott,* German!" she said with a flash of sarcasm. "And the bastard bit? That was appalling. I was shocked."

Cal remained lying where he was, as though it would cost him too much of a physical effort to get up. "Steve is the natural son of one of our biggest beef producers," he explained. "A man called Gavin Lancaster. Lancaster took a fancy to Steve's mother many long years ago and Steve is the result. He's so much a Lancaster everyone in the Outback knows."

"And Lancaster knows presumably?"

"Of course."

"But he chooses not to recognise his own son?" There was a throb of outrage in her voice.

"I'm very sorry to say the answer's yes."

Gina felt a great rush of pity for Steve Lockhart. "This Lancaster can't be a man of character and heart. That's terrible, Cal. And Steve's mother?"

"She was married at the time. Somehow managed to patch the marriage up. The family—he has two half brothers and a half sister—moved to New Zealand when Steve was fourteen. He's been on his own since. Surprisingly, however, they did put him in a very good boarding school before they left."

"Oh, that was nice of them!" Gina scoffed.

"Wasn't it? He was with other boys from landed families. That's how he remained on the land. Love for the land is something that runs deep in the blood. Steve has it."

"Poor Steve!" Gina looked towards the moonlit verandah and beyond that the night under stars. "The bar-b-que must have folded. The music has stopped."

"I think Dad's performance put paid to the evening," Cal groaned. "But they got a good few hours in."

"Steve's in love with Meredith," Gina said, a poignant expression on her beautiful face.

"He may well be but he's a proud man. Come here a moment." He raised his dark head slightly off the bed.

"You can't stay." She didn't move.

"Shall I get out now?" he asked, and gave a low laugh.

"No, you don't have to go *right* now."

"Many thanks, *principessa!*" he mocked. "Bear with me for a little while. That's all I ask."

All? She was near mad for him to touch her. Their sexual attraction was so strong she did right to fear it. Excitement was growing at a great pace inside her. She tried, but failed to keep it down. He knew exactly how to press her every last button. To move nearer the bed, would be akin to going in at the deep end.

When she was little more than a tentative foot away, he suddenly made a grab for her. "Gotcha!" He pulled her to him with a fierceness that still held an element of cherishing.

They were both on the bed in one swift motion, he half on top of her, running his hand down her shoulder to her waist to the top of her long slender leg, stopping while he looked deep into her eyes.

"I finally get you home and it's all bad news. Well, not entirely. Robbie has the magic key to everyone's heart. I'm sorry for the way my mother behaved at dinner. I apologise for her. I get mad just thinking about it, but it wasn't the time to bring on a big family argument. That might have to wait, but you can bet your life she got an earful from Dad."

Gina felt like she was going to cry but decided she could not. He lowered his face into her neck, his mouth moving against her skin. "Oh, you smell *wonderful!* Like a million wildflowers!"

She could feel the weight of his head on her shoulder. He had his eyes closed, just lying there breathing her in. "Things have got to change, Gina," he muttered against her skin. "Just hang in there. I'm going to make them change. I know how." *I can't lose her,* Cal thought. *Not all over again.*

The ache of tears was in Gina's throat. She couldn't help herself. She placed her palm very tenderly against his cheek. When she surrendered, she surrendered. It was part of her nature. What was the point of all this alternating between love and hate? They were tied to one another, weren't they? They shared their son.

"Gina?" He opened his eyes to stare at her. She had never seen eyes like his before she had met him. That amazing jewel-like green. Now she had a child with those same eyes.

Cal lifted his torso supporting his body with his strong arms. "Would you let me love you?"

Heat grew to flame. She knew he would be true to his word, giving her the opportunity to say yes, or decline his advances. If she said no would she always look back at this moment and regret it? Or should she open herself up to him? She had kept maintaining the past was best forgotten. She even acted on it, in not implicating his aunt in her banishment from the island. Shouldn't she look to the future? Shouldn't she take the first step?

As if to goad her the voice inside her head said: *Because you want it…want it…want it!* Sexual needs had their own sovereignty. Her need for him was urgent.

Cal saw the change come over her. He saw the powerful feelings that drove her. Feelings that left little place for pride or any other consideration. Nothing could stand up against the raw passion they had for each other.

Gina's hand came up compulsively and found the buttons of his shirt. She slid them free from their buttonholes. She could smell the special male fragrance of his skin, as intoxicating to her as her fragrance was to him. She could feel his warmth, the texture of the whorls of dark hair on his chest, spearing through it with her fingers while his whole body tensed. She must have been taking too long because abruptly he helped her, stripping his shirt roughly from him and flinging it away.

His shadow fell over her. He held her hands away as he bent to kiss her open mouth, pouring such passion into and over her she was drenched. Then he was removing her clothes, folding his face into them, and when she was naked his hands began to move over her commanding her body to obey. It was a primitive kind of mastery; dominant male over female, but it was made all the more fantastic because it seemed to Gina to be overlaid with a ravishing tenderness. He wasn't so much intent on his own pleasure. He was intent on *hers*.

"Tell me you can find it within yourself to love me?" His hands enclosed the golden globes of her breasts, the darkening rose-coloured nipples swollen and erect.

"I *did* love you." Her eyes were closed to him, as though open they would reveal too much of herself to him.

"Or so you said." His hand began to trace a line from her navel down to the quivering apex of her body with its delicate cleft. He dipped his head and kissed her there.

Sensations shot through her as keen as a blade.

She shuddered, her voice barely audible. "I believed all *you* said to me then." Her back began to arch and flex. The impact of his mouth on her sex was enormous.

"But you can't believe me now?" He took his time over his ministrations, all the while watching her face, a clear barometer for the raging emotions he was arousing in her.

"All I want is for our son…to…be happy." She could only gasp out the words, her body was in such a throbbing state of arousal.

"*I* don't matter?" Now his fingers found their way inside her.

"Of course you matter," she gasped, her back arching off the bed as he explored deeper. "I can't talk. I can't *talk*." Sensation was eclipsing everything else, requiring her most intense concentration.

"You're going to marry me."

His voice sounded deep in her ear.

"Yes!" she moaned hoarsely.

He levered himself over her, a lean powerful man yet she

couldn't seem to feel his weight. She *adored* his body on top of hers. Worshipped it. Now her own hand began to move, certain of what he wanted. She heard with a certain triumph, the harsh catch of his breath.

"Gina!" He groaned as if he were in the most exquisitely excruciating pain.

"I'm here!" She carried on tormenting him, until he could scarcely bear it. Then in a galvanic surge he reversed their positions. She was on top of him, her legs locked around him, muscles taut, her long hair tumbling forwards as she bent to kiss his marvellous mouth.

"Will this pass for love?" she softly taunted, armed with the knowledge in her lovemaking he found her faultless.

His voice was a near-satiated growl in his throat. "If it isn't, don't let it ever end."

From long habit Cal awoke in the predawn. The sky outside was a luminous pearl-grey, the horizon shot through with filmy layers of pink, gold and mauve. They were lying spooned together, front to back, her beautiful body curved into his, his arm lying over the top of her, the tips of his fingers resting on her breast. He felt his body instantly react, but first he just wanted to look at her sleeping face, to savour the miracle of her presence beside him. He no longer had just memories to live with. He had the woman. Whatever the difficulties of the past, the difficulties that lay ahead, this part of their relationship was perfect. He couldn't imagine lovemaking more ravishing. He swore he could hear the beat of her heart. Surely it matched his own?

She sighed deeply and began to turn, eyelids flickering, a frown shadowing her face, her lips murmuring, *"No!"*

His hand tightened over the satin slope of her shoulder. "Gina, you're dreaming." He shook her. "Gina?" There was real anguish in that moan.

A handful of seconds later and she opened her eyes, huge and velvety dark. "Cal!" She looked as if she were still lost in a wilderness of emotions.

"Are you okay? You were having a bad dream."

She shivered though the room was pleasantly warm. "I was back on the island."

"So why did it make you want to cry?"

She stared up into his eyes. "What *did* you really feel for me then, Cal, *what?* Please tell me."

He pushed her back gently into the pillows. He couldn't bear to tarnish the memory of what they had.

She closed her eyes against that telling expression on his face. "I'm sorry."

"You should be sorry." He bent and kissed her. A kiss that seemed to go on and on for ever. "I'm crazy about you," he muttered as he withdrew his mouth from hers. *"Crazed."*

This time when they made love it couldn't have been more different from the night before. This time their coming together was more a clash. It was almost as though each was still out for revenge. Unresolved revenge for four long years of pain and grief. Were they damned by all their complex issues? A man could be crazy about a woman without wanting it, without even loving her. Gina had believed herself abandoned at the most crucial turning point in her life. She had had to bring a child into the world without the love and support of its father; Cal felt himself betrayed by the girl, who in the shortest space of time, barely six weeks, had become everything in the world to him. The girl who had the power to destroy his ordered life. The girl who had denied him all knowledge of his son. There were, without question, powerful issues yet to be worked through.

But physically, they thrashed in the bed together, in an orgy of desire, playing out their past torments while their demons were let loose. Cal thrust into her powerfully, one hand behind her high arching back, her hoarse little cries serving only to drive him on.

When it was over they lay back utterly shaken by the primitive forces that had taken them over.

"Did I hurt you?" God, had he intended to, even for a moment? he castigated himself.

"No, though I seem to have left my mark on you." She could see her nail marks on his shoulders and on the small of his hard muscled back. "Let's take a shower," she suggested, aware her voice sounded as fragile as she felt. "That's when I can get my breath back."

"Here, let me help you." He rose from his side of the bed and came round to her, the splendid male, lifting her naked body high in his arms.

Under the warm silver stream of water, she let him cover her with a soft lather of sandalwood-scented soap: over her face, the long stem of her throat, down over her breasts, the smoothness of her stomach, between her legs, right down to her toes. She had thought herself satiated, yet she was trembling all over again, her stomach sucked in. She realised she couldn't get enough of him. Quite simply he filled her with passion in every pore of her skin. He was holding her strongly beneath the arms as the torrent of water washed over them; virtually holding her up. Her back was pressed up against the cold, slick tiles. He was moving into her body, moving rhythmically, driving slow and deep until he found her very core. The expression on his downbent dark face glistening with water was heart poundingly rapt.

Gina had the strangest sensation they were becoming one person. Then all thought was lost in a rush of violent desire.

* * *

Cal had been sitting outside the overseer's bungalow for maybe ten minutes before Steve drove up. He got out of the station ute, mopping the sweat from his face with the red bandana he had worn around his neck. He walked up the couple of steps with no sign of surprise.

"I've sent Mike and a couple of the boys to bring in the clean-skins at the ravine."

"Good." Cal nodded. "Have you decided what you're going to do?"

"I reckon your dad decided that," Steve said. "Look, would you like a cup of coffee?"

"I won't say no." Cal stood up, both men going inside the comfortable bungalow furnished in a simple palette of white with a turquoise-blue feature wall in the living area to offset the polished timber floor, the big Thai coffee table and the brown leather sofa and matching armchairs. The station had provided all the furnishings. Steve had added a few pleasing touches.

"Take a seat. This won't take a minute." Steve walked into the small kitchen and set to making the coffee with excellent freshly ground arabica coffee beans brought in from New Guinea.

While the coffee was perking he rejoined Cal, taking a seat opposite him in one of the armchairs.

"I don't want you to go, Steve," Cal said. "You do a great job. I rely on you and I trust you."

"I appreciate that, Cal. I really do but I can't have one of the McKendricks for me and one bitterly against."

"What about Meredith?"

Steve fought to speak calmly. "What have I got to offer her, Cal? A woman like that."

"Okay, so we can fix things," Cal said. "Do you love her?"

Steve lowered his head. No response.

"Steve?"

When Steve looked up there was misery in his golden eyes. "I was in love with her from the word *go*. Nothing has happened between us, Cal. Just a few kisses."

"One kiss can change a man's life, Steve."

"Tell me about it. It's not as if I've even got a name to offer her. My own mother and Lancaster did that to me."

"That's quite an indictment," Cal said.

"You don't know what it's like, Cal. I know you feel for me but you can't really put yourself in my shoes. You're a McKendrick. That's a proud, pioneering name. You know who you are."

"And you know who *you* are," Cal responded. "You're a top man. Every last person on the station likes and respects you."

"You're leaving out the most important people. Your parents."

"It's quite possible to love one's parents or some member of the family, for that matter, without liking them. I know my father and mother have a certain view of themselves that doesn't jell with the times. Right from the early days Coronation Hill was run more or less on feudal lines. Even Dad's extraordinary attitude to Merri's suitors, and she's had quite a few very serious about her, is feudal. It's the sheer size of the place and the isolation."

"Plus the money, the power and the influence," Steve added harshly. "I really should have taken my mother's maiden name instead of staying with Lockhart. But I guess it's too late to change now."

"Meredith will be tremendously upset if you go."

"I'll think of something," Steve said, his mind jam-packed with mostly crazy ideas. How did a working man win an heiress? A working man with pride?

"I've thought of something," Cal said. "Want to hear it?"

"Just let me get the coffee," Steve said, rising and moving back to the kitchen.

"Thanks," Cal said when Steve returned with a tray wafting

a rich aroma. "What do you think about this? What if I send you to Jingoll?" Jingoll was a McKendrick outstation close in to the McDonnell Ranges in the Territory's Red Centre. "And bring Cash Hammond back here. He's a good bloke. He's not you, but he does the job."

The constriction around Steve's heart eased up slightly. "But wouldn't your father object to that, too, Cal?"

Cal looked untroubled. "Dad's the king of the castle in name only these days, Steve. You know that. *I* run the chain. If I say I'm sending you to Jingoll, Dad will accept it."

"And I never get to see Meredith?" Steve drank his coffee too hot.

"That's up to the two of you, Steve. Merri has a sizeable trust fund."

"God, Cal!" Steve set his mug down so hard it might have been a hammer on an anvil.

"Hear me out," Cal said, holding up a hand. "I'm well aware of your scruples, Steve. All I'm saying is Meredith has the freedom to do what she likes."

"But if she came to me then your parents would give up on her?" Steve met Cal's eyes directly.

"It all translates into choices, Steve. We all have to make our own choices in life."

When Cal returned to the homestead an hour later he went in search of his sister. He needed to tell her what had transpired between him and Steve. Steve moving away from Coronation Hill was an undoubted loss for the station, but a plus for Jingoll. He didn't know what Meredith would think of it however. Jingoll was around eight hundred miles away, the distance between Darwin in the Top End and Alice Springs in the Red Centre being close to a thousand miles. He entered through one of the rear doors of the house, hearing voices coming from down the hallway. As he drew nearer to his father's study he recognised the voices. His mother and Gina were having a discussion. Ordinarily he would have let the sound of his boots announce his arrival, but this time for some reason he trod very quietly along the thick Persian runner, hesitating a few feet from the open doorway.

"So that's how it was done?" Gina was saying, her voice resonating with what Cal thought was quiet resignation.

"Something had to be done," his mother snapped back. "My son was to marry his childhood sweetheart. They were as good as engaged even before that unfortunate holiday."

"So that was the plan," Gina continued as though she was scarcely listening to his mother. "Your sister—a most convincing, beautiful society lady—told me Cal was to marry the girl the entire family loved. It had been known for ages. Sadly for me, I was little more than a bachelor's last fling before Cal tied the knot. A few months on he would be settling down to a splendid marriage—one made in Heaven."

"And so it was!" Jocelyn responded, her tone showing not a skerrick of remorse.

Again Gina didn't sound as if she were listening. It seemed more like she was simply speaking her thoughts aloud. "So you and your sister came up with a plan. She told Cal—who trusted her implicitly—and why not? I saw how sweet and loving she was with him—that I had gone to her, begging her to have me spirited off the island. She was a powerful lady. I was in awe of her. I was so young, the product of an ordinary working-class family. I thought your family lived on a scale I couldn't even imagine. The owner of the island was your sister's good friend. She could do anything. So the two of you concocted the story that I had confessed to her I had given my promise to marry *my* childhood sweetheart. My *fictional* childhood sweetheart. My father was a control freak, Mrs McKendrick. Something like you. I had no boyfriend. Then your sister told Cal I'd become panicked by the situation I found myself in. I had got myself in so deep I wanted only to run away. I was already promised to a young man my father approved of. I remember the exact words she used to me. She seemed so kind, so wise and mature, trying to prevent me from making a fool of myself, but she was playing me for the naive girl I was. *'My dear child, you do realise my nephew is very far above you?'*"

"True, too true!" Jocelyn answered so strongly. Cal winced. "Only by then it was too late. You were already pregnant."

"How could I possibly regret it?" Gina said. "Nothing was easy. My father was so devastated by my fall from grace, he banished me from our home. But I had Cal's son, my beloved Robbie. It may not be what you want, Mrs McKendrick, but Cal and I will be married very soon. Our son is the most important person in the world to us. If you wish to hold on to your son's love it might be in *your* best interest to turn over a new leaf."

There was a shocked silence, then his mother's well-bred voice rising in outrage. "You're advising me, are you?"

Cal judged it high time to make his appearance. He stood framed in the open doorway of the study, trying to keep calm if only on the surface. His mother was wearing her famous pearls. She was seated behind the huge partner's desk that was singularly free of paper work. Meredith, the unsung heroine, took care of all that with her usual quiet efficiency. Gina was standing in front of the desk, with her back to him.

His mother saw him first, her skin draining of all colour. "Cal, how long have you been there?" she quavered.

Gina spun around. Her face, too, betrayed shock. "Cal, we never heard you."

He closed the distance between them, folding an arm around

her. "For once I was eavesdropping. I should do it more often, especially with so many dishonest people about."

Gina's sigh was ragged. "We didn't mean for you to hear anything." She had been trying to effect a private understanding with her future mother-in-law, not drag Cal into it.

"I did tell you to shut the door," Jocelyn snapped, some colour returning to her face. As ever she was determined on braving it out.

"I'm sorry. I should have, but you rather upset me…"

Jocelyn sucked in a breath. "And I'm *not* upset?"

"If you are you deserve to be, Mother," Cal told her bluntly. "You and dear Aunt Lorinda. Just goes to show what a fool I was back then. I *trusted* her. She was family. She'd never shown me anything but love. She's a wonderful actress, too. I was sucked in good and proper."

"Exactly what she wanted," Gina said bleakly. "I believed her, too."

"Let's be very clear here," Jocelyn interrupted, a frown between her eyes, "Lorinda's only motivation was love and concern. She didn't want you, Cal, to make a terrible mistake."

"The terrible mistake was getting engaged to poor Kym. The fact is the two of you conspired to ruin my relationship with Gina," Cal said with a hard condemnatory note Jocelyn had never heard in his voice before. "I won't forget!"

"But, Calvin, we did what we thought best." Jocelyn threw up her hands. "You were set to marry Kym. She was just right for you. I was very grateful to Lorinda for letting me know what was happening on that island. It might be hard to believe now, Gina, but Lorinda quite liked you. She thought you very beautiful and clever, but unfortunately not one of us. She was seriously worried that you may have got hurt."

Gina gave a brittle laugh. "I did get seriously hurt, Mrs McKendrick."

"Please don't let's overlook the damage done to me," Cal broke in, his expression severe. "I'm only just getting to know my son. Robbie is only just getting to know his father. Or did the three of you think it was all *women's* business?" He turned his head to stare Gina down.

Gina didn't answer. Jocelyn sat stricken under her son's weight of judgement.

"What, no replies?" Cal asked, curtly. "No, sorrow, no remorse?"

Jocelyn delicately licked her chiselled lips. They were bone-dry. "Robert is a splendid little fellow." She offered like it was some sort of olive branch. "A true McKendrick. I'm sure the two of us will become great friends. Your father is already very proud of him, Cal. Robert is a beautiful child."

"You would never have laid eyes on him, only Merri happened to see that article about Gina in a paper," Cal pointed out coldly. "It was Merri who drew my attention to it. We have her to thank for bringing Robert into our lives."

"Fate sometimes takes steps to put things right," Gina murmured, lifting her drooping head.

"So where does that leave us?" Jocelyn asked.

Cal clipped off his answer. "It leaves us with the hope *you'll* take a good long look at yourself, Mum. You cross Gina, you cross me. Gina is to be my wife. She's the mother of my son. I love you—you know that—but I won't tolerate your trying to destroy the life the two of us want for our son. You messed up once. You're not allowed to do it again."

Cal turned about and stalked from the room, leaving the two women staring at one another. It would have been an exaggeration to say they were suddenly allies but they both felt the weight of his deep abiding anger.

* * *

Robbie, running around the ground floor, in an ecstasy of exploration, found Jocelyn some time later in the big room with all the plants. It was a dazzling world for a small boy used only to the confines of a two-bedroom apartment. In the room where his grandmother was, there were *trees* that nearly reached the ceiling. There were lovely big fat pots taller than he was, like the pots full of golden canes Aunt Rosa had in her garden. Huge hanging baskets were suspended from the ceiling, tumbling masses of beautiful ferns and flowers. He had never seen so many flowers in his life.

Mummy always had flowers in the apartment. He and Aunt Rosa used to go out into the garden late afternoon and pick some for her before she came home. Mummy liked lilies. There were beds and beds of lilies out in the garden, which seemed to him more like the Botanical Gardens Mummy used to take him to. He had never seen anything in his short life like this place called Coronation Hill. Not just the great big castle, but all the little houses and long dormitories for the stockmen grouped around it. There were no streets or streetlights, no highways, on Coronation; no tall buildings, no buses or trains, nor lots of cars whizzing up and down. There were no coffee shops and restaurants, none of the shops where Mummy normally went to buy things. Instead there were planes and a helicopter, lots of heavy machinery, thousands and thousands of really marvellous-looking cattle, emus, kangaroos—he'd heard *crocodiles*—zillions of birds and best of all *horses*. He couldn't wait until the special pony his daddy had ordered for him would arrive. But above all there was this enormous, empty land! It spread out to the horizons and they had it all to themselves! That was amazing! Coronation Hill was an enchanted kingdom. And it was his home.

"Hello, Nana!" he carolled, delighted to see her. His grandmother was sitting quietly with her back to him so he ran around the front of her, stopping short in dismay, "Oh, Nanna, you're *crying!*"

Jocelyn tried very hard to stem the flow. She had been sitting there coming to terms with what was going on in her life. It seemed to her she had never been so alone, darn near ostracised. Of course she was to blame. Her attitude was so negative. Even she could see that. Ewan was very upset with her. Their argument the night before had badly affected her. Cal, her beloved son, was starting to think badly of her. Of course she was jealous. *Go on, admit it!* She had been the Number One woman in her son's life. She wasn't any more. That was hard to take, especially for a possessive woman like her. A winner all her life it seemed to her all of a sudden she could finish up a big loser if she persisted with the hard line she had taken. Maybe there was something dreadfully wrong with her? The only answer was to express an abject apology directly to Gina, her soon-to-be daughter-in-law and suggest they start again.

"Nanna?" Robbie asked uncertainly, worried his grandmother might be sick or something.

Jocelyn came out of her unhappy reverie. "Just a few little tears, darling boy. Nothing for you to worry about. I'm fine now. What have you been up to?" she asked, trying to speak brightly.

Robbie moved close to her, putting his elbows in her lap and staring into her face. "Why are you so sad?"

Jocelyn gave a funny little groan. "How can I be sad with you around?" She gave him a lovely trembling smile.

Robbie leaned upwards and kissed her on the cheek. "It's so wonderful here, Nanna. I *love* it. It's my home now, isn't it?"

"It certainly is," Jocelyn responded, the icebergs that had all but held her heart fast, starting to melt away. "Coronation Hill is where you belong."

"And Mummy?" Robbie asked earnestly, taking her hand. "Don't you think she's beautiful?"

Jocelyn saw a far-reaching question in her grandson's highly intelligent eyes. *Her* eyes, wasn't that remarkable?

"Yes, darling, I do," she said, allowing herself to be drawn to her feet. "Mummy is very beautiful and she's raised you beautifully. She should be very proud. We're going to have the greatest time ever on the wedding day. I expect you want to be page boy?"

"Page boy, what's that?" Robbie looked up at her a shade anxiously.

"Come along with me and I'll show you," Jocelyn said. "I can show you photographs of your daddy when he was page boy at several big society weddings. That was when he was around four or five. He said he was too old thereafter and refused. Aunty Merri was flower girl at lots of weddings. It's all in the albums."

"Please show me," Robbie said with the greatest interest. "Are there photos of you, Nanna? Mummy said you would have been a fairy-tale bride?"

Jocelyn's gratified smile flashed out. She bent and kissed the top of her grandson's glossy head. "Oh, I was, my darling," she said. "I can show you. I used to have hair like your mummy's. It flowed all the way down my back."

"Like Rapunzel?" Robbie giggled.

"Rapunzel didn't stand a chance!" Jocelyn joyfully squeezed his hand.

CHAPTER SEVEN

MEREDITH rode until she and the gelding were close to exhaustion. It was the gelding's condition far more than her own that had her reining in at the creek, a place that she loved, all the more so now, because it was the place she and Steven had first acknowledged what they could mean to each other. The lead up had been slow—the going was tough—but finally when left alone together caution had given way to feelings of the heart. She just knew in her bones Steven wouldn't stay after the harshness of the way her father had spoken to him. He had insulted Steven in the worst possible way. It was so cruel, so unfair. Steven was the victim of the illicit affair between Gavin Lancaster and his mother. Steven was blameless. Yet he had been saddled with a burden almost too heavy to carry for most of his life.

Meredith sat down on the bank beneath the willowy melaleucas, with hundreds of little wildflowers, purple with yellow, black-spotted throats, growing all around the base of the sweet sapped trees. Above her, she could see chinks of the smouldering blue sky. There could be a late tropical thunderstorm though a cooling breeze had sprung up. It was moving its fingers through her hair and quelling the heat in her skin. A pair of brolgas were standing on their long legs amid the reeds at the water's edge. Brolgas mated for life. These days humans weren't taking sacred vows all that seriously. When she married she wanted it to be for ever.

She thought about the way Steven had kissed her; the way he held her; the depth of feeling he had transmitted to her through his mouth and his hands. Yet she had been much more certain yesterday that he loved her than she was today. At least *in love* with her. That very first kiss had been to her, the start of something big. She asked herself if it had really been that way for him.

A flight of pygmy-geese with their glossy green upper parts and breast bands had arrived, hovering above the mirror-clear surface of the water as though admiring their reflections. On the opposite bank brilliantly coloured parrots were alighting in the trees with wonderful flashes of emerald, deepest sapphire, scarlet, yellow, orange. Australia was famous for the numbers and varieties of its parrots. Almost certainly they had originated on the ancient southern continent of Gondwana. For once the sight of them didn't give her the usual pleasure. At that moment she felt as though all pleasure had been drained out of her.

She *had* to speak to Steven.

Back home at the stables, she turned the gelding over to one of the stable hands to take care of, and then she cut through the home grounds, narrowly dodging her uncle and Rosa who appeared to crave one another's company. She made for the staff quarters beyond the home compound, encountering no one along the way. She prayed Steven would be at the bungalow even if he were packing to leave. It amazed her now, the amount of interference in her affairs she had tolerated from her father. She had to stop living that kind of life. But it also struck her Steven was the first man she was fully prepared to fight for. She had taken a long time to truly fall in love. Maybe that was it.

She was running up the short flight of timber steps when Steven faced her at the door.

"Hi!" he said, his strong face impassive.

"May I come in?" She felt incredibly nervous.

"Sure." He stood away from the door. "You look tired." There were shadows beneath her beautiful, intensely blue eyes.

"I couldn't sleep. How could I what with everything that's going on."

"Would you like some coffee?" he asked. "Cal was here. I made him some, but I'm ready to make fresh."

She shook her head. "No, don't bother unless you want some. I haven't seen Cal. I've been for a ride because I was in the mood for a darn good gallop. Trying to clear my head. So what did you and Cal decide?"

"Sit down, please." It struck him she looked more fragile than he had ever seen her.

Meredith sank into an armchair, looking around her. The bungalow was comfortably and attractively furnished. Steven had kept it immaculately. No one could describe him as a careless man. "Two years later and this is the first time I've ever been inside your bungalow." She gave a brittle laugh. "Doesn't that say something?"

"It says you're Ms McKendrick and I'm the overseer," he clipped off.

She swallowed on her dry throat. "May I have a cold drink if you've got it?" she asked.

"Mineral water?" He glanced back at her, wanting desperately to take her into his arms. Determined not to.

"That'll be fine." She clasped her hands together. "Well, how did you end up?" she asked when he returned. "I must know."

"How did we end up?" He put the frosted glass into her hand, his shapely mouth compressed.

"Steven, please answer me," she begged. "You know how much I care about you."

"Enough to take off with me today?" He stood staring down at her, his expression taut and challenging.

Her heart jumped. "What, on the freight plane?" *Could* she, would she? What could she throw in a bag? Where would they go? Their flight from Coronation would be the talk of the Outback.

"Yes," Steve said. "You look mighty nervous."

"But it's a stunning suggestion, isn't it, Steven?" Her sapphire eyes pleaded with him to understand.

"You'd come if you loved me."

She thought, *Is that right? Is that what I should be prepared to do?* "I don't know, Steven." She shook her head from side to side. "I just don't know." She needed a little time.

"It's okay," he replied, as if he never for a moment expected her to say yes. "I'll put you out of your misery. Cal has made the decision for me. I'm to go to Jingoll and Cash Hammond is to come here."

"What?" For a moment she thought she would burst into tears. But shouldn't she be used to hiding her feelings by now? "Jingoll is outside Alice Springs."

"So?" His heart rose a little at her evident distress.

"How do I get to see you?" she demanded emotionally. "I wanted to learn to fly the plane but Dad wouldn't hear of it. Even Cal couldn't shift him. What am I supposed to do, drive all darned day and all darned night?"

"You've got money." He shrugged, pretending indifference to her plight. "You could call up a plane just like that! Fix it with Jim Pitman today. He could fly you down to me. Stay a week or two." *To hell with it! Make it easy for her to make the break.*

"Do you love me, Steven?" she asked with her heart in her eyes. "Or are you just a little bit *in* love with me? We don't entirely know one another."

"No, we don't," he replied soberly. He could see the way

things were shaping up. Put to the test she was getting cold feet. And why not? He had no reputation to protect. *She* was Meredith McKendrick. "I should be finishing off packing," he said, just short of dismissively.

A tight hand closed over Meredith's heart. "Maybe we can meet again in a little while?" She stood up, trying unsuccessfully to pin his eyes.

"Why not? There are always rodeos, bush races and what not."

Her head dropped. "I'm sorry, Steven. So sorry for everything." She went to move past him to the door, fighting down a storm of tears, only he suddenly caught her to him, golden eyes glittering. He forced her head back into the crook of his arm, his mouth coming down on hers. Passionate. Heated. Punishing.

When he released her she put a hand to her breast. Her heart was hammering unnaturally.

"Just something to remember me by," Steven offered tonelessly.

Steve headed almost directly south to the McKendrick holding that was situated close to the fantastically coloured McDonnell Ranges of the Red Centre. Here the landscape was as different from the tropical north as it could be. The Red Centre seemed as old as time itself, the mystique of the place amazing. Jingoll ran Brahmins, beautiful cattle crossed with the best Queensland Brahmans and going further back, fine American Brahmin stock. Jingoll's Brahmins were well-known in the industry.

The change-over went remarkably smoothly, Steve assuming the top job of manager caused no problems whatever with the staff. Everyone knew he had been the overseer at the McKendrick flagship, Coronation Hill, but the rumour was, as Cal McKendrick's man, he had been sent to make Jingoll an even bigger outfit than it was. That was okay by all. Steve Lockhart might be young but if he'd been overseer on Coronation, he really knew what he was about.

Steve set about proving it from day one. The best way he could cope was to bury himself in hard work. Work shifted the burden of his wretchedness a little. But he thought about her every minute of the day. Then again he had to admit Jingoll gave him a breathing space, while he tried to think how best to go about the difficult task of wooing an heiress which was far more a hindrance than a help. During his first few weeks he made several trips to Alice Springs or "The Alice" as everyone called it. The Alice almost in the dead centre of the continent was a big supply depot for the outlying cattle stations, mines and aboriginal settlements. In addition to being an important commercial centre it was also an enormously popular tourist spot for visitors from around Australia and overseas. The Alice was the jumping off point for the Red Centre's great monuments and beauty spots; *Uluru, Kata Tjuta, Mount Connor, the Devil's Marbles, Rainbow Valley, King's Canyon* and the extraordinary *Palm Valley,* a sight Steve found staggering, blooming as it did in all its tropical splendour in the middle of the red desert.

On that particular day Steve having completed station business allowed himself a couple of cold beers and a big wedge of Mediterranean sandwich, a freshly baked round loaf stuffed with half a dozen delicious ingredients, before he made the long drive back to the outstation. He was sitting at the bar counter alongside a chatty local called Pete, when an old fellow with the long grey hair of an ancient prophet and a matching grey beard burst through the pub doors jabbering something with his mouth wide-open. Despite that, his voice was so agitated, so high and reedy, most of those in the pub couldn't make out what he was carrying on about.

"What did he say?" Steve asked, not really interested. Pete was polishing off his own sandwich with gusto. It was seriously good.

"Hang on!" Pete swung around in his chair. "That's old Barney. Should be Balmy. He's a terminal alcoholic. Has been for the last forty years." Barney was still into his high decibel hollering but it took a moment for everyone to work out what he was on about. By the time everyone did, the humming bar inhabited by tourists, locals and stockmen having a day off in town, shut down to a stunned silence.

"Struth!" said Pete as though someone important had just died without warning. As, indeed, they had.

The pub owner, ponderously moving his huge frame and smoothing back his remaining strands of sandy hair, came from behind the bar. "News is just in, folks," he announced. "No need to mind Barney though he got it right for once. I have to tell you Gavin Lancaster, his son, the station overseer and another passenger, not yet identified, have been killed in transit to Darwin. Their Cessna with Lancaster at the controls went down some thirty kilometres north-east of the ranges. Apparently there was no emergency call, nothing. The wreckage was spotted by the Flying Doctor on a routine flight. So there it is! Lancaster is dead, when most of us thought he'd live to be a hundred."

Pete immediately swung to face Steven, studying him with unblinking light blue eyes almost too big for their sockets. "God, mate, that's your dad, isn't it?" he burst out. "Isn't Lancaster your dad? Hell, you're the living spit of him. I spotted it right away. I tell yah, mate, I'm shocked. *Shocked!*"

Steve didn't say anything. He couldn't trust himself to open his mouth even if he could find his voice. Instead he had the urge to bolt. As always he had been aware of the curious stares coming his way ever since he had entered the pub. It happened all the time. What could he possibly tell this guy, Pete, he didn't already know?

"Do you think there are things like justice in this world, mate," Pete put the question to him in a philosophical kind of way.

"What's your point?" Finally Steve managed to find his tongue, though even to him it sounded like a croak.

"My point, Stevo, is this!" said Pete. "And remember you got it from me. They've always said Lancaster was scared of nobody—but maybe he was a little bit scared of the Almighty? I know I am. It could well be Lancaster decided to do the right thing at long last and put you in his will."

Steve wrenched up a sad, bitter laugh. "He didn't know me." He stood up wanting to get out of the pub as fast as possible. For one thing everyone was now staring his way. That's what happened when you had the Lancaster brand on your forehead.

"I dunno, mate," Pete said, shaking his head, "my feeling is you're being a bit hard on yourself. I recognised you right off. Didn't say nuthin' then, o'course. Didn't want a punch in the nose. Only jokin', mate. You look a real good guy. Different from old Lancaster, God rest his soul," he added piously. "My bet is, you might be hearin' from his lawyers yet."

"*You've* got a better chance of hearing from them, Pete," Steve said, and moved off.

When he got back to Jingoll homestead, several voice messages were waiting for him. All of them related to the crash of the Lancasters' plane. The news had circulated through the Outback with the speed of a high-priority cyclone. One message was from Cal saying he was sorry so many lives had been lost. No more. The family would be attending the Lancaster funerals as a matter of course. These Outback courtesies and marks of respect were understood.

Well, the high and mighty McKendricks might be there, but I sure as hell won't, Steve thought, though the news had powerfully upset him. Lost lives he supposed. Light aircraft coming down in the Outback was a fact of life. One of the dead was his biological father, another his half brother, Brad. Even so he wouldn't be attending any funeral. The family had never had any use for him. He had no use for them, either.

But there he was wrong.

Once again Fate had made the decision to step in.

The day of the funerals was one of scorching heat with banks of grape coloured clouds shot through with streaks of living green, piled up on the horizon. No one took much notice. Outback skies could turn on truly ominous displays without one drop of rain falling. The heat and the threatening sky didn't prevent mourners from all over the country making their pilgrimage to the Channel Country in the extreme South West pocket of the State of Queensland. This was the stronghold of the cattle kings. The select band of families and pastoral companies ran the nation's greatest concentration of beef cattle in their unique, riverine desert. The Lancaster fortress, *Euroka,* an aboriginal word for *blazing sun* was the flagship, but the Lancaster chain like the McKendrick empire spread its life lines through adjoining States.

Gavin Lancaster's two daughters, Catherine and Sarah, both in their early forties, tall, elegant women, stood tearless, but their faces spoke of controlled grief. Standing with them at the graveside was their half brother, Steven. It was Catherine, the elder sister, who had persuaded Steven to attend. She had been adamant he should finally take his rightful place by their side. It was something Steve found enormously touching and, yes, *healing.* The family resemblance between all three siblings was so strong it made it much easier for them to identify with one another. The husbands were unable to attend so Steven stood in for them both. One was a brilliant economist at present a speaker at an overseas conference; the other a cardiologist with a very tight schedule.

Much had happened in the week since the fatal plane crash.

The man who appeared to have ignored Steve's existence for all of his life had left him by virtue of his elder half brother's death a sixty percent controlling interest in Lancaster Holdings. It had been a shock on a monumental scale. Steve had gone on to learn from the family's high-powered lawyer, who strangely enough had looked and acted more like a kindly parish priest, that Gavin Lancaster had secretly supported him for most of his life. Lancaster had made it possible for him to attend his prestigious school. Lancaster, too, working behind the scenes, had been instrumental in those early days, when Steve was fresh out of school, in getting him placed on a top station.

There were more shocks in store. Steve learned Lancaster had kept copies of his school reports and his sporting achievements along with a whole batch of photographs. Steve in his wildest imaginings had never conceived of such a thing. Looking through the photographs, he'd had to swallow many times on the hard lump in his throat. So the man Steve had spent most of his life despising had looked out for him all along, though Gavin Lancaster had chosen to live his life without his *other* son.

Perhaps his wife wouldn't have tolerated me beneath their roof, Steve thought. Who would know?

Steve could hear the Lancaster lawyer's voice in his head. "I never truly understood why your father did what he did, Steven. You're obviously a fine young man, but he tried to make up for it in the end. You won't have any problem whatever with the daughters. They're women of depth and character. Both married now to outstanding men with no connection to the industry. Their interests lie elsewhere, so you'll have a free hand to run Euroka. Cal McKendrick speaks very highly of you, so you're up to it. Needless to say my firm is ready to support you in any way we can." He had smiled encouragingly as he took off his glasses. "Let me be the first to offer my congratulations. It's your father's wish that you be known from henceforth as Steven Lancaster. And perfectly right it is, too!"

Rags to riches! Steve thought. But riches couldn't be measured against the lifelong abandonment of a father. So far as he was concerned they could take it all away in exchange for the chance of having belonged.

Afterwards at the reception at Euroka homestead, Steven found he couldn't have been treated better. Amazing what being handed a grand inheritance could do, he thought cynically. Some of the mourners even greeted him with a touch of reverence. Overnight a lot of power had been put into his hands. He and his half sisters made their way around the two large reception rooms briefly greeting people with a few words and a handshake. It might have been kind of crazy, but Steve felt he was supporting Cate and Sarah, far more than they were supporting him. But then it was obvious they had loved their father no matter what his faults and they had certainly loved their brother who, they had told Steve, had been overwhelmed by the thought of his future responsibilities.

"You see, Brad wasn't a cattleman," Cate had told him with tears in her eyes. *"The thought of stepping into Dad's shoes used to terrify him. Brad really wanted a quiet life. Now he's got it. None quieter than the grave."*

Steve turned to find himself face-to-face with the McKendricks. To anyone watching—and a great many were—it would have appeared the Lancaster heir was being comforted and consoled by close family friends.

Ewan McKendrick even got a little carried away with his words of reconciliation, Jocelyn McKendrick offered Steve her sincere condolences when she really meant congratulations. "I'm sure Catherine and Sarah are going to depend on you a lot!" She gave him a little encouraging pat on the arm.

Now I'm *one of them!* Steve thought, just so tired of all the hypocrisy.

Cal and Gina came to him, saying exactly the kind of thing he wanted to hear. When they moved off he was left alone with Meredith.

"Isn't life amazing?" He spoke with great irony.

"Maybe that's why it's so interesting?" she said, staring up at him, soaking him in. From somewhere he had found a beautifully tailored black suit, pristine white business shirt, obligatory black tie. Probably one of his half sisters had organised it, getting it in from the city. It fitted perfectly. He looked extraordinarily handsome and strangely daunting. Almost another person. "How are you *really?*" she asked, striving not to feel rebuffed.

"Well, most importantly I'm *rich.* Even your mother and father are prepared to accept me. Let bygones be bygones and all the rest." He glanced over her head to where Cal and Gina were standing at the centre of a small group. "Cal and his Gina make a beautiful couple. Where's young Robbie?"

"He's at home with Rosa and Uncle Ed. After ten years on his own Uncle Ed looks set to remarry. Rosa has reminded him of all the lovely things he had forgotten."

"Good. I like your uncle Ed. He deserves to rediscover some happiness. Cal and Gina working things out?" Gina, as if sensing she was being spoken about, suddenly turned to give them a little smile and a wave.

Meredith waved back. "They *appear* to be, yet I feel both of them are struggling with a lot of hurt. We've since found out there was a conspiracy going on to keep them apart. My mother and my aunt Lorinda I'm sorry to say."

"Why doesn't that surprise me?"

His tone stung.

"You'll be getting your invitation to the wedding," Meredith continued, very uncomfortable beneath his searing gaze.

"I expect I will. *Now.*"

"I know how you must feel." It was a great strain being with him in this mood.

"You don't know how I feel, Meredith." The sight of her was playing havoc with his nerves. He wanted to haul her into his arms and scream at her, as well. "How could you? You look lovely, by the way. Black suits you." With her long arched neck and her hair pulled back into some sort of roll she was as graceful as a swan.

Meredith stared over to where her brother and Gina were standing. "Cal wants to take us home, Steven," she said, aware of the flight plans. "I made a mistake coming here. The family is represented. I'm sorry."

"You *didn't* make a mistake, Meredith," he said crisply, his manner changing. "We have to talk."

She looked up at him startled. "About what? You're in a strange mood."

"Why wouldn't I be? I've had so many shocks this past week I scarcely know how to handle myself."

"You look perfectly in command to me. Your half sisters genuinely care about you. I've spoken to both of them."

"They're lovely women." His expression momentarily softened. "I'll never forget it was they who approached me. Far too much of my life has been wasted."

"You can change all that, Steven," she said gently.

"Sure!" His tone was falsely expansive. "I have the solution to all my problems. I have money, position, the running of one of the country's legendary cattle stations. I can even get the girl I want. I can't buy her, of course. She's got money of her own. But I'm pretty sure if I talk to her dad, he'll give me the green light."

Her hands were trembling. "Do you think that's all you need, my father's approval?" She threw up her gently determined chin.

"Meredith, did you think I was talking about *you?*" he asked suavely. "Wait and see if I don't make the most eligible list like Cal. There won't even be a scandal. The media will turn it all into a biblical tale. Prodigal son comes home. All anyone cares about is *money* and who's got it!"

She pressed her palms together to steady her hands. "On the contrary, *I* don't care about money, Steven. I don't think I even care about you any more. You're eaten up with bitterness."

He shook his head at her, a demonic sparkle in his golden eyes. "While *you're* a rich young woman who hasn't yet learned to stand on her own two feet."

Sparks rose into the air around them. "I'm surprised you saw anything in me in the first place," she said. "I'll say goodbye, Steven. I hope you have a good life. I mean that."

"How sweet!" He surprised her by catching her wrist, locking his fingers about it. "You leave now and you'll never see me again." He bent to her, speaking very quietly.

The strangeness of his manner was undermining her. "Surely you can't be asking me to stay?"

"I'm *telling* you to stay." Now his voice was full of authority. "Did you really think you could get away from me as easily as that?" He drew her so close to his side, its significance couldn't be lost on the room.

"You're mad!" There was no way she could break away without causing a scene.

"That's too ridiculous. I'm nothing of the kind. Pop along now and tell the family you're going to stay over. Tell them I have lots to tell you. Tell them your new life begins *now.*"

* * *

It was inevitable at some point Cal and Gina would encounter Kym. Sad occasion or not Cal could see the simmering jealousy just below the surface of Kym's murmured greetings, so civil and proper. Cal knew she took not the slightest pleasure in meeting Gina, but she was doing a fairly good job of hiding it. Though not from Gina he fancied. Gina was extraordinarily intuitive. Kym was busy assessing her from head to toe, working very hard to find a flaw.

You won't find one, Cal thought, wishing all the hurt would seep out of him, believing it would take time. His big question was, why when Gina had found herself pregnant, did she not try to contact him? Even had he been engaged to Kym—never mind that hadn't happened—but even *if*—he would have broken his engagement and married her. He had put the question to her heavy heartedly and she had recoiled.

"My worst fear was you would take my baby from me."

"How could you possibly have thought such a thing?"

"Because I was scared. Scared of you. Scared of your family. Why are you trying to blame me?"

The sad truth was, he *did*.

As for Kym, desperately unhappy after the break-up of her engagement to Cal, she now found herself desperately unhappy once more. It showed in her paleness which she hoped would be interpreted as sadness. She had truly believed—with Jocelyn's encouragement—she only had to bide her time and Cal would come to his senses, accepting she was the best possible choice for him. Now he had presented them all with the object of his mad passion from years back. Not only that, a ready made heir, who according to a besotted Jocelyn was "the image of Cal." In one fell swoop Cal McKendrick, the man Kym had fixated on for so many good years of her life was lost to her. She had ceased to exist for him. She could see it in his eyes as they rested on her, the outsider.

Even as she entertained such thoughts, Kym was murmuring to this woman who had stolen her heart's desire from her. "I do hope we're going to be friends, Gina. May I wish you both much joy." It was a lovely little speech and it tripped sweetly off her tongue. She would *hate* it to be barred from Coronation Hill. Hate it still more not to retain Cal as her friend.

"So that was your ex-fiancée?" Gina remarked quietly as Kym drifted away. "She still loves you." Her voice softened with pity. Gina knew all too well the pain of loss.

Cal couldn't be drawn. He had caught sight of some people he wanted Gina to meet. "Kym will find the right guy to make her happy," he said. "I certainly hope so. She's wasted years of her life on me." He began to steer Gina across the crowded room.

First, Kym has to forget you, Gina thought. She doubted she and Kym would ever become friends. Thank God for Meredith! It made Gina happy to know she had Meredith supporting her. Their friendship had progressed rapidly. Meredith was a lovely person. She deserved happiness, a full life. Gina had the presentiment all roads led to Steven Lockhart, or Steven Lancaster as he was now known. She'd had to bite down hard on her lip when Cal's parents had offered Steven their condolences. The acquisition of land and a proud pioneering name really did make extraordinary things happen, she thought.

CHAPTER EIGHT

By MIDAFTERNOON the last of the mourners had left the station in their private planes, charter planes, helicopters, trucks, one bus and all manner of four-wheel drives. Catherine and Sarah were among them. The sisters had spent a few hours of the afternoon discussing Lancaster family matters with Steven, grief-stricken about the deaths of their father and brother, but enormously relieved, even jubilant at the back of their minds a Lancaster would take over the running of Euroka and its several outstations.

"Lord knows what would have happened had Fate not brought you into the family frame, Steven," Catherine said.

Both women were anxious to return to their children; each had two girls, not present at the funerals, because the sisters hadn't deemed it advisable to uproot them from school, and if the truth be known, their father and brother had shown little interest in any of them. Both sisters put that down to the fact they were all girls. It was a sad fact of life—one that Meredith could attest to—some fathers had little use for their girl children.

"Fortunately *our* girls' fathers adore them," Cate assured them.

Steve's response was immediate and sincere. "Well, I want to meet them at the earliest opportunity."

"Oh, they'll love you!" Sarah had turned to him, blinking tears out of her golden-brown eyes.

Another prophecy that turned out perfectly true.

Meredith and Steve returned to the empty homestead in a near silence. Both of them had been treading around one another almost on tiptoe. It was amazing how greatly humans tortured themselves, suffering in silence, often unnecessarily, devising strategies for containing emotions, strangely frightened to reveal what was really in their hearts lest they be met by rejection. Love was such a terrible ache.

Meredith went to stand at the balustrade staring out at the horizon. The sky was piling higher, ever higher incandescent storm clouds, great plumes of purple, indigo, black, slivers of silver. Their depths shot through with the crimson rays of the sinking sun. It was a fantastic sight against the burning red of the pyramids of sand that lay to the north and the south-west of the station. The mirage was abroad, busy playing its usual tricks. Silhouettes of tall, slender trees stood out amid the wavy silver lines. Little stick people ran about in the somnolent heat and in the roughest driest areas blue lagoons glittered like polished mirrors, overshadowed by thickets of palms. These were the phantom pools and water holes the explorers of old had been tricked into trekking towards with no hope of ever reaching their destination. If only they had met up with some aboriginal tribe, Meredith thought. Aboriginals knew the exact location of wells and springs in the most forbidding country. She knew of many pioneer lives that had been saved by the kindness of the tribal people, including her own family.

The heat had increased not diminished with the closing hours of the day. It was difficult to believe such an extraordinary celestial display might not amount to a powerful electrical storm. At least it might clear the air, she thought.

Doug Winstone, the station overseer, was making his way towards the homestead. He had a curious rolling gait, the result of a serious injury some years back when an enraged bull had gored his leg.

"I'll go and have a few words with him," Steven called.

"Righto, and please tell him to thank Julie once again." Meredith lifted a hand to Doug who doffed his dusty hat.

"Will do."

It was Doug's wife, Julie, who had cooked and cleaned for the homestead over a number of years, but she and Doug had never been asked to take up residence in any part of a very large house. Instead, Julie had gone back and forth from the overseer's bungalow. It was she and the other station wives who had served at the funeral reception, although Cate had ordered in the mountain of sandwiches, biscuits and small cakes that had disappeared beneath the mourners' famished onslaught.

She watched the two men talking earnestly, no doubt discussing job priorities. She, herself, had been greeted most respectfully as if everyone on the station expected that she and Steven would make a match of it after an appropriate period of mourning. They looked an odd couple, Steven and Doug. Steven so tall and young man lean, Doug short of stature, top heavy, with a bull neck, powerful shoulders and a barrel chest. He and Steven had reached an understanding right away. It showed in the body language. These were two men who already trusted each other.

She moved back from the balustrade that badly needed repainting. The verandah wrapped the lower floor but not the top floor. She thought that a shame but it could easily be added on. The homestead was a mix of Regency and Victorian architecture. It had symmetry about it, but it was definitely not a welcoming place. All houses had an aura and this house badly needed its aura changing. It was an unremarkable building compared to

Coronation's homestead, but she was certain it could be turned into something far more impressive. The size was there. The interior rooms were all large, with high ceilings, and well proportioned. A lot of charm could be added to the exterior simply with adding some decorative details; certainly a repainting of the shutters on the large sash windows and all the timberwork, columns, balustrading, fretwork, etc. The broad, canopied verandah was very attractive, but the timber columns needed to be wreathed in flowering vines, maybe a beautiful violet-blue to go with the shutters that could be painted darkest green. She knew *exactly* what had to be done, even if she could see it would be a big ongoing job.

They had seen Cate and Sarah off at the airstrip. Neither sister had appeared the least bit surprised she should stay back with Steven. There was only one possible reason for that, Meredith thought. They believed what Doug and Julie Winstone believed; she and Steven were lovers. Her breath came sharp and jagged at the very thought. She felt herself on the very brink of a major turning point in her life, even if it looked as though the two of them were in retreat. It was a travesty of her true feelings.

The two men concluded their conversation. Doug tipped his hat to her once again. She responded with another wave, while Steven strode back to her. How she admired the wide line of his shoulders, the narrow waist, the lean hips.

"What exactly am I doing here?" she asked him as they moved into the unattractive entrance hall when such an area should always be inviting. It was long and fairly narrow with a timber staircase that led to the upper floor set just outside the drawing room. Something else that needed relocating.

"I would have thought that was obvious." Steven spoke with a false nonchalance, thinking all this past week he had been moving in a dream. He, who had always been on the outside, was in overnight. "You're keeping me company. Otherwise you would have gone home with your family."

"I suppose!" She answered coolly enough, when she was all but delirious with anticipation. She was, after all, quite, quite alone with him and she had taken steps to ensure she was safe.

"So this is Euroka homestead," Steve muttered, as they moved into the drawing room. "It's rather a scary old place, isn't it?" He lifted his handsome dark head, staring about him. "That was my dominant impression. It could even be haunted."

Meredith couldn't control a shiver. "It does seem to have a coldness at its heart." She too began to look around her, making changes inside her head. It wouldn't be all that hard to make the room look more natural and inviting simply by pulling down the heavy velvet curtains. Velvet in the Outback! She would introduce cool colours for a start. Maybe citron and white? The drawing room was furnished with a number of fine antique pieces—indeed, to Meredith's eye it looked like a drawing room of the Victorian period—but the spacious room had an air of neglect about it. It even looked dusty though there wasn't a speck of actual dust in sight. Julie Winstone and her helpers had made sure of that. But a home was not complete without the woman at its heart.

Steven's voice broke into her reverie. "No woman!" he said, echoing her own thoughts. "No woman's touch! How long ago was it the girls' mother died? They didn't say and I didn't like to ask."

"Quite early I think. Cate and Sarah are in their early forties. I think their mother died when they were still in their twenties." Meredith fingered the heavy velvet curtains, wanting to give them a good yank. They were stiff with age. "I know both of them married young."

"Probably broke their necks to leave home," Steve observed dryly. "Hell, this is a terrible place. It looks like it's been caught in a time warp."

"It's *your* place now," Meredith reminded him. "Men left alone generally let things slide. The house is shabby, but that can be easily fixed."

"It's not only shabby. It's unnaturally quiet."

Indeed, the only sound was the soft fall of their footsteps on the massive Persian rug. That at least was splendid, all jewelled medallions and floral arabesques. "It knows one era has ended and another has begun," Meredith hazarded, into the deathly quiet.

"Maybe the house doesn't approve of me." Steven had caught sight of his reflection in a tall gilt-framed mirror. It seemed to him he had changed. Maybe it was the sombre funeral clothes Cate had flown in for him. He had never owned such clothes in his life. "Have I changed or is it just me?" He turned to Meredith, a strikingly handsome young man who now had a chance at achieving some measure of greatness.

She didn't have to consider. "Yes, you have."

"In what way?" He didn't know if he liked the sound of that.

"You're a cattle baron now and you're behaving accordingly. Or to put it another way you've been given the opportunity to be your own man."

The corners of his mouth compressed. "It might come as a shock to you, Ms McKendrick but I thought I *was*."

"Oh, please, I didn't mean to offend you." Meredith gave a little grimace. "You know what I mean. Money gives one confidence if nothing else."

"It hasn't given confidence to *you*."

"You want to hurt me back?" Her intensely blue eyes met his.

"I suppose I do." He shrugged, slanting her a half smile. "A little anyway. This place is unnerving me. How am I going to make a home here?"

"You will." Meredith continued to gaze around her. She might have been an interior designer he had called in with all the answers at her fingertips. "Some pieces should be kept, others put into storage. You need new custom-made sofas, new curtains, a cool colour scheme. Maybe the sash windows knocked out and replaced with French doors. One or two Asian pieces wouldn't go astray and an important painting. I like the mix of different styles, don't you? This is just one of those awful days."

"Isn't it just!" He sighed deeply. "I've buried a father and a half brother I never knew. Wouldn't you have thought my half brother at least would have tried to meet me?"

Something in the way he said it brought her perilously close to tears. "You've heard enough about Gavin Lancaster to know he was a strange, hard man, Steven. I'm certain he had great power over his family. He probably ordered them not to make contact. Your existence was no secret, but he had decided to shut you out." Meredith half turned away, quite upset over it.

"At least I now know Cate and Sarah had wanted to meet me." Steven spoke in a gentler voice. "I'm most grateful for that. But things could have been so different. No use talking about that now, of course."

"Fate has stepped in," Meredith said. "You were always meant to come home."

His expression was disbelieving. "You're not saying Euroka is home?" That idea struck him as downright peculiar.

Meredith nodded. "You can't damn your father for everything. At the end he gave you back your heritage. Your job is to keep it safe."

Steve picked up a smallish bronze sculpture of a horse and rider, balancing it in the palm of his hand. It was a work of art. "He didn't know he was going to die. He didn't know his son and heir would die with him."

"Fate, Steven," Meredith repeated. "We have to leave it at that."

They were at the far end of the drawing room, moving into

the adjoining room when Steve asked, "Are you sure there's not someone following us?" The hairs on the back of his neck were standing up.

"You've got a lot of imagination for a tough-minded man," Meredith countered briskly, when she really felt like grabbing his hand.

"And I'm not on my own. *You* can feel it, too," he accused her. He knew if he touched her he wouldn't let her go.

"I wish I couldn't," Meredith confessed. "I don't fancy sleeping on my own."

"Who said you had to?" He gave her a down-bent golden glance. He was overwhelmed by her loveliness yet he felt an immense pressure on him to behave well. He didn't lack commitment, but the last thing he wanted to do was panic her.

"*I* said. I'm here on the understanding you keep your distance." Deliberately, she walked ahead of him, in retreat again. They were in a smaller room, a sort of parlour. It was enormously gloomy even with the lights on. There were a number of portraits hung on the walls around the room and she went to study them one by one.

"Not a one of them seems happy!" Steve observed, looking over her shoulder. He had the urge to place his hands on her silk clad shoulders, to bend his mouth to her beautiful swan's neck and kiss it but he kept his hands and his mouth to himself.

"They do look a touch subdued," Meredith remarked. "You've inherited the family face."

"Meredith, I've heard that for years and years," he told her in a satirical voice.

"Well, it's a very handsome face. It could have been ugly."

"That wouldn't have worried me if I'd had a *name*."

She moved on to the portrait of a very fragile-looking lady in a white silk morning gown. "It was all very sad, Steven, but you've been acknowledged now."

"Yes, indeed!" he agreed dryly. "My new status has certainly made a huge difference to your mother and father. Let's get a glass of something."

"I wouldn't mind a glass of wine," Meredith said, all her nerves jumping. She knew she couldn't count on herself not to surrender to anything he wanted. Indeed, she felt her entire tingling body belonged to him. Wasn't that proof perfect she loved him? "I don't expect there's a wine cellar."

"This isn't Coronation Hill, Ms McKendrick," he pointed out suavely.

"There might be, you never know." She sounded hopeful. "Let's take a good look upstairs before we go in search of one. I want to take this dress off anyway. It's depressing me. Sarah left me a couple of things to tide me over until I go home *tomorrow*," she stressed. "We're pretty much of a size."

His glance swept her. It held so much heat it sizzled her to the bone. "Sarah's actually thin," he said a little worriedly. Sarah was, indeed, too thin. "But you're very slender and lithe. You stand very straight. I like that. But I know what you mean. I'll change myself, then we can hunt up some food. The piles of sandwiches didn't take long to disappear and I had nothing."

"Neither did I."

"Nevertheless funerals evidently make a lot of other people hungry."

"And thirsty," Meredith added, thinking it hadn't just been tea and coffee that had quickly been downed. Whiskey decanters had been drained.

"I don't like this staircase," Steve said, not able to prevent himself from admiring her legs. High heels on a woman were infinitely sexy.

"Neither do I," she said, not about to let him in on the idea she had for relocating the staircase. She had her reasons for keeping him guessing. In fact, she had to confess to herself she was rather enjoying it, even on such a sombre day.

"So which bedroom do you want?" Steve asked, as they moved along the wide corridor.

Meredith spoke up so casually they might have been cousins. "I'll take Cate's. It's been aired and made up. Julie has been so good. She's quietly seen to a lot of things." She walked into the large old-fashioned bedroom that looked towards the front of the house. A verandah to walk out onto would have been perfect, but that would have to wait.

What am I thinking, for goodness sake! She was actually re-decorating the house in her head.

"What about you?" she asked airily, stepping back to admire the embroidered silk coverlet on the bed.

"I think I'll just head across the hall." He turned his crow-black head in that direction.

"To Sarah's room?"

"I don't want to get *too* far away," he told her with a mocking smile. "You're not mentioning you're damned nervous, but I know you are."

"It's an unfamiliar house," she replied, defensively. "More-over, one expects some kind of nervousness on such a day." In reality she was spooked.

He nodded, beginning to walk away. He might pretend to be at ease but all his senses were doing a slow burn. "All the signs augur for a thunderstorm during the night. If you're frightened you don't have to wait for an invitation to come over."

"Sorry, Steven," she called after him. "I come from the Territory, remember?"

He paused at the door, his face the face of the portraits down-stairs. "It might shock you to learn, Ms McKendrick, the electri-cal storms here are even worse. Now, I'm going to change out of this undertaker gear. Knock on my door when you're ready to go in search of the wine cellar. Let's hope Julie has done us a service leaving us some food."

Left alone Meredith looked quickly at what Cate had left her. A pretty loose dress in an ink-blue and white pattern, a sort of trapeze dress with short ruffled sleeves and a double ruffle at the hem. That would do nicely, lovely and cool. There was a pair of navy flatties a half a size too big but she was glad of them. She rarely wore high heels; a pink cotton nightdress, pintucked and embroidered with tiny grub roses, matching robe, very virginal. Both sisters were easy to like. She saw how life might have been hard for them without their mother, and knowing they had a half brother somewhere they had been forbidden to meet.

Meredith went to the solid mahogany door and closed it, without actually turning the lock. Would she forget to lock it tonight?

"I'll be damned if this isn't the best room in the house," Steven was saying, his surprised glance sweeping the large cellar with its attractive rustic ambience. The ceiling was dark beamed, the walls stone, as was the floor with a wide stone archway dividing the wine storage area with its long rows of racks from a seating, dining area if needs be. There were two big leather armchairs in front of a fireplace obviously well used—the desert could grow very cold at night—and a long refectory table with eight Jacobean style chairs set around it. There was even a strikingly realistic rural oil painting of a herd of cattle fording a coolibah-lined creek.

"Someone spent a lot of time here," Meredith observed, hunting at the bottom of the canvas for the name of the artist.

"So what do we want?"

"White for me," Meredith said, shivering a little because the cellar was so much cooler than the house. "A sauvignon Blanc."

"A sauvignon Blanc it is." Steve picked a bottle up, passing it to her while he hunted up a Shiraz for himself. Maybe there was a steak or two in the fridge? Euroka was a cattle station after all.

No steaks, but a leg of ham, bacon, plenty of eggs, cream, milk, cheese, a basket full of bright red tomatoes, a brown paper bag full of mushrooms; and in the bread bin a loaf of sour dough bread, obviously freshly baked.

"Looks like ham and eggs," Meredith said. "We can pretend it's breakfast."

"Ah, to think we really *will* be having breakfast together." Steve said, mockery in his expression. But the emotion was there. "Look at you, a little housewife!" Meredith had tied a clean apron around her waist to protect Cate's dress.

"Do you think you can get away with this because we're on our own?" she asked, briefly lifting her eyes to him. He was wearing a red T-shirt with his jeans and he looked extraordinarily vivid, vibrating with a physical energy that was like a force field around him. It was very impressive.

"Get away with what exactly?" he asked, though he knew precisely what she meant. He was goading her. He didn't want to, but he was.

"Your resentments are evident, Steven," she said, but went no further. The atmosphere between them was inflammatory enough.

He shrugged. "You're better off with me than at home I'd say."

Meredith didn't acknowledge that, either. She took six large eggs out of their carton. "Shall I scramble them? There's plenty of cream."

"Are there no ends to your talents, Ms McKendrick?" He tipped out the mushrooms that needed a wipe over. "Scrambled will be fine. Why don't you have a glass of the red while you wait for your wine to chill?"

"I think I'd drink anything at the moment." She gave a faint sigh. The strain was telling on both of them. She began to break the eggs into a bowl adding the cream.

"I'll find us some glasses. *Nice* glasses." Steve hunted through the numerous cupboards before he hit the mother lode, crystal. He filled two glasses and put one beside Meredith's hand.

"Thank you." Meredith took a good sip of the wine. It was ruby-red and very good.

A sudden gust of wind blew strongly through the back door, pungent with bush incense. Steve went to close it. "I know we'll get rain," he said. "I just know it."

Lightning was a dazzling white illumination, searing the retinas of her eyes. Meredith hid her head beside a stack of pillows. She could have pulled the curtains but she had no desire whatever to sleep in the pitch-dark. The bedroom was oddly cold. Could she risk getting up and finding a blanket? Why not? Steven wasn't going to come to her. She had to bow low before him. The truth was he hadn't forgiven her for her apparent rejection.

You'd come if you loved me.

And if you don't, I'll disappear out of your life.

That had been the implication. What had she done? She'd waffled on about meeting up again in a little while. That had been a mistake. Now, apart from ensuring she had stayed with him, he was acting as cool as you please.

"Good night, Meredith!"

"Good night, Steven." She was far from happy, but she managed to sound as cool as he.

Both of them had been hungry, leaving not a morsel on their plates. There was ice-cream to follow; she found a tin of peaches. They finished the wine and then Steven made coffee. Afterwards they talked a good deal about running a big operation, something with which Meredith was well acquainted. She made a number of suggestions that he picked up on immediately, saying they were excellent and facetiously offering her a job. They talked about what would be expected of him, who might replace him on Jingoll, anything and everything except their personal relationship and where it was going, if anywhere. It was a huge jump from desire to consummation. She realised she wasn't going to be allowed to get away with that perceived humiliation.

Surely he realised she couldn't have turned her back on everyone and eloped with him on the spot? She had obligations. It would have taken her a little time to put her affairs in order, then pack her bags if that was what he wanted; not that she didn't understand where he was coming from. Steven had lacked real commitment from childhood. His family had virtually abandoned him by the time he reached adolescence. What a blow that must have been! What a heartache for a young boy! When he had suggested she go with him to Jingoll, a *yes* answer had been crucial. In some ultrasensitive corner of his mind she had failed him, even if he could rationalise the difficulties of her position.

Then there was her parents' embarrassing back flip. Who could blame him if he was contemptuous of that? Surely he couldn't think his change of fortune had had any influence on her? All her adult life she had kept herself very much under control. She had been waiting for the right moment to make her move. She had, in fact, been working steadily towards it when Fate stepped in.

Around three in the morning the rain advanced from the north like a large army on the march. Meredith heard it coming minutes before it actually arrived. Then when it did, the storm broke with ferocity, a driving deluge that changed direction within seconds as the wind chopped this way and that. Now it was pelting through the open casement windows, whipping up the curtains that went into a wild dance.

Meredith turned on a bedside light, then sprang out of bed, but by the time she got to the windows the rain was lashing the bedroom floor. Half blinded, she managed to get one window down without much trouble, apart from being drenched—indeed, the flimsy nightgown was almost ripped from her body—but the sash on the middle window abruptly broke as she was lowering it. It came crashing down with fragments of glass flying like steel chips.

Instantly she jumped back before the chips could stab her, curling up her bare toes against the broken glass that now lay on the floor.

"Meredith?"

It was Steven banging on the door, his voice charged with anxiety.

"It's open!"

He burst into the room, shirtless, his jeans pulled on in obvious haste, zipped but not buttoned. She could see the low line of his navy hipsters. "Don't move!" he ordered, taking in the situation at a glance.

"You've got bare feet, too," she warned him, rain all over her face and in her eyes.

He yanked up a cushion and swished it a few times over an area of the wet floor. Then he pitched it into a corner. One armed he lifted her away and carried her that way back into the centre of the room. "You're soaking wet."

"I *know*. So are you!" His black hair, his bronze skin and his upper body were glistening. Yet he felt warm, whereas she was chilled.

"Hang on, I'll get a few towels." He rushed to turn on the lights in the bathroom, but she went after him her wet nightgown draped to her body like a second skin.

A few seconds more and she was swaddled in a large bath towel while he took a smaller one to her hair. "You'd better get out of that nightgown."

"*Excuse me,* not while you're looking!" She spoke huskily from behind the towel he was so energetically wielding.

"Then I'll turn away."

He did, throwing down the towel and turning his wide bare back.

"What are we going to do about the rain pouring in?" she asked, pulling the nightgown over her head in a kind of frenzy. Her heart was beating much too fast. She knotted the pink towel around her like a sarong, feeling incredibly nervous but her whole body aroused.

"We'll have to pray the storm passes over quickly or the wind changes. Or I can rig up something. Can I turn around now."

"Yes." She had never been more conscious of her own skin.

"Actually I could see you in the mirror."

She found that so electrifying her whole body broke out in a fabulous flush of excitement.

"Only joking," he murmured, his fingers reaching out to tidy her tumbled hair.

"Then I'm not amused."

"Neither am I. I've never felt less like laughing in my life." His eyes dropped the length of her body, and as he did so, his handsome face picked up a sharp shadow. "Your foot is bleeding."

"Is it?" She hadn't been aware of any cut or sting.

"Let me take a look," he said with concern. "Sit on the chair."

"Aren't we're supposed to be fixing the window?" She knew where all this was going but she wasn't about to stop it even for a tornado.

"I'll fix it when the rain stops. Right now I want to take a look at your foot."

"I don't remember standing on any glass." How could she

when she was concentrated on him? The bright light cast a mosaic of glittering jet on his hair, the whorls on his chest, the dark gold of his face, the skin of his shoulders, his strong arms and his sculpted torso. Who could blame her for feeling such piercing desire?

"You must have." He balanced her narrow foot in the palm of his hand. "It's not bad, just a bit of blood." He reached around for a box of tissues that were sitting on the counter. "I'll hold it until the bleeding stops." He glanced up at her, glittering sparks in his eyes. "You know, your toes are as pretty as your hands."

It might have been the most thrilling compliment she had ever received because she was instantly on fire. "Not a lot of people know that." She spoke shakily, finding the sensation of her foot resting in his hand incredibly erotic. She could even hear her heart banging furiously above the wild orchestration of the storm. It seemed to her to be passing over the roof in a dipping rush before swinging away.

He lifted her foot higher and pressed his mouth to her high instep. Then he began to lick it, curling his tongue over her soft skin down to her toes.

"Steven!" A moan came from the back of her arched throat.

"God, you're beautiful!" He said it in such a tender voice she couldn't help it. She burst into tears.

"Meredith!" His expression so frankly sensual, changed to concern. "You're all right? You're okay?"

She let her head fall forwards onto his shoulder, her breathing deepening. "I've missed you. Oh, God, how I've missed you! I want you back."

"And I want *you* back." He rose from his haunches, gathering her close up against him. "Tell me you love me. I'll never let you go otherwise."

She sank against his marvellous lean body, letting his chest hair graze her cheek. The pleasure she felt at being back in his arms was tremendous. "That's all right! I'm happy here." She gave a voluptuous sigh, pierced through with love.

"But I want to take you back to bed. *My* bed." His eyes had turned very dark with emotion. "You can't stay here anyway."

She lifted her face to him, blue eyes overbright, her hair in riotous disarray. "You're saying you want to sleep with me?"

"That's not the worst of it. I'm *going to!*" His gaze travelled down over her smooth shoulders to the cleft between her breasts barely concealed as the pink towel kept dipping lower and lower. "Surely you're overdressed in that?" he asked huskily.

Yearning poured into her. She no longer felt the need to deny or repress it. "Can I keep it on while I ask you a question?"

"Fire away." He pulled her in very tight, trapping her within his arms. "Ask me anything."

It rippled out with laughter. "What are your intentions, Steven Lancaster?"

He spoke against her lips. "Devilish!" His palms were running down over her silky shoulders, her sides, his fingers playing very gently with the folds of the towel. "Surely you already know? I want you. I'll never stop wanting you. I want to marry you."

She could see so clearly how wonderful that would be. Overcome with emotion, she dropped her head, barely able to speak.

"Look at me." He cupped her chin.

Tremors were shooting through her. She could feel the heat rising from his skin. She caught his musky male scent, the evaporated rain, saw the little pearl drops that still clung to him. She leaned forwards and tongued a few off. They tasted like some powerful aphrodisiac putting her in a fever of want.

"Would you have come to me if all this hadn't happened?" he asked. "Or would you have lost your nerve?" It was a serious question demanding a truthful answer.

Her throat was suddenly crowded with words. Then they came tumbling out as though to withhold them any longer would choke her. "Never. I'm so sorry what happened that last time, Steven. I wanted you to understand so badly. I know you felt I failed you. No, don't say anything. You *did*. But I was planning all the while. You stamped your name on me. Body and soul. I swear, I was never going to let you go." Her nerves were fluttering badly. She lifted her arms to lock them around his neck. "*Please* believe me." She was frantic he would. "Nothing and no one would have stoppe—"

She got no further. The flow of words was as abruptly cut off as the drumming rain.

His mouth was over hers, covering it, his tongue opening it up fully to his exploration. He kept going and going, thoroughly aroused, kissing her, staggering her with the force of his passion. The towel fell away unheeded, falling in a soft pile at their feet. She strained against him, while he grappled with her satiny naked body, her breasts crushed against his bare chest. For a long moment he held her back from him, studying her body, his glance alone ravishing her. She rose on tiptoes. She had never thought it possible to feel like this. He lifted her as though she weighed no more than a feather pillow.

Naked he put her down on his bed, leaving his strong hands on her shoulders, revelling in her expression that was wild with longing. For *him!*

"From this day forward we're bound together," he said in triumph, desiring her so much his entire body throbbed. He wanted nothing more than to bury himself deeply within her feeling the clutch of her around him. He wanted to merge himself with her. All his wildest dreams, his hopes, his expectations, so seemingly impossible had come true. He had made a great discovery. Meredith was the love of his life.

Blissfully, she sank back into the pillows and shut her eyes.

When she opened them again, *her man,* her lover was bending over her, staring down at her with such a world of longing in his eyes her limbs turned liquid.

She cried out his name in an ecstasy of need. "Steven, my true love, come here to me."

He obeyed, awed by the realisation he was about to take this wonderful woman in a way he hitherto had only dreamed about.

CHAPTER NINE

LIFE was always dealing out surprises. Almost overnight Jocelyn had undergone a remarkable sea change. The histrionics disappeared. Previously unable and unwilling to conceal her dismay that things were not what she had hoped for, Jocelyn now set about making the best of things. Robbie had a lot to do with it, Gina thought. There was no doubt in anyone's mind Jocelyn really loved Robbie. He was a beautiful child, his father's son, of course, natural, easy, comforting and loving with his grandmother. That was the irony of it, Gina thought. If Cal had brought only Robbie and not her back to Coronation Hill, Jocelyn would have been over the moon. As it was, Jocelyn had discovered it wasn't pleasant being the odd man out. Ewan and Meredith had accepted her. In fact, one would have thought she was the girl Ewan had in mind for his son all along.

Even Steven Lancaster—the young man Ewan McKendrick had appeared to hate so much—was now very much in the picture. Meredith had come home from the Lancaster stronghold, so happy, so radiant, so obviously very much in love, her imminent engagement to Steven was received with exclamations of congratulations and every appearance of pleasure. Even Jocelyn knew better than to risk a sarcastic comment.

"Marvellous, isn't it?" Meredith commented later to her brother. "It seems I've done something right at long last!"

Gina found Robbie in one of his favourite places, the beautiful Garden Room, Jocelyn always called the Conservatory. He was sitting at a small circular table flanked by Rosa and Uncle Ed who had taken over elements of his education. A big picture book was open in front of him, his glossy, dark head bent over it. Rosa saw Gina first.

"So where are you off to, *cara?*" Her brilliant dark eyes swept over Gina. She was in riding costume, which pretty well answered the question. It really suited her Rosa saw with pride and pleasure. Her Gina had a beautiful body. She wasn't so sure about Jocelyn McKendrick as a teacher for her beloved godchild. But it appeared Jocelyn had been a fine rider in her day and still rode, though not as frequently. She had offered to give Gina riding lessons on the quiet. It was to be a big surprise for Cal.

"Mummy, Mummy," Robbie broke in excitedly, "Uncle Ed found a book for me all about the planets. Do you know what the word *planet* means?"

Gina went to him and kissed his warm rosy cheek. "No, my darling, I don't. Please tell me."

"It means *wanderer* because the planets wander across the sky."

"Well, that's what the ancient Greeks *thought,* Robbie," Ed told him. "In fact, the planets all circle the Sun. They move in the same direction, in much the same plane and each spins on its axis as it orbits." He demonstrated with a finger and a twirling movement of his hand. "You have a very bright boy here, Gina." Ed looked up to smile at her. "He just soaks up knowledge. It's a pleasure for Rosa and me to have anything to do with his education."

Rosa reached out and covered Ed's hand with her own.

They'll probably beat Cal and me down the aisle, Gina thought as she moved off. But they'd have to be awfully quick. The wedding invitations had been sent out. It was to be a small wedding. No more than fifty people. Neither of them wanted a big affair. Each night he came to her. Lying beside her on the bed until she finally went off to sleep, her body wanting nothing more after the tumultuous passion they aroused in each other. Their sex life was glorious. It could hardly have been bettered, but their trust in each other lagged behind. The lost years, the old grieves, the needless suffering, needed time to be erased, before each had full confidence in the other. Both of them desperately required forgiveness of themselves and one another.

They had decided for Robbie's sake they wouldn't openly share a bedroom until after the wedding. Gina couldn't wait. They had talked about a honeymoon. They didn't want to leave Robbie. The love between father and son had developed at a tremendous rate. That was Cal's big problem with her, Gina thought sadly. She had deprived him of his son for three of the most precious years of life. Cal had taken that greatly to heart. She was terrified that deprival might in time be forgiven but never forgotten. What Cal required of her from now on, was her total allegiance.

She arrived at the stables complex a minute or so late. It was set amidst beautiful trees, with a training yard, almost a small track, enclosed by a high white painted picket fence facing it. Jocelyn, looking very trim and youthful, was waiting for her in the cobbled courtyard. Their horses had been saddled up by one of the stable boys—and there appeared to be quite a number. Gina's mount was a pretty liver-chestnut mare called Arrola—which meant *beautiful* in aboriginal—with a star on its forehead and four white sox.

"Just the horse for a novice like you," Jocelyn had decided briskly.

Arrola, who really did have a lovely nature, extended its velvety muzzle to be stroked. Gina made an affectionate, low clicking sound she had learned from Jocelyn that appeared to work. That first time she had prayed she would stay on. She was still praying after half a dozen lessons, but she had settled a good deal. She had to admit Jocelyn was an excellent teacher, very patient, showing no sign of disappointment or disapproval when Gina couldn't perform as expected. Gina had come to the conclusion—and she was being very hard on herself—she wasn't a natural as all the McKendricks were and Robbie would prove to be, but she was quickly gaining an acceptable level of expertise. Jocelyn wouldn't tolerate less.

Jocelyn always chose the route they would take, always away from where the men would be working. This was to be a surprise for Cal after all. The two of them always rode alongside, Jocelyn constantly offering instruction on some aspect of posture and handling of the reins. Today was a new route along a chain of billabongs densely wooded around the banks. The onset of the monsoon season had brought in a few storms but the earth beneath them was hard, giving Gina a feeling of security and solid leverage. Her leg and thigh muscles didn't ache half as much as they used to, either.

After twenty minutes or so, Jocelyn gave the order to quicken the pace. Ahead of them the giant landscape glimmered in the heat. The fragrance of wildflowers tossed up by the storms carried on the wind. In the distance, glittering through the thick screen of trees, some of them covered with scarlet flowers, were the billabongs alive with native birds and maybe the odd crocodile.

Gina, feeling a rush of excitement, lightly kicked Arrola's

flanks. She was beginning to appreciate how enormously exhilarating a gallop could be.

Riding up from the stream, Cal heard the drumbeats of hooves before he actually sighted the riders. Then as he cleared the trees a single rider burst into view, billows of dust rising as the rider's horse galloped out of control. A second rider came hot in pursuit; an expert this time. He recognised his mother's small frame.

"God!" he shouted, scarcely able to believe his eyes. Here was a tragedy waiting to happen. Galvanised, he swung into action, squeezing his big bay gelding's sides hard, urging it up the bank, then into a gallop. It couldn't be, it shouldn't be, but it was happening. That was Gina out there and she was in terrible danger. It struck him with tremendous force the devastation he would experience if she were injured. Or worse. He could see she had lost her hat, her long hair streaming on the wind. He recognised the horse. It was the little mare, Arrola, normally such a mild animal. Now it was clearly in a mad panic, galloping wildly towards the line of trees with Gina clinging desperately to its back. Her stirrups appeared to be lost. If she got flung off—and God knows how she was staying on—she would come down in a fearful mass of broken bones. If she managed to stay on, the mare would only continue its crazed gallop on to the trees. There she would have no hope. She would plough into a tree-trunk, or be hit by a large branch, her neck broken, her limbs snapped.

His heart froze. Why had he held back on telling her how much he loved her? he flayed himself. Why had he continued to blame her for not contacting him when she found herself pregnant? He had the right to know, sure, but why had he wanted to keep punishing her? Maybe she had kept a momentous event secret from him, but she must have suffered carrying their child alone. He had wasted so much time nursing his hurts, instead of trying to let them go. Even when he found out Lorinda and his mother had plotted against them, he had still kept on blaming Gina. She should have come to him. He could have put things straight. She hadn't trusted him. The grievances had gone on and on.

Now *this?*

There suddenly existed, right out of the blue, the dreadful possibility he might never get to tell her how much he loved her. How desperately he wanted her There had not been enough talk about matters of the heart. He had laboured to hide his very real love for her and he had to bitterly regret that. She could go to her death not knowing. That was unimaginable. No way could he let it happen.

His mother's horse, Dunbar, was a splendid animal. It never stumbled. It was eating up the ground but he realised it would never overtake the little mare. The mare must have had a considerable lead he calculated, his heart twisting in pain at the fleeting thought his mother could have been in some way responsible. Even as the thought came into his mind, he rejected it absolutely. His mother had her faults but she would never do anything to harm anyone. Even her efforts to break up his island romance didn't come under the heading of a malicious act. She and Lorinda would have truly believed, however mistakenly, they were doing the right thing.

He rode like he had never ridden before, his face blanched with fear and a boiling dread. If there was a God in Heaven, He couldn't do this to him. To have refound the woman he loved only to lose her to a violent death? How could he survive such a tragedy without undergoing some tremendous alteration in his character?

He galloped on. A lesser horseman would never have closed in on the runaway so fast. The gelding was wondrously surefooted in the rough. It didn't have the speed and power of his favourite stallion, but it was responding magnificently. They were coming at the runaway from an angle, cross country, whereas his mother was pounding straight after them. His mother, too, was in mortal danger, but still she kept going. She would have to get Dunbar under control soon, or she, too, ran the risk of getting pulped amid the wilderness of trees.

A final powerful surge and he was pulling the big gelding alongside. Immediately it and the little mare began to jostle for supremacy, the tall gelding easily winning out. On Gina's beautiful face was exhaustion and despair. "Hang in there, Gina!" Cal shouted, finely judging the precise moment to lunge after her reins.

Please, God, don't fail me!

The first line of trees, brilliant with flower loomed up.

His nerve held iron-hard.

Got them!

Now it was a ferocious battle to control two horses. He reined back hard. The gelding responded, the mare just wanted to keep on going as if it had a death wish. Superb horseman that he was Cal had to fight against being pulled from the saddle. Again he yanked back. The little mare was still putting up a mighty fight, hell-bent on hurling herself and her rider into the trees.

He gave her a bit of head, and then pulled back as violently as he dared without bringing them all down. "Whoa, now, easy, easy, easy…"

With the compliance of the gelding, so responsive to his every demand, he got the mare under some sort of control. "Easy, girl, easy!" The mare began to centre herself.

The thicket was no more than twenty-five yards away.

Gina fell into his arms, collapsing against him, burying her face against his chest. His strong arms encircled her as though he would never let her go. All his defences, all his efforts to keep his real feelings in check were swept away.

His mother rode up, her face paper white. "My God, Cal," she gasped, chest heaving. "Only *you* could have done it. Gina could have lost her life." She spoke with the tremendous relief of a person who had seen a horror averted.

One arm still strongly around Gina, Cal went to his mother's assistance helping her dismount. There were tears coursing down her face. "My fault, my fault," she kept saying. "I'm so sorry, son. We wanted it to be a big surprise for you."

"Whatever happened?" His mother looked too distraught to really question, but he had to know at least that. Gina was in shock. She was very pale and trembling. So far she hadn't spoken a word.

"A bloody kangaroo!" His mother who rarely swore, swore with gusto. Anything to relieve her pent-up feelings. "Gina has been doing so well I thought we could try a little gallop. All would have been well, only the 'roo just popped up in front of her, spooking that silly mare. Spooked good old Dunbar, too, for that matter. He did quite a dance. If Gina had had more experience she could have reined the mare in. Instead Arrola took off as though she was going for the post in the Melbourne Cup. I didn't know she had it in her. I'm so dreadfully, dreadfully sorry. I would never have forgiven myself if anything had happened to Gina." Jocelyn looked into her son's eyes, frightened.

"I know that, Mum," he said gently.

At his response Jocelyn rallied. "Well, we'd better get her home," she said, already swinging herself back into the saddle. "A shot of brandy should do it. Some good strong black coffee. Always helped me. I'll ride ahead. Get one of the men to bring the Jeep. Bear up, Gina, girl," she called down to Gina in such a bracing voice Gina might just have been blooded. "It's a miracle you managed to stay on. I can think of any number who would have fallen off."

Jocelyn kicked her sweating horse into a gallop, determined

to outrun her lapse of judgement. The girl had guts. Damned if she didn't!

Gina remained within the half circle of Cal's arm, dragging in fortifying breaths. She was very pale but he thought it unlikely at this stage she would go into a faint.

"This is just a suggestion," he murmured quietly. "I could take you up before me on the gelding. You would be quite safe and we'd meet up with the Jeep quicker. If you prefer not to, shake your head."

His tone was so gentle and comforting Gina nodded her head. "Okay!"

"Okay what, Gina?" His expression relaxed a little.

"I'll ride with you." She turned up a face that showed a mixture of trepidation and bravery.

"I'll never let you come to harm," he said, making no effort to hide his depth of feeling. "Just trust me."

"I do," she whispered. She had the sense many of the defences he had put up against her had toppled.

"I really don't deserve it." His brief laugh was ragged.

"You saved my life. Whatever would have happened to me if you hadn't turned up?"

"Don't even think about it." Cal shuddered.

"Death by freak accident."

"Hush!" Of course, it happened. Freak accidents weren't uncommon in station life.

"It was all for you, the riding," Gina wanted to reassure him. "Your mother had faith in me. I let her down."

"God, no," Cal protested violently, greatly upset even if he appeared in control. "The best station horses can be spooked. Horses are such nervous animals and the 'roos have a bad habit of popping up out of nowhere. You'll learn how to keep a horse under control."

"Is that why you want me to get on one again!" She gave a ghost of a laugh.

"Not today if you don't want to." His arm tightened around her. It was a relief to hear her voice strengthening and see colour coming back into her cheeks.

"Then I have to tell you the only one I'd do it for is *you!*"

Back at the homestead Gina found herself being fussed over.

"You can go off now, Cal," Jocelyn said after about an hour and several cups of tea later. "Gina will be fine now. We'll look after her, won't we, Robbie, darling?"

"We'll spoil her!" Robbie stoutly maintained.

Cal stood up, looked down at Gina, reclining on the sofa. "I'll stay if you want me to." God, he'd do *anything* she wanted.

"That's okay, I know you've got lots to do. I'm fine. Really!" In fact, she had never felt so safe and sound.

"We'll look after her, Daddy." Robbie gazed up at his father. "Won't we, Nan?" Robbie had taken to calling Jocelyn Nan of his own accord. "It bothers you, doesn't it, Daddy, Mummy got such a fright?"

Cal smiled down on his very perceptive little son. "You can say that again, pal!"

"Mummy's brave all the time," Robbie announced proudly.

At that moment, Rosa, who had been taking a leisurely drive with Edward, rushed in, closely followed up by a concerned-looking Edward, their gazes falling on Gina. "What is this I hear?" Rosa asked worriedly.

Gina thought it time to move. She swung her feet determinedly to the floor. "No fuss, Rosa, dear. I'm fine."

"You look upset?" Rosa's dark eyes flashed accusingly around the room, focusing on Jocelyn. Her baby needed protection.

"Mummy doesn't want to talk about it, Rosa, okay?" Robbie

jogged over to Rosa and took her hand in his. "She got a fright when her horse bolted, but Daddy saved her from any danger. No one is as good as my daddy. He's a marvellous rider. Now we're helping Mummy get over it. Would you and Uncle Edward like a cup of tea?"

Rosa blinked and caught her breath. "Coffee, I think, sweetheart," she said. "I must admit I panicked."

Jocelyn stood up immediately, all graciousness. "I'll go organise a pot. It won't be too long before it's ready."

For the rest of the day Gina took it quietly, but by evening she was over the worst of her shock. She was alive when she could have been a serious casualty. Or dead. Everyone appeared enormously grateful. For the first time there was genuine accord around the table, Jocelyn leaning over to touch Gina's hand several times during the meal. Even Ewan put his hand on top of Gina's and gave it a little squeeze. Gina didn't realise it but everyone thought she was standing up to a very frightening incident awfully well. Meredith, who had been staying with Steven for a couple of days working out how best to refurbish Euroka's homestead, had been startled and upset by the news when she phoned in earlier in the evening.

"It must have given you a tremendous fright, Gina," she said. "And Mum, too. When I spoke to her she was trying hard not to cry. What a miracle Cal was around to save you. You'll have to make it up to him tonight, girl!" This she proffered with a smile in her voice.

The very least I can do! Gina felt a rush of affection for her soon to be sister-in-law.

The household settled around eleven o'clock and a short time later Cal tapped on her bedroom door.

He stood looking down at her, a bottle of champagne and two

flutes in hand, a white linen napkin draped over his arm. "Room service, madam."

"Please come in," she said, as though he were exactly that, but her whole body was instantly a-pulse.

"Sometimes nothing else will do but champagne," he offered smoothly.

"It certainly helps." Gina turned and saw them both reflected in the mirror of the dressing table; he with his impressive height, densely, darkly, vividly masculine; she with her flowing hair and glowing skin, dressed only in a satin robe, the quintessential image of alluring woman. As an image it appeared incredibly erotic. "Do we have something to celebrate?" Her dark eyes watched him.

"You know we have. This has been quite a day." He leaned to graze her cheek. "There *is* a God," he announced.

"Of course there is." Gina moved to take up a position on the invitingly cosy chaise longue covered in a lovely pale green silk. "I've never doubted it."

"And I never will again!" Cal said, his voice filled with real gravity. He didn't think the memory of the immense blessing they had been granted that afternoon would ever leave him. Gently, he twisted the cork from the bottle, muffling the loud *pop* with the linen napkin. "I should have brought a wine cooler," he said, partially filling one flute then the other. "You do realise the silk on the couch is the same colour as your robe?"

"That's why I'm sitting here," she said, her voice silken cool. Gracefully she accepted her flute from him, deliriously close to swooning. "Sit beside me. There's plenty of room." She patted the smooth surface.

He gave her his achingly beautiful smile. "The damn thing is almost as wide as a double bed. We might try it here one night." Emerald eyes glittered as he moved slowly towards her. "To us!"

His breath ended on a faint groan. "For gut-pulverising moments this afternoon I thought I was going to lose you."

They clinked glasses, their eyes locking. "You do want me around then?"

He continued to soak her in. "How can you say that?"

She pushed back the long cuffed sleeve of her robe. "You've been very…conflicted, Cal. You can't deny it. I could tell."

He smarted inside, knowing the charge was right. "Tonight is going to be different," he promised, low voiced. "You tore the heart from me, Gina. Afterwards…" He paused, shrugged a shoulder, then settled opposite her on the chaise. "Some things you can't help."

"I know. I've gained a lot of experience these past few years. It wasn't supposed to happen like it happened," she said with profound regret. "I should have done something."

"*I* should have done something." The admission continued his liberation. "Think how different it would have been." He captured her free hand, studying her pearly fingernails, inflamed to be near her. "I should have married you four years ago. I had the wisdom to fall in love with you. I lacked the wisdom to see through Lorinda. She was enormously convincing and she was family. I believed she loved me and had my best interests at heart."

"And so she did by her lights." Gina spoke with intensity. "That's what made the deception so easy. You trusted her because she was family. I trusted her because I truly believed I wasn't good enough for you."

His hand pulled away. "Is that what she said?" he asked sharply, his face tautened into an angry mask.

Gina glanced straight head. A fresh arrangement of exquisite tropical orchids had been placed on the nearby table. "I believed it," she repeated, thinking it wasn't a good thing to store up the mistakes of the past. Life wasn't long enough to hold on to thoughts of vengeance.

"And what do you believe now?" he demanded, swiftly draining his glass, then setting it down.

She hesitated a moment. "*You* mightn't be good enough for *me!*"

He laughed aloud, charmed and amused by the little expression of hauteur. "Drink up," he ordered. "I'm going to make love to you far into the night."

"Really?" She exhaled voluptuously, unable to hide her sensual pleasure. "That will be wonderful! But I need more from you than desire, Cal McKendrick, however ravishing."

"Desire is only part of it, *Gianina*," he assured her. Those moments of terror when he had thought she could be killed, had clearly shown him his own heart. He loved her so much he wanted to go down on his knees before her.

"Then tell me about the other part," she invited, holding her empty flute for a refill.

He stood up. "You have a mind to make me wait?" He glanced back over his shoulder, seeing more of her golden flesh exposed as the robe slid off her ravishingly sexy long legs.

Gina's smile was slow. "It's more that I want these moments to last. You delight and astonish me with your lovemaking, Cal, but you have never said *I love you*."

He rejoined her on the couch, handing back her glass. "Surely that applies to us both? I've never heard it from you. At least, of recent times."

She tongued a bead of champagne around the rim of the flute into her mouth. Delicious! "Too much confusion. Too much pain. I thought the love you once had for me—or I thought you once had for me—had disappeared."

He leaned forwards to brush his mouth over hers, tasting the delicate yet intense fruity flavours on her luscious lips. He would never, never, never find another woman like Gina. "Where could the love go?" he asked. "It was always there. All locked up inside me." He drew his head back, murmuring, "You really do look like a goddess."

His desiring gaze enveloped her in flame. "A goddess?" She laughed shakily. "Not at all. I'm just a woman."

"If you were only *just* a woman I might have found it easier to forget you." When he spoke again his voice was edged with agitation. "I never got to be with you when our son was born."

She quickly set down her glass; cradled his beloved dark head. "And how I missed you! I cried out your name, not once but many times. Everyone in that delivery room knew the first name of my child's father if they were not to know the last."

He drew back, staring into her huge velvety eyes, brilliant with the glaze of tears. "I should have been there." His voice carried a mixture of great conviction and pain.

"You'll be there next time," she whispered, afraid she was going to break down.

"I couldn't forget you, Gina." His voice cracked with strong emotion.

"No more than I could forget you." She tried to encircle him with her arms, leaning into him to kiss his mouth. "Do you believe in Destiny?"

"I do now!" Cal's hands moved to her shoulders, peeling back her robe, then he dropped to his knees in front of her, his open mouth brushing against her throat, moving down lingeringly to the fragrant slopes of her full breasts. His strong hands were drawing her in nearer and nearer. Finally he eased the robe off her naked body cradling her back with his spread hand. "You're mine and I'm yours!"

Womanlike, she teased him, shaking her tumbled head. "I want you to prove it."

He didn't answer. He only smiled, picking her up and carrying her to the huge four-poster bed where he laid her down and slowly began to practise his magic on her.

"I truly, truly love you," he softly whispered.

"I truly, truly, love you."

"And I will to my last breath."

That night they made love not only with their bodies, but to the depths of their souls.

Days later Cal announced he was going to fly a blissfully happy Gina to Broome to buy her some pearls. "My wedding present to her. We'll only be gone a day or two."

Immediately Robbie piped up. "Can I come, too, Daddy?"

Cal placed his hand gently on his son's head. "Not this time, Robert, but I'll have a big surprise for you when we get home."

Robbie caught his mother's eye. "What *is* it?" he asked in a loud stage whisper.

"A surprise is a surprise, my darling," she told him, her mind already on giving him a little brother or sister to love. "But you're going to absolutely *love* it!" she promised.

Robbie gazed back at her steadily for a moment then he cried out in an ecstasy of excitement. "It's the pony!"

"Careful now, Robbie, you'll tip over your chair." Ewan reached out to steady it, looked at the child fondly. What a great little chap he was! Of course it was the pony. Every McKendrick had his own pony by Robert's age.

"Don't worry about Robbie, you two," Jocelyn said, flashing her grandson a big conspiratorial smile. "He'll be fine with me!" She couldn't help but hope at her rival for Robbie's affections the flamboyant Rosa would soon move off and take the besotted Ed with her. "I adore pearls as you all know. They'll suit you beautifully, Gina, with your lovely skin. Our South Sea Pearls are recognised all over the world as the finest of all white pearls. 'The Queen of Gems' they're called."

The multi-cultural city of Broome, with a vast red desert behind it and the azure-blue Indian Ocean in front of it, was a fascinating melting pot of nationalities Gina found. European, Chinese, Japanese, Malay, Koepanger and Aboriginal cultures were all represented. Broome had quite a history going back to its founding as a pearling port. It was the English seaman and pirate, William Dampier who was credited with having discovered Western Australia's fabulous Kimberley region for which Broome was the port. That was way back in 1688, when Dampier first visited "New Holland" bringing Britain's attention to the area's rich pearl shell beds.

Gina actually owned little jewellery outside the costume variety so the afternoon's shopping expedition was very exciting, especially when the sky seemed to be the limit. The pearls that were put on display for them took her breath away. At first she didn't know what size she should be looking at. Even strands of smallish pearls were worth thousands. The boutique assistant steered them towards another showcase.

More strands were laid out for her. They were all so beautiful she stood staring down at them not sure what she should pick. No price was being mentioned. The assistant must have taken her silence for some tiny sign of dissatisfaction because she turned away and came back with a shorter strand, a *necklet* of magnificent, large pearls.

"That's it!" Cal proclaimed immediately. "That's what we want. You should have shown us these first," he said, softening the remark with one of his smiles. "Turn around darling so I can put them on. We'll need earrings to match. Pendant earrings, maybe a little channel of diamonds above the pearl?"

The assistant returned the smile warmly. It was a long time since she had seen such a *gorgeous* couple. And they were so very much in love! She loved it when couples like that came in.

It was the grandest day, full of happiness and excitement and the day wasn't over.

Gina was finishing dressing for dinner—they had taken a suite—when Cal entered the bedroom. "I have someone in the sitting room I'm sure you'll want to meet," he announced casually.

She looked up quickly. That peculiar little tingle had started up at her nape. It didn't simply touch her, either. It actually began to *tap* away. "Okay. Do I look all right?" She presented herself for his inspection. She was wearing a new silk halter dress, very sophisticated, with a plunging neckline. Too plunging?

Cal didn't look like he minded. In fact, his eyes glittered with pure desire. "Yes, yes and *yes!*" he exclaimed, bending to kiss her on her luscious mouth. "But you must come along now."

"Who is it?" Her voice had turned quavery. "Or aren't I allowed to ask?"

"Oh, it's someone you know." He gave her a reassuring smile. *The tapping grew stronger.*

"Are you going to ask them to join us at dinner?" Was it a man, or a woman? she briefly speculated.

A man, the voice inside her head said.

She felt like she was travelling on some new stretch of road. Cal took her trembling hand in his, drawing her into the sitting room. "Gina, my darling, he might have been a very hard man to find but I'm sure you're happy to see him!"

Shock and triumph folded into one another. Gina stood speechless for a moment then she cried: *"Sandro!"* It was a cry that came from the depths of her heart. *"My* Sandro! Oh, Cal, will I *ever* be able to thank you? This is wonderful, wonderful!" One brilliant upwards glance at the man soon to be her husband, then Gina rushed towards her long lost brother who stood there with tears unashamedly coursing down his sculpted cheeks.

"How could you? How could you, Sandro?" Gina beat her fists against her brother's chest. "There's not a day I haven't missed you!"

"Forgive me," he begged. "I have so missed you, but I never knew Papa was dead. You know with him alive I could never go back."

"Well, you're not going to leave us again." Gina shook a warning head. "I won't let you."

Sandro, dark and handsome, perfectly beautiful to his sister's eyes, opened his arms wide.

Cal stood back watching with satisfaction their highly emotional reunion. He felt justifiably pleased with himself. "Back in fifteen minutes," he announced, moving smoothly to the door. Brother and sister could do with some time together before they all went down to dinner.

His determination to find Gina's brother had paid off. It had taken weeks for his agents to find him, finally tracking him to Broome, of all places. Sandro had changed his name without going to a whole lot of bother. He was now Alec Sanders, a valued employee of the largest pearling outfit in the region.

Nothing is going to part those two again, Cal thought, happy to bring Gina's Sandro into the family. Broome, after all, was on their doorstep. From now on they all were to look to the future.

EPILOGUE

The McKendrick-Romano Wedding
Zoe Caldwell
Aurora Magazine.

I DO, I do, I do!

You all know the words! But do you know just how much excitement a girl can cram into a week-end? I'll tell you, a thrill a minute. Not the end of story. There was hardly a dry eye at the fabulous McKendrick pad, a vast cattle station in the Northern Territory, after the most moving wedding ceremony held in a flower-decked folly erected in the extravagantly beautiful tropical grounds of the homestead where this lucky social editor was privileged to stay. These cattle barons sure know how to live! Bride and groom had opted for a small private affair (not the rumoured *huge* affair coming up for the McKendrick heiress, Meredith, in a couple of months' time) but all the more intimate because of that. The bride looked a goddess come down to earth in a strapless white sheath dress with gold detailing, and an exquisite gold headdress. A fortune in pearls adorned her neck and swung from her earlobes. She was attended by her matron of honour, Mrs Tanya Fielding, in a divine, strapless, yellow silk chiffon gown, and her sister-in-law, Meredith McKendrick, breathtaking in a matching strapless gown of a wonderful, harmonising shade of iris blue. Last but not least, there was the little page boy, the couple's adorable three-year-old son, Master Robert McKendrick who behaved perfectly throughout, or all the time I had my eye on him anyway! The bridegroom was attended by best man, Ross Sunderland, of North Star Station, another trillion square miles Territory spread, and his soon to be brother-in-law, Steven Lancaster, of the Queensland Channel Country's Euroka Station. Quite a turnout of the dashing cattle barons! The bride was given away by her stunningly handsome brother. The bride's mother, Lucia—boy, the stars were in attendance when they handed out *that* family's looks!—and Dutch born stepfather, Kort Walstrum, travelled from their coffee plantation in New Guinea to join in the celebrations, confessing themselves thrilled to be there.

The McKendricks will honeymoon in Dubai, returning through Hong Kong and Bangkok. It's understood the McKendricks Senior, now their son and heir is married, will be spending a lot of time at their luxury Sydney Harbour front apartment, with frequent visits to the legendary station. A little birdie whistled in my ear we're not looking at two McKendrick weddings, but *three!* Mr Edward McKendrick, the bridegroom's uncle, is said to be planning to marry the bride's glamorous godmother, Rosa Gambaro!

So get up to the Territory, girls, if you're looking for romance. It's contagious! Hire a Lear jet if you have to! I can't remember the last time I had so much fun!

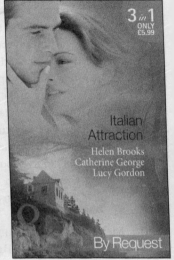

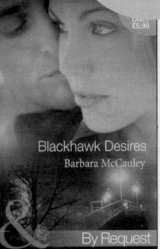

BAD BLOOD

A POWERFUL
DYNASTY,
WHERE SECRETS
AND SCANDAL
NEVER SLEEP!

VOLUME 1 – 15th April 2011
TORTURED RAKE
by Sarah Morgan

VOLUME 2 – 6th May 2011
SHAMELESS PLAYBOY
by Caitlin Crews

VOLUME 3 – 20th May 2011
RESTLESS BILLIONAIRE
by Abby Green

VOLUME 4 – 3rd June 2011
FEARLESS MAVERICK
by Robyn Grady

8 VOLUMES IN ALL TO COLLECT!

www.millsandboon.co.uk